LOVE IN THE LIMELIGHT

LIMELIGHT

VOLUME TWO

ANN CHRISTOPHER

ESSENCE Bestselling Author
ADRIANNE BYRD

LOVE IN THE LIMELIGHT

VOLUME TWO

 HARLEQUIN® KIMANI ARABESQUE®

Love in the Limelight Volume Two
ISBN-13: 978-0-373-09164-5

Copyright © 2014 by Harlequin Books S.A.

This edition published November 2014

The publisher acknowledges the copyright holders of the individual works as follows:

Seduced on the Red Carpet
Copyright © 2010 by Sally Young Moore

Lovers Premiere
Copyright © 2010 by Adrianne Byrd

Recycling programs
for this product may
not exist in your area.

HARLEQUIN®
www.Harlequin.com

Printed in U.S.A.

CONTENTS

Dear Reader,

Love in the Limelight Volume Two presents a pair of wonderfully inspired stories that will take you on an exciting journey of romance into the world of fantasy, fortune and fame.

Ann Christopher introduces supermodel Livia Blake in *Seduced on the Red Carpet*. Discovered at sixteen, she has lived a life most women only dream of. She is a woman afraid to fall for any man, and when Ethan Chambers comes along, he is determined to heal her heart.

In Adrianne Byrd's *Lovers Premiere,* Sofia Wellesley discovers her agency, Limelight Entertainment, is about to merge with its biggest rival—run by none other than Ram Jordan. From L.A. to Vegas, the spotlight's on passion as Ram fights for a future together—and the love that could be theirs at last.

We hope you will enjoy *Love in the Limelight Volume Two,* and look out for *Love in the Limelight Volume One,* available now wherever books are sold.

All the very best,

The Harlequin Kimani Editors

SEDUCED ON THE RED CARPET

Ann Christopher

To Richard

Chapter 1

Livia Blake consulted her list again and surveyed the small, neatly packed and nondescript suitcase on her bed. No Louis Vuittons for this little trip to Napa Valley, no, sirree; if you didn't have to make a grand entrance to impress the loitering paparazzi, you didn't need the expensive luggage. Nor did you need twenty bags crammed with false eyelashes, hairpieces, stilettos and tiny little black dresses that showed off your freshly waxed legs, so she hadn't packed them.

This getaway was, for once, solely for pleasure. No business. At. All.

Ha!

For the next several days, she could—and would—eat and drink whatever the hell she wanted without worrying about fittings and disapproving remarks regarding the amount of junk in her trunk or her buoyant cleavage (all natural, thank you very much) refusing to be strapped into a postage-stamp-sized bathing-suit top. There would be no swaggering runway walks for her, no fake smooches with egomaniacal designers and no over-the-top parties filled with airhead celebrities, socialites or steroid-puffed professional athletes trying to get into her panties.

That's right. She wasn't traveling to the Chambers Winery as Livia Blake, Supermodel. Until she had to report to Mexico for the photo shoot at the end of the month, she was plain old Livia Blake, civilian. Hallelujah.

But the question was: Had she packed everything?

Back to the list.

Hiking boots? Check. Bug spray? Check. Sweaters for those cool northern-California nights? Check. Also in her bag? A satisfyingly thick wine-tasting book, because she didn't want to look like an idiot in wine country; her jogging shoes, because, although she wanted to eat and drink while on vacation, she didn't want to gain thirty pounds while doing so; and her Jackie Robinson biography, which she was *finally* going to finish. She did love her some baseball.

Did she need thicker socks, though? And should she throw in one nice dress just in case—

The muffled bleat of her cell phone came from somewhere in the room.

Uh-oh. Where was it?

Scrambling for the remote, she hit Pause on the DVR (she'd been watching *The Dog Wrangler* in the background and wanted to hear what he had to say about the neurotic poodle with stress incontinence) and listened again. Aha. Nightstand. Unearthing it from beneath a pile of rejected scarves, she saw that it was her friend Rachel Wellesley—probably calling about her flight time and when she'd meet Livia at the winery—and clicked it on.

"What's up, girl?" Livia said.

There was no reciprocal greeting. Just a direct launch into the purpose of the call. "We *might* have a problem," Rachel told her.

It always made Livia nervous when Rachel used that easy-breezy tone. "Problem as in you broke a fingernail or problem with the trip?"

During the long pause that followed, Livia saw all of her vacation hopes—the walks along the river to enjoy the fall foliage, the five-star accommodations, the wine tastings—go up in a spectacular plume of black smoke.

After a good two or three beats, Rachel cleared her throat, an additional stall tactic that didn't fool Livia for a second. "Possibly with the trip."

Oh, no. No, no, no. NOOOOOO. No one was going to rain on her parade and spoil the first official vacation she'd had in years. "Spit it out, Rach."

"We can't come," said Rachel.

"What?"

"Not yet, but—"

"Why not?"

"—we want you to go ahead, anyway. We'll meet you there when filming's finished."

"Filming was supposed to be finished *today*."

"Trust me, I know. But what can we do? And like I said, you go on ahead. Start without us."

Wow. She had a comedian on her hands. "Will you kindly explain how I'm supposed to start without you when the whole purpose of this little trip is for you to see your fiancé's family winery and decide if you want to get married there? Do you want me to try on wedding dresses for you while I'm at it?"

"Someone woke up on the wrong side of crabby today, didn't they?"

Livia had to snort at that. Staring at her suitcase, she thought about her options.

Option 1: she could sit here on her butt and wonder if she should have her walls repainted.

Option 2: she could take herself to Napa, sightsee, eat and drink to her heart's content and wait for her friends to arrive in a few days. Then they could all eat and drink together.

Okay. Decision made.

"Fine," Livia said ungraciously. "I'll go by myself, but I'm not going to like it."

"Please forgive me."

"No," Livia said, smiling.

"Look at it this way," Rachel said with all the nauseating smugness of a happily engaged woman who could look forward to an orgasm or two that night when she went to bed with her sexy man, "maybe you'll meet someone nice while you're there."

Livia balanced the phone on her shoulder and went back to searching for socks, which was hard to do since she'd rolled her eyes to the top of her head. Meet someone nice? Puh-lease. Nice men were rarer than white tigers on the moon.

"Right. And maybe Donatella Versace will feature a plain white cotton dress with flat shoes during fashion week."

They both got a kick out of that unlikely image.

Napa Valley was, in a word, spectacular.

Having traveled all over the world, Livia didn't use the word lightly, but it applied here. Whereas Las Vegas was spectacular in a tacky, glittery sort of way, and the Great Wall of China was spectacular in a humbling, majestic sort of way, Napa was spectacular in a quietly peaceful way. The gentle mountains, the waves of green trees now

speckled with fall orange and the acres of lush vines—
row after row, some red (red grapes, she'd read), some
gold (white grapes), marching as far as her eye could
see and seemingly past the horizon—all touched something deep in her spirit. This was a place that felt like
it'd been transplanted from a previous century, and she
wouldn't be surprised if its lazy grace made the hands
on her watch move a little more slowly than they did in
New York or L.A.

This was, in short, a place she could love.

Once she got checked in to the guesthouse, that was.

She parked her rental behind the main bed-and-
breakfast, which was wedged into a hillside and larger
than she'd expected, and popped the trunk for her luggage. The charming redbrick building had several gables
and chimneys and—oooh, she liked those!—pretty little
flower boxes at every window, all of which were filled
with cheerful red blooms. Several guesthouses, one of
which she assumed was hers, were scattered nearby, and
there was a—

Oh, wait. Was that a little girl?

It was, about twenty feet away, peering around a tree
at her. She was brown-skinned and cute, about five or
six, with a head full of dark twists, a white T-shirt with
blue shorts and a red bandage on one knee. Could she
be any cuter?

"Hello!" Livia smiled and waved. She was never quite
sure about greeting strange children because she knew
they'd all been taught not to talk to strangers. Hopefully
she didn't look too threatening. "Hello," she called again.
"My name is—"

The girl scampered off, disappearing around the corner of the big house. Livia watched her go, trying not to get her feelings hurt. Well. So much for new friends, eh?

Yeah, she thought as she bent to grab her suitcase. She loved it here.

Something moved right behind her and smacked her in the butt. She shrieked, jumped, whirled and found herself face-to-face with a pony-sized creature who'd made himself at home sniffing her private parts.

Another shriek welled in her throat, gathering steam, and her frantic brain was wondering how many of her four limbs he could rip off and devour before help arrived, when something weird happened. The thing backed up a couple of steps, cocked his head and studied her with benign interest. Probably not typical predator behavior, true, but that was no reason not to scream. She opened her mouth nice and wide and—

Hold up. That wasn't a pony. It was a dog. The world's biggest and possibly goofiest dog.

Snapping her jaws shut, she stared at the animal, who stared back. The darn thing's head was well past her waist, which was quite impressive since she qualified for Amazon status at five feet eleven inches. He had big brown eyes, floppy ears, knobbly knees and gangly legs that made him look like the canine equivalent of a high-school geek. His fur was the kind of brown with black slashes that the Dog Wrangler called—what was it?—a brindle pattern.

A Great Dane. That's what he was. So. Was he going to eat her or not?

Apparently not. He had his big black nose working already, sniffing her, and she knew he'd like what he smelled because her signature fragrance was a light and lovely honeysuckle. Deciding to risk it, she reached out past his broad snout and scratched his ears. They were surprisingly silky, and the dog all but grinned at her in gratitude.

What a sweetie! He wasn't so bad—

Without warning, the dog began barking at her, and each bark was the rough equivalent of a kibble-smelling cannon blast right in her face.

Bark! Bark-bark! BARK!

This pissed her off. One second ago they'd been new BFFs and now he wanted to take her head off for absolutely no reason? Uh-uh.

Calling on the thousands of hours of *The Dog Wrangler* that she'd watched over the years, she stood her ground, arched her fingers into a claw and gave the dog a quick jabbing zap right on his hindquarters. Just like that—*zap!*

This startled the dog, thank God, and he shut up midbark. Better than that, he yelped, backed away, dropped to his belly, rested his snout on his front paws and eyed her with newfound respect, almost as though he was waiting for her next command.

Nodding with grim satisfaction, she put her hands on her hips and stared down at him, daring him to try anything funny with her ever again.

That's right, pooch. Don't you mess with me.

"Hey!" Running feet came up behind her, crunching on the gravel. "What'd you do to my dog?"

What? Was this clown for real? She was almost mauled by a schizophrenic Great Dane and then *she* got blamed for making the dog behave? Again—uh-uh. Wasn't gonna happen.

"Excuse me," she said, turning and letting the sarcasm

fly, "but maybe you didn't notice that Marmaduke here is a menace to society and—oh."

Whatever else she'd been about to say disappeared in a tiny little *poof!* when she locked gazes with the owner of that booming voice and those feet, who was clearly an asshole at heart hiding behind the body and face of a god.

The first thing she noticed was his height. He was taller—*taller!*—than she was, which was an event so rare in the non-NBA population that it might have been a full solar eclipse during a leap year. But he wasn't a beanpole, which she could clearly see because he filled out his Chambers Winery powder-blue polo shirt and khakis in spectacular fashion, with squared shoulders, heavy biceps, a flat belly and narrow hips that told her, quite plainly, that he spent a little time lifting weights when he wasn't honing his skills at being a world-class jerk.

He was brown-skinned and clean-shaven, with skull-trimmed black hair and eyes that blazed copper fire at her in the late morning sun. Unsmiling, he shifted his accusatory gaze between her and the dog at her feet. She had the nagging feeling that he was sorry the dog hadn't finished her off and planned to do the job himself.

Okay, Livie. Put your eyes back in your head and get a grip.

"That dog—" she pointed to the offender lest there was any confusion about the dog in question "—needs to be on a leash."

Mr. Personality, apparently deciding not to waste any unnecessary words on her, responded by raising one heavy eyebrow and holding up a black leash for her to see.

"Great." Mollified but still irritated, she matched

him glare for glare. "Are you planning to use it any-time soon?"

"If you don't mind."

His exaggerated politeness scraped across her nerves like tree bark. Still glowering, she stepped aside, gave him a be-my-guest flick of her hand and watched to see if he had any dog skills.

He didn't. Inching closer with a wariness that was an open invitation to the dog to cull this weak member from the pack, he reached out with the leash, ready to clip it on the dog's collar.

The dog's head came up. One side of his black-lipped mouth pulled back just far enough to reveal a white inci-sor that looked sharp enough to mince walrus hide, and the beast emitted a rumbling growl. The man froze, arm outstretched. Livia froze, too, and the dog wasn't even looking at her; she'd heard less fearsome growls com-ing from the lionesses on Animal Planet shows as they ripped hapless wildebeests to shreds.

The man, his cheeks coloring with either blind ter-ror or embarrassment, shot a glance at Livia and took a minute to regroup. Then he cleared his throat, licked his lips and tried another tactic.

"Nice doggy," he began. "I've got a cookie for you, you big monster, if you let me—"

Another growl, this one punctuated by the flattening of the hound's ears and the revelation of several more teeth.

Oh, for God's sake. Hadn't this guy ever seen *The Dog Wrangler?* He was doing it all wrong and she didn't have the inclination to watch the dog toy with him any longer.

"Here," she snapped, snatching the leash from his hand.

"Wait—"

The dog tilted his head in her direction and tried that growling nonsense again, but she'd had enough. Snapping her fingers at him, she held her index finger down in his face.

"Hey," she warned, keeping her voice low and calm.

The dog immediately dropped his head back on his paws and stared up at her with dewy eyes, as though he'd been waiting all his life for someone to appear, seize power and become the undisputed leader of his pack. Taking advantage of this peaceful moment, she clipped the leash onto his collar and handed it off to the man.

"That's how it's done." Since the man didn't know she'd never leashed a growling dog before in her life, she didn't bother keeping the smugness out of her voice. "No need to thank me."

The man clenched his jaw in the back, and she waited to hear the snap of his teeth breaking. "Like I said—what did you do to my dog? He doesn't behave for anyone."

Sooo…wait. He hadn't been accusing her of abusing the animal?

"I just, ah, tried to be assertive with him. Let him know who's in charge. You know."

"I don't know, actually." His jaw loosened but he still seemed grudging with his words. "Thanks."

"You should watch *The Dog Wrangler*."

"Right," he said sourly.

Wow. This guy and his dog both needed attitude adjustments. Big-time. Raising her brows—was there something bitter here in the water in Napa or what?—she turned back to her open trunk and suitcase.

"I'll just take my bag and check in—"

"Let me." Before she could object, and she planned to object because she hated it when overzealous bellhops or doormen snatched the bags out of your hand in their relentless quest for a big tip, even when you could clearly handle the bags yourself, he reached for her bag. "I'm happy to help."

She studied his grim face. "I can see that. But really, I've got it."

Ignoring her, he set the bag on the ground and walked around to peer inside the car's window for who knew what. Seeing nothing but empty car, he looked back up the drive, as though he expected the imminent arrival of someone or something.

"Where's the rest?" he asked.

"Of what?"

"Your luggage? Your entourage?"

Oh. Oh, okay. She got it. He, like other idiots world-wide, assumed that because she was a famous model, she was a diva-licious bitch. Or maybe he'd read some of her press coverage from back in the day, when she was young and stupid, and thought she was still as big an airhead as she'd ever been. Whatever. Clearly he needed a little schooling in both manners and customer service relations, and she was just the woman to do it.

"I take it you know who I am."

Nothing at all changed in his expression, but the quick skim of that light brown gaze down her body and back up again all but ignited sparks across her skin.

"Every man who's ever bought the swimsuit issue knows who you are."

Livia froze, her pulse galloping away like a bee-stung horse, because she realized, with sudden excruciating clarity, that this man was trouble. Men checked her out all the time, which was no big deal. She was used to and impervious to it.

This was different.

This was the subtle peeling away of her cute little capri pants and fluttery top. There was banked heat in those eyes, as if he could look at her now and see her as she'd appeared on that *Sports Illustrated* cover when she was nineteen: sun-kissed and dewy, wearing a white triangle scrap of a bikini bottom with the strings undone and dangling on one side, and a loopy crocheted top that displayed every inch of her upper body—except for her nipples—in vivid detail. She'd had her windblown hair in her face, her hips cocked to one side, her lips and thighs parted, and sand dusted across one side of her body while the blue waters off Fiji lapped in the distance.

She'd been a young dingbat then, but as beautiful as she'd ever been—or probably ever would be—in her life. This man, whoever he was, remembered all that. He'd looked at that cover shot and now thought he knew her, but he knew nothing about the girl inside that shell.

Men never did, and she was used to their snap judgments.

What she wasn't used to was the responsive curl of heat in her belly and the tug she felt toward this jerk, as though she'd been secretly magnetized and he was the North Pole.

Shake it off, girl.

"You might know who I am," she said, painfully aware that her Georgia accent was thickening the way it always did when she was upset, so that *might* became *maht* and *I* became *ah,* "but you don't know me. I don't travel with an entourage when my job doesn't require it, and I only brought one suitcase." She snatched it up from the ground before he could touch it again. "And I will carry it myself."

Propelled by her wounded dignity, she stalked off toward the house, well aware of the surprised widening of his eyes. She'd put several feet between him and his mangy dog when he spoke again.

"Whatever you want."

The subtle mockery made something snap in her brain, covering her vision with red. Halfway to a graceful exit, she discovered that she couldn't let this jackass have the last word. It just wasn't in her.

So she marched back up to stand in his face, suitcase in tow, and pointed her free index finger right at his perfectly straight nose. "You're very rude," she informed him. "You better believe I'm going to complain to the owners about you."

To her further annoyance, this pronouncement only amused him, if the slow smile creeping across his face was any indication. "You do that," he said. "They've had problems with me before. Make sure you tell them my name's J.R."

It would have been so nice to smack that wicked smirk right off his face and teach him a thing or two about the right way to treat a) women and b) paying guests, but that would have required moving and she found she couldn't do that. There was something so sexy about this man, so unabashedly masculine and unaffected, that he made her breath hitch and her heartbeat stutter. And that was something that athletes, actors and rock stars alike hadn't been able to do to her in more years than she cared to remember.

The amusement slipped off his face, leaving something altogether more disturbing and intense. Something that, as the old folks liked to say back home, scared the stuffing out of her.

Time to go, Livia.

Pivoting, she walked off toward the house.

The dog scrambled to his feet and ambled along after her.

Chapter 2

Man, what a day.

Hunter Chambers Jr. edged the pickup onto the road and beneath the cool tunnel created by the elms' outstretched branches overhead, heading home after a quick trip to the neighbor's winery. Rolling all the windows down, he enjoyed the rush of air on his overheated face and arms, although the refreshment came at a steep price: now he could smell himself. It wasn't pretty. Atop the mild funk of clean sweat was the not-so-clean aroma of mud. What a winning combination *that* was. It was like he'd rolled several miles in the muck rather than merely walked the vines, picked a few bunches of cabernet—almost ready now; another couple days should do it—and carried the load on his head.

Braking as he went into a switchback, he slid the baseball cap back and swiped his forehead with the back of his hand. Mistake. Big mistake. A glance in the rearview mirror showed an unfortunate brown streak across his skin, adding to the general pigpen effect.

Nasty.

Just the way he liked it.

There was nothing like a hard day outside from dawn to dusk to make him feel like he'd done something, and the sweat and dirt were badges he wore with honor. You couldn't grow grapes sitting nice and clean in the air-conditioned inside—no, siree. Today had been especially productive, especially grueling, and he couldn't be more pleased.

Especially since he'd worked off some of the agitation caused by that woman this morning.

Livia Blake—aka Trouble with a capital *T.*

Having put her out of his mind only through a lot of sweat equity, he wasn't going to think about her now. No, he wasn't. He would keep his mind on, ah…he'd keep his mind on…

Oh, yeah. Shower.

Yeah. An emergency shower was in his immediate future; possibly two. And then it'd be time to open a nice bottle of—

Holy shit.

He came out of the curve and had to cut the wheel hard and stomp the break to keep from plowing into a stupid-ass biker stopped on the shoulder. Hell, it wasn't even the shoulder. Biker and bike were standing on the edge of the road, which was where you hung out when your fondest wish was to be launched three hundred feet into the air and then smashed into roadkill beneath the tires of an oncoming truck.

The biker dropped the bike and jumped aside, way too late, with a shouted "Hey!"

Dumbass. Like he was the reckless one. And Hunter would have been at fault if he'd hit the idiot and culled a weak and clearly stupid member from the herd. Was that fair? Giving the horn a furious honk, he glanced in the side mirror to see if the fool needed help and that was when he realized who it was.

Oh, shit.

It was her. Livia Blake. Trouble.

His gut lurched with a crazy excitement that had nothing to do with playing the Good Samaritan and everything to do with her. *Keep going,* he told himself, but the damn truck was already reversing as though it'd been caught by an invisible tail hook and reeled in. A smarter man would've sent someone back for her, but he and smart hadn't been on speaking terms since he laid eyes on the woman that morning.

Stopping the truck properly on the shoulder, where all stopped vehicles belonged, he got out and took his time about walking back to her. Like the worst kind of Peeping Tom, he sent up a quick prayer of thanksgiving that his shades allowed him to study her with something like discretion. Which was shameful, especially for a man who had a mother and a small daughter. Women were not objects, and they should not be ogled. He was ashamed of himself. Truly. Deep down—deep, deep, *deep* down—in the farthest reaches of his soul, he felt like pond scum for checking her out so thoroughly. God would probably punish him later, and he'd deserve it.

He stared, anyway.

That was the funny thing, not that it was really funny. He'd been aware of Livia Blake, of course, and he'd ogled her in the occasional Victoria's Secret catalog that'd strayed across his path over the years. Certainly he'd seen that cover issue of *Sports Illustrated* and lusted, but that was in the generic way that all men universally lusted over all the women in that issue. *Wow. Sexy models... I wonder what's in the fridge.*

But this...

Seeing her in person was a whole 'nother kettle of

fish, and he wasn't quite used to it yet. Especially since she'd far exceeded his expectations and was beautiful in addition to intelligent, funny and intriguing.

Having scrambled back onto the road after darting out of the way, she now bent to pick up the bike. Which was the perfect way for him to appreciate the way her shorts highlighted both her round plum of an ass and her long, smooth and shapely brown legs. This was no tiny little five-footer who you'd be afraid of bending and breaking in bed if things got a little too enthusiastic. Oh, no. This was an Amazon who'd wrap those strong thighs around him—a man, he meant, not *him*—and give as good as she got before demanding more and then more again.

In a fateful move that made this one of the luckiest days of his life, she'd worn a stretchy little tank-top-type thing in white. *White!* Which, out here in the late afternoon sunlight, was really something to see. Maybe that top looked fine in a dressing room, but she'd apparently been riding that bike hard—lucky bike—and she was nice and sweaty. Wet and sweaty. And, as every man in the world knew, white top plus sweaty woman equals a spectacular view of breasts.

No doubt she'd die if she knew it, but he could see… Jesus, he could see everything. Rounded breasts just saggy enough for him to see that they were hers and not some pair purchased via installment plan from a Beverly Hills plastic surgeon. Dark areolae, pointy nipples, the thrilling valley between. Then all that bounty gave way to a narrow waist and curved hips. Anyone who thought all supermodels were bony anorexics with no hips, butt or breasts had never laid eyes on this fantastic creature; no wonder she got millions just for showing up and smiling.

She was one tall drink of water, and he wanted to lower his head and drink.

The face was even better, if that was possible. All the makeup was gone now, not that she'd been wearing much to begin with, replaced with the damp glow of a healthy woman who'd gotten some good exercise. Her hair was up, damp around the edges with curling strands skimming her neck. Those hazel eyes glittered with fire, and her pouty lips were ripe for kissing.

She looked, in short, as though she'd spent a thoroughly satisfying afternoon in bed, and this view of her was definitely not the sort of thing he needed burned into his brain if he wanted to ignore and then forget her.

"You." She kicked the stand down on the mountain bike, hung the helmet from the handlebars, planted her feet wide and jammed her hands on her hips. "I should have known. You're a menace on the road, you know that?"

His blood, he was beginning to discover, flowed a little faster when she was around, and his skin felt a little warmer. It wasn't his imagination and it wasn't just his generalized appreciation of a beautiful woman. There was something about *this* woman that made his heart pound, something intriguing in those bright eyes that he longed to explore.

"I like to drive on the road," he told her. "That's what it's for. Not loitering and admiring the scenery."

"I wasn't admiring the scenery, genius. I have a flat tire."

Yeah, he'd seen that already. He stooped to examine the tire in question, mostly because it brought him much closer to her. Close enough to admire the smoothness of her skin, the attitude in her expression and to smell the clean, earthy musk of her.

Mistake. Big mistake.

And yet, when he stood again, he edged even closer, within kissing distance, if that sort of thing had been on his mind. Only the bike separated them, and God knew they were both tall enough to lean over the bike.

"You and your flat tire should be on the shoulder so you don't get hit."

"That's where we were headed when you and your monster truck almost plowed us down." Here she paused to give him a pointed and disdainful once-over. "What have you been doing, anyway?"

"Working in the fields," he told her, unabashed. No doubt she'd never in her life raised her pretty little manicured hands for anything other than to signal for another glass of champagne. "That's what we do here at the winery."

She wrinkled her nose at him. "Shower much?"

Oh, she was funny. Stripping off his shades so she could see what he was doing, he gave her the kind of look-see she'd just given him, only his was quite a bit more lingering and appreciative. Her cheeks colored accordingly, but she didn't drop that haughty chin by so much as an inch.

"Yeah," he said. "You?"

Giving him a killing glare, she reached for her little pack on the ground and unzipped it. "Thanks for making sure I wasn't killed when I dove out of the way of your speeding death machine. Kindly leave me in peace while I patch this defective Chambers Winery bike tire."

What? Patch? *Her?*

To his astonishment, she withdrew a repair kit and

actually looked like she knew what to do with it, which really screwed with his preconceived notions of her as a partying airhead with nothing inside her skull but marshmallow fluff. But, of course, it'd only taken one look into this woman's keen hazel eyes for him to know that there was way more to her than what he could see on the outside.

He'd have to stop misjudging her and give her a chance.

Maybe.

If only he didn't have such fierce reactions to everything about her.

"There's nothing defective at the Chambers Winery, including the bikes. You must have ridden over a nail or something," he informed her gruffly. "And I'll do that for you."

"No, thanks."

"It's the least I can—"

"No, thanks. I can do it."

Yeah, he could see that. The sight of her, tired, dusty, sweaty and proud as she stooped beside the tire, was really doing a number on him. It was a terrible time to discover that he was a caveman at heart, but she shouldn't have to fix that tire, and he was incapable of standing by with his thumb up his ass watching while she did it.

He could do it for her. He wanted to do it for her. An irritating voice inside his head was egging him on, pushing him to prove to her that, even though he wasn't a Hollywood millionaire with flashy cars and a plane, he was strong and capable, and if she needed help while she was here on his land, then he was the one she could rely on.

Crazy, huh?

Insanity. But he still squatted on the other side of that

tire, stared at her startled face through the spokes and put his hand on top of hers where it rested on the rubber treads. Something sparked a shiver across his skin. He told himself it was the cooling sweat on his body but that was as blatant a lie as he'd ever told, even to himself. The contact between their flesh tied him up in knots. That, and the wary turbulence in the depths of those astonishing hazel eyes.

"I'll either do this for you or take you back to the bike rental. Your choice, Livia." Her tightening jaw reminded him of his manners. "Please."

"I'm not a spoiled diva."

The stubborn insistence in her voice said it all. She was tired of being stereotyped and dismissed on the basis of her looks, tired of being treated like a china doll that could break and ruin the franchise. She was a strong, capable woman, and she wanted him to see that about her, to acknowledge it.

That pride tugged at his heart. It shouldn't have, but it did.

"I know you're not," he said softly. "And if the truck gets a flat, you can change that for me, okay?"

That got her. A sudden laugh lit up her face and it was every bit as breathtaking as a vivid red sunset on the ocean's horizon or sunlight hitting a rainbow. He started to laugh with her, but halfway through the maneuver his throat seized up and he could only stare, wishing she'd release him from whatever spell she'd spun around him.

"You're just being nice because you know I'm going to try and get you fired."

He floundered, trying to get his voice back online. He wasn't quite sure why he hadn't told her that he was one of the Chambers that owned the winery, or why he'd given her his old nickname, J.R. for junior, rather than his real name, other than the idea of her trying to get his parents to fire him was hilarious.

This woman… She did things to him.

"Can we go now?"

"Yeah." Her smile faded, probably because she'd seen—she had to see—how she intrigued him, how he wanted her. There were lots of things he was good at, but controlling his reactions to her didn't seem to be one of them. Their touching hands became a fulcrum, the ground zero of a growing wave of heat that would ignite a fire capable of torching all these surrounding elms if they weren't careful. "Can I have my hand back now?"

"Yeah," he said, meaning it, and his brain sent the command to his hand: *let go.*

It took three or four beats after that for his hand to obey.

He stood, flustered, and she stood, clearing her throat. They didn't look at each other. This unspoken signal made them look in other directions while he loaded the bike in the truck's bed and she gathered up the helmet and her pack. They got in and he started the engine. No eye contact. They buckled up, staring out of their respective windows.

It didn't matter. The damage had already been done and the air between them vibrated and sizzled accordingly, reminding him of the crackling energy created by the light sabers in the *Star Wars* movies. Which wasn't a good sign.

He put the truck in gear and gripped the wheel with palms that were now wet like the rest of him but for an entirely different reason.

Drive, man. Keep your trap shut and drive. The sooner she's out of your truck, the better.

Don't say anything stupid.

"Livia?"

There was all kinds of yearning in his hoarse voice but it didn't seem to reach her. She kept her head resolutely turned toward her window and didn't answer.

"Are we developing a problem here?"

"No," she said flatly.

Right.

Recognizing the lie for what it was, he drove off toward the winery.

Okay, girl, Livia told herself. *Okay. This is not a big deal. There're only a few miles to go back to the winery and you'll be safe there. Not that you're in danger or anything.* Physical danger, that was. *Just ignore the sexy man because you're not here in Napa for a hookup or any other kind of romantic adventure. Stare out your window and think about what you need to pack for the shoot in Mexico at the end of the month.*

She thought hard, possibly damaging her discombobulated brain in the process.

What did she need? Mexico was hot, right, so she'd need—what?

Oh, wait. *Sunscreen.* Good! Good start! Great job ignoring the sexy man!

Yes. She could do this. She'd need sunscreen, and she'd also need—

"Are you cold?" he asked, adjusting the vents.

Damn. Was he doing that on purpose or what? Was his voice always this velvety rasp that crept its way under her skin—when he wasn't barking at her, that was? And why was he being so thoughtful and considerate all of the sudden when she knew darn well he'd already written her off as a Tinseltown flake with a worthless job flashing pretty smiles at the cameras for big money?

Why did his presence tie her belly up in crazy little knots?

He was dirty like a field hand, for God's sake! Dirty, grouchy and arrogant. What was so thrilling about that? True, he wore a Negro League baseball cap—the black background with red lettering of the Indianapolis Clowns—so he couldn't be all bad, but he was definitely mostly bad. So why was he making her unravel like a ninth-grader crushing on the prom king? Why did the musky scent of him and the indecipherable light in his golden eyes turn her into a quivering pool of mush?

At least he'd stopped touching her. Thank goodness for small favors.

"Ah, no," she said, clearing her throat. "Thanks."

They rode in silence for a way, which was good. Using the least amount of words possible seemed to be his thing, so as long as she kept quiet and didn't babble or engage him in any way, this whole disconcerting interlude between them could pass without further incident.

Nice. She had a workable plan.

"What exactly do you do at the winery?" she asked.

He hesitated, keeping his eyes on the road. "I grow the grapes. And I make the wine."

A lightbulb went off over her head. She'd known this guy was way too intelligent to dig irrigation ditches or some such all day, despite his appearance.

"Oh. So you're a viticulturist and enologist?"

His jaw hit his lap with surprise and he glanced over, all wide-eyed astonishment. "Yeah."

Annoyance warred with dark triumph inside her gut. So he was surprised she knew a couple multisyllable words, was he? Did he think she was too dumb and clueless to do a little reading about a vineyard before she showed up at one? Bozo.

"Keep your eyes on the road, please," she snapped. "I don't know why you're so determined to kill me with this truck."

He jerked his gaze back to the road. "Sorry. Not many people know the words."

"Well, I'm not like many people, am I?" She didn't bother keeping the ice out of her voice; she wasn't ready to accept his apology just yet.

"No." A muscle ticked in the back of his jaw. "You sure as hell aren't."

"So you're a scientist. Did you go to UC Davis? I know they've got a program there—"

"No." The edge of his lip curled, as though he was fighting a smile. "I went to Washington State."

"So how long have you been working here?"

He paused. "Long time."

"Do you like it?"

"Yeah."

"Is it true that you can tell when the grapes are ripe by squeezing them and seeing if the juice makes a little star-shaped pattern?"

His brows crept toward his hairline. They drove a good several hundred feet before he answered, "Yep."

Irritated all over again, she glared at the side of his face. "Feel free to jump in anytime and tell me some fun facts about making wine. Maybe we could carry on a conversation."

"I doubt there's anything I could say that you don't already know."

"What a great ambassador for the Chambers Winery you are," she muttered. "I can hardly wait to go back home and give this place a one-star rating on all the review sites."

They rolled up to a stop sign just then and he took the opportunity to stare into her eyes with what seemed like bewilderment and sincerity. "Livia," he said tiredly, "at this point, I'm just trying to keep my head from exploding off my shoulders."

Well, what the hell was that supposed to mean? Was that an insult? A compliment?

Stymied, she snapped her mouth shut, crossed her arms over her chest and kept her head turned toward the window. See? She knew she should've kept her mouth shut. Why'd she let her weird fascination with this guy overwhelm her good sense? They were oil and water, in case she still hadn't gotten it through her thick head, and any conversation between them was impossible, notwithstanding all her best intentions.

Luckily, they'd arrived. Driving past the tasteful stone sign that read Chambers Winery, he pulled up to the crowded bike rental stand and put the car in Park.

"Thanks for the ride," she snapped. Desperate to get out of his truck and be done with him, forever, she snatched her pack off the floor and reached for the door handle. "I can get the bike myself—"

"Here." Something soft tapped her on the arm and she looked over her shoulder to discover that he'd produced a clean powder-blue Chambers Winery T-shirt from somewhere. "Put this on."

"I don't need it."

"You're cold," he insisted.

Cold? Did he not see her sweat-slicked face? "Are you crazy?" she began, but then he gave her chest a pointed once-over and she glanced down with dawning understanding.

Oh, God. Everything—everything!—was on display down there; she might as well have photographed her girls and posted them on the nearest billboard. Cheeks burning with humiliation, she snatched the shirt and jerked it on, taking two attempts to get her right arm into its sleeve.

"You could have mentioned that earlier," she snarled when her head emerged.

He shrugged. "I couldn't resist the view."

Would it be wrong to scratch his eyes out? The local police would understand given the circumstances, right? And why did she *still* feel this strong connection to him and, worse, the driving need to understand what went on behind the honey-colored crystal of his eyes?

"I can't get a read on you." It wasn't the wisest confession she'd ever made but she couldn't hold it back. "I can't figure out if you're the world's biggest jerk or a great guy."

Renewed heat swallowed up his amusement and that smirk disappeared, giving way to naked intensity that had her belly fluttering and her toes curling.

"Does it matter to you which one I am, sweet Livie?"

"No," she lied. "It doesn't matter to me at all."

Chapter 3

Livia tiptoed through the small foyer and inched the door of her guesthouse open just enough to let in a sliver of early-morning sunshine. Peering out, she saw, to her delight, that the heavy mist seemed to have burned off since she woke from a near-dead sleep forty-five minutes ago (something about this wonderful mountain air really did it for her), and it looked like it'd be a great day for—

Bark!

Aaaannnd he was still there.

Resigned to her fate, she sighed, gave up her covert routine and stepped out onto the porch, where Marmaduke had taken up residence on one of her Adirondack chairs. Had he slept there last night, keeping a sweet but misguided watch over her little temporary home? She was beginning to think he had. He'd definitely been guarding his post when room service arrived with her breakfast oatmeal, granola and fruit earlier. Clearly she shouldn't have slipped him that tiny piece of banana; she could see that now. It'd only encouraged him, and the Dog Wrangler wouldn't approve of a dog being fed people food. Now she was apparently stuck with the monster.

Served her right for being softhearted.

The dog, sensing weakness, cocked his enormous

head, regarded her with those melted chocolate eyes and managed to look less goofy and more cute.

"Hello, poochie," she murmured, scratching his ears again and wishing she knew his name. His tail wagged, thumping the chair hard enough to cause splinters in the wood. "Are you trying to get more banan-aaa? Well, I don't have any. I don't have annn-yyy."

The dog showed every indication of forgiving her. He gave her hand a sweeping lick with a tongue the size of a slab of beef and lurched to his feet, tail swinging and ready to begin a full day of following her around.

Right.

First thing on her agenda: complaining to the owners about J.R.

The main house was a hive of activity with people converging around bicycles lined up on the cobblestone courtyard beyond the huge front porch. This must be the daily tour she'd read about in the brochure; she'd have to sign up for the one tomorrow. Riding down these country roads through the swaying vines and past the river sounded like heaven to her, and the tour ended with a winery tour and tasting. Who could turn that down?

Skirting the friendly crowd, several of whom smiled at her with respectful recognition but showed no signs of wanting an autograph or picture with her, thank goodness, she and her four-legged shadow entered the huge main lobby.

It was incredibly beautiful in that Western open-sky kind of way. Huge windows, vaulted ceiling, an enormous stone hearth with a roaring fire to ward off the morning's chill. Seating areas with leather sofas and chairs invited people to sit, stay awhile and visit, and the hearty scent of good brew wafting from the fully stocked coffee bar in the corner invited her to never leave. Ever.

Another cup of coffee was just the thing she needed before—

Wait. Was that the little girl again, over there peering at her from behind the grand piano? It was. Crouched down with only her face visible around the gleaming ebony bench, she was all wide-eyed interest and quivering excitement.

Livia smiled and waved.

The girl giggled, clapped her hand over her mouth and disappeared into the shadows.

Livia laughed. She'd gotten a giggle out of her little stalker this time, so that was progress, right?

Helping herself to a huge powder-blue Chambers Winery mug, she filled it with her morning drink, which was essentially a cup of milk with just enough coffee in it to turn it tan. No nasty skim milk for her today, thanks. On this vacation, she was going to eat and drink to her heart's content, and that meant—oh, wow, look at the creamy deliciousness!—whole milk.

Taking a sip, she moaned in ecstasy. The dog, who was nothing but a blatant opportunist, whined with hope.

"None for you," she said sharply.

He whined again, ears drooping.

"Okay," she muttered to herself, glancing at all the blue-shirted employees for the one she wanted. Time to talk to…oh, there she was at the reception counter. She recognized her from her photo on the winery's website. "Excuse me. Are you Mrs. Chambers?"

The older woman, who'd been typing something into the computer, looked up and smiled. "I certainly am. So if you love it here and you're having the time of your life, you have me to thank. But if you're having any sort of problem with the food or service or anything, it's my husband's fault and I had nothing to do with it. You can blame him."

Laughing, Livia stuck out her hand. "I'm Livia Blake. I'm great friends with Rachel Wellesley. You've got a fantastic place here."

"Well, any friend of my son Ethan's fiancée is practically family. It's so nice to meet you." Mrs. Chambers was lovely, with salt-and-pepper natural waves and happy eyes that crinkled at the corners. She had a warm, double-handed grip and wide smile that made Livia feel like a long-lost niece or something. "Your pictures don't do you justice."

Livia flushed. "Thank you so much."

"I see you've met Willard."

"Willard." The dog, hearing his name, perked up and waited at attention. "So that's his name. Wait—*Willard?*"

"Don't blame me," Mrs. Chambers said. "My granddaughter named him. He's not bothering you, is he? We're still trying to civilize him. He's a stray."

Willard, the manipulator, chose that exact moment to rub his big fat head against Livia's leg, leaving a splotch of saliva on her cargo pants. What could she do but give him a nice scratch under his collar?

"Oh, he's fine," Livia said. "I'm used to him now."

"Well, you let me know if he doesn't behave."

"Actually, there's someone else here who isn't behaving—"

"Oh, no."

"—J.R.? One of your employees?"

Mrs. Chambers gaped at her. "J.R.?"

Livia hated to sound like a tattletale, but she wasn't

going to pull her punches. "He was very rude to me when I arrived yesterday. I thought you should know."

"J.R.?"

"Yes, and he said you'd had problems with him before. So, I just—with a bed-and-breakfast this lovely, I thought you probably didn't want employees giving paying guests a hard time. Maybe you'll want to speak to him about that."

A sudden speculative gleam sparked to life in Mrs. Chamber's eye, almost as though she knew Mr. Arrogant had made Livia's belly flutter with unmentionable desires. It figured. A man like that—all muscles, dimples, testosterone and bad attitude—was nothing but trouble to any nearby female guests, a fact of which Mrs. Chambers was probably well aware.

Sure enough. "I certainly will talk to J.R. and get to the bottom of this right away," Mrs. Chambers said. "Don't you worry."

"I don't want to get him fired or anything," Livia said quickly.

"I understand." Mrs. Chambers looked utterly sincere but Livia couldn't shake the feeling that there was a teensy bit of amusement in there somewhere, and she didn't get it. "You leave him to me."

"Well." Livia hesitated. Was there some punch line she was missing here? "Thank you."

"Have a lovely day, dear. Feel free to explore."

"I will." Livia drifted away, with nowhere in particular to go.

O-kaaay.

Now that her complaint was officially lodged, it was time to dooo…

Nothing. Absolutely nothing. Yay!

The light and easy feeling of being an eagle, soaring high and free, was so overwhelming she had to sit in one of the cozy chairs before the fire and let it sink in while she sipped her coffee. For once she didn't have to check her watch every three minutes and then dash off to a flight or a shoot. For once she didn't need to have the cell phone glued to her ear and take every urgent call that came through from her agent, manager or personal assistant. For once she could sit on her bee-hind and be as lazy as she wanted.

Feeling ridiculous and happy, she grinned down at Willard, who'd collapsed atop her feet for an impromptu rest. Ever watchful, he peered up at her, brows raised, and lounged patiently while she finished her drink. Yawning with a startling display of sharp white teeth, he waited for his marching orders.

"All right, you big oaf. If you'll get off me, we can get going."

Apparently the dog spoke a little English. After another jaw-cracking yawn and stretch, he heaved himself upright—what'd this beast weigh, anyway? One-eighty? Two hundred?—and trotted over to a back door, which seemed as good a place to start as any.

Out they went. It hadn't warmed up much but the bright sun had burned off the last of the mist and it was already a gorgeous day. She wandered past the open-air restaurant with its green market umbrellas and enormous trellis twined with wisteria vines thicker than her arms and paused on a stone terrace overlooking the rolling hills and the grapes.

Leaning her elbows on the thick stone wall, she breathed in the sweet air, which was so different from the low-hanging and unidentifiable gray cloud that smothered L.A. and the exhaust-filled fumes of New York. It was so clean and pure she was surprised her lungs didn't seize up in shock.

In the far distance she could see workers walking between the rows, probably assessing the grapes for ripeness. It was, she knew from her pretrip research, almost harvest time. Maybe she could even pick a grape or two before her trip was over.

Pulling out her 35mm camera, which she'd slung over her shoulder earlier, she took a few shots. Maybe she could start a Napa Valley scrapbook. She did love scrapbooking. Willard obligingly posed for a couple of pictures and then they were off again, wandering with nowhere to be.

Wasn't there a heated pool around here somewhere? And a spa? Wait…yeah. Over there. Inside an enormous wrought-iron fence was one of those deep blue natural pools that looked like a pond carved out of a hill. There was even a stone waterfall, as though they'd stumbled into some sort of hidden jungle oasis. People lounged on towel-covered chairs beneath market umbrellas, chatting happily and sipping wine from oversized glasses.

Livia focused her lens, snapping a few more shots and wishing she could stay here in this laid-back and peaceful environment forever, or at least discover somewhere in L.A. that made her feel this mellow.

"Not swimming?"

So much for relaxation. J.R.'s deep voice way too close to her ear wound her up tight, making her skin tingle and her breath come short. Resolutely determined to ignore him, she kept her elbows on the fence and the camera up to her face, taking pictures of God knew what in her sudden distraction—probably scattered flip-flops, empty orange-juice glasses and the corners of people's noses. He didn't take the hint. Big surprise. Doing the worst possible thing, he rested his elbow on the fence beside hers, igniting her skin with the slight brush of his.

God.

"Hello, J.R.," she finally said, keeping her voice tart and refusing to look at him. "Stalking me again?"

Too bad the smug amusement in his voice disturbed her as much as his touch and masculinity. "Actually, I've been staking out the pool. I don't want to miss it if you take a dip. Will you be putting on a two-piece anytime soon?"

That did it. Jerking the camera down, she glared at him, meeting that honey gaze and feeling its kick right in her solar plexus. He wore the Chambers Winery colors and a Negro League cap again today, but he was fresh and clean, smelling of soap and masculine deliciousness. The lethal combination of his arrogance, proximity and boyish wickedness—he had dimples! *Dimples!*—was making her agitated and hot enough to burst out of her sensitized skin, and it really pissed her off.

"I spoke to Mrs. Chambers about you a little while ago. You should probably update your résumé."

He laughed and that was sexy, too. "Thanks for the warning. So you like being on the other side of the lens, eh?"

"Yes. Not that it's any of your business."

"Are you any good?"

"Naturally," she said, hoping he didn't ask to see any of her last few shots. "Don't you have some work to do in the fields? Mud to wallow in? Something?"

He tsked. "If you're not nice to me, Livia, I'm not going to give you your present."

Present? Really? That sounded interesting, but she couldn't be swayed from her absolute and unadulterated dislike of him. This man disturbed her way too much. "Thanks, but I don't want anything from you. Except maybe your swift departure."

"Really?" That amber gaze skimmed over her, silky-smooth and smoldering. "You sure about that?" he wondered softly.

She stared at him, her dry mouth and tight throat rendering her incapable of answering. That was bad enough. Worse was the sudden fullness in her breasts and the subtle but insistent ache between her thighs.

The moment lasted way too long, until she managed to find her voice and create a diversion. "I wouldn't mind taking your Black Yankees cap."

His eyes widened with surprise. "You know the Negro Leagues?"

"I…love baseball. I'm reading a Jackie Robinson biography right now."

"Oh," he said faintly.

So much for her diversion. This revelation that they had baseball in common seemed only to sharpen his interest; she felt it swirling around her and wrapping her up tight in its cocoon.

He didn't seem to like it any better than she did and his next words came with great reluctance, as though he was kicking them out of his mouth.

"You're really something. You know that?"

She couldn't answer. The air was pregnant with so many things between them that she couldn't trust her voice.

He blinked and recovered and, unsmiling, presented her with a bowl that he'd hidden behind his back.

Oh, wow. It was filled with the most beautiful dusty-purple grapes.

"Oh," she said helplessly, feeling special and decadent, like a latter-day Cleopatra who'd been gifted with all the treasures this wondrous land had to offer. "Thank you."

He dimpled again, but the piercing intensity with which he studied her didn't diminish by so much as a watt. Was this a seduction? Did he know that she would have thrown a diamond bracelet back in his face, but her driving curiosity would never let her reject a bowl of grapes from a vintner?

"You're welcome. They're pinot noir. Do you drink pinot?"

"Yes. Are they ripe?"

They had to be; she could smell their fragrance already.

"You tell me."

He pulled one off the stem for her and her unwilling gaze went to his hands, which were long-fingered and even with short, clean nails. That hand had touched hers yesterday. That hand had made her feel all kinds of unwanted sensations. That hand was trouble.

To her agonized dismay, he wiped and then squeezed the grape in a careful grip between thumb and forefinger, making her wonder how a man this size could be so gentle. The grape burst open into a star pattern with a bead of dark juice that was one of the most sensual things she'd ever seen as it trickled down his brown skin.

Her gaze flickered up to his face. She couldn't breathe. "It's ripe."

"What does it taste like?"

He held it to her lips, utterly still and watchful, as though the earth would stop revolving for him until he saw what she would do. There was only one thing she could do. Opening her mouth, she took the grape, taking care to brush his thumb with her tongue as she did.

His breath hitched. "What does it taste like?"

His skin tasted salty and warm, absolutely delicious. But he was probably asking about the grape, so she pressed it to the roof of her mouth, crushing it and letting the flavors wash over her. "I don't know—"

"Yes, you do," he urged.

She thought hard, struggling to put it into words. "Strawberry, maybe…or is it raspberry? With something that's a little, I don't know…a little spicy."

That pleased him. Those eyes of his crinkled at the corners, thrilling her beyond all reason. "I'll make a world-class viticulturist out of you yet, Livia," he murmured.

With that, he pressed the bowl into her hands and turned to go, granting her wish to be alone, and she stared after him, wanting him to stay.

Chapter 4

The next day, after a bicycle tour in the morning and an open-air lunch on the terrace, Livia resumed her exploration of the winery grounds. She still hadn't seen the stone chapel that was around here somewhere—the whole point of her visit was to scope out the chapel and report back to Rachel on its suitability for her wedding—and there was no time like the present to find it.

There'd been no sign of J.R., and she was glad about that.

Really. She was glad.

"Come on, Willard." Heading to the far end of the terrace, she consulted her map and clicked her fingers at her sidekick, who'd again been outside her door this morning and had waited for her at the bike stand during the tour.

No answer.

"Willard?" She raised her head and looked around.

Nothing.

Had that silly dog finally abandoned her? Feeling unaccountably disgruntled, she put her hands on her hips and scanned in all directions for her unfaithful companion, but there was no sign of him.

Well, fine, Willard. *Fine.* She could explore by her damn self.

At the edge of the terrace, though, she discovered a surprise. A pretty little rock waterfall had been carved into the hill like stair steps and the water flowed into a small pond with the kind of relaxing trickle that people back in L.A. acquired through the use of programmable sleep machines available in high-end gadget stores. Potted plants, flowers and lush grass surrounded the whole area, and there, at the end of several enormous stepping stones, sat the biggest doghouse Livia had ever seen. At least she thought it was a doghouse.

Wait—was it a doghouse?

Fire-engine red with a black roof and honest-to-God wraparound porch with white rails, it had a white bone-shaped cutout over the arched doorway, so…yeah, it was definitely a doghouse. Oh, and there behind it were King Kong–sized stainless-steel food and water bowls, so—

"Are you a princess?"

Whoa. Unidentified small-person voice. Was this the girl that'd been following her? Livia glanced all around but there was no one in sight. "Uh," she said, still searching and beginning to feel dumb, "are you talking to me?"

"Yes."

"Where are you?"

"Here."

That time she got a bead on the voice. It came from the general direction of the doghouse… There it was! A flash of movement inside the house and the unmistakable glint of a pair of large eyes that did not belong to Willard.

Creeping closer, Livia squatted and squinted into the dark depths of the house. At the same time, a flashlight clicked on, settled under a small chin and illuminated a girl's face—it was her shy little friend—with the eerie up-lighting usually seen only in horror movies and at sleepovers.

Deeper into the doghouse—geez, how much square footage did this thing have?—lounged Willard, chomping on a chew toy of some kind. In front of the girl was a collection of lunging and snarling plastic dinosaurs and dragons that overflowed from their plastic bin.

"Hi," Livia said.

The girl regarded her solemnly, the effect intensified by the flashlight's glow, and spoke in a Vincent Price–like, creepy voice. "You may enter the dragon's den if you utter the secret password."

"Ah," Livia said, not at all certain she wanted to fold her body up in there with that dog, no matter how much space there was. "I don't think I know the secret pass—"

"Guess."

"Ah. Okay. Hmm. Is it *please?* No, that'd be dumb. *Princess? Pterodactyl?*"

"It's pteranodon."

"Sorry. I knew that. Pteranodon?"

"No."

"Umm… Belle? Aurora? Snow White? Mulan? Pocahontas?"

The girl took mercy on Livia and apparently decided she'd made enough of an effort, which was good because Livia's knees were beginning to creak.

"The password is *Tiana.* You may enter."

Livia was afraid of that. "Tell you what. Why don't I just sit right here and—"

"Enter," the girl commanded in that ghostly voice.

"Enter. Right."

What else could she do but drop to all fours and crawl into the doghouse? She sincerely hoped that there were no paparazzi loitering nearby in the bushes. The cover shot on the week's tabloids would include a close-up picture of her butt, which would look like a double-wide trailer, and the headline would read something along the lines of "Guess Which Supermodel is Losing the Battle with Cellulite?"

Nice.

To her immense surprise and relief, though, once she got through the cramped opening the house was quite spacious. More like a dog mansion. Willard seemed happy to be reunited with her and, when she sat cross-legged, put his head in her lap.

Thus settled, she turned to the girl. "What's your name?"

"You may only speak when you have the light of truth."

"Oh. Sorry." Livia accepted the flashlight and turned it on to her own face, trying to match the girl's somber tone. "What is thy name, little girl?"

The girl giggled, revealing half an adult-sized tooth, a gap and what seemed like several dozen pearl-sized baby teeth, but didn't answer until she'd taken the flashlight back.

"My name is Kendra Chambers." Aha. This must be Mrs. Chambers's granddaughter, the one they all had to thank for christening Willard. "What is thy name and is thy—?"

"Art thou," Livia corrected.

"Art thou a princess?"

Another flashlight switch. "Livia Blake is my name. I am no princess, fair maiden, alas. My parents were neither king nor queen."

"Alas," Kendra agreed solemnly.

They stared at each other for one long beat and then burst into laughter. The girl was adorable, with that perfectly smooth, beautiful baby skin that most women in L.A. achieved only through Botox, dimples, eyes of an indeterminate dark color and bouncing curly twists that reached her shoulders.

"What're you doing in here, you silly girl?" Livia asked, dropping the spooky voice and flashlight routine. "Don't you know this is a doghouse?"

"Willard doesn't mind sharing."

"Oh, yeah? Well, where's your mommy? Who's watching you right now in case Willard wants to eat you for lunch?"

Oh, no. That was clearly the wrong thing to ask because the girl's sweet little smile slipped away, leaving her forlorn and lost. Still, she blinked back her tears in a stunning stab at bravery. "Mommy died three years ago."

"Oh, no."

"When I was three."

"I'm so sorry." Livia touched the girl's soft chin and then decided that more silliness was required. "So if that was three years ago, then that makes you, what— sixteen right now?"

"Nooo!"

"Seventeen?"

"I'm six! *Six!* And three-quarters."

"Wow. I thought you were a teenager for sure." Grinning, Livia pointed to the dinosaur display. "What's all this?"

Kendra perked right up again and reached for that favorite prehistoric beast of kids the world over: a T. rex. "This is a Tyrannosaurus rex. *Rex* means king because he was the king of the dinosaurs and usually ate everyone else. This one's a brachiosaurus, and he was really tall—see his neck?—but he only ate plants and stuff. And this one…"

There was more, but Livia was too busy staring at this adorable chattering child to absorb it. What a precious angel, so smart and strong, so funny and interesting. Guided by some long-dormant mothering instinct that overrode social niceties like, say, not touching kids who didn't belong to you, she reached out and stroked Kendra's cheek, which was the finest caramel velvet. Then, when Kendra kept on yakking and didn't miss a single beat in her dino lecture, Livia smoothed one of the girl's bouncing spiral twists. The satiny feel of it between her fingers was more wondrous than that of any of the five-figure couture gowns she'd worn over the years.

An ache of longing gripped her around the throat and settled in her chest.

Beautiful little girl.

"Which one do you like?" Kendra was asking.

"I don't know." Trying to get back in the game, Livia sifted through the plastic, looking for her favorite. "Do you have one of those—I can't think of the name, but they're the ones with the scary long claws that hunt in a pack."

"Velociraptor?"

"Yeah. Velociraptor."

"Here it is!" Brimming with triumph, Kendra located the model in question and handed it to Livia. "Did you know these guys were related to birds?"

"No way."

"Yuh-huh. And some of them maybe had feathers."

"Get outta here."

Nodding vigorously, Kendra scooched around, scrambled out of the doghouse and held out a tiny hand with sparkly purple nail polish to help Livia up and out. "I'll show you! It's in my book in my room. They have drawings, too, so you can see."

Oh, thank goodness. Another minute sitting on the ground like this would make her butt go numb and her hips and knees seize up. Unfolding her long limbs, Livia was in an undignified crawling crouch, half in and half out of the doghouse, and had just reached for Kendra's hand when that familiar male voice, acid once again with disapproval, boomed over her.

"What did you do to my daughter?"

Hunter stared at the scene in front of him, wondering when he'd slipped through the rabbit hole and into Wonderland with Alice. Or maybe he'd plunged into the twilight zone or been out in the fields too long this morning with the bright sun beating down on his unprotected head. Possibly he was just insane.

Whatever.

The bottom line was he couldn't believe his freaking eyes.

Because there, emerging from the doghouse, was Livia, the woman who'd become his recent obsession even though he'd spent the last day or so trying to avoid her. Livia, a supermodel who, if *Forbes* could be believed, had made about, oh, forty million last year, give or take—an intelligent and intriguing beauty so statuesque and stunning she was as fantastic and unreal as a unicorn sitting next to the pot of gold at the end of the rainbow.

Livia. In the doghouse. With his daughter and her goofy dog, Willard.

And here's where it got weird.

Kendra was talking to her. Kendra, the girl who'd been so severely traumatized by her mother's death in a car accident three years ago that she'd lost most of her words at age three, scaring the whole family to death. Kendra, who shut down in new situations with new people.

Kendra "The Silent" was talking. Livia Blake had, in a few short minutes, achieved a breakthrough with his child that was nothing short of a miracle.

Holy shit.

"What did you do to my daughter?"

Finished straightening and smoothing her clothes, Livia scowled at him, her hazel cat eyes narrowed into a killing glare. "I didn't do anything to her, just like I didn't do anything to your dog the other day. Why are you always accusing me of wrongdoing? We were talking and playing. She showed me her dinosaurs. No harm done."

Brilliant, Chambers. Way to bark at the pretty lady and piss her off. Again. You should try to bottle that charm and sell it. Eau de Knucklehead. You could make a fortune.

"I didn't mean—"

"Save it." Though clearly angry, she dialed it all back and stooped to face Kendra with a smile. "Thanks for letting me into the dragon's den, sweetie. I'll see you later."

"No!" Kendra grabbed Livia's hand and whirled on him with a healthy dose of six-year-old ferocity. "Livia's going to—"

"*Miss* Livia," he corrected.

Now hopping from one foot to the other, Kendra amped up her plea. "Miss Livia's going to come see my dinosaur books because she doesn't believe dinosaurs are related to birds. O-kaaay? Please? Please, please, please?"

"That's okay," Livia told Kendra. "We'll do it another—"

"Actually, we'd love to have you come for dinner," he said.

Livia gaped at him, probably because he'd crossed over the line they'd been skirting. Flirting was one thing. An attraction—and Lord knew they had an attraction going here—didn't have to lead to anything. But if they spent time together, then they'd start down a road that inevitably led to them sleeping together and who knew what after that.

It was a bad idea; he understood that. Their different worlds had collided for only a few days while she was here in Napa, pretty much as if a zebra had taken a submarine into the Caribbean and taken up with a dolphin, but what could he do? Ignore the power of his infatuation with this one special woman who was good with dogs and children, loved baseball, had a nose for grapes *and* was sexy as hell?

No.

If he'd ever had a choice about it, he didn't now. If he didn't at least try to get to know her better, regret would haunt his steps for a good long time.

Livia still hadn't recovered from her surprise, so he took advantage of the momentary silence to send Kendra on her way. He had no idea what he thought he'd say or do next, only that it involved him and Livia alone. "Go on up to the house, Dino-Girl. Grandma's looking for you."

Kendra didn't want to go. "But Miss Livia—"

"I'll see if she wants to come to dinner. So tell her you'll see her later."

Being no dummy, Kendra whirled on Livia and

turned on the charm. "Please will you come to dinner? Pleeeeaaaaase?"

There were many advantages to having the world's cutest kid and he was witnessing one of them right now: people couldn't say no to her. It made his life tough when she turned those big baby browns on him and he had to be the bad guy, but right now he thought his daughter was pretty spectacular. Hell, he ought to buy her another dino figure later as a reward.

Livia's uncertain gaze wavered between the two of them, and then she caved. "I'd love to come to dinner. See you later, okay?"

"Yay," Kendra sang, already hopping down the path. "Bye!"

"Bye," they called.

Then the girl disappeared, leaving awkward silence behind.

It didn't take Livia long to fill it with an accusation. "You're Hunter *Chambers.*"

"Right."

"How the hell do you get J.R. out of Hunter? A typo on your birth certificate?"

"It's for junior. My dad is senior."

"Your family owns this vineyard."

"Right."

"So you're not some random employee that I could get into trouble or fired say by complaining to your mother, are you?"

"Nope."

Her kissable lips flattened into a sexy little pout and her faint drawl intensified. "So you had a nice laugh at my expense."

"I sure did." Matter of fact, he was having a hard time

not laughing now but, judging by the steely flash in her eyes, she wasn't above taking a swing at him, so he kept his current amusement to himself.

"Have I offended you in some way?" she asked sharply.

"No."

"Because you've had an issue with me since the second I got here. First you accuse me of doing something to your dog, and then you accuse…"

There was a whole lot more in that vein, but his mind wandered.

They were attracted to each other, he and Livia Blake, supermodel. When they were near each other, they all but ignited the air between them. Maybe she wished she didn't feel it, but he could see it in her overbright eyes and flushed cheeks, and he'd definitely felt it when she licked that grape juice off his thumb.

"…and we were just sitting there! In broad daylight, looking at dinosaurs! Is that a crime now? What did…"

It'd been a long time since he'd had anything other than the occasional booty call with a woman, and an even longer time since he'd felt this fascinated by anyone, this enthralled.

"…I am a nice person! I don't care what you may have heard about me on *Entertainment Tonight* or some other show. And I don't appreciate…"

She wasn't for him. A woman like this could snap her fingers and have any man she wanted, from European royalty to billionaires, from professional athletes to U.S. senators, and he was only fooling himself if he thought he was anything other than a farmer. A grape farmer, true, with one of the best labels in Napa, but still just a farmer. Phylloxera could attack the roots of his vines tomorrow, the crops would be ruined and he'd be in a world of hurt. He was doing pretty well for himself, but there was no danger of him being able to afford his own plane anytime soon.

"...what happened to the benefit of the doubt? Or doesn't that apply here in northern California? Do I have horns on my head? Is that it?"

Still.

He wasn't a bad guy even if he wasn't rich and famous, and she, when it was all said and done, was just a woman. He was here now, and she was here now. They were attracted to each other and that was pretty basic no matter how you sliced it. And he really, really wanted to get to know her.

Great. Decision made. He tuned back in to her rant.

"...think you owe me an apology?"

Oh, man. He liked this one. A lot. All attitude with just enough sweetness thrown in to make him sweat. He'd bet she had those hands on her hips again and— yep. There they were.

"Hello-ooo! I am talking to you—"

"Livia, do me a favor and shut up a minute so I can kiss you, okay?"

The second her mouth popped open in surprise, he made his move. No point in giving her time to protest or manufacture more denials about being interested in him. Cupping her face between his hands—Christ, when had he ever felt something so soft and fine?—he leaned in to taste her.

Chapter 5

He'd meant it to be an easy brush of lips, a nibble at most. A quick, simple and nonverbal statement of intent—assuming, of course, that she didn't smack him away. But then they were connected and she made one of those sounds that women do. It was a coo, raw and sexual, and it sent him over an edge he hadn't even known was there. He pulled back, shaken and burned, and stared at her. *Livia.* She was all shocked, wide eyes, heaving breasts and wet lips, and he wanted her.

He *wanted* her.

Tightening his grip into her nape, he pulled her in again, devouring her this time without any need or ability to be gentle. She made it easy for him, opening her sweet mouth and slipping her tongue into his. *God.* This woman did something dangerous to him, and he was so far gone he couldn't expose his jugular fast enough.

Someone moaned; it was impossible to tell who because there was no separation between them, nothing but a perfect, seamless whole. And when he found himself delving into her hair, caressing her back and reaching for her ass to press her writhing hips against his, he let her go because the time wasn't right.

But, he now knew, the time would definitely come.

The sound of their mutual panting filled the space until he could talk again.

"Thanks for your help with Kendra. You're really good with her."

She'd backed up a step and put her fingers to her lips. Now she blinked off some of her sensual daze and studied him with a keen focus. "I wasn't helping her. I was enjoying her. Why wouldn't I? She's a bright, beautiful child."

"A bright, beautiful child who never talks to strangers and has a tough time coming out of her shell."

"She wouldn't stop talking."

"I know," he said. "That's not normal for her. Ever since my wife died—"

"Oh." Something in her expression darkened, closing off from him and shutting him out in the cold. He didn't like it in the cold. "So that's what that was? A gratitude kiss?"

Is that what she thought? Was she insane? "No, but I'm happy to give you a gratitude kiss if you're in the mood."

"What was that, then?"

Some questions didn't need answering, so he simply stared at her until a knowing flush crept over her face and that glittering light behind her eyes came back on again.

"You know what that was, Livia," he said softly.

She met his gaze, not quite smiling but not looking away, either.

Taking that as agreement, he leaned in for another kiss, a quick one this time, because he was already addicted and he couldn't help himself. Just that simple touch made her sigh and soften, and he realized she couldn't help herself, either.

This was dangerous, what they were doing.

And he couldn't hurtle toward it fast enough.

"Dinner's at six-thirty," he told her. "I'll be waiting for you."

Hunter watched Livia go and barely resisted the overwhelming urge to call her back. What the hell was wrong with him? You'd think she was departing for a one-way trip to a neighboring universe, forever taking the secrets to food and air production with her. Was this normal? Hell, no. Yet seeing her walk away opened up a yawning ache inside him and the feeling was so compelling that he had to take a minute. Shake his head and clear it. Remind himself that he'd see her again in a few short hours.

Well, they wouldn't be *short* hours, apparently, but a few hours.

In the meantime, he had something to do. Something important.

Too bad he couldn't remember what it was.

The feeling of Livia's lips moving beneath his? Now that, he could remember. Maybe he should take a quick dip into the icy river and clear the remnants of her touch out of his thrumming blood. Maybe then his mind would be able to access the other parts of his life, of which there were many.

Think, man. He'd already met with the production manager this morning and spent an hour walking the vines, checking the grapes...

Lunch! He was supposed to be having a late lunch with his mother and daughter up at the B and B, where his parents lived in a private wing away from the guests and spent a lot of their time.

Right.

By the time he got there and made his way to the small

family dining room off the huge kitchen, however, Kendra was gone and Mom, who had a disquieting gleam in her eyes, was clearing the dishes.

"Sorry, Mom." He paused to kiss her cheek before taking his seat at the weathered oak table that sat in front of an enormous bay window overlooking the pool in the distance and, beyond that, the tennis courts. "What'd she eat today?"

Kendra, with the unerringly faulty taste buds of a six-year-old, ignored all the delicious farmer's market produce, fresh fish and gourmet dishes the chefs prepared for the guests here, preferring to eat chicken fingers, hot dogs, pizza and peanut-butter-and-jelly sandwiches in an endless and disgusting rotation. They'd long ago given up trying to fight city hall and instead focused on sneaking her an occasional carrot stick or grape.

"PB&J." Mom made a face in case there was any doubt about her thoughts on this particular selection. "But I did get her to drink a big glass of milk and eat some pineapple slices."

"Fresh?" he asked hopefully.

"Canned."

Sighing, he accepted the soup and salad she passed across the table to him—creamy lobster bisque, field greens with grilled salmon and balsamic vinaigrette and all the hot sourdough rolls he could eat, which was usually about four—and bowed his head for grace. When he sensed her hovering over him, waiting to pounce, he kept his head down for a few seconds longer. Eventually that just became silly, and his bread was getting cold.

He braced himself for the coming inquisition, took a fortifying bite of soup and decided to take the bull by the horns. "Something on your mind?"

Mom looked around from where she'd begun wiping the counters down, all bewildered innocence in an Emmy-caliber performance. "Hmm—what? No. Why do you ask?"

Snorting, he tore into a roll and reached for the butter.

"Kendra went to find her dinosaur books." He kept chewing as his mother spoke. They were getting closer now. "Because she wanted to show them to Livia Blake—" almost there "—and she seems to be a lovely woman. I thought she'd be one of those Hollywood-diva types, but she wasn't like that at all. She's very good with children, but she wasn't too happy with *you*. Said you were rude to her or something. What's that about? You're never rude to anyone, especially paying guests. What do you think of her?"

Bam. There it was. The elephant in the room.

Mom had sniffed something in the air and was now on the trail of a potential romance for her widowed son. Any roads that might lead to additional grandchildren must be followed with due diligence—that was the woman's philosophy in a nutshell.

Shrugging, he focused all his attention on pouring a glass of iced tea from the pitcher without spilling a drop. Fortunately, his hands didn't shake. Unfortunately, he couldn't prevent the hot wave of…something from crawling over his face and making him feel sheepish.

"She's fine."

"Fine?" Gaping, Mom tossed that sponge on the counter.

"Fine."

"That's all you have to say, Hunter Chambers? Or should I call you J.R.?"

"That's all I have to say, Mama Chambers."

Mom returned to wiping all nearby hard surfaces with a frustrated vengeance; she hated it when he stonewalled her. You'd think she'd stop with the pointed questions now that he was damn near forty, but no.

"Well, I like her. Kendra really likes her—"

"Willard likes her, too."

That was when that shrewd gaze zeroed in on him, cutting off all means of escape. "I'm guessing you like her best of all."

He shoveled salad into his mouth, willing her not to notice his burning cheeks. "Guess all you want. It's a free countr—"

Ah, shit.

She walked over, cupped his face in her soft hand like he was three years old again and gave him a shot of that maternal understanding that always made him want to press his face to her belly and lean in for a comforting hug that lasted two to three hours. He was lucky to have a mother like this and he knew it. He just wished she didn't know him so damn well.

"It's time, Buddy Boy," she said gently. "It's time."

That old familiar misery inside him woke up, yawned and stretched and reported for duty. Though it might take a break for an hour or two here or there, or even a few days when he was lucky, misery always checked back in with him and kept him from getting too far away.

In the three years since he, Annette and Kendra had climbed into that car for a day trip down to San Francisco and only he and Kendra climbed out alive, he'd learned to master misery a little bit, to keep it at arm's length by focusing on something else like, say, Kendra or the winery, and he tried to do that now. To shrug it away and laugh.

"You're not fooling anyone." He smiled around his sip of iced tea but it felt strained and weak, as though his mouth muscles weren't strong or experienced enough to manage expressions of pleasure. "You just want more grandchildren."

"I just want you to be happy."

As if that wasn't a big enough test of his emotional control, she bent down and kissed him on the cheek, leaving a powdery fresh scent in her wake. And he damn near lost it.

Was he allowed to be happy when Annette was dead and his daughter had been motherless since the tender age of three? Really? Who said? Where was the fairness in that? Why did he get his mother's blessing on living his life when Annette was gone and he'd had to scatter her ashes down into the vine-strewn valley she'd loved so much? Wouldn't it be better if he kept his existence utilitarian and tormented into the indefinite future? And if his whole life didn't need to be given over to grief and penance, wasn't a mere three years way too short a time to mourn the wife he'd loved and lost to a slick road?

This time the casual shrug and smile didn't come so fast. They didn't come at all, especially after he stared up into the bottomless understanding in his mother's wise eyes.

"Is it that easy, Mom? Being happy?"

"It might be." She dimpled at him in that reassuring way she had, opening the door to the possibility that things may not be quite as bad as he feared. "With the right woman, it just might be." Disappearing into the pantry, she left him to digest this kernel of wisdom in peace.

Until his father banged into the kitchen through the back door, stomping his work boots on the mat to get rid of mud and smacking his leather gloves against his dirt-smudged jeans. Harvesttime and walking the vines always got his juices flowing, but that did not, Hunter knew, explain the brilliant sparks of excitement in the old man's eyes.

"What's up?" Hunter wondered.

Dad gave one of those low, appreciative whistles that never needed an explanation, especially among the male of the species. "I just got a glimpse of that model, Livia Baker—"

"Blake," Hunter said, starting to get the picture and trying not to laugh.

"—and let me tell you—"

Mom reappeared in the doorway of the pantry, carrying a jar of cookies and glaring.

Dad's cheeks flushed but to his credit, he never missed a beat. "—that she is nowhere near as pretty as she looks in the magazines, poor thing. They must do a whole lot of airbrushing with that one. Oh, hey, honey. Can I have a cookie?"

"Absolutely not," Mom said, stalking through the kitchen and into the main dining room, leaving the door to close behind her with an irritated flap.

"She's here! She's here! Miss Livia's here!"

Livia, who was used to creating a stir when she entered a room and had stepped out of more limos, walked more red carpets and runways and stared into the flashing lights of more paparazzi cameras than she could possibly count or remember, paused at the corner of the Chambers family's private terrace, Willard on her heels, feeling a) humbled by Kendra's exuberant greeting and b) nervous.

Really nervous.

She hesitated, taking in the sweeping valley view, the planters overflowing with greenery, the wrought-iron table with market umbrella, the flickering white candles, a pair of older adults and…oh, God, there he was, over in the bar area opening a bottle of wine and studying her with those unreadable eyes.

Hunter Chambers, the man who'd planted such a fine kiss on her that her lips were still tingling hours later. *Okay, girl. Pull it together and don't stare unless you want his family to think you're a complete and unmitigated flake.* Hoping for the best, she opened her mouth and prayed that her voice cooperated.

"Hi, sweetie!" Bending just in time to catch the girl as she hurled herself at Livia's legs, Livia took a moment to wonder if she'd worn the right outfit. "It's good to see you!"

Over in the four-star restaurant on the main terrace, the female diners were wearing a lot of black. Black dresses, black slacks, black pumps—black, black, black, black…and, yes, black. But she'd only brought the one LBD (little black dress), and it was too much for a small dinner that included a child wearing—she glanced down at Kendra for a closer look—a T-shirt with several colorful dinosaurs on it, including a T. rex, some terrible flying thing with teeth, a triceratops and a legend that read It's More Fun in the Cretaceous Period.

Yeah. If there were kids in T-shirts, she didn't need to be wearing Chanel. So she'd scrounged around in her suitcase and produced a crocheted blue sweater, which she'd thrown over the off-white sundress she'd be wearing for the rest of the trip. It would have to do.

And, oh, man, was she crazy, or was there something

special about this little girl who was so sturdy and strong and smelled so sweetly of baby lotion and fruity shampoo? Planting a kiss atop the snarled curls of her little head, Livia pulled her closer and went ahead and wished it—that she had one at home just like this. Yes, she did. In fact, she'd give back a good portion of the millions she'd made last year if only she had a little balance in her life, a little more peaceful quiet and a lot more hugs just like this one.

Without warning, it was over. Having had enough affection even if Livia wasn't quite ready to let go yet, Kendra pulled free and yanked on Livia's hand, towing her to the table. "You can sit right there by me, okay? See the place card? I made it. So that's your seat."

Livia peered at the place card in question. Kendra had clearly used every crayon in the box producing this one, which had surprisingly good flowers on it and her tragically misspelled name in neat green letters: *Leviah*.

Livia stifled a delighted laugh.

"And I brought my dinosaur encyclopedia and some other books and you can see—" Mrs. Chambers stepped forward, put an indulgent hand on her granddaughter's shoulder and steered her a few steps away from Livia. She made a discreet face that Kendra wasn't able to see.

"You probably won't believe this, Livia, but I swear we only gave this child one pot of coffee today."

"I don't mind," Livia said, laughing and accepting Mrs. Chambers's kiss on the cheek. "I love to talk dinosaurs. And thank you for having me for dinner."

"Thank you for coming." Mrs. Chambers held her arm wide, drawing her husband into the conversation. He was tall and handsome, like his son, and wore rimless glasses along with a white dress shirt and dark pants that made him seem like a charming college professor. "Livia Blake, this is my husband, Hunter."

Mr. Chambers took one game step forward, held his hand out and then lapsed into what appeared to be dumbstruck paralysis. His unblinking and wide-eyed gaze latched on to Livia's face and wouldn't, Livia suspected, let go even if a flying saucer buzzed by overhead.

"I…" he said, and then apparently lost his train of thought.

Livia waited a beat to give him the chance to recover, but…nothing.

There was no helping it; she laughed. It'd been a while since she'd had quite this effect on someone and she'd be lying if she said it didn't make her feel good. Grabbing his hand, she shook it.

"So nice to meet you, Mr. Chambers. You have a beautiful winery."

"I… Yes, I… Thanks, and…nice to—"

"Oh, for God's sake," Mrs. Chambers hissed. "I asked you not to embarrass the family."

Mr. Chambers flushed, shot an abashed look at his wife and swallowed audibly. Livia had high hopes for a recovery and an actual sentence or two out of him, but when he looked her in the face again, he reassumed his deer-in-the-headlights expression.

"I—" he began again. "I—"

"Okay, Dad." Hunter made a quiet appearance beside them. Extracting his father's hand from Livia's, he passed the old man off to Mrs. Chambers, who yanked him over to the side for what looked like a pretty good talking-to. "That's enough staring at the beautiful woman for now. You can try again later if you stop drooling on your shirt."

Livia smiled after Mr. Chambers—what a sweet-heart!—at least until Hunter slid his palm against hers and twined her fingers in his strong grip. As though they'd done it multiple times daily for the last twenty years, he took her hand to lead her to the table and it felt stunning and yet absolutely natural.

Heat trickled over her face, making it hard to look at him. When she risked a sidelong glance, she discovered a wry glint in his eyes, which were like polished copper in this light.

"You have a strange effect on the males in this family, I've noticed."

Oh, man. More flirting. Her foolish heart was going to give out before she even got to sample their wine. "Is that so?"

"You know it's so."

She paused, letting him pull out the designated chair for her before she sat. Some little devil made her glance over her shoulder and peep up at him from under her lashes.

"But you're not kicking me out...?"

"Oh, no." Leaning closer on the pretext of scootching her in, he let his nose skim her hair in a brushing touch that made her toes curl in her strappy sandals. "You smell way too good to kick out. Have some wine."

He passed her a glass of something rich and red, showing no sign that he had any idea of his disturbing power over her or how he made her skin tingle with absolutely no effort on his part. She, meanwhile, wondered when this intriguing man was going to kiss her again and what she could do to speed up the process.

That was when Livia knew she was in trouble.

Deep, serious and unavoidable trouble.

Chapter 6

The edible part of dinner was wonderful, a feast of everything that was fresh, colorful and delicious: olives from the groves surrounding the grapes, salad, caviar on sourdough crostini, grilled salmon with parmesan risotto, cheeses and fruits and a chocolate torte for dessert. To Livia's immense pleasure, she even got Kendra, who was apparently a finicky eater, to try the risotto.

"I don't like it," Kendra said, glaring at the single bite Livia had scooped onto the fork for her.

"You didn't even try it. I don't see how you can eat a hot dog and not try any of this fantastic food your grandmother cooked, Kendra," Livia told her. "Taste one bite. It's sort of like macaroni and cheese."

"Well…okay."

Around the table, there was a ripple of excitement as the girl took the bite and chewed, as though they'd all just witnessed the birth of a rare giant panda or something equally auspicious.

They waited. Kendra smiled. "Can I have some more, please?"

Everyone laughed with relief. In that delicious moment, Livia's gaze was drawn to Hunter's, and when he winked and mouthed *Thank you,* a shivering thrill filled her heart to bursting and she had to look away on the pretext of reaching for her goblet.

And the wine...

Livia drank two glasses of zinfandel produced by vines that were, they told her, over a hundred years old, and then enjoyed a chardonnay that Hunter claimed was so creamy because it tasted of butterscotch, with scents of pear and apple.

Ambrosia. Nectar of the gods. Liquid heaven.

Thinking about her agent's horrified reaction if she could see her eating and drinking like a starved sow at the trough, Livia shuddered. And had another slice of torte with an extra splash of raspberry sauce.

Wonderful as the food was, though, it was the company that made the dinner. As the sun settled on the horizon and Hunter watched her from across the table, the candlelight flickering against his eyes, she learned all about cooking from Mrs. Chambers and winemaking from Mr. Chambers, once he recovered his tongue and the powers of speech, and dinosaurs from Kendra.

After two hours of the food, wine and laughter, Livia could claim, with absolute certainty, that she wasn't anxious to leave this enchanted valley and go back to L.A. anytime soon.

Displaying what she was beginning to think of as a delightful possessive streak, Hunter took her hand again—right in front of his parents, he took her hand!—and spoke to his daughter, who was naming the dinosaurs on her T-shirt for the second or third time that night.

"Say good-night to Miss Livia, Kendra. I'm taking her for a walk and it's time for you to go to bed. We already talked about you sleeping in your bed here tonight."

Kendra frowned, her pointed index finger hovering

around the parasaurolophus covering her navel. "But I don't want to go to bed."

Hunter folded his arms across his chest, clearly girding his loins for battle but determined to be patient. "I understand that. It's still bedtime."

"But—" Kendra began.

"Maybe," Livia interjected, slipping between girl and father, who were now wearing identical intransigent looks, "we could play in the dragon's den tomorrow after school—"

Kendra began to hop from one foot to the other, glowing with supreme happiness.

"*If* you go to bed without giving your father a hard time," Livia finished.

Kendra's expression soured, and her hovering foot hit the flagstone with an annoyed stomp. "But I—"

"Take it or leave it." A sudden spark of maternal instinct made Livia put her hands on her hips, the way her mother always did when she wanted to scare Livia and her brothers spitless, and it seemed to work. "Last chance."

"Okay," Kendra said in a hurry, as though she feared Livia would rescind the offer forever. "Okay, okay." She turned to Mrs. Chambers. "Can you read me a story first, Grandma? Pleaaaaase?"

"And the stalling begins," Hunter murmured in Livia's ear. She stifled a grin.

"I certainly will," Mrs. Chambers said. "Livia, you come back real soon now, you hear?"

Livia kissed her cheek. "If you feed me like that again, I'll be here for three or four meals a day."

"That'd be fine with us," Mr. Chambers said eagerly, earning himself a big eye roll from his wife.

The goodbyes continued, stretching into a procedure that was beginning to remind Livia of the "Goodnight, John-Boy" portion of *The Waltons*. The family, especially Kendra, didn't seem to want to let her go. She didn't want to go. Except that she was excruciatingly aware of Hunter's thumb stroking over the back of her hand and of the frustrated tension thrumming through his big body. Feeling the same delicious agitation herself, she recognized it for what it was: he wanted to be alone with her. Now.

Finally he lost all patience. "You will see the poor woman tomorrow, people. She's not going to disappear overnight, okay?" He didn't bother keeping the exasperation out of his voice. "Can you let me walk her to her cottage, please? Kendra, you have school tomorrow, so you need to get cracking."

After a last whiny response from Kendra, he gave Livia's hand a gentle tug and they were off, skirting the terrace wall and heading through the cooling night and into the relative darkness of the path that led to her guesthouse.

Livia was still grinning with a ridiculous amount of delight. This dinner had felt just like the ones back home in small-town Georgia, with relatives crammed around a table groaning with good food, all of them talking at once. None of the fancy-schmancy dinners at trendy L.A. restaurants she'd been to lately could top that. Please. Most of the time, those places only served half a spear of asparagus with some unidentifiable sauce in a starburst pattern on the plate and called it a meal.

Yeah. She wasn't anxious to go back home.

"Your family is so great," she gushed. "I wasn't sure

your father was ever going to talk to me, but when he finally—"

Midstride, and without warning, Hunter swung her around, into his arms and up against the hard length of his body. The shock rippled through her and she only had time for a quick *"Oh, God,"* before his mouth found hers and they were kissing—urgently, sweetly, amazingly— in the shadowed privacy of a huge tree at the edge of the grounds, where terrace and stone path gave way to hill.

Livia crooned and fell deeper into sensation, her body's reactions so far outside her control they may as well have been operating from different time zones. He smelled like sunshine and air, earthy outdoors and fresh, clean man, and the delicious tartness of red wine in his mouth made her want to swallow him whole, right now.

Other men had tried this kind of thing with her before, most notably the arrogant rapper-turned-fashion-designer who thought that a couple of text messages, a nice dinner and a hundred-dollar bouquet of lilies entitled him to a blow job in the limo on the way home. For them, she had a verbal smack-down. For Hunter, she had a willing body and a mouth that opened eagerly to let his tongue slip inside.

God, he felt good. She wanted...

He pulled back but his hands kept their hold on her face, and his fingers relentlessly massaged her nape, driving her abso-freaking-lutely wild.

"I needed that."

"So did I," she breathed.

"Should I apologize?"

Huh? "For what? Being the world's greatest kisser?"

Another little licking kiss was her reward for that compliment, and she mewled and surged up, closer, wanting more. He pulled back for a second time and studied her with a troubled gleam in his eyes.

"Is there some billionaire planning to pick you up on his private jet for a luxurious trip to Fiji I should know about?"

Was he jealous? How fun!

"Wow. That's the longest sentence I've ever heard you string together."

"Is there?"

"No."

"Are you just killing time until one shows up?"

What? *"No,"* she said, starting to get annoyed.

His eyes narrowed. "Maybe you're just killing time between parties," he mused. "Taking a little break here in the country and gearing up for the next premiere or something?"

Okay, hold up. What was with him and the never-ending accusations of bad behavior? Were these garden-variety insecurities because she was rich and famous and he wasn't? Or had he heard those tired rumors about her party-girl reputation?

"For your information," she snapped, "I severely curtailed my partying several years ago, when one of my friends was injured by a drunk driver. I rarely drink. Tonight was an exception. Is there anything else you'd like to accuse me of since your opinion of me is so low? You think I'm, what—a diva, an airhead, a party girl, oh, and a dog- and child-hurter. Anything else?"

Gazes locked, they engaged in a wary stare-down for several tense beats and then some of the sudden harshness bled out of his expression. A wry smile curled one edge of his lips and, taking her hand again, he kissed it.

"Like I mentioned," he said by way of apology, "you do strange things to me."

Lord, she knew that feeling, didn't she? "I don't believe that's *quite* what you said."

"That's all the confession you're getting out of me. Other than it's hard for me to believe I'd get this lucky."

Huh?

Mr. Presumptuous needed to be smacked back to earth, didn't he? Arching a brow, she folded her arms across her chest. "Pardon me, but who says you're going to get lucky? That remains to be seen, doesn't it?"

She put a lot of frost in her voice, which was pretty funny since she'd been a kiss and a rub away from orgasm mere seconds ago, and he'd accomplished that fully clothed and without a bed.

"Does it?"

Man, he was nothing but trouble, saying it without male arrogance and making it sound like genuine puzzlement. *Gee, Livia, are you really so delusional that you honestly think we can keep a lid on the explosive passion we're feeling right here? Wow, you should get that checked out by a professional.*

"Yes," she lied.

"A thousand apologies. Let me rephrase. I can't believe I'd get lucky enough for an amazing woman like you to wander across my path, and I didn't even have to leave home."

Oh, man.

She wished he wouldn't make her foolish heart skitter like that.

His cheeks dimpled with a repressed smile. "Better?"

Hitching up her chin, she tried to look haughty and no doubt failed spectacularly. "Maybe."

He grinned and took her hand to get them started moving again. She fell into step, matching his long stride with no trouble, but sudden doubts and fears followed right behind her, bringing a chilling dose of reality with them.

"What are we doing, Hunter?"

Staring up at his profile as he studied the path ahead, she saw the subtle tightening of his jaw and knew he understood the question. Still, he chose not to answer it.

"We're taking a walk."

"I'm only here for a few days," she reminded him.

"I know that."

"I don't do casual relationships," she continued. "I'm past that young and stupid phase of my life, and I never handled them well, anyway."

"Got it."

Was he always this frustratingly evasive? "So what are we doing with each other?"

He twitched his shoulders, shrugging this away the way he might get rid of an aggressive fly at a picnic. "I don't know. My crystal ball's in the shop."

Okay. Enough with the walking. Yanking her hand free, she darted in front of him, giving him the choice of stopping or plowing over her. He stopped. Grudgingly. And huffed out an exasperated sigh that did nothing to soothe her increasing agitation.

"I don't think you understand that I can't just—"

"You talk a lot," he told her. "And you think too much."

He thought *this* was talking a lot? Boy, was he in for a rude awakening.

"Get used to it," she warned.

"Anything else I should get used to?"

"Yes. I'm a big control freak. Very anal-retentive. I make lists. I check things twice. I don't just make willy-nilly decisions without thinking about the consequences."

"That's the city in you. Here in the country, we know we can't control the weather and we can't control every opportunity that pops up along the way."

Something about the O-word made ice form in her gut. "Is that what I am? An opportunity? So now you can cross 'had wild sex with a supermodel' off your bucket list and move on to the next item?"

He stilled, his displeasure so obvious and overwhelming it was like a fire hose blast to the face. She had to fight the urge to duck and run.

"Is that what you think about me?"

It was hard to hold his gaze and not shrink inside her skin like a chastised teenager. That low, irritated voice of his must be *very* effective in keeping Kendra in line, poor child, because it made Livia feel like a slime-trailing slug, and she was a grown woman.

"No," she said, staring at the ground.

Considering her for a minute, mollified for now, he tilted his head and tapped his index finger against his lips. "You want a formal declaration, Livia? Is that what this is about?"

"A formal decl—"

"How about this?" He swallowed roughly, making his Adam's apple dip, and she seriously wished it wasn't so dark outside because she'd swear he was blushing. "For the first time since my wife died, I'm interested enough in a woman to let her spend a little time with my daughter and introduce her to my parents."

"Oh," she said, her heart skittering to a stop.

"I've never gotten involved with a guest at the winery, and if I did want to get involved with a woman, it wouldn't normally be with a celebrity who lives four hundred miles away and is wanted by most of the men in the English-speaking world, most of whom have way more money than I do."

Livia's stare froze into a gape.

"However, I am so intrigued by you that my doubts seem ridiculous. And, in case you didn't notice, the train has already left the station on something developing between us. So, if all that makes sense to you, and if you're on board with me not being able to predict the future, I'd really like to get to know you better while you're here. Okay?"

She nodded frantically.

"Can we walk now?" he asked.

"Yes."

"Thank God for that." He started off again.

Undone, Livia gripped his hand tighter and leaned her head against his shoulder, knowing that if she wasn't careful—if she wasn't really, *really* careful—she was going to fall crazy in love with this man.

Chapter 7

"I want you to see something," Hunter said as they turned a bend in the path.

"Oh, yeah?" Livia lifted her head and stared up at him with avid interest, as though he might whip out a Ferrari and present it to her. That was one of the things he really liked about her, the enthusiasm that made everything feel like a great adventure. Was she always like this? So bright-eyed and enthralling? "Is someone finally going to give me an official tour of the winery?"

"We can do that tomorrow."

"What is it, then? Ooohhhh. *Stars*."

They'd come to the hillside's edge, where the path ended, opening up to a sweeping view of the dark valley and, beyond that, the gentle beginnings of the mountains. Above all that, a sprinkling of stars glittered like diamonds spilled on black velvet.

"Oh, my God." She tipped her head toward the sky, gaping with open delight. "How amazing."

Grinning, he wrapped his arms around her from behind, rested his cheek against her temple and enjoyed the feel and smell of her. How did she maintain that country girl's spirit of delight in simple things even though her modeling career had no doubt molded her into the most sophisticated woman who'd ever crossed his path? Why did this woman thrill him beyond all reason?

"Is this okay?"

He nuzzled the sweet column of her long neck and prayed she didn't push him away anytime soon because there was a serious question in his mind about whether he could let her go or not. But, in answer, she relaxed against him and rested her arms atop his to keep him close.

"It is not okay at all. I plan to call the police and have you arrested for assault in a couple hours or so."

"Well." He shifted enough for his raging erection to settle into the cleft of her amazing ass, just so she could see what she did to him. For emphasis, he ran his tongue up the side of her neck and nipped her earlobe. "As long as I'm already in trouble…"

Her breath did an excited little hitching thing that went a long way toward unraveling what normally passed as his self-control. That was strange and problematic. Self-control and he were buddies. They hung out with discipline and perseverance. As a gang, the four of them managed both his winery and his daughter, and kept his dog from being any more unruly than he already was.

That made for smooth sailing, right? *Keep your nose to the grindstone, Hunter, build your winery and raise your daughter. Keep the blinders on and look neither left nor right. Other people might have more of a life, yeah, but not you. Fun with a woman is strictly off-limits to you, so don't even think about it.*

Normally, that was all well and good, and he embraced his duties with enthusiasm.

But normally he didn't have Livia in his arms, and damn…she felt good. Really good. So good that he wasn't in any hurry to return to the house and tuck his daughter in bed. Nor was he anxious to attack the paper-work waiting for him after that. Nor, come to think of it, did he see any need to work like an indentured servant tomorrow. Ownership had its perks, and he was pretty sure that the winery wouldn't turn to salt and dust if he took tomorrow off.

He wanted to play, just this once, and he wanted to play with Livia.

In more ways than one.

The fact that this woman could make him think un-precedented thoughts like these should have made him run for the hills. Instead, it made him feel...he felt...it was like...

He felt alive.

With Livia, he felt as though he'd put one foot through the door back into the land of the living. Was that al-lowed when his wife was dead? Probably not, but until a bouncer showed up to throw him out, he'd spend as much time with her as possible.

Livia swiveled her hips, grinding into him, and this time it was his breath that did the hitching, especially when a female murmur of appreciation hummed in her throat.

"Wow." Underneath her sudden breathlessness, he heard the strain in her voice as she tried to keep this light and easy when really this growing thing between them was enough to scare any thinking person to death. "Do the stars always get you this excited?"

Nuzzling his way to her ear, he whispered the truth.

"This is all about you, Livia, and you know it."

If a person could melt and stiffen at the same time, that's what she did. It was like she wanted to relax and enjoy this moment with him, but wouldn't give herself permission.

He could almost hear her doubts cranking like a hamster on a wheel. "There you go thinking again. Maybe you should ease up on that a little."

"What, relax? Me?"

"Aren't you on vacation?"

She grinned, causing her cheeks to plump against his lips. This was nothing less than an invitation to kiss her sweet skin again, so he did. "It's hard to relax when I'm always dashing off to do the next thing. Plus, it's hard to relax in a great new place when I'm anxious to explore it."

"Anything else?"

"Yeah." She paused, apparently fighting the urge to hold tight to her secrets. "It's hard to relax when you're touching me."

Was that it? No. His gut told him there was more, and he wanted all of it.

"Because..." he prompted.

Turning her head just enough, she looked him in the eye and let herself be vulnerable. "Because you make my skin hum."

Something happened between them in that moment. Maybe it was the connection of their gazes or her willingness to let him get a little closer or, hell, the starlight. He couldn't pin it down to one single cause. All he knew was that a tenderness for her opened up inside him, blossoming like a daylily in the sun, and the feeling was familiar and not unwelcome. He'd felt it before, with Kendra, of course, and he'd felt it with...

Whoa.

Time to slow this down a little.

But…one more kiss first. He had to.

So, letting all of her go except her hand—he wasn't made of stone, and he could only control his skin's craving for her so much—he smiled a little to tell her it was all right and brushed her lips with his.

Then he towed her to the nearest wrought-iron bench, where they sat. And then, because you couldn't properly stargaze while sitting upright, he eased her back until her head was on his lap and he could stroke the fine hair at her temple while they talked.

Bit by bit, Hunter felt the tension ease out of her and he considered it a triumph, something as big and significant as the invention of movable type or the discovery of penicillin.

"Do you have stars like this in L.A.?" he asked after a while, because some foolish and insecure corner of his brain needed to know that he and Napa had things to offer her that the City of Angels—and the rest of the world, for that matter—didn't.

"Who knows?" she answered. "No one in L.A. has been able to see the sky in living memory."

"The smog isn't that bad, is it?"

"Not really. But this is spectacular." She pointed at something that held her rapt attention. "And there's the North Star—"

"Actually, that's Jupiter."

"Jupiter," she murmured, her body loosening a little more. "I've never seen it before."

It made him happy to introduce her to something new. Ridiculously happy. Too happy, because the feeling could easily become addictive and he was already addicted to both her smile and the feeling of his hands on her body and hers on his.

For a while there was a wonderful silence broken only by the occasional rustle of the wind through the trees. She stared at the stars in the sky, he stared at their reflection in her gorgeous dark eyes, and life was good. Quiet didn't bother him. He'd never been one to talk just for the sake of hearing his own voice. But then it occurred to him that he had everything to learn about her and only a few days to do it, so he'd better get started.

"Tell me one thing about you," he said.

Her brow scrunched. "One thing?"

"One thing I need to know to really get you. Other than you love baseball."

She grinned, her confusion clearing. "I'm from small-town Georgia."

Being from northern California himself, this needed some clarification.

"And therefore...?"

"And therefore I'm a country girl at heart. I like peaches fresh off the tree and my mama's snap beans drenched in butter. Also, lumpy grits drenched in butter and biscuits drenched in butter. If you don't have biscuits, I'll take cornbread, but I prefer the biscuits. Or I'll just take the butter. I like to have my sisters and brothers around, with all their screaming children, and it's best to sleep with the windows open so you can get the cool night air. It's good for sleeping." She paused and seemed to think it over. "That's about it."

"That's you in a nutshell?"

"That's me in a nutshell."

This information needed a little bit of analysis; the

scientist in him required it. "You didn't mention anything about your career."

"Hmm. Guess I didn't, did I?"

Wow. For someone who made money hand over fist, that was really strange. And so was the fact that everything she'd just said was inconsistent with modeling as he understood it.

"Correct me if I'm wrong, but is anything you just named possible as, one, a model, and, two, a model based on the West Coast? I mean, do you get down South much? And do they serve grits to the models in Paris during Fashion Week?"

Her snort and dramatic eye roll needed no interpretation. "Honey, if anyone in the business knew I ate grits, they'd probably cancel all my contracts tomorrow. Grits go right to the hips."

Well, he liked her hips just fine, thanks, but he didn't want the conversation to get diverted because this seemed important. "Answer the questions, please."

Something in her expression dimmed. She shrugged, studiously avoiding his gaze. "It's my life," she said simply. "My career has pluses and minuses. Everyone's does."

He kept quiet. Naturally, she noticed.

"Oh, come on." Turning her head, she frowned up at him. "Are you telling me there's nothing about your job you don't like?"

"I could do without the mud."

"That's it?" she demanded.

How could he explain how he loved it here? It wasn't something to quantify in ten words or less, or even a few paragraphs, but the grapes were in his blood. Corny, but true. He needed the hills and the river, the vines and the olives and the air.

Some people lived in concrete jungles with canned air, traffic and smog, but not him, not ever. The idea of being far away from the leaves and the harvest was enough to make him break into a sweat. If he didn't have to worry about parasites, pests and the weather, he'd think he'd died and gone to heaven.

"That's it." He smiled wryly, telling it like it was without the varnish. "I'm a farmer. I love my farm. That's what you need to know about me."

Snuggling closer, she settled her head in the crook of his arm, rested her cheek against his belly and circled her arms around his waist. Her lids fluttered with drowsiness, reminding him of Kendra at bedtime, fighting sleep.

"I love your farm, too," she murmured, trying to pout. "I only hope someone'll take me on a tour of it before I leave."

He stroked her hair again, fighting the growing tenderness he felt for her and losing big. "I'll show it to you first thing in the morning, baby. If you keep working on relaxing. Deal?"

"Deal."

She was true to her word. After a couple minutes, her breathing evened out, and before he knew it, she was asleep. Content in a way he hadn't been for years, he sat there with her long past the time he should have returned to his house and to work.

The pounding continued.

Livia crawled out from under the delightful jumble of warm linens and cracked one bleary eye open against the faint predawn light trying to creep past the fluttering curtains. The open window, which had seemed like such a brilliant idea when she went to bed, now let in an arctic chill that would soon create conditions ripe for icicles and frostbite. It also didn't help that she'd cleverly worn only a tank top and panties last night, thinking that'd be more comfortable than the new nightgown she'd brought. The floor was a frozen lake for her poor tootsies—her flip-flops were nowhere to be seen—and she hadn't bothered packing a robe.

Some idiot, meanwhile, was trying to break down her door.

Cursing, she hurried through the cottage, ran into an end table that'd moved two feet to the left sometime during the night and peeked out the nearest window to see what the big freaking emergency was and who she needed to blame and possibly kill for this rude awakening.

Oh, God. Hunter. It was *Hunter. Nooooo.*

He looked annoyingly bright-eyed beneath his baseball cap (today it was the Pittsburgh Crawfords), and was dressed in jeans and a jacket. His hands were filled with two disposable cups of coffee, which made her wonder what the heck he'd been knocking with.

Gasping, she let the curtain drop, ducked back into the shadows and wished she could hide beneath the nearest rug. Maybe if she was really still and quiet, he'd go away and—

"I saw you," he called from the other side of the door.

Of *course* he saw her.

With no other choice available, she sucked it up and tried to be a woman about this. All she could do was sweep her hands through the rat's nest snarl of her hair and thank the stars she had good skin, although what woman on earth couldn't benefit from a quick swipe of lip gloss? Ah, well. No time for that now.

Swearing she'd get even with him for this if it was the last thing she ever did, she cracked the door open enough to stick her head out and glare.

He grinned, the bastard. "Good morning."

"It's the crack of dawn. Less than the crack of dawn. The roosters haven't even had their coffee yet."

"I thought you wanted your tour today."

"I do want my tour. You said 'first thing,' which to me means sometime after the sun actually rises. I'm on vacation."

The bright amusement in his expression left no room for sympathy for her lack of sleep. Of course, he didn't know that after he'd woken her from that wonderful spot with her head resting on his lap, walked her back here and left her with a chaste kiss on the doorstep, she'd spent several hours writhing around the bed in sexual frustration.

She'd wondered, in no particular order, whether he was sleeping, what, if anything, he was sleeping in, what kind of bed he had, whether he was thinking of her and whether he wanted them both to be in the same bed anywhere near as much as she did. The result was a solid fifteen minutes of sleep for her, which was something less than what she was used to, even with her frantic work schedule.

"We start early here," he informed her.

"Have mercy," she begged.

His smile dimmed, leaving behind that naked intensity that made her skin sizzle. "I can't." The sudden roughening of his voice signaled that maybe he was struggling, too, that maybe he'd also been doing some serious yearning. "I had a tough time sleeping. I wanted today to start so I could get back to you."

Breathing suddenly got a whole lot more difficult. "Oh," she said in a stunning display of eloquence.

"Did you sleep?"

God. It was so hard to think when he looked at her like that, as though her face held the answers to all his prayers and he could study her forever. She shook her head, hating to be so honest but unable to deny him anything.

A deepening of his dimples told her that she'd just made him happy, and that made her happy. Like a hormonal junior high schooler who'd been caught passing a note to her crush, she flushed to the roots of her hair.

"Here's your coffee. Get dressed, okay?"

Turning to go, he passed the cup to her and their fingers brushed. With that simple touch, all bets were off. He paused, his shoulders squaring off with a new tension that radiated out from him and tightened something deep inside her belly.

Then he turned back. "Just out of curiosity…what're you wearing?"

A nervous titter flew out of her mouth before she could choke it back.

"You're kidding."

The early-morning shadows hit his face just right, heightening the gleam in his eye and making him wicked. Dangerous. Irresistible.

"Do I look like I'm kidding?"

Absolutely not. "Panties," she said, swallowing hard. "A tank top."

His gaze, speculative now, flickered over her face and down the door, as though he wished his X-ray vision would kick in and help him see past her hiding place.

"That's it?"

"That's it."

A beat passed.

"Show me," he said softly.

Wow. She'd known that was coming, hadn't she? "I haven't been retouched and airbrushed," she warned.

He almost smiled. "I'll try not to scream."

She hesitated. In that moment, she had lots of options available to her. She could laugh and make another joke. She could slam the door in outrage. She could read him the riot act for suggesting such a thing.

She didn't do any of that.

Instead, she held his gaze, tossed her hair over her shoulder to shake off her wild nerves and stepped out from behind the door in all her nearly naked glory. He didn't look right away; he seemed far more interested in interpreting whatever he saw on her face. And then, at last, he looked down, his gaze gliding over her thin white tank and string bikinis with the ease of an Olympic skater on the ice.

Livia was comfortable with her body. As a model, she'd sashayed down runways all over the world, often more naked than clothed, and she'd posed for more than her share of magazine bikini shots. There'd even been that Times Square billboard of her in a teeny-tiny dress that'd barely covered her privates, selling her line of perfume.

None of that bothered her.

Hunter's eyes on her—now that bothered her. Correction: Hunter's gaze on her made her hot and bothered. It also made her ache with repressed needs until she felt the wet clench between her legs and the insistent swelling of her nipples.

He wasn't unaffected. All of his desire for her was obvious in his high color, glittering eyes and growing bulge in the front of his jeans. Watching him stare at her and feeling their effect on each other without even touching, she wondered how long they could hold out and why they even wanted to.

Some things couldn't be fought.

"Turn around," he said.

Putting one hand on her hip, she turned the way she'd been trained to do. There was an audible hitch in his breath and, spurred on by a tiny devil whispering in her ear, she looked over her shoulder at him. After a lingering look at her ass—judging by the open appreciation in his expression, he didn't think she had too much junk in her trunk, or anything like it—he stared into her face again.

That sharp electrical current flowed between them, making her feel like she'd been zapped by those defibrillator paddles they were always using on medical TV shows.

"Soon." His voice was raw now, husky with a passion that yanked against its restraints. "Okay?"

Soon? Was that, like—what? *Now?*

Now would be good, but she didn't want to be needy or brazen. Although that horse had, clearly, raced out of the barn hours ago.

Still, if he could be patient, then so could she. Sort of.

"Yeah," she said. "Soon."

He blinked and then dimpled again, breaking up some of the tension. Her mouth, on the other hand, had used up all of its skills on those last two words, so speaking was out of the question for her, at least for now.

Stepping back, he put some much needed distance

between them. Not that it helped or anything, but it was a move in the right direction.

"Get going. Oh, and Livia?"

She waited.

"Don't forget to brush your teeth so I can kiss you good morning."

That snapped her out of it. Roaring with outrage, she slammed the door in his laughing face.

Chapter 8

"Help me lift it, please," Livia said.

Hunter stared at her with what was beginning to be a familiar mixture of exasperation and admiration. After a quick breakfast, they'd started their day in the pinot-noir vines with the workers. He'd meant to show her how the picking was done and move on to the next stop on his nickel tour, but was that good enough for Livia, she of the bright eyes and endless curiosity? No. "I want to pick some," she'd said. So he'd found her a tub, showed her how to cradle the bunches and angle the curved blade just right and watched as she'd worked quickly and efficiently to fill it with purple grapes.

Now she wanted to lift the damn thing onto her head to carry it to the nearest gondola the way everyone else was doing.

"Livie." He chose his words with care because making it sound like it was too heavy for her would have the effect of doing the red cape shimmy in front of a charging bull. "These tubs weigh forty pounds."

As he could have predicted, this didn't slow her down any. Squatting to get a grip on the tub's handles, she gave him a pursed-lipped glare.

"And therefore…?"

"And therefore I don't want you to get hurt. Your beautiful swan neck could snap in two and all your sponsors would come after me when you wind up stuck in traction for six months. I don't want to get sued."

Rolling her eyes, she stood, hefting the tub waist-high. "You're full of it, Chambers. Are you going to help me or not?"

Ernesto Sanchez, his foreman, chose that moment to stride by. Overflowing with amusement, he gave Hunter a "don't fight city hall" sort of shrug. "Do yourself a favor, *el mero mero.* Help *la muñeca.* She's picked more grapes than half the no-accounts on the payroll, you know? I think we should hire her."

Livia grinned. "*'La muñeca,'* eh? *Eres un coqueto.*" *You're a flirt.*

"*Siempre.*" *Always.* Winking at her, Ernesto disappeared down the path.

Feeling unaccountably annoyed, Hunter gave her a look. Was there no end to this woman's charms or talents? "You speak Spanish, eh?"

"Who doesn't?"

"Yeah, well." Lifting the stupid tub onto her head, he made sure she had a good grip on it before he let go. "If you need someone to flirt with, *doll,* you can flirt with me."

Laughing and happy now—hell, if she liked manual labor so much, he should put her to work mopping the floors in the cave; that'd make her weep with joy—she called over her shoulder to him. "Yeah, but his accent is so sexy, big boss. Or do you prefer *el mero mero?*"

He got his own tub settled on his shoulder and grumbled. "I'd prefer getting out of this hot sun and not working so hard. A big boss shouldn't have to sweat."

Pausing, she swung around to face him, all sun-kissed enthusiasm and light. A waking dream that made his breath hitch and his thoughts scatter. "Have I mentioned how full of it you are? You love every second of being out in your fields."

Yeah, he did, but how did she know that? Was she that intuitive or did she have a secret window into his soul that no one else could access?

"I'm not that easy to read."

"Of course you are. I don't blame you, though." She glanced around, absorbing the natural beauty in every direction. "I'd never leave here if I were you."

"I never plan to."

She paused, a shadow flickering across her face that had nothing to do with the vines or the clouds. A thousand things went unspoken between them in that second, things he didn't want to think about until he absolutely had to. That he belonged here and she didn't. That while he would never live anywhere else, she did. That this interlude between them, this moment, this connection, had a shelf life that would soon expire. That she would leave to return to her real life before he knew it, and he was beginning to fear she'd take the sun with her when she went.

But then she smiled again, delaying anything sad or serious between them.

"Let's go. I want to make sure I fill out the paperwork so I can get the employee health plan you owe me."

"So." Livia turned in a slow circle, feeling as though she'd been trapped in a Schwarzenegger/Stallone movie in which a thirty-foot wall of water would soon flood through, leaving little to no chance of survival. "Is this where the tortures are carried out?"

They stood inside one of the caves, which was a cool subterranean tunnel with naked overhead bulbs providing the only dim lighting. Shadows surrounded them on all sides, and she didn't peer at them too closely lest she spy an eight-legged critter and humiliate herself by screaming her fool head off.

Enormous wooden bins two rows deep lined either side of the path through the cave, and inside of each were about a hundred upside-down bottles of sleeping wine. The overall effect was more than a little eerie, and she was glad, in the farthest girly-girl corners of her heart, to have a big, strong man with her if she had to spend time in this dungeon.

"This is where the wine rests until it's ready," Hunter told her.

"Have you ever been trapped in here?"

"No."

"Have the lights ever gone out on you?"

"Only that time Ethan flipped the switch on me."

"I can see him doing that."

He leaned against one of the bins, rested one ankle over the other and studied her with shrewd interest. "I forgot you know my brother from the show."

"That's right. *Paging the Doctor.* I was a proud guest star for a few episodes."

"Did you like acting?"

"It was fun, yeah. But I can tell by that scowl on your face that you're not wild about acting."

Caught, he crossed his arms over his chest and tried to shrug off his disapproval. "Ethan left the vineyard to become an actor. If that's what he wants to do with his life…" Another shrug.

"Oh, you're funny. If that's what he wants to do

with his life, then—what? You support him a whopping two percent?"

The corners of his eyes crinkled but he withheld the full smile. She had the strong feeling he wished she couldn't read him so well or would at least stop doing it when he wasn't prepared.

"I'm not cut out for acting, or life in Hollywood," he told her. "But if that's what Ethan wants to do, then that's fine with me."

"He and Rachel seem very happy together, you know."

"Yeah. I can hear it in his voice when he calls."

"He's a good guy."

Hunter frowned. "You seem a little too fond of him. He didn't hit on you, did he?"

"Of *course* not," she said. "He was all over Rachel. I don't think he ever even looked at me."

He snorted as though this was as unlikely as surfing on Mars. "Get real."

She flushed and their gazes locked, leading into another of the deliciously silent moments they'd been sharing all morning. He had a way of studying her face that was so darkly, frankly appreciative that she suspected he'd swallow her whole if given half the chance.

The funny thing was, she couldn't wait to give him the chance.

They'd settled against opposite bins, both leaning, neither moving. The three or four feet of path separating them felt suddenly like a yawning canyon—way too wide and nearly impossible to cross.

"You know," she said, wishing he would take all decision making out of her hands and touch her. Hold her. Because she needed him to, even if she had a terrible time figuring out how to ask. "I brushed my teeth this morning. I even gargled. You never did give me my kiss." Trying to pout, she waited for him to react and meet her halfway. "Do I smell bad?"

"Your smell is not the issue, trust me. I love honeysuckle."

Whoa. Had he just correctly identified her body cream? "How did you—?"

"Like I told you. I'm a farmer. I know my flowers."

There was so much intensity in him, so much in the two of them together. If only she could figure out whether she should be running toward it or away from it. Right now she knew they were circling an issue that could be awkward, but did that really matter next to her consuming need to be close to him? Hell, even her pride was beginning to matter less.

"Are you dodging the question?" she wondered.

He cleared his throat and studied his shoes. Ran his hand over the top of his head and scrubbed his jaw. Showed every sign of being a man about to come out of his skin with agitation. The one thing he didn't do was come closer.

"The thing is," he said finally, his voice low and hoarse, "the more I kiss you, the harder it is for me to stop."

"Then don't stop."

There it was. Carte blanche. It didn't get much clearer than that, although of course they'd already discussed this a little bit this morning. He could have her any way he wanted her, as soon as he decided it was time. The rational part of her knew this was probably a bad idea that would lead to doom in the end. The rest of her just didn't care.

"We need to get this on the table right now." He stared

at her, giving her a clear shot of the unhappiness in his eyes, the turmoil. "I'm not going to want you to go when your vacation is over."

God. That was exactly the kind of thing she should never hear.

Exactly the kind of thing she needed to hear.

There was no real way to lighten the mood or divert the conversation, but she felt she needed to point out the obvious. "You'll probably get sick of me in the next day or two, don't you think?" Funny how she said the words so easily when the mere possibility of this happening made her stomach drop; the chances of her getting tired of him anytime soon were somewhere between the probabilities of harvesting gold for food and spinning straw into usable petroleum. "We hardly know each other, Hunter."

"I know enough," he told her. "More than enough."

"Pick," Hunter said. "*A* or *B*."

After a delightful lunch on the terrace, he'd loaded her into his truck for the second half of what she was already thinking of as a fairy-tale day. Possibly the best day of her life, although she hated to make that concession before the sun even set on the horizon. Holding hands in a wonderful silence, they drove down a peaceful road with valley views of orange and gold in every direction. Now they'd come to a dead end, and Hunter, who seemed to be brimming with a kind of smug excitement, expected her to select the next activity.

"B," she said, grinning and hoping she hadn't chosen between, say, a trip to either a mall or museum. Neither idea appealed to her. While she was here in Napa, she

fully planned to spend as much time outside in the crisp air and sunshine as possible.

"*B* it is." Shooting her a return grin, Hunter turned right.

They drove a little farther and then, suddenly, the trees gave way to reveal flashes of startling color and—

"*Balloons.*"

Clapping a hand over her frantically beating heart, she tried to keep some of her excitement inside lest they were planning to drive on past and head to an art museum after all. Four balloons, in various stages of inflatedness, stretched out in the valley before them, their baskets—gondolas, right?—waiting nearby. One was rainbow striped, one rainbow swirled and the other two were mostly blue with red zigzags. Did he know she'd always wanted to ride in one?

"Are we going on a balloon ride?"

Laughing, Hunter parked and cut the engine. "That's the plan. Unless you're scared of heights."

"Of *course* I'm scared of heights! Let's go!"

If she'd given herself more time to think about it, she'd have behaved with a little more decorum rather than leaping out of the truck and clapping and hopping like a two-year-old. She probably would have said her prayers and called her life insurance company to make sure she was paid up. But she was too excited and happy, and the sun was shining and she was free to play for once in her life.

Why not wallow in the joy?

"Thank you!" Racing around the truck's cab, she launched herself into Hunter's arms, nearly knocking him over with her Amazonian enthusiasm, poor guy. He was a good sport about it, laughing and holding her tight, and he didn't even protest when she planted sloppy kisses all over his face. "Thank you, thank you, *thank you!*"

"You're welcome, angel."

He set her back on her feet, staring at her with such glowing tenderness that she fully understood, deep in her gut, how much trouble she was in. This wasn't about having a bittersweet vacation fling and taking fond memories with her for the rest of her life. This was about falling crazy in love with a man who didn't belong in her world any more than she belonged in his. This was about her life changing into something unrecognizable, and if she was smart, she'd walk away now.

Instead, she held her hand out for his and they walked, together, to their balloon.

"We can sit here all night if we need to," Hunter said.

Kendra, who was sitting at the table with him, stared unhappily at her plate, which featured the healthy food selections they'd forced on her but no chicken nuggets, pizza or fries, and…wait for it…rolled her eyes at him. Again. For good measure, she clicked her tongue, too.

Down on the rug, his snout resting on his paws and his mournful brown eyes reflecting hope, Willard waited in utter stillness, clearly hoping that someone would drop a morsel of some kind on the floor.

Hunter had foolishly thought that he had at least a couple more years before being confronted with this kind of withering female attitude from his little girl, but he'd been wrong. The child was in a serious snit and would, any second, commence with the finger snapping and head bobbing.

Picking up a piece of asparagus with two fingers, she

hung it upside down and eyed it the way she would a dead snake. "I'm not eating this."

After sneaking a quick peek at his watch—only 6:33, thank goodness, so he still had plenty of time to argue with the diva here and cook dinner for Livia—he shrugged.

"Suit yourself. But you're going to have a long and hungry night with no dessert if you choose not to eat it. And Grandma made peach ice cream."

He waited.

Folding her arms on the table (he waged an inner debate with himself but now was not the time to engage in an additional battle about elbows and manners), she regarded her plate with utmost gloom. After a shuddering sigh, she opened her mouth and took half a nip off the end of the asparagus, probably not enough for the vegetable's flavor to reach her taste buds.

"Eww." Scrunching her face, she stabbed a bite of salmon and let the fork hover one inch from her lips. "Why can't Livia eat with us again tonight?"

Mom sailed in through the patio doors just then and did a poor job of suppressing her smile of glee.

"Don't mind me," she said, not quite meeting his eye as she set the bushel of tomatoes she was carrying on the counter. She, along with Kendra, Dad and Willard, all seemed to bitterly resent his commandeering Livia for his own tonight and were unlikely to forgive his selfishness anytime soon. Mom, in fact, was only too happy to watch him squirm on Kendra's hot seat for a little while. "I don't want to interrupt."

"Why?" Kendra demanded again.

"Well," he said, reaching deep for his patience and finding none, "as I've already explained forty or fifty times, Livia and I are having dinner alone together in a little while. So you can see her another time. And it's not like you haven't seen her today. Didn't she stop by the doghouse—"

"Dragon's den," the girl corrected.

"—earlier?"

"But why can't I have dinner with you?"

"Because then Livia and I wouldn't be having dinner alone, would we?"

This logic didn't come close to piercing Kendra's intransigence. Lifting her head up again, brimming with the spirit of peaceful compromise, she decided to sweeten the deal.

"But I can be quiet. Really quiet."

Hunter snorted. "What, quiet like you were at last night's dinner? With your nonstop yakking about dinosaurs? No, thank you."

Willard, who seemed to have grown tired of the passive approach to food acquisition, sat up on his haunches, rested the very tip of his nose on the table, one inch from Kendra's plate, and snuffled at the salmon.

Kendra looked affronted with Hunter, her little brows flattening with the implication that her two-hour monologue on all things dinosaur had been anything less than scintillating. "Livia loves dinosaurs like I do. And I need to show her my shirt."

She pointed to today's model, a white one featuring a snarling tyrannosaur and the caption I'm a T. rex Trapped in a Human's Body.

"She saw it earlier," Hunter reminded her.

"But she really liked it. It made her laugh."

While he understood the idea of people becoming addicted to Livia's laughter, especially since he was confronting this issue himself, there was no way he was going to bring his six-year-old along on the romantic date night he had planned. Wouldn't happen, not even for a million tax-free dollars.

"Sorry, Charlie."

"But why-yyy-yyy?" Kendra whined, producing a remarkable number of syllables out of those three letters.

Grappling for the right words, which were nowhere in sight, Hunter made the mistake of looking up and catching Mom's eye. She winked, a tiny gesture that told him she understood his turmoil even if Kendra never would.

Why couldn't Kendra come?

One: because he was a greedy bastard and wanted Livia all to himself tonight.

Two: because he didn't want his daughter getting too attached to a woman who'd be gone from their lives all too soon.

He was a grown man; he knew what he was getting into. Well, no, he didn't. Not with Livia, not really. But he was a grown man and he knew about consequences and knew he'd chosen to deal with them, painful as they'd inevitably be when Livia went back to her real world and left him here in his.

But Kendra was a six-year-old who'd already lost both her mother and most of her words for a long time after. Her emotions were not in play here and never would be if he had anything to say about it, and he did.

Protecting this precious child from further heartbreak was his sacred duty as her father and he didn't plan to fall down on this job. Wasn't making hard decisions for the greater good in his job description? Kendra may not like it, but she didn't get a vote on the issue any more than she got a vote about whether she needed her vaccinations or not.

Kendra could spend time with Livia, in small, controlled doses, where Livia wouldn't have the opportunity to ingratiate herself into Kendra's routine too much and the chances of the girl falling in love with her were remote.

His plan was to guard his daughter's affections and he needed to stick to it, no matter how difficult it might be. And it would be very difficult because his beautiful supermodel—when had he begun thinking of Livia as his?—had a way of enchanting those around her without even trying.

So he stared into the hopeful face of a child who was starved for a mother figure and gently told her the painful truth, "We can't expect Livia to be around here too much, okay? She's going home soon, and we won't be able to see her anymore after that because she lives so far away."

Kendra stared at him in uncomprehending silence for two of the longest beats of his life. And then, her face twisting with bitter disappointment, she shoved her plate across the table and slumped her forehead on her arms.

Beside her, Willard whined in sympathy and rested his head on her knee.

Chapter 9

"Are we almost there yet? I can see lights."

Livia and Hunter turned a corner on the stone path and she tugged his hand a little harder. They both had long-legged strides but he was moving way too slowly for her tastes right now, and she couldn't wait to see what additional wonders this day held for them. He'd met her at the cottage just as the sun was setting, walked her down this lovely path—everything in Napa seemed to be lovely; apparently the region had received more than its fair share of beautiful spots when God was handing them out—and kept up a sphinxlike silence about his plans for their dinner.

Aaaand…he still wasn't talking.

As though he knew it would make her explode with impatience, he laughed and shrugged with smug satisfaction rather than answer her question. Luckily for him, the trees gave way at that point, revealing a beautiful setting and sparing him from a sharp smack on the arm.

"Oh, wow, what a pretty house!" she cried. "Is that yours?"

"It's mine."

Mission-style, with the typical white stucco and red tiled roof, the small house sat tucked into the hillside.

Everything about it was beautiful and welcoming, from the overflowing flowerpots to the drapes fluttering in the open cloverleaf-shaped windows and the warm glow of lamps from inside. Even the air around here smelled good, like grilled steaks and vegetables or something, and, if she wasn't mistaken, the homey crispness of wood smoke.

She headed for the front door, propelled by her unreasonable curiosity about All Things Hunter and dying to see what kind of furniture he had, but he steered her around back.

"This way," he said, grinning.

That smile of his distracted her, the way it always did. All dimples and boyish delight, it was a thing of wonder that should be marked on tourist maps as a not-to-be-missed local sight.

"You have the sexiest smile," she blurted. *Way to throw yourself at the man, girl. Mama would be so proud.* "I can't believe I ever thought you were the world's grumpiest man."

He changed in an instant, the amusement vanishing in favor of dark desires and naked heat. "Is that so?"

"Oh, yeah."

"Are you trying to seduce me?"

"Is it working?"

"It's working." Leaning in, he gave her a nipping little kiss that began with the tip of his tongue and ended with a gentle tug of her bottom lip. She gasped with a sudden, twisting need that felt like a living thing inside her and fought the urge to reach for him, to bring him close. "You have no idea how well it's working. But I promised you dinner, didn't I? Come on."

Dinner had just dropped to number nine-hundred-eighty-five on her to-do list, but it seemed polite to show some interest since he'd gone to a lot of trouble. So she let him lead her around the path, which was lit with white lights strung through the bushes, to the back of the house.

Where the most amazing wonderland awaited her.

"Oh." Multisyllabic words failed her. *"Wow."*

"You like?"

"I *love.*"

What wasn't there to love? Beautiful potted trees and flowers—a man who grew things for a living had to have a spectacular yard, right?—wove their way down a lush green hill that ended in a wooden dock and, beyond that, a rippling pond. A trick of the moonlight—or maybe it was the glowing white Japanese lanterns he'd strung overhead that did it—made white spots shimmer on the water, creating an effect like diamonds sparkling over satin.

The dock seemed to be their ultimate destination for the night, because it was edged and illuminated by several flickering column candles and a domed fire pit that crackled merrily. Inside the ring of light was a spread blanket, a wicker basket and a champagne bucket.

And people said you had to die to reach paradise.

Who knew?

Emotion gathered in her throat, requiring her to clear it once or twice. It wasn't that men never tried to impress her with romantic gestures; they did. All the time, in fact. It was that it was meaningless if some rapper had his personal assistant order her a ruby bracelet while also ordering emerald and sapphire ones for the other models he had his eye on.

This simple picnic meant more to her than anything had since...

Since...ever?

Was that giving him too much credit? Or had her life, and the people inhabiting it, simply become that shallow and meaningless over the years?

"Is this all for me?" She swiped at her tears, hoping he wouldn't notice if she started bawling like Kendra probably did at bedtime.

He widened his eyes with fake shock and dismay. "Is that what you…? Oh, man, this is awkward. This is for my real date, who's due any minute. I was just hoping you'd tell me if you thought she'd like it."

"Stop it!" Laughing now and feeling like a complete idiot, she smacked him on the arm. "You know what I mean."

"Of course it's for you."

"This is a lot of effort," she pointed out.

"You're worth it."

That disarming honesty of his really did a number on her. Back in L.A., people practically gave themselves whiplash with their overenthusiastic and utterly insincere efforts to kiss her ass at every turn. All that was bull, and she knew it, but, hey, if it got her a nice table at a restaurant every now and then, well…so be it.

Hunter, on the other hand, seemed incapable of that kind of nonsense. The little bit she knew of him so far screamed that what she saw with him was what she got.

Wasn't that a refreshing change?

Taking a step closer, she decided to lay it all on the line. "Can I tell you something?"

He studied her for a few seconds, not answering, and that sizzling hyperawareness of him and his every reaction almost made her shiver, it was that acute. What did he see in her face when he looked at her so intently? Why couldn't she shake the certainty that he knew and understood things about her that she'd never suspected about herself? And why did that feel okay?

"You can tell me anything."

"You scare me to death," she said helplessly. "I'm almost shaking with it."

The edges of his eyes crinkled with the beginnings of a smile, softening all those harsh planes and angles, making him tender but no less fierce.

"So that's it, then? We walk away?"

She tried to take a nice, deep breath to calm herself, but that swooping sensation remained in her belly, as though her little boat was bobbing along in the waves with no way to control the tide's sweep. If she was about to capsize and drown, she almost didn't care.

"That's the funny thing," she told him. "The thought of walking away scares me more than staying."

"Well, then." Touching her with a vibrating restraint, as though he only trusted himself on a very short leash, he smoothed a fluttering lock of her hair away from her face. "Stay."

Hunter led her to the dock, to the quilted picnic blanket, and stretched out on it, intending to lay her down with him. Livia had another, better, idea. With the light wind ruffling her hair and the firelight making her skin glow and giving her eyes a wickedly female glint, she arched her back and, in one fluid movement, pulled her sweater off over her head, dropping it to her feet. Holding his gaze, she unzipped her jeans and shimmied out of them, tossing those away, too, and revealing herself to him with a generosity and raw sensuality he could only have dreamed about.

Levering himself up on one elbow, he stared.

She was so freaking amazing in so many ways he could hardly wrap his brain around it. Long and lean, but curves—and plenty of them—everywhere that counted. She wore a lacy black bra that cradled the perfect plump ovals of her breasts and revealed every detail to his searching eyes. Nipples, aroused and jutting, perfectly centered within dark areolae.

Belly that was fit and toned but still rounded and feminine, made all the more intriguing by the winking stone in her navel. *Note to self: check that out at first opportunity.*

Wide hips that would give him plenty to hang on to during the thrusting he planned to do, and skimpy little panties that did nothing to hide the bare cleft he intended to taste in the next three minutes. Strong thighs that he wanted up around his shoulders and then, later, wrapped around his waist in a death grip. Shapely legs, gleaming skin, knowing eyes, as though she fully comprehended that she'd just blown his mind and wasn't done with him yet.

Cracking open his dry mouth, he spoke in an urgent and guttural voice he barely recognized as his own. "Come here."

A slow grin, as lazy as it was dangerous, crept across her lips, heating his skin and tightening something inside him to the snapping point. Taking way too long about the whole process, she crouched and then dropped to all fours, crawling up the length of his body with a tiger's grace and a centerfold's in-your-face sexuality.

Thank God she wasn't shy; there were too many things he wanted to do to and with her, too much ground they had to cover while she was here. If he had to hold himself back long enough to bring her out of a shell, he'd suffer cardiac arrest and then spontaneous combustion.

No. This was a woman who knew how to give and, more importantly, to receive pleasure. Which was good because, while he'd planned a picnic for tonight and would've waited if she wasn't ready, this was what he'd wanted.

Exactly this.

When she was almost within range of his reaching hands, she paused, her face level with his groin. Then, flashing him a smoldering look that had his blood flowing as hot and thick as boiling honey, she nuzzled him with her cheeks, laughing a soft laugh of such wanton satisfaction that he hardened as though she'd already sucked him deep into her mouth.

Right about then, his head became too heavy to hold up and he let it fall back to the blanket and gathered fistfuls of her silky hair to hold her in place. Jesus. He hadn't known he could get this aroused from just the hint of a sex act, hadn't known he was still capable of the kind of desperate need that clawed at him from the inside out.

A drumbeat began, thudding in time with his pulse, and it felt so powerful that he was surprised it didn't echo all around the pond.

Livia…Livia…Livia.

Had he known her for only a few days? It felt like he'd waited a thousand lifetimes for this, and he couldn't get her close enough to stop that rising need from driving him wild. When she laughed again, reaching around to wedge her hands beneath him to squeeze his ass, something in his head snapped.

Letting go of her hair, he grabbed her shoulders and jerked her back. After a groaned protest, she raised her defiant and disgruntled gaze to his. They stared at each other for an arrested second, long enough for him to feel her frustrated restraint shudder through her.

"I need you," she said. "Now."

He couldn't control himself. Not when she played dirty like that. "You're playing with fire," he warned.

"Then burn me."

There went all of his fantasies of finessing her and being a gentle and considerate lover, up in a cloud of lust-induced smoke. In a burst of movement that he really hoped didn't scare the hell out of her, he reared up over her, grabbed her hips and unceremoniously pulled them out from under her, until she was flat on her back.

Impatience made him shake; he needed two tries to tug his sweater off over his head and three to unbutton his jeans and work the zipper over his straining erection.

It took her too long to unfasten the front of her bra, and she had no business doing that, anyway, when he was itching to touch her. So he caught both of her hands in one of his and pinned them to the blanket over her head, where they were out of his way.

"I'll do that," he said, undoing the clasp.

Wrong move. Because the sight of those breasts bouncing free, the nipples dark and distended and just begging for his mouth, brought out the poorly hidden animal in him. Growling—yeah, he actually made a crazy rumbling sound like a dog going for his bone and protecting it from the rest of his pack—he filled his hands to overflowing with all that firm flesh, squeezed them together, and tasted. Licking and suckling, rubbing and nipping, he hoped, in a distant corner of his overwrought mind, that she liked what he was doing because it sure as hell was working for him.

He couldn't get enough of all the sensations of her. Like the way when he drew hard on a nipple, using his tongue to stroke that sweet deliciousness against the roof of his mouth, her fingers tightened on his head, scratching his scalp in a desperate effort to keep him close. Or the way her back arched, making her rise up to meet him, and her strangled cries coalesced into a symphony of all the things he wanted to hear.

"Hunter…ah, God, don't stop. Don't stop…*please*."

She was everything. In the entire world, there was only her body in his hands, her voice in his ears, her taste in his mouth and the faint and earthy scent of her arousal filling his nostrils. She was everything, and he couldn't get enough.

Thrilling as these breasts were, he had other ground to cover.

Sliding lower, he rubbed his face all over her heaving belly, encountering that tiny little ring he'd seen earlier. Interesting. Wonder what she'd do if he dipped his tongue—

"Hunter." She writhed, her hips twisting and apparently beyond her control. *"Hunter."*

Oh, yeah. He liked that.

And he liked those sexy little panties but they had to go, and he didn't have time for sliding them down her ten miles of legs. What else could he do? Using both hands, he ripped them apart, pulled them off and threw them…somewhere.

There she was. That beautiful cleft between her thighs was swollen and ruddy, glistening with cream that he needed to taste. Leaning down—man, he was about to explode here—he breathed her in, making himself high with her scent, and then he ran his tongue over her with the kind of greed that would be right at home at an all-night buffet. Above him, she'd gone silent, either too stunned by this raw pleasure between them to speak—or asleep.

He was betting she wasn't asleep.

"Stop torturing me." Her breathless voice was the tiniest whisper, something he felt more than heard. "I need you inside me."

Yeah. He needed that, too.

Shoving his jeans and boxer briefs just far enough down his hips to free himself, he rose up, hooking her behind the knee with the crook of his arm and spreading her wide as he went. There was a second as he looked into her face and saw the stars' reflection in her heavy-lidded eyes and those dewy lips of hers, swollen now, curled in a half smile, that he absolutely couldn't breathe. Poised to enter all that slick heat, he felt something swell inside him that had nothing to do with the orgasm gathering strength and getting ready to let loose.

Had he done something right? Was that it? Because he'd never imagined he had an experience like this—a woman like this—coming to him.

"Livia," he said, but beyond that he was mute.

Her answer was to widen that smile by an inch, tip her chin up and give his bottom lip a long, slow stroke with her tongue.

Anything he'd been holding back from her was unleashed by that single act.

Groaning, he palmed the engorged length of his penis and entered her with a single hard thrust.

Chapter 10

Jesus.

The feeling of all that honey-slick tightness closing around him almost stroked him out on the spot. Paralyzed with exquisite sensation, he didn't dare move below the waist but couldn't stop his eyes from rolling closed or his head from dropping into the fragrant hollow between her neck and shoulder. She smelled like honeysuckle and felt like an unspeakable new heaven that he hadn't had to die to reach. This fitting together of their bodies also felt like home.

Never in his life, not ever once, had being with a woman unraveled him like this.

Moving against him, she circled her hips and moaned with such unabashed delight that she snapped him out of it and fired him up even more, if that were possible. Pulling out to the tip, he thrust, setting a punishing pace that made him both lose his mind and also settle more fully into her body than he'd been before.

Those long legs of hers wrapped around him with the strength of a vise grip and he went deeper. Felt more.

Every detail came into excruciating focus: the cool night air against his back, the candlelight surrounding them, the slapping contact of his tightening balls and her ass, her flattened breasts against his chest, the hard twin points of her nipples, the silk of her hair in his hands, the wet fullness of her sucking tongue in his mouth and the encouraging croon in her throat.

It was all too much; he wouldn't have been able to hold anything back even if the punishment was death.

Just as her cries reached a thrilling crescendo and her inner muscles began their rhythmic pulse around him, the orgasm roared through him with the force of an arrow shooting out of an Olympic archer's bow.

He came. And came and came and came, shouting her name and pouring so much of himself inside her that he had no hope of ever being whole without her ever again. The whole time they rode it out, he gathered her closer, held her tighter, and even when his body's urgency had begun to cool and it should have been enough, it wasn't.

They melted together into the blanket, still joined, and the kissing subsided into nuzzles until, finally, he shifted enough of his weight for her to breathe and rested his forehead against her cheek.

When sated exhaustion should have been claiming him, his thoughts danced to life and twirled through his brain as though someone was throwing an impromptu party with four hundred dancing couples in there.

Wait a minute…what the hell just happened?

He hadn't finessed her.

He hadn't managed to take his jeans and underwear all the way off and was now hobbled about the ankles like some unfortunate horse.

He hadn't remembered to use a condom.

None of that particularly bothered him. In fact, he couldn't wait to do it again.

That was what bothered him.

What had happened to his life since this sweet siren showed up in it? What was she doing to him? What the hell was he going to do when she left?

Apprehension shivered through him, making him cold.

"What's wrong?" she asked.

He lifted his lids to see those clear hazel eyes staring into his, waiting for an answer he couldn't provide. What could he say? That he had the growing fear that he couldn't live without her? That he hadn't thought about his dead wife, Annette, during this interlude, not even once? That the more time he spent with Livia, the more living he wanted to do, even though he'd spent years wishing the accident had killed him, too? That this thing between them was so much bigger than he'd anticipated?

Of course not.

"I meant to use a condom," he said instead. "I'm sorry."

"We'll use them next time. I'm on the pill, anyway."

"Yeah?" he said, trying to act like this was good news when his gut was doing a sickening little lurch.

"So." Turning her head, she ran the backs of her fingers against his cheek and kissed him again, slipping her tongue into his mouth, where he wanted it. "Should we eat some of that dinner you cooked?"

"Yeah," he said, rolling over her again and giving those spectacular breasts a bit more of the attention they deserved. "In a minute."

Hunter walked her back to her cottage just as a pink-tinged dawn was breaking against the mountains on the horizon. What was that saying? Oh, yeah—*Red in the morning, sailors take warning; red at night is sailors' delight.* Or something like that. So that meant rain today, for the first time since she'd arrived. She could already touch the growing damp in the breeze and it felt like an omen worth noting.

Something had changed. Sometime between their glorious night on the dock, huddled under the quilts, making love, talking and eating the world's best grilled steaks, the walk to the cottage and now, Hunter had stopped touching her. For good measure, he'd even shoved his hands into his jeans pockets and had them balled into unmistakable fists.

That was bad.

What was worse was his shifting gaze, which seemed to land on everything that wasn't her. The growing awkwardness between them felt like approaching doom, and if she'd looked up to see a rampaging herd of elephants heading in their direction, she'd have this same suffocating tightness in her throat.

Still, she didn't have to act needy. For one, Mama didn't raise any fools, and for two, he'd never promised her a lifetime, or even more than one night, of that heart-stopping sex.

He was a man, she was a woman, they'd enjoyed each other and maybe now it was over. Fine. Big deal. She was a grown woman and she'd get over it without lowering herself to the level of burrs clinging to his pants as he walked.

Her? Please. She was so far above all that kind of nonsense it wasn't even funny. Many people considered her to be one of the most beautiful women in the world, so she didn't need to fret and wonder about any particular man. Someone else would turn up soon.

What was it that Beyoncé sang? "I can have another you by tomorrow," wasn't it? Yeah. That.

Opening her mouth, she prepared to say something witty and unconcerned so she could demonstrate her sophisticated understanding of what sex meant and didn't mean.

"Will I see you later?" she blurted.

At last he looked at her and she wished he hadn't. Gone was her lover from last night, replaced by the cool-eyed, granite-faced stranger who'd confronted her in the parking lot that first day. This was the man she didn't know and wasn't sure she wanted to know.

As though he knew something was going on and she needed moral support from wherever she could find it, Willard materialized just then, providing a much needed, though temporary, distraction. Yawning and shaking that huge body to wake himself all the way up, he woofed, trotted over and sat at her feet, bumping her hand with his head in case she needed a hint.

Grateful for his comfort, she scratched his ears and clung to his warmth, since she wasn't getting any from Hunter, who ignored her question altogether.

"When are you leaving?" he asked.

Ah. Was that the heart of the matter, then? Did he prefer she pack and head out right now or was the thought of her going home killing him? Looked like the former.

"Ethan and Rachel are due this evening. We'll check out the chapel, I guess, and then head out as early as tomorrow."

"Tomorrow," he echoed.

His face gave nothing away, which was a real trick. Though she'd done a little acting, she wasn't good enough to stand here and play it cool for another second, so it was time to wrap this up.

Forcing a smile, she kept her voice light. "Thanks for the picnic."

There went his gaze again, shifting off toward something over her shoulder while he jerked his thumb over his own. "I should get going. Kendra'll be getting ready for school soon, and I need to—"

"I understand," she said quickly, beginning to hate him with a seething virulence that they should really bottle and use as a pesticide, it was that strong.

He nodded, already a thousand miles away from her before his steps took him to the edge of the porch. There was no kiss. No hug. Nothing but the generic "See you later" that he might've said to the cashier at the farmer's market.

"See you later," she replied.

She watched him go as the first drops of rain began to fall.

The rain came down in driving sheets that did nothing to help Livia's gloomy mood. Going out in that mess was unthinkable so she never even considered it. After showering and a room service breakfast, she took up a listless post on the living-room sofa, watching a *Dog Wrangler* marathon (the episode with the bulldog's obsession with skateboarding always made her laugh) on the B and B's satellite TV system and hunkering under a down blanket for comfort.

Willard, who'd apparently decided he was her pet, sprawled atop her legs, which was something like cuddling with an overweight fawn. To her surprise, he was a fine companion, except for when he barked back at the barking dogs on the show. That, she could do without.

Hunter didn't call.

Not during the morning and not after she shared her paella lunch with Willard, who loved the shrimp but wasn't so big on the mussels. When three o'clock-ish came, she figured he was getting Kendra off the bus from school, and when four o'clock came, she wondered if she should maybe think about changing her clothes for when Ethan and Rachel arrived.

Buuuut…nah.

It was so much better to wallow in her self-pity for being stupid enough to fall more than halfway in love with a man she'd met on vacation.

The loneliness was excruciating, which was pretty funny considering she'd only known him for a few days. If she'd never met him, she'd've been fine. If she'd merely kissed and flirted with him, she'd've been fine. Hell, if she'd merely had sex with him, she probably would've been fine.

But the agonizing combination of their wonderful daytime hours yesterday followed by the best sex of her life, followed by snuggling and talking and more sex, followed by today's absolute absence of him from her life, made her feel as though she was dying. As though the best part of her had been ripped away and wasn't coming back. As though this echoing hollowness inside her could never be filled.

How crazy was that?

She levered herself up just enough to gaze down at the dog, who had his snout resting on her knees. "Am I insane, Willard?"

That mournful look of his was answer enough.

Yeah. It figured.

Slumping back with emotional exhaustion, she tried to refocus on TV.

Screw Hunter Chambers. *Screw him.*

Her cell phone bleated, the sound echoing off the walls like the crack of a rifle. First she jumped ten feet in the air. Then her pulse went haywire on account of her soaring heart. Then she scrambled upright and grabbed it off the end table, simultaneously smoothing her Medusa-worthy hair out of her face, like *that* mattered.

True, she'd written Hunter off and never wanted to see him again. But that didn't mean she wouldn't take his call and read him the riot act for this shabby treatment today. Oh, yes. If he thought he could do this to her, then he'd better— "Hello?"

"Hey, girl," said Rachel.

"Oh." It was impossible to switch gears between crashing disappointment that it wasn't Hunter and happy surprise that it was Rachel instead, so she didn't even try. "Rachel. Hi."

"Okay, what's wrong with you? Did you get hit by a truck?"

Friends. That was both the good thing and the bad thing about them—they knew when you were feeling down in the dumps and didn't have the decency to ignore your misery and let you wallow in peace. Normally she told Rachel everything that was going on, but then she'd never had her life turned upside down quite the way Hunter had done. Now wasn't the time to get into it; she'd barely had time to process anything herself, and there'd be time enough to dissect her tragic love life once Rachel and Ethan arrived.

"Hello?" Rachel snapped. "What's wrong?"

"Cramps," Livia lied. "Are you on your way?"

"Ah. About that..."

"No way. No. Freaking. Way."

"We can't get away yet, Livie. Sorry. This thing is running long and I—"

"Well, are you talking another day or two delay or—"

"Three weeks."

What? Three—*what?*

Dropping the phone away from her ear, Livia gaped at Willard, who yawned and scratched his jaw with one of his hind legs in an underwhelming display of support.

Okay. Okay, girl. Pull it together.

"Did you just say three weeks, Rachel? Is that what I'm hearing?"

"I'm sorry. I'm really, really sorry. But there's nothing we can do. This thing is so far behind schedule—".

"I'll just come home." Yeah. That made the most sense. "I'll come home tomorrow, and you and Ethan can come on your own, when you have time. You don't need me to scope locations for your wedding."

"No! I need you, and I was looking forward to this! You can't let me down like this—"

"I can't stay here for three more weeks." A desperate, lonely vista opened up before her at the idea: twenty-one days spent on this very sofa with Willard, longing for Hunter and remembering the good old day—yes, it'd only been one day, hadn't it?—when he'd pretended she meant something to him. She and Willard could order pizza. They could have joint massages and manicures. It'd be great.

Not.

"Yeah," she said, the decision made. "I'll come home. I'll get the first flight I can."

"Well, at least stay a couple more days. I thought you had all that sightseeing to do, and it's been so long since you had a vacation."

"Yeah. I don't think so."

Rachel heaved a big sigh and Livia could practically see her deflating over the phone. "Did you have a chance to meet Ethan's family?"

"I did."

"Well, don't keep me in suspense. What were his parents like? I've only talked to them on the phone so far. I can't wait to meet them."

A sudden stab of jealousy, her first ever toward Rachel, hit her. Soon Rachel would have those wonderful people for in-laws. Soon Rachel could call this vineyard home. Soon Rachel would belong here, with this family, and Livia never would.

"They were great. You'll love them."

"And what about Hunter? What's he like?"

Hunter.

Even the sound of his name hurt right now.

"He's a great guy," Livia said, fighting a mighty battle to keep her voice even and her sudden tears from falling. Blinking furiously, she got control of herself, but only just. "You'll love him."

I love him.

The words were right there on the tip of her tongue, waiting to be said, but she bit them back. Love. She couldn't be in love with a man she'd known for only a few days. That was impossible. Ridiculous. Over-the-top romantic nonsense.

Wasn't it?

"What's he like?"

Lord almighty—what was with the questions? She

was coming out of her skin here and Rachel wanted Hunter's personality profile? Was this a cosmic joke on her?

"I don't know, Rach," she said, the strain breaking through in her voice. "You'll have to see for yourself—"

Someone knocked at her door and her heart, foolish to the point of recklessness, leapt with renewed excitement and hope like a tongue-dangling retriever going after a ball.

Hunter? Was that Hunter? Did he care about her after all? Hunter? *Hunter?*

Pathetic.

"Hey, Rach," she said, already leaping from the sofa and making another futile effort to smooth her hair as she raced for the front door. "Someone's here. I gotta go, okay? Call you back."

"But—" Rachel spluttered.

Livia clicked the phone off and tossed it back on the side table as she went past. Slowing down on the last couple of steps, she swung the door open and held her breath as—

"Kendra," she cried. "What're you doing here?"

The girl looked up at her, those big brown eyes filled with tragic despair, her chin trembling. Today she wore a green Future Paleontologist T-shirt with her shorts and carried a small square makeup suitcase circa 1960 or earlier in her hand. When Willard raced over to greet her, she patted his neck and gave his furry face a lingering kiss. Then she looked up at Livia, gathered all her courage around her with one dramatic breath and spoke in a heartbroken voice that would do a blues singer proud.

"Can I come in?" she asked.

"What are you doing here?" Livia asked again.

"I ran away."

"Oh," Livia said, trying not to laugh at this solemn moment. "Is that why you have the suitcase?"

"Yeah."

"What's in there, anyway?"

"My dragons and dinosaurs. Oh, and I packed a granola bar in case I got hungry, but I ate it already."

This child was too precious for words. "What about a change of clothes, underwear, a toothbrush and some money?"

Kendra's face fell. "I forgot those."

"I see."

Apparently tired of waiting for permission, she edged past Livia and headed into the living room, making herself at home on the sofa. There was nothing for Livia to do but shut the door, follow her and sit on the coffee table facing her. Willard, who wouldn't let his pack go anywhere without him, trotted along and settled at their feet.

"What happened?"

"Daddy was mean to me."

"Oh, no."

"He yelled at me. And he wouldn't let me come see you."

Oh, really? Wasn't that interesting?

"Well," Livia said carefully, knowing it wasn't cool to interrogate a six-year-old, "daddies yell sometimes. Did you not clean your room, or—"

"*No.*" Kendra's voice was adamant, her outrage absolute. "He was grouchy when I got home from school. I didn't do *anything*. Even Grandma said he needed to get his act together or leave her kitchen."

Livia gaped at her, overwhelming hope making her head spin. "What do you think was wrong with him?"

Kendra shrugged, looking bewildered and victimized. "And then," she said with the rising excitement that told Livia she was getting to the juicy stuff, her father's worst offense against her, "I asked if I could come see you, and he yelled at me and shook his finger and said—" Kendra puffed herself up, wagged her finger and deepened her voice in a remarkably good imitation of Hunter "'—Miss Livia is on vacation and she'll be leaving tomorrow, so there's no point getting too attached to her!' And then he marched out and slammed the door! Really hard!"

"Hunter slammed the door?" Livia tried to get her mind around the image of Mr. Calm, Cool and Collected having a meltdown, but it was as incomprehensible as a hippopotamus being a principal dancer in *Swan Lake*. "Maybe he's just, you know, having a bad day, honey. I'm sure he didn't mean it."

"I can't live like that!"

"Ah…" Livia kept her lips pressed tightly together, fighting that urge to laugh again, because Kendra was clearly embracing her inner diva with this dramatic performance. "You can't just run away when—"

Moving in for the kill, Kendra hopped down from the sofa and scrambled into Livia's lap, where her solid weight and fruity-fresh little girl's fragrance were much too wonderful for Livia's overwrought nerves. Livia tried to brace herself against all this cuteness but that was no use, especially when Willard, who hated to be excluded from any nearby affection, rose up, rested his snout in the girl's lap and gave them both the soulful eye.

"Can I live here with you, Miss Livia?" Kendra begged. "Pleeeeeeeaaaaase?"

Allowing herself one precious minute of fantasies, Livia hugged her and kissed her fat cheeks. Both of them. What would it be like to have a child like this in her life, playing and giggling, whining and just sitting, like this, in quiet moments that were only special because they were together? What would it be like to tuck an angel like this into bed and wake up to her bleary smile in the mornings? What would she give to have a family of her own, with a husband and a child and a home that was really a home and not just the place where she landed in between shoots all over the world?

Would a million dollars cover it? Done. Ten million? No problem. And if her career interfered with the proper raising of a bright girl like this, the career would have to go, no question. Much as she'd worked and bled to get where she was right now, one of the top models in the world, she was coming to a painful realization that she should have known all along, just like Dorothy should've known, there was no place like home.

Money didn't do you a damn bit of good when you had a yawning ache inside you that only a family of your own could fill.

But she didn't have a family of her own and this child, meanwhile, was waiting for an answer. So she gave Kendra's forehead a kiss, because she'd missed it on the first round of kisses, swallowed the growing tightness in her throat and gave the kind of understanding but regretful smile she imagined a good mother would give in this kind of situation.

"You can't live here with me, honey—"

"Pleeeeeeeaaaaase?" Kendra clasped her hands together, ramping up the enthusiasm. "I promise I'll—"

Livia held up a finger to silence her. "But..." she said.

Kendra snapped her jaws shut.

"If you're finished begging and whining…"

Kendra nodded violently.

"Then you can call your grandma to tell her where you are and apologize for scaring her, because I'm sure she's wondering if you've been kidnapped or eaten by cougars or something."

More nodding.

"And we can have snacks and give each other pedicures with this pretty pink polish I brought with me. How would that be?"

"Great! Thank you! Thank you, thank you, *thank you!*"

"Here's the phone."

Livia watched her dial and then chatter with her grandmother, certain that when she left Napa tomorrow, she'd be leaving a big chunk of her heart right here with Kendra.

The rain was relentless, pounding against Livia's windows until late in the evening and doing nothing to lift her spirits.

After the impromptu but delightful pedicures with Kendra, she'd walked her and Willard back to the big house and then, thoroughly sick of her own company and disgusted with her pity party of one, which had gone on long enough, she bundled up, had a quick sandwich at the winery's bistro (no sign of any of the Chambers family, thank goodness) and came back to finish her Jackie Robinson biography, which was excellent.

The Dog Wrangler marathon was still on at that point (they were now up to the episode with the nonretrieving golden retriever, a canine who also didn't know he could swim), so she watched it for a while and then decided to call it a night at eleven-thirty. She was making a last lap around the cottage, clicking off the lamps, when someone knocked on the door.

Hunter.

It was him; no one else would disturb her at this hour, not unless it was the local authorities trying to evacuate everyone at the winery on account of an impending flood or mudslide. Indecision nailed her feet to the floor while an excited hope made her lungs heave like giant bellows.

Her brain was just pissed.

Recovering just as the second round of knocks began, she marched through the foyer and flung the door open for the simple pleasure of telling him to go to hell. But then their gazes connected and her thoughts scattered like rioters being fire hosed.

The overhead porch light was bright enough for her to see that he looked drowned-rat terrible. His clothes and jacket were soaked, and the idiot didn't even have the sense to wear the baseball hat he'd had glued to his head the other day. Rivulets of rain ran down his forehead and dripped into eyes that were flashing dark and ferocious but otherwise unreadable. His jaw was tight, his lips thin. And she was so relieved, so unbelievably and unspeakably happy to see him after today's long hours without him, that it absolutely infuriated her.

He was the jerk, yeah, but she was the fool.

"Livia," he began.

She slammed the door in his face.

Better to cool off and deal with him later—or never— than risk letting him see what he'd done to her today and how she'd unraveled at the loss of his attention after their glorious night together. He'd either come because his guilty conscience was forcing him to put a nice period at the end of their little fling—his parents were decent folks, after all, and they'd probably taught him to treat women the way he'd want to be treated—or he'd come to stammer out some lame excuse in the hopes that he could have a no-strings-attached booty call.

Either way, it wasn't happening.

A sharp curse came from the other side of the door, and then pounding. "Livia," he said, and the husky aggravation in his voice made her want to break into a few joyous steps of the Electric Slide. "We need to talk. *Please.*"

She flicked off the porch light and bolted the door.

Is that a clear enough message for you, Hunter?

Filled with a savage satisfaction, she dusted off her hands—*buh-bye, jackass!*—took her time about folding the throw and draping it over the sofa's arm and turned off the last couple of living room lights before heading down the hall.

So he thought he could just play her, did he? Thought he could rock her world last night, kiss her off this morning, ignore her all day and then reappear tonight to a warm reception and her open legs?

No way, buddy. No. Freaking. Way.

She swept her sweater off over her head, thinking maybe she needed a shower to decompress before bed. The steam would help soothe her raw nerves and the water—

"Oh, my God," she shrieked, backing into the nearest wall with a thunk.

Hunter stood in the middle of the bedroom, looking grim.

Chapter 11

A tense second passed, during which Livia tried to catch her breath and settle back into her skin. She opened her mouth to demand to know how he'd gotten in there, but the open window and displaced screen behind the fluttering curtains said it all so she snapped her jaws shut.

Who'd've thought her love of Napa's cool nighttime air would bite her in the ass in such a big way?

Since she hated being outflanked and outmaneuvered, she let both her temper and her sweater fly, hurling the latter at him. Naturally he deflected it with a casual swipe of his arm, the bastard.

"Don't scare me like that, you son of a—"

"Kindly don't slam the door in my face again."

That quiet calm of his was more than she could take at the end of this long day of feeling abandoned and strung out. "Are we talking about manners here? Because I don't take kindly to being blown off, and I don't do booty calls. So you can get out right now."

"That's not why I'm here."

Too late she regretted the rashness of throwing her sweater at him, which left her both half-naked and vulnerable to the quiet pain in his eyes. It was more than that, actually. Those harsh facial lines, tight lips and the flashing brown turbulence all added up to one thing.

He'd spent his day every bit as tormented as she had.

That mattered to her but that didn't mean she was a marshmallow.

"What do you want?" she demanded, crossing her arms over her lacy white bra and praying he couldn't see the way her breasts swelled and her nipples tightened for him or the goose bumps rising all over her skin.

"Thanks for taking care of Kendra earlier."

"My pleasure."

"I hope she wasn't too much trouble."

"She was no trouble. I'm crazy about her."

"We're crazy about you."

Whoa. Something shifted just then, charging the air with enough electricity to power the Vegas strip for a month or so. She told herself that physical chemistry didn't amount to much, that keeping this roller-coaster ride going with him would lead to inevitable heartbreak for her, but none of that mattered when her skin was starved for his.

"'We'?" she echoed.

"I," he said softly. *"I* am crazy about you."

That raw ache in his voice went a long way toward soothing her bruised feelings and reassuring her. It was terrifying to fall, yeah, but how bad could it be if they both fell together? And he was falling, even if he didn't say it. She had eyes; she could see his fear.

Still. A reminder of recent events seemed like a good idea. "You didn't seem that crazy about me this morning. You couldn't leave me fast enough."

"This morning it was all I could do to remember that I have grapes to harvest and a winery to run." He swallowed hard, making his Adam's apple dip in a rough bob, and then confessed something else that made her knees weaken and her heart pound. "It was all I could do not to lose it when you told me you're leaving tomorrow."

The words came before she could think about the wisdom of telling him. "I don't... I don't have to leave tomorrow. Rachel and Ethan have been delayed again—"

"How long?" he demanded urgently, cutting her off.

"Three weeks."

His face twisted, although whether it was with a sob or a grin, she couldn't quite tell at first. "Three weeks," he repeated, and he said it with the wonder of a man who'd been gifted with a room full of beer, pizza and a recliner parked in front of a theater-sized TV tuned to ESPN. "Three weeks."

Much as she wanted to fall into his arms right now, they had to get some things straight. She couldn't spend another day like this one. No one had died, true, but another day like this one just might kill her.

"You hurt me this morning," she told him.

He stepped closer, his voice dropping to a whisper. "And you're making me feel things that scare me to death."

"So why come back now?"

"I can't stay away from you," he said simply. "It's out of my control."

That did it. She was now, officially, in love with this man.

With a glad sob, she launched herself into his arms.

They came together hard and fast, with a grappling urgency that bordered on violence. Hunter caught her face between his hands and angled it way back, imprisoning her and using aggressive licks and nips to possess her mouth. She opened up for him, a flower unfolding her petals for her sun, sucking him deeper, needing him more, needing it all.

In this world full of frightening new feelings between them, this was the scariest: he had her. She couldn't seem to give herself over to him fast enough. Not her body, certainly, and not her heart, either. They were his. All of her growing whimpers and cries belonged to him, and her swelling breasts and weeping sex were his, too. Did he know that she'd never lost herself like this before? That his presence sparked a fever in her and his smile made her head light?

Could he see this terrible weakness in her?

The words came and kept coming because he'd unlocked a hidden mechanism that wouldn't let her hold things back from him; everything she had and was belonged to him and she gave it freely. It wasn't enough that her shaking hands shoved aside his jacket and dove under his sweater, hungry for the hot skin underneath. She had to narrate everything, paint him a picture and draw him a map.

"I missed you." It was hard to kiss him and talk at the same time, but she somehow made it work, brushing her lips against his and tasting him with her tongue even as she rubbed her breasts against his unyielding chest and raked her nails up his back. "I missed you so much. I couldn't breathe with it."

"I missed you, too." Beneath all that smooth skin, she felt the flex of his tightening muscles, the vibrations as he tried to hold himself in check. He ran his hands all over her torso, zeroing in on her breasts and freeing them from her bra with a flick of his fingers. "You were all I could think about. This was all I could think about."

Stooping just enough, he pressed her breasts together in his rough grip, circling her nipples with his thumbs and then licking, sucking and biting them with primitive abandon, as though he'd been given only thirty seconds to claim every part of them and the only thing that mattered was not missing a single millimeter.

"Hunter…God. Don't stop. Don't stop, Hunter. Hunter. *Hunter.*"

"Shhh. It's okay, baby. It's okay—"

"I needed you inside me. Don't you know that? I need you…I need you…I need you, Hunter. Stay with me, okay? Stay with me. Please. *Please.*"

Was that her voice sobbing like that? Chanting like that? Which of them was making that animalistic sound— part growl and part purr? Who was shaking worse?

Leaving her breasts, he focused in on her cargo pants, undoing the button and then yanking with both hands to separate the zipper and pull them off over her hips. They fell to her ankles and she had just enough time to kick them away before he planted his hands on her ass and hefted her up.

Apparently no one had ever told him that she was an Amazon, taller and heavier than a lot of men she knew, because he tightened her thighs around his waist and swung her around toward the bed. Through her heavy-lidded eyes, she had a quick glimpse of him staring up at her, his expression glazed and alight, his lips swollen and his forehead damp. Then he dipped his head again, latched on to a nipple and suckled with long, rhythmic pulls that shot electric jolts of pleasure to the depths of her belly and made her inner muscles clench.

Blinded with the sensation, she clung to his neck for dear life but let her eyes roll closed and her head fall back. The next thing she knew, he was lowering her to the cool sheets and resting her head on the pillow, and there was no world but this, nothing but him standing by the bed, squirming out of his jeans and boxers to reveal a heavy erection that she needed inside her right now.

Reaching for him, she spread her thighs and angled her hips. "Now." There she went with the chanting again. It would have been funny if the need wasn't suffocating her alive. "Now, Hunter. Please. Now."

His feverish gaze locked with hers, his movements choppy and uncoordinated, he fumbled with something in his pocket and produced a tiny package wrapped with green foil. Something in her overwrought mind protested as she watched him rip it open and roll it on. They'd used them last night after the first time, yeah, but it seemed unnatural to have anything between them even if it was the smart thing to do. Worse, the delay took too long and she needed him buried deep when this gathering eruption roared through her as it was threatening to do any second.

"Hunter," she began again.

"Turn over."

Scrambling to obey, she rose up on all fours, presenting him with the tiny white whale tail of her thong panties between her cheeks. Since she and shame had parted ways a while back, the second he laid his hands on her, she dipped her back into a U, making herself as open and accessible to him as humanly possible.

Just in case he needed a hint.

"Christ," he muttered, then crawled onto the bed behind her and sank his teeth deep into her rounded flesh.

"Oh, God."

Jerking her hips back and up against him, he pulled off her thong and stroked the swollen flesh between her legs in an excruciating caress that had more sobs collecting in her throat. A rumble of approval was her only warning before he thrust deep, stretching her beyond endurance and hitting a hidden spot inside her body that made stars spark in front of her eyes.

"Yes," she said with what was left of her voice. "More."

Sliding up over her, he surrounded her on all sides, giving notice for the record. Her back was his because he'd covered it with his chest. Her neck was his because he'd clamped it between his teeth, using that exquisitely sensitive spot to hold her in place. Her dangling breasts belonged to one of his exploring hands and her engorged sex belonged to the other.

He thrust sharp and deep, taking it all and demanding more, letting go of her neck only to bite her ear as he spoke. "Say my name."

Hey—if he wanted it, it was his. Everything was his.

"Hunter," she gasped.

He withdrew to the tip and surged again, harder. "Who do you belong to?"

"You."

"Huh?"

"You, Hunter. *You.*"

"Do you want it like this?"

Funny guy. Laughter began in her throat only to be choked off by another moan of pleasure. "You know I do."

"Harder?"

"God, yes," she said, but even as the words were coming out of her mouth, she wondered how she could take any more before her body disintegrated. "Yes."

His rhythm picked up until their bodies slapped together and she felt like a very wicked girl for being punished like this. Deliciously wicked. Breathless and triumphant, she let the pleasure fill her up until she laughed.

He growled in the most primitive kind of masculine warning but she could hear the amusement in his voice. "This is funny?"

"You feel so good."

"Yeah?"

"Oh, yeah."

"Are you going to come for me?"

"Maybe."

The teasing sealed her fate. Unleashing anything he'd been holding back, he thrust into her with sharp strokes, in and out, biting her neck again and pinching one of her nipples for good measure.

She flew apart, shouting her release with an abandon she'd never felt before. And just at the moment she needed his driving force between her thighs, prolonging the ecstasy, he stiffened to concrete and refused to move.

"Don't stop," she begged. "Please don't—"

"Are you going to come again for me, Livia?"

"Please don't stop—"

"You're not holding back on me, are you?"

As if she could. "No," she gasped. "Just a little more. I just need a little more."

"Good girl."

He surged again, harder and deeper, and she dissolved into spasms of such intense pleasure she didn't know how she could survive. She opened her mouth to let it out, but she had nothing left because he'd taken it all.

She collapsed into the pillows, sated and exhausted, and listened to his raw voice say her name in an endless stream as he drove into her, again and again, and then, with a hoarse shout, went rigid all around her.

When it was over, they stretched out, fitting together so well they could only have been made for each other, and she drifted toward peace and oblivion with his lips brushing back and forth against her nape.

"Do me a favor," he murmured just as she was falling asleep.

"Hmm?" Turning her head to receive his kiss on her cheek, she brought his hand to her breasts to make sure he didn't let her go during the night and settled her butt more firmly into his lap.

"Think about how we can see each other when your vacation is over."

Now this was worth staying awake for. Lifting her heavy lids, she twisted her neck a little further so she'd be able to see his eyes. They were smiling. Intent. Happy. Knowing that she'd had something to do with putting a look like that on such a man's face was overwhelming. Incomprehensible.

"Yeah?"

He skimmed the corner of her lips with a featherlight kiss that made tension coil in her belly and heat pool— again!—between her legs. "Can you do that for me?"

Yes was the answer, but before she could give it, he slid his mouth a couple of inches in the right direction, beginning the dance all over again. As she turned in his arms and sucked his tongue deeper into her mouth, her last coherent thought was that they were going to have another deliciously sleepless night.

"Should we be doing this?" Livia asked, her voice hushed.

He had to grin. The woman who'd made a fine living displaying her body for the world to see was turning shy on him over a late dip in the B and B's spa. Was that funny or what? Despite the fact that it was two in the morning, the whole place was asleep and he'd only turned on a couple of discreet lights inside the fenced and landscaped area, Livia was bundled up tight in the white floor-length terry-cloth robe he'd nabbed from the massage area for her. Looking worried, she watched him relax into the churning water and dipped one toe in.

"What if someone catches us?" she wondered.

Closing his eyes, he rested his arms on the ledge and leaned his head back. Heaven. The hot water against the cool night air on his face (it had finally stopped raining) was absolute heaven. Well, no. Being buried inside Livia's body, making love to her—that was absolute heaven. This was…heaven's basement.

"If someone catches us, then we'll apologize and leave. In the meantime, I'm staying here until my skin wrinkles." He cracked one eye open. "You coming in or not?"

With a final, furtive glance in all directions, she unbelted the robe, slipped it off—yeah, he needed both eyes open for that—and slid into the spa and onto the bench beside him.

"Oh," she breathed, her eyes rolling closed and her head tipping back with exaggerated ecstasy. "*God.* Why didn't you tell me?"

"I tried. You didn't listen."

"Hmm."

They sat in silence for a minute, melting into the relaxing swirl, and he figured now was as good a time as any to bring up a subject that'd been nagging at his brain for a while now.

"Can I ask you something?"

"Course," she murmured.

He stared at her, wanting to see her reaction. "Why haven't you ever gotten married?"

Those hazel eyes opened and crinkled in a wry smile. "My life isn't exactly conducive to successful relationships, is it?"

Why did that simple truth sting so much? And why did he feel this relentless compulsion to tiptoe down this road with her? "Why's that?"

"I'm always traveling, for one. For two, a lot of the men I meet are, ah—"

"Unworthy?" he supplied sourly, thinking of rumors he'd heard a while back about her dating some producer who'd later run off with an actress.

That made her grin. "*Unworthy.* I like that."

This should've been answer enough but it wasn't. "They can't all be unworthy."

"No," she agreed. "Some are intimidated. Some could be worthy but are more concerned with a trophy on their arms and don't bother to ever see me."

What did that mean? "*See* you?"

"Me." Lifting a hand out of the water, she touched it to her heart and he got it. *"Me."*

For reasons that eluded him at the moment, this explanation made him unreasonably happy. Maybe it was because he wasn't rich or famous, didn't have his own jet and couldn't give her a part in a movie that would make her acting career.

But, unlike those other men, he saw her. Not just the outer shell—her.

He saw the fierce pride and the keen intelligence, the sweetness and the strength. He saw the beauty of her smile, yeah, but he also saw the greater beauty of her heart.

Did she know that? Should he tell her?

Covering her hand with his, he pressed it to her chest, where the water thrashed and her heart thudded. When her breath caught and her uncertain gaze flickered to his, he leaned in to give her lips a gentle but lingering kiss.

"I see you, Livia."

"Yeah?" she whispered.

"You're beautiful." Nudging her hand aside, he settled his fingers against the silky slickness of the valley between her bobbing breasts. "*This* is beautiful."

Because he didn't trust his voice to say anything further, not now, he slid his hands to the curve where waist met hips, pulled her around until she straddled his lap and showed her just how special he thought she was.

Chapter 12

"Hey, sexy."

Rolling the driver's-side window down a little farther, Hunter leaned his elbow on the door and steered the truck alongside Livia. She liked to ride her bike for an hour or so after lunch every day and, as luck would have it, he just happened to be traveling this very same road, on his way back from picking up a few things in town.

What a delightful coincidence. Or not.

Why burden the poor woman with the information that he was finding it increasingly difficult to make it through the long hours between when they left each other's beds in the mornings and their afternoon glass of wine together? Was there any reason to tell her he'd been driving up and down these roads for the past fifteen minutes, hoping to catch a glimpse of her? No way. God knew he'd already lost his head enough over her; there was no reason to confess it outright. What if she thought he was a stalker?

"You need a lift?"

Grinning, she hopped off the bike and stared over her shoulder at him, her eyes hidden and mysterious behind dark sunglasses. Along with her helmet, she wore those same sexy shorts from that day he ran her off the road, and, unbelievably, the same tank top, although she had another shirt of some type tied around her waist and apparently planned to use it when she got back to civilization. Pulling the glasses down to the tip of her nose, she gave him a once-over and pretended to give it serious thought.

"I don't know," she said. "Mama always told me to watch out for strange men."

"Honey," he said before he backed the truck under a tree just off the road, "if your mama knew the kinds of things I wanted to do with you, she'd call the police."

There it was again: that delighted and delightful laugh, the sunshine in his life that had nothing to do with the bright sky overhead. How this woman had worked her way this deep under his skin and into his blood in only a few short weeks was a mystery he really needed to figure out at some point.

If only he wasn't too whipped to think.

"I'm not sure." Taking her helmet and glasses off, she tipped her face up to his as he approached, revealing flushed skin that was dewy with sweat and musky with the best fragrance in the world—healthy woman. *This* healthy woman.

He kept coming until he felt the blaze of her body's heat all up and down his front, happier than he'd been since…man, he didn't even know when. Annette was drifting more firmly into his past, and the more he looked into Livia's beautiful face, the more appropriate it seemed that he turn the page on that first part of his life. It didn't mean that he hadn't loved Annette. It just meant that he had more living to do, with Livia.

"Is it safe in that big truck with you?"

"Absolutely not."

Another laugh. "Let's go, then."

After he'd loaded the bike into the bed, he snapped his fingers as though he'd just remembered something. "I forgot to mention one little thing. Sorry."

"And what's that?"

"Payment. You don't think you can ride in my truck for free, do you?"

Her face fell into a pretty pout. "Oh, no. I'm not sure I have any money with me."

He shrugged. "I'll try to be flexible. What do you have to offer?"

"What did you have in mind?"

This time, he was the one to pull off his sunglasses. Taking his sweet time about it, he let his lazy gaze drift over her. To the drops of sweat gathered in the hollow between her collarbones; he wanted to lick those. To her beaded nipples under that little top; he wanted to lick those, too. To the V between her legs where he wanted to bury himself to the hilt. Now.

The hot pulse of his blood wouldn't leave him alone until he did.

"What do you think I have in mind?"

A wicked light flickered to life in her eyes. Her lips curled with the beginnings of a smile and that smile widened when she checked him out below the waist and saw how hard he was behind the tight button front of his jeans, how ready.

"Well," she said softly, "I always try to pay my debts."

"Glad to hear it."

Taking her hand, he pressed it to his erection, which was all the encouragement she needed. She stroked him up and down, rough, the way he needed it, and if that wasn't enough to drive him to the brink of insanity and several miles beyond, she jerked his head down with her free hand, opening her mouth so he could slide his tongue inside and taste her.

Lord. She was hot and slick, minty fresh and delicious. And suddenly playtime was over and he couldn't wait. Breaking the kiss, he towed her around to the rear door, which he opened.

"Have I introduced you to my backseat?"

She hesitated, taking inventory. Her gaze scanned the long stretch of deserted road in both directions, the protective overhang of tree branches and the truck's blacked-out windows. Then she eyed the spacious and comfy stretch of leather seat and, finally, the front of his jeans.

The decision apparently made, she looked him in the eye.

And peeled that stretchy top off over her head, baring her breasts to him. Dry-mouthed and astonished, he glanced to the cloudless blue sky overhead and said a silent thanks to whoever was responsible for Livia's appearance in his life. After that, he had a quick second to enjoy the way those plump handfuls bounced back into place and her nipples darkened and tightened down into jutting buds before she bent and, still watching him, shimmied out of her shorts and shoes, straightened, and stood before him in all her considerable glory. "Jesus," he muttered.

You'd think that after all their long nights together, the sight of this body might be losing its breathtaking effect on him, but no. You might also think that sex two or three times a day for a man who'd spent the last several years having sex once a month, if he was lucky, would be more than enough, but no. And if you thought having constant sex with Livia made him want to do anything other than have more sex with Livia, you were dead wrong.

Creeping closer, she went to work on freeing him from his pants. "Were we going to do this today, or…?"

"Hell, yeah."

He dove headfirst into the truck and pulled her in after him. Slamming the door shut, she straddled his lap and all but mauled him with her urgency. Her mouth caught his with aggressive, biting little kisses, and she rubbed her sweaty torso all over him, arching those breasts into his hands…his mouth…her own hands. Squeezing them together, she offered herself to him, brushing those hard nipples against his lips until, with a harsh groan, he sucked the way she liked.

"Ouch," she murmured. "Too hard. Take it easy on the girls, okay? You wore them out last night."

"How's this?" Trying to be gentler, he traced circles around her areola with his tongue. "That better?"

"Oh, yeah." Her head fell back—God, she was flexible—and she moaned and laughed in the most delicious combination his ears had ever heard.

Which was all well and good, but there was creamy white honey between her thighs—he could see it glisten and smell its musk—and he was dying here. Desperation making his movements choppy, he fished a condom out of his wallet and ripped it open with his teeth. He hated those little bastards, hated that there was a layer of anything between his flesh and hers, but he knew that wearing them was the right thing to do and—

"Wait," she said, slipping off his lap and to her knees on the floor in front of him. "Not so fast."

"Don't." Down to the last fumes of his control now, he couldn't possibly—

Too late.

Those dewy lips of hers slid down his length and sucked him inside, to the farthest, hottest part of her slick mouth, and he gasped with the unbearable pleasure. Damn near passed out.

"Livia," he croaked as his head fell back against the seat and his eyes rolled closed. "You have to stop." But the vibrating hum in her throat sounded suspiciously like smothered amusement and his hands were already twining into her damp hair to keep her bobbing head in place. "You have to…to…"

At that point he just shut the hell up. It was hard to launch a decent protest when you couldn't maintain blood flow to your brain. Limp and boneless except for his hands, which had curled into a death grip against her warm scalp, he accepted her gift until he absolutely couldn't take it another second.

"Come here."

She straddled his lap again and he rolled the condom on with lightning speed. The next thing he knew, he was buried to the base inside her, her frantically flexing ass was in his hands and her tongue was in his mouth.

At least for a few more thrusts, until the orgasm roared through her and she had to pull back and open her mouth to a high-pitched cry that was the world's best music. The sound of it, naturally, drove him over the edge, and he pumped and shouted until there was nothing left inside him except for his growing feelings for this woman.

Spent, they laid across the seat with her sprawled atop him like a rag doll.

After enough time had passed for them to catch their breath, she raised her head and gave him a kiss that was sweet and lingering.

"Hi," she said.

He grinned. "Hi."

"How was your day?"

As if she didn't know. "My day was excellent. Yours?"

"Oh, I'm having a great day. But I have a question for you."

"Oh, yeah?" This sounded like it could be serious, so he made a pillow by stacking his palms beneath his head. "What's that?"

"Are you ashamed of me?"

This was so unexpected that he couldn't stop a disbelieving snort. "What? No!"

"Have I embarrassed you?"

"*No*. Why would you ask—"

Sudden unhappiness darkened her eyes, turning the hazel muddy. "Because you haven't had me around your parents again and I'm getting the feeling you don't want me spending too much time with Kendra."

"Oh," he said, stunned and absolutely incapable of forming a decent answer. And then, because that wasn't lame enough, he said "Oh" again.

Silence, unless you counted her now red-hot cheeks, which all but sizzled with growing humiliation.

"Sorry," she backtracked, sitting up and grabbing her clothes. "I don't want to put you on the spot—"

"Livia."

His body protested the loss of her even as his floundering brain struggled for something acceptable to say. Options? Well, there was "I don't want you breaking my vulnerable daughter's heart when you go back to L.A.," but that sounded too much like "I don't want you breaking my vulnerable heart when you go back to L.A.," and that, in turn, was too close to "Please don't ever leave me and go back to L.A.," and he wasn't ready to say that yet.

Hell, maybe he was only fooling himself. Maybe he'd been ready to say it since he'd laid eyes on her. But that didn't mean she was ready to scale back her career and the thrilling single life of fun and travel in favor of his cozy little ready-made family here in the country. And it also didn't mean that Kendra was ready for a new mommy.

How had they managed to duck and dodge the issue of the future of their relationship this whole time? And why couldn't he get a couple of words unstuck from his mouth before he completely blew it?

By the time he'd finished hemming and hawing, she had her clothes back on and her hurt face firmly in place. He may not have all the answers—yet—but he knew he'd sell his soul to the nearest passing demon to get her to smile again.

So he cupped her face and smoothed her silky cheek with his thumb.

"Hey," he said.

It took her a minute to flick her sulky gaze up to his. She raised a brow.

"Why don't you come for dinner at the big house with us tonight?"

"You don't want me."

"The hell I don't."

Thank God. For once he got something right; maybe it was the vehemence in his voice that did it. Whatever it was, she dimpled in the beginnings of a smile.

"We'll see," she told him. "I'll check my calendar and get back to you."

* * *

"Can you help me with my homework, Livia?" asked Kendra.

"*Miss* Livia," Hunter corrected.

Kendra, catching Livia's gaze, gave her an eye roll of utmost disgust. Livia, who was trying not to laugh and trying harder not to let Hunter see what she was doing, winked at the girl. Kendra laughed. And Hunter looked over from the kitchen counter, where he was pouring coffee with his mother, and frowned.

"What're you two females giggling about over there?"

"Nothing," answered Livia and Kendra together, doing a poor job of stifling more giggles. Hunter gave the two of them an exaggerated glare and then returned to what he'd been doing.

Livia couldn't stop grinning. The Chambers household was warm, loving and fun, and she'd enjoyed every minute of tonight's dinner there, even if she had put Hunter on the spot and basically forced him to invite her. What was a little lost pride when a night like this was at stake?

After welcoming her with smiles, hugs and mutterings about taking so long between visits, Mr. and Mrs. Chambers had treated her to flavorful beef stew, homemade biscuits and apple pie. Livia, feeling it was only polite, had eaten second helpings of everything, and was now stuffed like a Thanksgiving turkey. If there was a better way to spend a cool fall night, God hadn't invented it yet.

Now she sat in the leather chair closest to the great room fire, curled her legs under her and held her arms open for Kendra. The girl scrambled into her lap, bringing a hefty book with her, and settled in as though they'd spent a thousand other nights in this chair together. For extra coziness, Kendra pulled a fringed blanket off the back of the chair and spread it over their laps.

"There," she said, smoothing a last wrinkle and tucking one edge under Livia's thigh. "So you won't get cold."

"Thank you." Livia kissed the girl's cheek and took the book. "So what's the homework? I didn't even know first-graders had homework."

"I have to read for fifteen minutes." Kendra produced a small kitchen timer and set it. "You can listen."

"Okay. What're we reading? Oh, wait. Dumb question." She checked the book's spine and the tiny print. "*The Mammoth Book of Dinosaurs, Volume II.* Just a little light reading for a six-year-old, eh?"

The sarcasm went right over Kendra's head. "It's my favorite. I'm on page three-twelve."

"I hope you'll explain all the big words to me, girl," Livia said.

Livia flipped to the right page, glanced at Hunter to see how he was coming along with her after-dinner coffee and got an unpleasant shock. On his way from the kitchen, with two steaming mugs in his hand, he'd paused to stare at a framed photograph that was at eye level on the bookshelf. The expression on his face was so rapt… so bleak…so lost…that she felt her heart contract in response.

Trying to pretend she didn't know what he was doing or that she'd never seen the picture didn't work. She'd seen it. It was a casual shot taken at his wedding to his dead wife, Annette. Wow. Even the other woman's name made her heart ache. *Annette,* Mrs. Chambers had told her. His wife's name was Annette. The name of Kendra's mother was Annette.

Annette.

It was one of those tight close-up shots of the two of them laughing into each other's faces, as though they couldn't believe their luck in finding each other and making it to such a fabulous day.

Annette, in her cloud of white, was the kind of beautiful and glowing bride that graced the pages of all those wedding magazines and catalogs. And the expression on Hunter's face in that frozen moment in time screamed things like love, passion and forever.

So there it was, in Livia's face for the first time: Hunter, the man she'd fallen in love with, had passionately loved and lost his wife, Annette. Now Annette was gone and Livia was here, and Hunter had never spoken his wife's name to her, not even once.

What did that mean? Nothing? Everything?

As though he felt the weight of her gaze on him, and the hurt, Hunter chose that moment to blink and snap himself out of it, giving Livia just enough time to look away and pretend she hadn't seen. If only it was that easy to erase the memory of his expression from her mind.

"Hey," he said, coming over and handing her the mug. "We didn't have that vanilla-flavored cream that you like, but—"

Whatever he may have said after that was lost to a wave of nausea that hit her the second that coffee smell hit her nose. It rose up out of nowhere, gagging on the back of her tongue, and for one horrified moment she saw herself spewing all that delicious food on Mrs. Chambers's polished floor.

Surging to her feet and unceremoniously dumping Kendra off her lap and into the chair, she hurried into the kitchen, poured herself a glass of water from the sink and took a couple of tentative sips.

"Livia?" Mr. Chambers, who'd been sweeping the floor, glanced around with concern. "You okay?"

"What's wrong, sweetie?" Mrs. Chambers hurried over and rubbed her shoulder.

Livia looked into their worried faces and called upon all her limited acting skills to force a cough and a smile. "I just, you know—" she coughed again and took another sip of water "—got strangled."

Relief brightened Hunter's face, but he kept a watchful eye on her, apparently ready to spring into some kind of action if another spell hit her. She stared into his face, wondering what the hell she'd do now because several things had just occurred to her and collectively added up to a huge issue.

One, she hadn't had a period in about six weeks.

Two, her breasts were unusually tender.

Three, the smell of coffee had just about made her vomit, and Mama always said that one of the earliest symptoms of pregnancy was an aversion to certain food smells.

Oh, God, she thought, stunned. *Oh, God.*

"Thanks for bringing me," Livia said. "I'll just be a minute."

"Take your time."

Hunter watched her disappear down the aisle into the depths of the pharmacy area and tried to use the time alone to collect his scattered thoughts. At some point between apple pie and this impromptu emergency trip to the twenty-four-hour drugstore for Livia to get several toiletries that she absolutely, positively had to have tonight, things had gone seriously wrong. A night that had begun so promisingly now seemed…bewildering.

Well, why pretend? He knew when things got weird. It was when he caught that unexpected glimpse of his wedding picture and Annette's image came back into sharp and painful focus for the first time in a while. For the first time since he'd begun falling for Livia.

Annette had been young and exuberant, the radiant sun at the center of his universe, and on that wonderful day so long ago, when he'd promised her forever, he'd had no idea that her forever would end in a few short years, snuffed out in a smashed car on a dark road.

Now here he was, still alive, and alive in a way he'd never been before, thanks to Livia. Was that okay? Was that fair? Was this the course his life was supposed to take?

Guilt and loss were part of his issue tonight.

The other part was primitive, gut-wrenching fear. It wasn't cool, a big guy like him being scared shitless, but it was real. Spending time with Livia and his family, seeing again how effortlessly she made herself at home and won the hearts of everyone around her, watching his daughter sit on her lap and snuggle with her... it was too freaking perfect. Too much of a dream come true to be real.

What if—and this was where the fear came in—what if it wasn't real? Livia's idyll here in the country with him was ending soon, and they'd managed to spend her time here making love and talking about everything in the world *except* where, if anywhere, this relationship was going. What if she thought it wasn't going anywhere? He'd barely managed to scrape his ruined heart up off the floor after Annette died. He didn't think he could do it again if Livia said goodbye and sailed back off to L.A., into the world where she belonged and he never would.

The killer was that this whole time he hadn't worked up the nerve to just ask her. How crazy was that? If you wanted to know what someone's plans were, and you had a question, the normal and sane thing to do was just ask. Except there was that fear again, keeping his throat on lockdown—because what the hell would he do if she blinked up at him with those gorgeous eyes and tried to let him down gently as she told him that she'd had fun in the country, thanks, but it was time for her to get back to the glitz and glamour of her real life?

Jesus.

His head felt like it was seconds away from explosion. Rubbing his hands over his temples didn't help and neither did pinching the bridge of his nose until he could all but feel the cartilage snap. Headache. He had the mother of all headaches.

And what was the solution to that overwhelming and complex problem, genius? How about you look around, since you're in the middle of a, you know, drugstore, and find some drugs? Didn't they always keep those little travel packets of aspirin and whatnot next to the candy in the checkout line? Why not look?

Abandoning his post holding up the customer-service desk—what was taking Livia so long? Had she been abducted out the back door?—he went to the nearest open checkout lane and skimmed the offerings. Candy… candy…more candy…lighters…dangling air fresheners for the car…tabloids…tissue packets…

Wait.

Go back.

With dread inching up his spine and creeping across his scalp, he shifted his gaze back to the tabloids. He knew they were trash, yeah, and that he was having a vulnerable moment here and that he shouldn't look closer. If he was smart and had a single self-protective molecule in his body, he'd just walk away and pretend he'd seen nothing.

Only he'd never been one for being an ostrich.

Shooting a quick glance around to make sure Livia wasn't returning right this very second, he grabbed the ridiculous magazine with hands that were suddenly both damp and shaky and looked down into the smiling face of the woman who, it turned out, he only partially knew. And got a nice kick-in-the-gut glimpse into the other part of her life.

There she was, at a table at one of those glittering parties, looking like a million sexy bucks, with the hair, the makeup and the skimpy little dress that tastefully hinted at one of the world's greatest bodies. There was the obligatory champagne glass and there was the inevitable NBA MVP grinning and whispering something in her ear as she laughed.

To tie the image up into a nice fat bow for him, there was the caption, which was just enough to knock the remaining wind out of his sails: "Athletes and Their Supermodels—Why These Relationships Work."

Chapter 13

Pregnant. She was pregnant.

Livia stared at the plus sign on the little pee stick thingy, trapped in a weird world between fierce joy and abject terror. She was going to be a mother. Hysterical laughter bubbled up in her throat, but since Hunter was on the other side of that bathroom door and she didn't want to babble like a loon, she clapped her hand over her mouth and choked it back.

A baby. There was a baby inside her. She'd made a baby with the man she loved.

Did she look different? Staring hard at her reflection in the mirror, she didn't think so. Well, except for that glowing happiness on her face. That was different, but, in fairness, Hunter had put that there long before she'd known there was a baby.

How had this happened? They'd used condoms, all except that first time on the dock, but, as they'd taught her in health class in fifth grade, one time was all it took. What about the pill, though? She religiously took it every morning, right after she brushed her teeth and she never missed a day. Ever. So how on earth did—

Oh, wait. Oh, God. It was the antibiotics she'd taken to get rid of that never-ending sinus infection from hell that did it. Hadn't the doctor mentioned that she'd need to use other forms of birth control when he'd written the prescription all those weeks ago? Since she'd been celibate with no prospects at the time, the advice had gone in one ear and out the other. Too bad the doctor hadn't had a crystal ball in his office. Then he could have warned her that she'd soon be having nonstop wild sex and needed to be more careful.

So what did she do—

"Livia?" Hunter called from the living room. "Did you fall in or what?"

Peeking her head around the door, she tried to sound normal. "Sorry! I'll be out in a second."

"Hurry up," he grumbled. "It's lonely out here."

"Okay."

Okay. She shut the door again and tried to think. What did she do? Should she tell him now or should she confirm with her doctor before she went off half-cocked? Maybe she wasn't pregnant after all, and this would be a big scare for nothing.

The blaring red *99% accurate!* on the blue box in the trash can put an end to that desperate speculation. Yeah, she was pregnant. In addition to the breast thing and the nausea thing, she just knew. There was a baby in there. And she couldn't be happier about it.

Still, they'd never talked about their future and she was supposed to leave for Mexico soon. Hunter couldn't very well run the winery from L.A., but he hadn't asked her to stay here with him, either.

Other *hadn'ts?*

He hadn't told her he loved her.

He hadn't raised the subject of their future.

He hadn't exposed her to his daughter and his parents

except in very small doses, as though he didn't want them getting the wrong idea about her place in his life.

He hadn't ever talked about Annette and whether he was over her.

He hadn't looked like he was over Annette when he'd stared at their wedding picture earlier.

The doubts crept, one by one, into her mind, banding together and gathering strength to use against her, like a pitchfork-carrying mob. When they'd all assembled, they formed one unmistakable truth:

Hunter might not be happy about this.

What the hell would she do then?

The distant bleat of her cell phone distracted her, pulling her away from her increasingly dark thoughts. She should get that. It might be Rachel calling about tomorrow's arrival time, assuming, of course, that it wasn't Rachel calling to say, yet again, that she wasn't coming.

Taking a deep breath, she hurried out to the living room, where Hunter was sprawled on the sofa watching ESPN and looking sulky, with Willard drowsing on the floor at his feet. They both looked around at her appearance and Hunter picked her blinking cell phone up from the coffee table and passed it to her.

"Thanks." She glanced at the display. "It's my agent. I'll just be a minute, okay?"

His jaw tightened. There was definitely something off about him tonight; was it the whole wedding picture thing still? Maybe. She'd have to ask after she got off the phone.

"Okay," he said, his gaze shifting back to the TV.

Clicking the phone on, she headed back into the bedroom. "Hey, Susan."

"How's Napa?" Susan asked in her usual crisp tone.

She'd never been one for niceties and always wanted to get them out of the way ASAP so she could get to the only part of any conversation that interested her: money. "You ready to get back to work?"

"Well," Livia began.

"We need you in Cabo in two days for the fittings, right? So you'd better start packing your little bags. Or were you going home first?"

God. Livia slumped on the bed and rested her head in her hands, sudden exhaustion making her crazy. Ten minutes ago she'd discovered she was pregnant with a man who'd never even said he loved her and she was supposed to talk travel logistics and photo shoots?

"I'll just go straight there."

"Good. And Giancarlo's hosting a dinner party for you that night. Only about fifty people, nothing big."

"A party?" Was this some sort of a cruel joke? Another stupid dinner party given by another one of her idle-rich friends when her life was at such a dramatic crossroads? "This is the first I'm hearing about that."

"It's an early surprise. For your birthday. So don't let on, okay?"

"Fine."

"I'll call you tomorrow to check in."

Checking in was Susan-speak for accepting a ridiculous number of new assignments and scheduling Livia's time for the next six months or so. Since Livia would be preparing to give birth, and since she'd already decided to take an extended break from modeling even before she found out she was pregnant, she'd have to put the kibosh on that plan, but it could wait until tomorrow. One big conversation per night was all she could handle, and she and Hunter had a baby that needed discussing.

"Great," she told Susan. "Bye."

Hanging up, she went back to the living room and perched on the coffee table in front of Hunter. He sat up, looking grim, turned off the TV and swung his feet to the floor. Willard yawned his overwhelming enthusiasm for her arrival and went back to sleep.

"Hi," she said. "Maybe we should talk."

"You're leaving," he said flatly.

"Yeah. I have a photo shoot in Cabo San Lucas. It's been scheduled for a while."

"And a party."

So he'd heard that, eh? "There's always a party."

"I see."

Those golden eyes of his were dark now, and his shoulders were so rigid that they might have been replaced with a slab of concrete. The tension radiating from him felt black and dangerous, like a negative force field, and she watched him scrub his hands over his head and across his tight jaw with growing anxiety.

Finally he met her gaze and they stared at each other for several beats. The whole time she searched for a sign of the laughing man who'd made love to her in his truck earlier that day, tried to find evidence of his existence, but he was so far gone right now he might have only ever been a figment of her imagination. Right now, the only thing she could see was the cold, aloof man who'd confronted her in the parking lot the day they met, and it terrified her.

"What's wrong?" she whispered.

He shrugged and raised a wry eyebrow, and the gestures were so casual and unspeakably wrong for this moment that they were like slaps to the face.

"So this is it, then."

She licked her dry lips and took a deep breath, trying to formulate a scenario where those words and that detached look on his face didn't add up to things being over between them.

"This is...*it?*" she echoed.

"Well, we knew it couldn't last, right? Now it's time for you to leave Napa and go back to your shoots and your parties and your life."

"What about you?"

Another dismissive shrug. "I'll stay here."

Oh, God. Blinking back sudden hot tears, she looked at Willard's sleeping body and tried to pull it together. Falling apart now wouldn't solve anything and neither would begging. Though her pride told her to keep her big mouth shut and not make this moment more awkward than it needed to be, her stupid heart forced her to reach out, to try.

"But we'll see each other, right? We can fly back and forth because it's only a couple of hours, and I don't see why we couldn't—"

A crooked smile distorted one corner of his mouth. "What's the point?"

"I thought the point was that we cared about each other. Am I wrong?"

That, for the first time, put a dent in his composure. Resting his elbows on his knees, he dropped his head between his hands and squeezed his temples so hard she was surprised she didn't hear his skull crack.

Forever passed, and then another forever, and then he raised his now red face and ran his tongue along his lower lip in a clear attempt to keep his composure. It didn't work. He was fighting back a grimace that made him look like there was something disgusting in his mouth that he needed to spit out.

"This isn't about us caring for each other." He wouldn't look at her and could barely get the words out, his voice was so rough with gravel. "This is about what will work and what won't work."

Okay. Okay, so she needed a minute to choke back the rising sob of frustration and fear, and for some of the burning in her throat to cool enough for her to talk. *Breathe, girl. Breathe. You can do this. Think of the baby.*

Blinking furiously and pressing her lips together until they'd gone numb, which was better than the quivering they'd been doing, she focused on the logical argument. "If we care for each other enough, Hunter, we can make it work."

At last he looked at her and she wished he hadn't. His golden eyes were nothing but a sheet of ice now, a wall of amber behind which he'd locked himself down so tight she'd never be able to get close to him.

"How can it work?" His tone was so light and conversational they could have been discussing whether a three-pronged plug could fit into a two-pronged outlet. "You think I'd ask you to sacrifice your career for me? Or maybe you think I'd be just fine leaving the winery and, I don't know, spending my days on the beach in Malibu and my nights attending movie premieres and restaurant openings with you? Is that it?"

Wow.

Way to hit below the belt, Hunter. Way to slice through all her attempts at compromise and make her feel vulnerable, foolish and, best of all, shallow. If ever there was a time for her to just shut up and walk away, this was it, but she just couldn't let him go. What they had together couldn't be destroyed so easily.

So she swiped away the embarrassing tears that trickled down her cheeks, took yet another deep breath and swallowed enough of her remaining pride to try again.

"It doesn't have to be about sacrifice. This is my last shoot for a while and then my calendar is free. I could do whatever I wanted. And they have these newfangled inventions called airplanes, don't they? We both have cell phones and email. Why couldn't we try for a while and see how—"

He stared at her with not one spark of pity in his hard eyes. "When did a long-distance relationship ever work?" he wondered. "And how could my young daughter and I fit into your glamorous world of celebrities and fashion and parties?"

Something snapped inside her. Broke neatly down the middle, leaving the two ruined parts to disintegrate to dust. Much as she'd wanted to be calm, gracious and classy, she couldn't do it when he was this anxious to destroy everything they'd shared.

"Those are just *excuses,*" she shrieked. "Excuses! If you don't love me enough to try, then why don't you just say—"

"Don't." The big L-word made his mouth contort with disbelief or discomfort or something terrible like that, but, hey, at least he didn't laugh right in her face. "Don't do this, Livia."

A lightbulb went off over her head, bringing this whole situation into terrible HDTV clarity, and she had to ask, even if the truth killed her.

"This is about Annette, isn't it?"

The name made him flinch and wasn't that a clue enough for her dimwitted brain? "What about Annette?"

"I saw you." The rising hysteria was making her voice shake and she backed off for a minute, shuddering with her effort to remain rational and lower the volume. "I saw the way you looked at her picture tonight."

Cursing, he dropped his head again, squeezing it between his fisted hands as though he'd love nothing better than to smash his skull and end this excruciating conversation. Which was just too damn bad because he owed her at least this much of an explanation.

"And I'm wondering if you're not over her yet. I'm wondering if you'll ever be over her."

When he raised his head this time, he was deathly pale and still, his eyes feverishly bright. And his voice was absolute and unyielding as he threw a live grenade into the middle of all her hopes and dreams, blowing them to kingdom come.

"No," he said softly. "I'll never get over my wife."

Livia consulted her list in the bright-morning sunlight and surveyed her bag, which was packed to the gills with various little Napa Valley purchases and would, therefore, be a lot harder to close and zip than it'd been when she came nearly a month ago. Her toiletries were still in the bathroom, but she'd remembered her camera, her shoes, not that she'd brought that many pairs, and her Jackie Robinson biography, so she could cross all those off the list. The only other things were—

Someone knocked at the front door.

Since it wasn't Hunter's brisk and assertive knock, she didn't really care who it was, but the car to take her to the airport may have come a little early so she should probably answer it.

Taking a final inventory as she passed through the living room—no forgotten shoes half-hidden under the sofa, thank goodness—she opened the door.

"Rachel!"

Screeching like ten-year-olds, they latched on and hugged as though they hadn't seen each other for fifty years of desperate searching. Since Livia was a giantess and Rachel was a cute little pixie, Livia swept her off her feet and swung her in a circle, which Rachel tolerated with good grace. Then Livia plunked her back down and, keeping her at arm's length, checked her out to see how she was doing.

Boy, was she glad to see her.

She needed a friend after the horrible night she'd had.

"You look great." Livia smoothed Rachel's dark Halle Berry hair and admired her turquoise necklace; Rachel always wore the prettiest artsy jewelry and whatnot, which probably had something to do with her eye for color and her success as a makeup artist. If you wanted a great accessory, Rachel was the one to consult. "I thought you weren't coming until later."

"We got bumped up to an earlier flight."

"Come on in." Taking her hand, Livia led Rachel into the living room, where they both sat on the sofa. "What's new? What'd you decide about the wedding? You got my emailed pictures of the chapel and all, right?"

"Yup. It'll be here in about a month."

"A month!"

"Oh, and the merger is going through."

Wow. So Limelight Entertainment Management, the agency that represented Livia and had been started by

Rachel's parents before their death twenty-five years ago, would merge with their rivals at A.F.I.

Sofia, Rachel's sister and second-in-command at Limelight Entertainment Management, *hated* A.F.I. and had been fighting her uncle for months, arguing against the merger.

This was going to be interesting.

"I can't believe it," Livia said. "I never thought it'd happen."

"Tell me about it."

"Where's Ethan?"

"He's catching up with Hunter."

"Oh, yeah?" Livia glued that painful smile on her face and focused on keeping her expression from falling at the mere mention of his name. If she didn't watch it, she'd slip up and do something to clue Rachel in that she'd just had the love affair of her life, and she wasn't ready to discuss Hunter, her feelings for him or the baby with anyone. Not even Rachel. "Did you meet him?"

"Yeah. It's a shame he's so ugly. A real tragedy."

Livia tried to laugh.

"But is he always this glum? He looked like he'd lost his best friend, his house and his dog. Is that what running a winery does to a person?"

Livia shrugged, her gaze shifting away from Rachel's. This was dangerous territory and they really needed to talk about something else.

"Come to think of it," Rachel said, taking a closer look at Livia's face with those eagle eyes of hers, "he looked a lot like you look. Have you been crying? You have, haven't you? Your eyes are all swollen."

"Rachel," Livia began, trying to work up a plausible denial but it was already too late.

"Oh, my God! You and Hunter?" Rachel clapped her hands over her mouth, trying to stifle a giggle of startled comprehension and excitement. "I'm right! There's something going on with you, isn't there?"

"I can't get into it, Rachel."

"But—"

"Rachel." Livia held up a hand, pressed her lips together and struggled not to cry. "Please. I can't do this right now. Please understand."

"Oh, honey." Rachel squeezed her arm in a show of concerned support. "Do I need to kill him for you?"

Livia spluttered out a laugh. "I'll let you know, okay? Right now, I just need to get out of here. I think Mexico will do me some good."

Sometime during the long and difficult night, when she wasn't replaying the coldness in Hunter's eyes and the lack of inflection in his voice as he hit her with the joyous news that he'd never be over his dead wife, she'd convinced herself that the trip to Mexico, though inconvenient, was exactly what she needed.

She'd throw herself into her work, get some sun and think. The time away would give her some perspective and, hopefully, enough emotional distance to manage this situation. In a few days, she'd come back, tell Hunter she was pregnant and would raise the baby whether he decided to be involved in their lives or not, and it would all be good.

In a few days.

Right now, though, all was not good.

"How about another hug?" she asked Rachel. "I could use one."

"You got it, girl."

Holding her arms wide, Rachel pulled her in close,

and Livia, feeling exhausted and empty, rested her head against the reassuring warmth of her friend's chest and wished she could stay there forever.

Chapter 14

This was so hard.

This was so incredibly, unspeakably, unbelievably hard.

Livia loitered outside the doghouse, blinking back her tears and trying not to fall apart. Kendra had ignored her with steadfast determination for the last five minutes and Livia was nearing the end of her depleted emotional reserves.

"Kendra," she called again. "Please."

No answer from the dark depths of the doghouse. The flashlight was out today, intensifying the gloom inside. Even Willard, who was also in there with Kendra, had his face turned away from Livia, as though she was also letting him down and he didn't plan to let her forget it anytime soon, if ever.

Swiping at her face, she made a quick decision and sat down. "If I'm not welcome in the dragon's den today," she said, "I'll just sit by the entrance. I hope that's okay."

No answer but at least now she could see what was going on in the den. Kendra sat in the far corner, with Willard's big head in her lap and her stuffed diplodocus hugged to her chest above that. As Livia peered inside, Kendra stared off in the other direction, resolutely refusing to either acknowledge her presence or accept her goodbye.

It hurt. In a twenty-four-hour period that had pretty much maxed her out on the hurt thing, what with that final talk with Hunter, the all-night crying and a poignant goodbye to Mr. and Mrs. Chambers, the wounded silence from Kendra was, quite possibly, the worst. Was this what she'd been like when her mother died? Was this what Hunter had had to overcome? How had he managed it?

"Kendra." Swiping away another of her never-ending tears, she focused on not sniffling and keeping her voice upbeat. "I have to go to Mexico for my work, okay? I really wish I could stay here and play with you for a little while longer but I have to do my job. Can you understand that? It's like when you have to go to school. Sometimes you don't want to go, but you have to, anyway. And I don't want to leave here, but I have to, anyway."

Kendra pressed her lips into the green fur of her stuffed animal and said nothing.

"But I'm going to send you a postcard when I get there. And they have lots of fossils and stuff in Mexico, so I'll see if I can find one for you. And maybe a dinosaur T-shirt. Could that work, do you think?"

Kendra shrugged.

Oh, thank God! A shrug was communication, right? It wasn't a sentence or anything but it was a definite step up from being ignored, wasn't it?

"Kendra," she said helplessly. "You're a wonderful girl. I'm going to miss you so much." *I love you. I wish you were mine. I wish your father wanted me enough to let me into your life a little more.* "Can I please give you a hug before I go?"

This time the communication was a lot more painful: Kendra scooted farther into the corner, away from Livia. The sight of that tiny little figure so stiff with disapproval and disappointment was more than Livia could take. Dropping her head into her hands, she gave in to the despair and sobbed as quietly as she could manage, grateful that Kendra wasn't looking and hopefully didn't know that she'd fallen apart.

But three seconds of that nonsense was enough. She needed to work on getting her emotions under control. No time like the present, right? Wiping her face dry, she tried to smile and tried harder to keep her voice upbeat and positive.

"Bye for now, Kendra."

If only she could tell the girl that she'd be back soon when she returned to tell Hunter about the baby. If only she could tell her that she'd become a big sister next year. If only Hunter would share his wonderful family with her and maybe let Kendra visit her in L.A. when the baby came. If only…

Wow. She had enough *if onlys* to fill up a stadium, didn't she?

"Bye, Willard." The dog, at least, looked around to acknowledge her existence. When she held her hand out to him, he crawled forward on his belly and let her scratch his soft ears one last time. From here on out, she'd have to watch *The Dog Wrangler* by herself and that would never be as much fun as enjoying it with him. "Silly dog."

Okay, Livia. Stop stalling. Time to go.

She stood, dusted off her jeans and headed for the cottage to grab her bag. She'd turned in her rental bike already and printed her boarding pass. The only thing—

Running footsteps came up behind her and she turned

and saw Kendra sprinting after her. With an incoherent cry of happiness, she stooped in time to catch her and swung her up into her arms, thrilled with the weight and heat of that sturdy little body and the sweetness of her skin and the fruity fragrance of her twisted hair.

"I love you, Kendra." Livia kissed those fat little cheeks over and over again and let the words come, because they were the truth and the girl had the right to know. "I love you."

Kendra wrapped her strong arms around Livia's neck, nearly strangling her with affection, and she hung on for much longer than Livia ever could have hoped. Then she pulled back and offered Livia her stuffed diplodocus.

"Take him with you," she said. "He's always wanted to see Mexico."

"Can someone tell me who died?"

Hunter, who was sitting at his parents' kitchen table at the B and B, looked up from the cup of stone-cold cappuccino he'd been nursing for the past half hour and glared at his younger brother. With his usual flair for the dramatic, Ethan was standing in the middle of the room, putting on a show. Though Hunter was glad to see him, he'd have to cut the youngster down to size if he kept up like this.

"I mean," Ethan continued, "what could be wrong? The grapes are harvested, the prodigal son—that would be me—is back and the sun is shining. Where are the smiles and the laughter? What the hell's gotten into you people?"

"Watch your language," muttered Mom, who was manning the cappuccino machine. "I don't know what they teach you in L.A., but around here, we don't swear."

"Damn right." Dad, who was pouring a bowl of kibble for Willard, winked.

"We'll get right to work on killing that fatted calf for you, Ethan," Hunter said. "Would that make you feel better? What about a parade?"

"A parade would work." Ethan accepted a steaming cup from Mom, leaned against the counter and sipped appreciatively. "I'm serious, though. What's wrong?"

Mom put her hands on her hips and frowned over at Hunter. "Should you tell him or should I?"

Ah, shit. Mom had been in a rare mood ever since Livia stopped by to say goodbye earlier, and the last thing he needed right now was Mom launching into him in front of everyone. No good could come of that. He already felt like he was crawling out of his skin what with Livia leaving to resume her glamorous life far away from him.

Even now he couldn't quite believe it.

Livia was gone. She'd gotten on a plane and flown away. Just like that. And had he begged her to stay? Had he told her he loved her? Had he thrown his body in front of the plane to stop it from taxiing down the runway?

Hell, no.

He'd done everything but plant his foot in her ass as she walked out the door, and now he couldn't shake the sickening feeling that he'd made the worst mistake of his life. At the time, he'd thought that a clean break was best. Now he felt like he'd cut off his right hand for no good reason.

Still, he didn't plan to spill his guts to this crowd.

"There's nothing to—" Hunter began.

Mom snorted with disgust and waved him to silence.

"Hunter found a wonderful girl," she explained to Ethan. "We all loved her. Livia Blake—"

Ethan goggled. "What? *Livia?*"

"Sweetest girl in the world. Now they've had a falling-out and Livia left. God knows if we'll ever see her again. And this one—" Mom jerked her thumb in Hunter's general direction, apparently too irritated by his actions to look at him directly "—just let her go." She snapped her fingers. "Just like that. *Idiot.*"

Great. Now, on top of Livia leaving, Kendra falling into the depths of despair and his own broken heart to nurse, his own mother thought he was an idiot. It was shaping up to be quite a day, wasn't it?

Ethan clunked his mug on the counter and looked at Hunter with alarm. "Is that true?"

Dad, now patting Willard's hindquarters while the dog crunched loudly over his bowl, answered for him. "It's true," he said grimly.

Okay. That was enough.

"First of all," Hunter said, raising a hand to stop this discussion before it got any further out of hand, "I can speak for myself. Second, my personal life isn't up for discussion, so let's just drop this—"

"Yeah, but who knew you had a personal life since Annette died?" Ethan interjected. "I think that's worth discussing. Livia, eh?" He tipped his head, giving the matter serious consideration. "She's great. I actually think she'd be a good match for you. What happened?"

"Did you just hear me say that I'm not discussing—"

"I don't know," Mom answered, ignoring his statement. "Getting this one—" another thumb jerk in Hunter's direction "—to talk is like getting blood from a stone."

The three of them gave him baleful stares. Hell, even

the dog paused in his chomping to nail him with a look that said, quite plainly, *You dumbass,* and the negative attention was more than he could take. He was sick to death here because Livia was gone and he'd sent her away, but even if he got her back, he didn't see how it could work.

He exploded. "Do I look happy? Why the hell are you blaming me? If any of you geniuses know how I can run a winery while Livia is flying all over the world, going to her little parties and whatnot, then I'd love to hear."

Both Mom and Ethan stared at him as though he'd begun babbling in pig Latin.

"That girl doesn't want to fly around and go to parties," Mom said, aghast.

"Yeah," Ethan agreed. "She's not a partier anymore. I'd have heard—L.A.'s a small town. And Rachel claims she's phasing out the modeling. I'm not sure about that."

"That girl helped me with the dishes." Mom ticked off her points on her fingers. "She asked for my beef stew recipe. She wanted to talk about how Kendra's doing in school and she grilled me about what I do here at the winery. It's as plain as the nose on my face that she's got her mind on family and children. How much partying can a person do, anyway? I'm betting she's got all that out of her system and now she's ready to settle down. Too bad you let her go."

Stunned and deeply disturbed, Hunter planted his elbows on the table and rested his head in his hands. Could any of that be true? More unbearable was the possibility that it was all true and he was such an idiot that he'd never even discussed it with Livia.

Mom was right about the sorry state of his mental prowess, wasn't she? He was such a genius he'd never even asked Livia what she wanted or if she'd consider staying here with him. He'd been so afraid of her rejection that he'd preempted it with a rejection of his own.

And then when he saw that tabloid photo last night...

"I have a daughter to consider," he reminded everyone.

"Kendra and Livia love each other, boy," Dad said. "Can't you see that?"

Yeah, he'd seen it. Maybe he hadn't known what to make of it but he'd definitely seen it.

The question was: What should he do now? He rubbed the top of his head, wishing he could make his brain work and kick out some sort of a plan, a solution, but he just couldn't.

"Oh, I get it," Ethan said in that soft taunt that only brothers could manage. "He's scared."

This accusation was, naturally, a red cape to a bull, and Hunter snapped his head up, ready to throw down in front of God, Mom and everybody.

"I am *not*—"

To his surprise, Ethan smiled, and it wasn't a sneering smirk or anything like it. It was the understanding expression of a man who'd been there himself and knew what it felt like to walk in those shoes. "Let me tell you something, my brother. I didn't want to fall in love. Trust me. I wanted to try all the women I could get my hands on—"

"I'm not hearing this," Mom said loudly.

"But life's short, you know? And if you're lucky enough to find the right woman—actually, you're lucky enough to find *another* right woman, aren't you? You gonna throw that away? You think that's what Annette would want? You don't think she'd be glad to know that a great woman was taking care of her little girl?"

Shit. That actually made sense. A whole lot of freaking sense. Why hadn't he seen it that way last night? What was wrong with him?

Mom gave him a pitying look. She could probably detect that his overwhelmed circuits were about to melt down and wanted to give him a reprieve to gather his thoughts.

"Let's give the boy a minute," she told the others. "He needs to—"

Purposeful rubberized footsteps came into the kitchen just then, and they all glanced around in time to see Kendra arrive, looking grim and determined.

Oh, Lord. What now?

She wore her little pink Windbreaker and carried that same square suitcase from the other week. Willard's leash was in her other hand and she wasted no time clipping it onto the dog's collar.

"Ah, Kendra?" Hunter asked, not at all sure he wanted to know. "What're you doing?"

"I'm running away. Can you take me and Willard to the airport right now?"

Inside his chest, his heart began to pound. With fear, yeah, and with trepidation because he'd dug himself a pretty big hole with Livia last night, but mostly with hope. "Why, sweetie?"

"We want to go to Mexico and bring Livia back," Kendra informed him.

"Why?" he asked again.

"Because Willard and I want her to be our new mommy."

Chapter 15

There she was. Finally. Thank goodness.

Relief overwhelmed Hunter, roaring through him like an avalanche down a mountainside. He was lucky it didn't knock him flat on his butt.

After prying Livia's itinerary and trip details out of Rachel—who didn't seem too keen on him, to tell the truth—he'd scrounged up his passport, thrown a few clothes in his overnight bag and caught the next available flight south, which wasn't until late that night. There'd been no delays, praise be to God, because in his current state of high agitation and extreme nervousness, he'd probably have flipped out and run afoul of the flight attendants if the captain had reported mechanical trouble or cloudy skies.

He'd landed, taken a cab to the swanky hotel where Livia was staying and decided to wait, just a little while longer, and take the time to decompress and gather his thoughts so he didn't blow it again—which, given his unfortunate record when it came to communicating with Livia, was a distinct possibility.

Now here he was, on a white beach in front of a startling backdrop of sparkling aquamarine water beneath a sky of piercing blue, and there she was, doing her job, not fifty feet away.

He wasn't the only avid onlooker, which shouldn't have surprised him but did. Standing on the periphery in a crowd of about fifty people, he watched the photo shoot, which was quite the production. A photographer and a videographer both stood barefoot in the lapping surf, getting their shots and murmuring words of encouragement. Miscellaneous other people surrounded them—probably makeup people and stylists and the like.

In the center of it all, like a statue of a goddess on a dais, was Livia.

Her hair was wild and blowing free, and her skin had already acquired a tropical glow that it hadn't had in Napa. Draped over an outcropping of black rock, posing for the camera with utmost concentration—smiling… pouting…seducing—she wore a red bikini that he'd be wet-dreaming about for the rest of his life.

She was a glittering jewel. A siren. A dream.

But then the clouds shifted, the photographer said, "That's it. We've lost the light," and she took off her supermodel's mask as though she'd unzipped her dress, stepped out of it and hung it in the closet.

The sultry expression left her face and she was, suddenly, just Livia, the woman he loved. But the light was gone from her eyes and her shoulders drooped. She was lost and forlorn but struggling to do her best, and he was to blame.

He'd made her sad but, with God's help, he'd spend the rest of his life making her happy.

Hit with a sudden inspiration, he blended into the crowd surging forward for her autograph and waited for his chance.

* * *

"Livia! This way, Livia! Sign this!"

One of the stylists passed her a tie-dyed sarong and Livia made a dress out of it, wrapping it underneath her arms and tying it in the front. Then she plastered that damn smile—each fake smile these days felt like it was taking twenty years off her life, no joke—back on her face, waved at the people who'd come to watch the shoot and wandered over to sign a few autographs and pose for a few quick camera-phone shots. Exhaustion and growing nausea (this baby was really starting to make himself known, the little stinker) were no reasons to ignore her fans and act like a diva.

"Hi, guys," she said, accepting markers and scrawling her name on whatever surface was thrust her way, which included T-shirts, iPods, scraps of paper and, notably, the bare shoulder blade of a scrawny teenage American boy who swore he'd never shower again. "Are you enjoying Mexico? Yeah? *Que pasa?*"

It went on. And on.

"Sign this, Livia."

Another hand thrust forward, passing her a folded cocktail napkin from the hotel. Raising her pen, she started to sign it, but there was already huge block writing on it: "Marry me."

Ah, geez. Another marriage proposal from a starstruck, hormone-poisoned fan. What photo shoot would be complete without at least one man begging her to marry him? At least he hadn't asked for her bikini bottoms or anything. She looked up, ready to let the guy down easily and call for one of the bodyguards if necessary—

"Oh, God," she cried, clapping her hand over her mouth to choke back the sob before it erupted.

It was Hunter.

Hunter.

With a cry, she threw herself into the crowd and at him, possibly knocking several people to the sand in her enthusiasm; she didn't know and didn't care. Then his arms were closing around her, holding her too tight, hurting her, and she could only laugh and cry as he rained kisses all over her face, all but choking on her emotion.

"You came, Hunter. I can't believe it. You're here."

"Where can we talk?" he whispered urgently in her ear.

"Over here."

Taking his hand and ignoring the disgruntled murmurs of the last couple of fans, she towed him to the other side of a folding screen beneath a huge palm frond umbrella. This was where she'd changed and it wasn't exactly a private room, but it would do for now. The second the crowd was out of view, he grabbed her face in his hands and kissed her, which was no easy job since they were both crying.

"I'm sorry." Pulling back at last, he swiped at his eyes and tried to get control. "I've got some begging to do."

"You sure do," she said, doing her best to look furious through her face-splitting smile. "What have you got to say for yourself?"

"I should be on my knees after what I said the other night."

"Well, why don't you correct the record right now?"

"I'm happy to. I love you. You know that, right?"

"Oh, God," she said, sobbing again.

"After the accident, I really thought my life was over. I wanted it to be over—"

"Don't say that."

"I didn't think I'd ever be happy again, and I certainly never thought I'd find a woman who makes my heart stop in a way no one else has ever done before."

"But why?" Holding his hard cheeks between her hands, she stared up into his turbulent eyes and tried to understand what he'd said and done. "Why did you act like you'd never be over Annette?"

"Because I was scared," he said simply, the confession stunning her. "Why would a woman like you want to be with a man like me when you've got this—" he flapped a hand toward the shoot and the fans "—this life?"

Silly man. "Why? Because I'm crazy in love with you, and your daughter, and your winery and your parents. Oh, and your dog. That's why."

"So…maybe you'd want to live there with us?"

"That'd be nice. Since that was my last shoot and I won't have much income anymore. It'd be great to have somewhere to stay."

"I'm not asking you to give up—"

"I'd already decided before I ever went to Napa. The modeling thing is over. Been there, done that. Yawn."

"Are you sure?"

"Oh, I'm sure." She hesitated but now was as good a time to tell him as ever. "Besides. Kendra and the new baby deserve a full-time mother, don't you think?"

"Speaking of Kendra, that girl tried to get me to take her and the dog to the airport so she could fly down here and—wait, *what? What* did you say?"

Taking his hand, she pressed it to her stomach. "I'm saying that Chambers Winery is a fertile place. Must be something in the air. I hope that's okay with you."

"Okay?" His voice cracked and his face twisted with utmost, blinding joy. She had a one-second glimpse of

renewed tears in his amber eyes before he dropped to his knees, wrapped his arms around her waist and pressed his face to her belly. "Yeah. I think that's okay."

Epilogue

Nine Months Later

"Shh," Hunter said. "You have to be quiet."

"I can be quiet," Kendra shouted, dancing on her toes. "I can be *very* quiet. Watch me. You'll see. Willard can be quiet, too, can't you, Willard?"

Willard began to bark.

Hunter rolled his eyes. So much for that. So much, also, for keeping the dog, his slobber, his dandruffy hair and his canine germs away. It was probably okay, though, and sometimes it was best not to fight the system. At least he'd gotten Kendra to pause in the bathroom to wash her hands after she got home from summer camp.

Okay. Here goes.

With a deep breath, he opened the nursery door and hoped for the best.

But of course he already had the best possible life, didn't he?

There she was, over in the rocking chair amidst a sea of flowers, presents and balloons, with a shaft of sunlight from the open window hitting her hair just right, shooting it through with streaks of gold. Looking up from the bundle in her lap, she caught his gaze and smiled, stopping his heart the way she always did. The way she always had, since that first day.

Livia. His wife. His life.

"Hey, guys," she said. "How was camp?"

Kendra ignored the question. Creeping forward with Willard on her heels, she accepted Livia's kiss on the cheek and peered down at the newest member of their growing family.

"Is this the baby that was in your belly?" she breathed.

"Yes," Livia said.

"What's her name?"

"Jayla Marie."

"Does she know I'm her big sister?"

Livia smoothed Kendra's hair. "Why don't you sit on my lap and tell her?"

Kendra didn't need to be asked twice. Vibrating with impatience while Livia shifted Jayla to one side, she hopped up and—it figured—insisted on holding the baby herself.

"Hi, Jayla," she cooed. "Hi, Jaaay-laaa. I'm your sister. You have to do everything I say. And leave my dinosaurs alone, okay?"

Hunter, who'd come over to keep a closer eye on Willard, who was sniffing the baby's bare pink toes with great hope, laughed. So did Livia. Then they stared at the miracle they'd created together.

Despite all his dire warnings about being quiet so the baby could sleep, Jayla was awake, her eyes, which were an indeterminate shade somewhere between his whiskey color and Livia's hazel, focusing on Livia and then Kendra with bright interest. Her fat fists waved. Her plump legs kicked, ruffling the skirt of her little pink dress. And her perfect rosebud of a mouth curled into a smile so beautiful he didn't even care that it'd only been caused by gas.

He stared down at his girls, stricken silent with joy.

Livia, in that knowing way she had, glanced up and held his gaze. "Well, Daddy," she asked, taking his hand and squeezing it, "what do you think?"

Blinking back his sudden tears, he smiled.

"I think I'm the luckiest man in the world. That's what I think."

Willard, taking advantage of his distraction, licked Jayla's toes and then stared up at them both, his tongue dangling in clear agreement.

* * * * *

LOVERS PREMIERE
Adrianne Byrd

This book is dedicated to A.C. Arthur,
Ann Christopher and Brenda Jackson.
It was a pleasure working with you talented ladies.

Prologue

"Sofia Wellesley, will you marry me?"

Ten-year-old Sofia's amber-brown eyes sparkled at the bundle of wild daisies Ramell Jordan thrust toward her. Daisies were her favorite flower and always put an instant smile on her face—which he knew very well. As for his ridiculous question, she just rolled her eyes and pretended not to have heard it.

"For me? Thank you." She took the flowers and shoved them under her nose so she could inhale their fresh spring scent.

Ram waited and then his wide smile crumbled into a frown when his girlfriend walked away. "Aren't you going to answer my question?" he asked, as they strolled through the back gardens of the Wellesley estate.

"What question is that?" she asked absentmindedly, still drifting away from him in her bubble-gum-pink sundress.

"C'mon. You know." He stopped following her and folded his arms under his chest. "I've only been asking you every day for the last two weeks."

Sofia kept walking and smelling her flowers. About

a minute later, Ram ran and caught up with her just like she knew he would.

"Well?" he tried again.

"I told you that I needed to think about it. Marriage is a very important decision in a girl's life and it's not something to be taken lightly," she said, quoting her mother perfectly. "And just because I've known you all my life doesn't mean that we're destined to be together. We may grow up and want to see other people."

Ram frowned. He didn't like the sound of that. "See other people like who?"

Sofia shrugged her thin shoulders. "I don't know. There's like a gazillion people in the world."

"You want to date a gazillion people?" he asked with his eyes practically bugging out. "Do you have any idea how long that would take?"

"I don't know. Probably like five years."

"Well, five years is a looooong time."

Finally, she stopped walking and turned toward him. "Momma said that if a boy really liked you then he would wait, no matter how long it takes."

Ram tossed up his hands. "That's ridiculous! What am I supposed to do while you're out dating a gazillion people—play Atari and drink juice boxes?"

"Oh stop being overly dramatic." Sofia rolled her eyes. "You're going to do what all boys do—work and save a lot of money."

"Wait a minute. I work while you date other people? That hardly seems fair."

"Oh, I'll work, too," she said, beaming. "I'm going to work with my dad and Uncle Jacob. I'm going to work with movie stars, directors, writers—you name it."

"You're going to do all that *and* date a gazillion people?" He rolled his eyes and then shook his head. "All of that is going to take forever. We'll be *old*—like thirty or thirty-five."

Sofia's brows stretched upward. "Are you saying that you won't want to marry me when I'm old?"

"What? No. I didn't say that," Ram backtracked. "I'm just saying that I want to marry you while you're young, too."

"Well we're young now. And we see each other every day as it is so what's the problem?"

"I didn't think we had a problem until you said you wanted to date a gazillion people. If you can lower that number down some then maybe…"

"Okay. How about a bazillion?"

He crossed his arms and gave her a stern look. "Lower."

"A billion."

"Lower."

"A million."

"Lower."

"Umm…a thousand?"

Ram shook his head. "No."

"Lower than a thousand?"

"Definitely."

"A hundred."

"Lower."

"Fifty."

He paused as if it was a number he could work with but then started shaking his head. "Lower."

"Oh, I give up. You're being totally unreasonable." Sofia turned and stormed toward the sprawling mansion.

"Fine. If you're going to start dating other boys then I'm going to start dating other girls—starting with Twyla Henderson."

Sofia stopped in her tracks and turned around. "What did you just say?"

Pleased to see that he'd finally gotten her attention, Ram thrust his chin up and puffed his chest out. "You heard me. I'm going to date Twyla Henderson. She's pretty enough and I know for a fact that she likes me."

"And you also know very well that I don't like that big bully. All she does is talk bad about people and think that everyone should kiss her butt because her father knows a bunch of famous people."

"Whatever. She's always nice to me." Ram turned and started to stroll in the opposite direction, mimicking one of Sofia's slick moves. He smiled when he heard her stomping up behind him.

"Ramell Jordan, I *forbid* you to go out with that knock-kneed cow."

He turned around, laughing. "Knock-kneed?"

"You heard me." She pushed up her chin. Her anger made red splotches on her smooth brown skin.

"I don't know." He shook his head. "Hardly seems fair that you can date millions of people but I can't see *one* girl that goes to our school."

"You can date anybody but her!"

"Okay. How about Jill Marshall?"

Sofia's face twisted in disgust. "The girl that makes bubbles in her milk every day at lunch? Why would you want to go out with her?"

"Connie Woods?"

Sofia opened her mouth but then closed it. She liked

Connie. Everybody did. When she hesitated, Ram took her silence as a stamp of approval.

"Great! I'll go over to her house right now. Maybe she'd like to go to the arcade or the roller rink." He started to march off.

"Ramell Jordan, you'll do no such thing!"

He had her now, but he quickly fixed his face so that he looked confused. "Why not?"

"Because I forbid it," she said, as if it made all the sense in the world.

A smile ballooned across his face. "Admit it. You don't like the idea of me dating other girls just like I don't like the idea of you dating a *gazillion* boys."

Sofia pressed her lips together like she wasn't about to admit to any such thing.

Seeing that she was going to continue to be stubborn about the issue, Ram shrugged his shoulders and said, "Fine. I guess I'll go see what Connie is doing."

He took one step forward and Sofia grabbed his wrist so fast that she dropped half of her fresh-picked daisies. "Don't go!"

Ramell cocked his head and waited for the words he wanted to hear.

"All right. Fine." She snatched her hand back and folded it across her chest with her other one. "I don't want you to date other girls. There. Are you happy?"

"Extremely." He turned toward her. "So how about getting married?"

"Sofia! Dinnertime! Time to come in!" Gloria, the Wellesleys' housekeeper, hollered out through the French doors.

Sofia's face split into a smile. "See you tomorrow!" She turned and shot off toward the house.

"Wait!" Ram called after her, but it was no use. She was already running as fast as her long legs could carry her.

He crossed his arms dejectedly. "Women!"

Sofia raced into the house, laughing because she had managed to get away from Ram once again without having to answer his proposal. Of course their game would resume tomorrow and she'd have to come up with a whole new set of stall tactics. Heaven knew that she wasn't opposed to marrying Ramell. The two times that he'd managed to sneak a kiss from her from underneath the oak tree in her backyard she actually thought it was rather nice. Sofia liked Ram. She especially liked how his dark brown eyes would shine like two new marbles when she'd let him. But they were only ten years old. What was a girl to do?

"Go on and wash up," Gloria said, pulling her from her reverie. "Your parents are busy with something in your father's study, but when they're done they'll join you and your sister in the dining room."

Sofia nodded and then ran through the house and up the long spiral staircase to her bedroom. Once inside, she hurried over to the pink vase on top of her chest of drawers and added the four remaining wild daisies she clutched in her hand with the other ones Ram had given her this week. It was starting to look like one of the huge bouquets her father usually sent her mother.

"Mrs. Sofia Jordan." She practiced saying the name a few times in the mirror. "Mrs. Ramell and Sofia Jordan." It had a nice ring to it, she decided. After standing there and admiring her wildflowers for a minute, she sighed and then turned toward her adjoining bathroom to go wash her hands for dinner. On her way back down the hallway, she stopped by her sister's bedroom to peek inside.

A year ago, when her parents first brought Rachel home, Sofia was absolutely not in favor of the whole kid-sister idea. But the moment her mother had put Rachel into her arms for her to hold for the first time, things changed. Sofia didn't expect the new baby to be so cute and adorable. It was love at first sight. She knew from that moment on that she would be like a second mom to her sister. And so far, that's exactly what she turned out to be.

Seeing that Rachel was still fast asleep, Sofia carefully tiptoed backwards and continued to head back downstairs. However, she hadn't even reached the middle stair before a tide of angry voices rose from her father's study. If she had been told once, she had been told a million times not to go into her father's study when the door was closed. But given the amount of yelling that was going on, her curiosity took over and the next thing she knew she was creeping into the room.

As she poked her head in, the first thing she noticed was her father's handsome face distorted and inflamed with anger.

"You think that I don't know what the hell is going on in my own house?"

"John, John. Calm down," Uncle Jacob, her father's twin, tried to pull him away from Emmett Jordan.

"No, Jacob. Wait until you hear about this…this low-life son-of—"

"JOHN," Sofia's mother yelled.

"This *backstabber,*" he yelled, "has been sneaking

around here with my own wife!" His narrowed gaze shifted to his wife. "Isn't that right, Vivian?"

"No, John!"

"Don't lie to me!" He charged toward her, but once again Uncle Jacob jumped in and blocked his path.

Vivian gasped and stepped back.

"I know what's going on! I've seen you two with my own eyes!"

Her mother dropped her head into her hands and sobbed.

Her father's rampage continued. "Fine! You want her...you can have her. But it'll be a cold day in hell before I let you take my children and my company away from me!"

"John, please," Sofia's mother wailed.

Uncle Jacob kept his hold around his brother. "Everybody just needs to calm down."

"Calm down?" John questioned wildly as he twisted his way out of his brother's arms. "You know what? *Everybody get the hell out of my house!"*

A hand landed on Sofia's shoulders and she nearly jumped ten feet into the air.

"What are you doing in here?" Gloria hissed.

"I was just... I was..."

"Sofia?" Vivian Wellesley turned her stunned, tear-stained eyes toward her and the housekeeper. "Get her out of here!"

"Yes, ma'am." Gloria grabbed Sofia's arm and dragged her out of the study and shut the door.

"What's going on, Gloria?" Sofia asked with panic settling in her bones. She'd never seen her father so angry before.

"Don't worry about it," the housekeeper said, escorting her to the dining room. "That's grown-folks business. None of that concerns you."

Doesn't concern me? Her father had just yelled at her mother and Ramell's father for sneaking around and then accused him of trying to steal his company—a company that he and Uncle Jacob had poured blood, sweat and tears into. Everyone knew how much her father worked and loved that company. And her mother…how could she?

Sofia plopped down at the dinner table and folded her arms in a huff. She knew how. Emmett Jordan was every bit as much of a charmer as his son, Ramell. Clearly, neither one of them could ever be trusted.

Ever.

And that belief would be held for a long time, because Sofia's parents were killed in a plane crash two days later.

Chapter 1

Los Angeles, Today

Sofia sat on the edge of the doctor's table with her cell phone tucked between her shoulder and her ear while her fingers raced across her iPad as she fired off one contract counteroffer after another.

"Sorry, Larry, but that's not going to happen. You've only locked down Ethan Chambers for two seasons of *Paging the Doctor.* And you got off cheap, if you ask me. If you want to get him on board for another four years then you're going to have come up with a figure that doesn't insult my intelligence."

She only half listened to Larry Franklin's response because she knew that this was the part when studios start crying broke or downplaying just how important her client is to their hit shows. But in this case, it would all be irrelevant because Ethan Chambers dominated the tabloids and magazine covers—despite the mild hiccup with him, her sister and the paparazzi a couple of months ago.

"Larry, if you feel that way then we can just let the contract run out and I can dedicate more attention to the numerous *movie* offers that have been flooding my inbox. You know Denzel Washington started off on a medical show and then exploded on the big screen. That just might be the way to go here. Ethan has the looks and the talent, after all."

"Damn, Sofia. You're really going to bust my balls over this."

That managed to put a smile on her face. "I don't have any idea what you're talking about."

"I'm sure you don't." He laughed. "Just like I'm sure this hard bargain you're driving has nothing to do with Ethan Chambers being in queue to become your brother-in-law."

"You're right. I fight for all my clients."

"Duly noted. I'll get back to you with a counteroffer."

"I'll be waiting," Sofia singsonged before disconnecting the call. But as soon as she had her phone started ringing again. She was about to answer when Dr. Turner's bored baritone startled her.

"You think you can fit in time for your checkup?"

Sofia nearly jumped and flashed him with an apologetic smile. "Sorry about that, Brian." She quickly put her phone on vibrate and set it and her iPad down.

"How long do I have before you pick that up again?" he asked, flipping open her chart.

"Two minutes," she answered honestly. Her addiction to her gadgets was well known and quite frankly *not* a laughing matter.

Her longtime friend and doctor shook his head. "I said it before and I'll say it again. You work too much, Sofia."

"Don't be ridiculous. When you love what you do then it's not considered work."

Still shaking his head, Dr. Turner reached for the blood pressure cuff and wrapped it around her arm. "When was the last time you had a vacation?"

Exhaling, Sofia rolled her eyes while she tried to recall the date. "Honey, I don't know. A couple of years ago, I think." She reached over to take a peek at her vibrating phone.

"Let it go to voicemail," the doctor ordered while pumping air into the cuff.

She withdrew her hand from the phone and tried to pretend that she wasn't about to look at it.

"Not good," he said, listening through the stethoscope and watching the needle on the cuff.

"What?" Sofia looked down as if she could decipher the numbers he was reading.

"Your blood pressure is up...*again*." He pulled the cuff off of her arm and leveled her with a stern look. "Look, Sofia. I'm talking to you as both your doctor *and* your friend. You have to do better about controlling all this stress. You keep going down this road and you're going to have a meltdown."

"Ugh." She fought hard not roll her eyes. If she had a nickel for every time someone told her that—mainly her uncle Jacob—she'd be...well, she was already rich, but she would Bill Gates rich.

"I'm serious, Sofia. You need to cut your stress levels," Brian warned, pulling out his prescription pad.

"What are you doing?" Sofia asked when he started scribbling.

"What does it look like? I'm putting you on medication."

"Great. Then what's the problem? I just pop a pill and everything is cool." She picked up her phone and Dr. Turner quickly took it out her hands.

"No. You don't just pop a pill. You still need to try and slow down, watch what you eat and what you drink or you're going to go down the same destructive path that all workaholics go down that leads to an early grave." He handed over her prescription.

Sofia frowned at his scare tactics. "Will that be all?"

"How's your love life? Are you seeing anyone?"

"What the hell does that have to do with the price of tea in China?"

"I'm going to take that as a no." He folded his arms. "You need to get out. Relax. Get a life. Meet someone."

"Limelight is my life. It's all I need."

Thirty minutes later, Sofia strolled into Limelight Entertainment Management while switching back and forth between two different business calls on her Bluetooth. Still, she flashed smiles to staffers while she continued to chew studio executives and directors out without missing a beat.

"Ms. Wellesley, your uncle wants to see you in the conference room," Sarah Cole, perhaps the best assistant in the world, whispered to her. "He said to direct you there as soon as you walk into the door."

Sofia just smiled and ignored the order by continuing her march toward her office. Her uncle Jacob was the last person she wanted to talk to. His little stunt to merge their *family* company with Artist Factory, Inc.—Emmett and Ramell Jordan's company—despite her numerous verbal protests, was a slap in the face that she just couldn't ignore or bring herself to forgive him for anytime soon.

But when she entered her office, she stopped short upon seeing her uncle sitting on her office couch.

"Larry, something just came up. I'm going to have to call you back." She tapped her ear once. "Frasier, I have to call you back." She pulled the gadget from her ear and made a beeline toward her desk. "What are you doing in here?"

"I came to see you since I knew that you wouldn't come to the conference room like I requested."

"I'm busy, Uncle Jacob. What is it?" She asked absently as she plopped into her seat and turned to face her computer.

Jacob heaved himself up from the couch and strolled toward her desk. "First things first. How was your doctor's visit?"

She cut a look toward him as if to ask *are you serious?* Still he stood there waiting so she answered with a slight lie. "Fine."

His brows lifted slowly until they stretched to the center of his forehead. "So I look like an idiot now? The shakes, the occasional vertigo and chest pain is all normal for a *healthy* thirty-five year old woman?"

Sofia gasped. "Allegedly thirty-five." She glanced around him to double-check that they were alone in the room together. Then she said quietly, through clenched teeth, "A woman, especially in this town, never reveals her age."

"Come on, Sofia. It isn't really your age we're talking about, anyway. Tell me the truth."

"Fine. Dr. Turner said something about my blood pressure being *slightly* elevated. He gave me a prescription. It's no big deal." She glanced at her watch. "Now if we're finished discussing my health, I have a ton of calls to get through today."

"They can wait. We need to discuss details about this merger with A.F.I. I've been calling your assistant for weeks now to book a joint meeting with all the parties involved so this transition can go smoothly, but the one person I can't seem to get on the phone is you."

Sofia tossed her hands up in the air. "I don't know what you need my help for. You certainly didn't want to listen to me when I told you that I thought that this merger was a big mistake. Apparently my opinion doesn't matter around here despite supposedly being second in command."

Jacob sucked in a frustrated breath. "I'm not going to keep going around and around with you on this. This merger is a done deal. I know in my heart that this would've been something that even your father would've approved of."

"Like hell he would have."

"Sofia!"

"What? I'm just being honest here. You used to appreciate my honesty. Has that changed, too? Just let me know and I'll just keep my mouth shut."

Jacob slammed his hand on her desk. "How about you just keep the attitude?"

Stunned, Sofia was momentarily unable to respond.

"Now I appreciate and respect your opinion on this matter, but *I'm* still president of this company, and our merging with A.F.I. makes sound financial sense. Plus, Ramell can go a long way in helping to lighten your load around here and you need to take advantage of it."

"I *don't* need Ramell Jordan's help with anything."

"Use him, anyway. In fact, I'm ordering you to delegate some of your workload to him. No more ninety-plus-hour workweeks, Sofia. You need to start taking better care of yourself."

Sofia opened her mouth to protest, but her uncle cut her off.

"You fight me on this then I'll have no choice but to fire you."

"What?"

"You heard me. Since you're too hardheaded to take care of yourself then it looks like I'm going to have to force you to do it."

With her mouth still hanging open, he turned and started to march out the door.

"By the way, Ramell Jordan is waiting for you in the conference room. You have five minutes to get in there."

Chapter 2

Ramell glanced at his watch and then resumed pacing back and forth in the conference room. He was more than a little annoyed about wasting a whole hour to meet with Sofia to discuss the transition between the two companies. This was a power move, plain and simple. He knew Sofia well and he knew that she was still fighting this merger tooth and nail.

He, like her uncle Jacob, saw the financial advantage in merging their two companies together. Together they would be able to give some of the big-name agencies some real competition in this town. When his father and the Wellesleys started their family agencies back in the day they were more like boutique operations serving a niche market for African-American actors. For Limelight, it was Sofia who expanded their clientele to include other artists in the entertainment field, but now it was time to expand their scope to include all actors, musicians, models and directors, no matter their race, in order to compete in today's mainstream market.

On top of that, merging their Los Angeles and New York offices would also free up capital to open new offices in Paris and London. As far as Ramell was concerned this was a no-brainer. Sofia—not so much. In fact, the only thing she'd said to everything proposed so far was a steadfast *no*. Limelight was a family company and she wanted to keep it that way. End of story.

By now he shouldn't be surprised. He'd been running into the same brick wall with Sofia for the past twenty-five years. He would've thought by now that he would be used to the pain, but he wasn't. The main reason being that he was still in love with Sofia, despite the fact that she made it clear that she couldn't stand to be in the same room with him.

The reason? That was one thing he didn't know. One day they were best friends, talking in her backyard about marriage, and the next she was avoiding him like the plague. Thinking she was just playing games again, he'd gone through with his promise to date Connie Woods, only for it not to faze her. Or if it did, she sure as hell didn't let it show.

Before he could get to the bottom of it, John and Vivian Wellesley were killed in a plane crash. They were flying into Aspen, Colorado, on their private jet. Their death sent a shockwave through the Black Hollywood community and even caught the attention of the rabid mainstream paparazzi.

The whole thing came as a shock to the Jordan family, as well. Ram remembered his father being distraught over the whole incident because there had been some kind of falling-out a couple of days before their death. Ramell tried to get to the bottom of what happened but whenever he tried to discuss the matter, his father would clam up, even to this day, which was odd considering how close he was to his father. If Ram didn't know any better, he would've sworn that his father blamed himself for what went down and that just didn't make any sense.

Regardless, he thought that eventually the whole situation would settle down after some time had passed and Sofia and her sister, Rachel, moved in with her aunt and uncle. That never happened. Whatever the story was, Ram suspected that Sofia knew what really happened and she was equally determined to keep him as in the dark as everyone else.

Still, his love for her remained true. If anything it only grew. From a distance Ram watched as Sofia transformed from a pretty young girl into a gorgeous woman. A tall, willowy woman who looked more like the models that graced glossy fashion magazines than a woman who represented them. Sofia stunned everyone who met her because she was as smart as she was beautiful.

The only balm for his broken heart was the fact that he hadn't been forced to watch her settle down with another man and bear a house-load of children. He didn't know whether he could survive something like that. Still, he did have to watch her turn herself into a workaholic in order to carry on what she perceived as her father's dream. Of course, that was a little bit like the pot calling the kettle black since Ram also put in long hours since he took control of A.F.I. But he still managed to squeeze in *some* time off and even the occasional vacation.

Sofia did not. She lived and breathed Limelight. It was her husband, her children—her life.

"I'm sorry to have kept you waiting," Sofia said, breezing into the conference room and not even bothering to glance in his direction.

Ram's head swiveled toward the tall hurricane that just blew into the room. His eyes immediately landed on her long, cinnamon-brown legs streaming from a short dark blue miniskirt. He quickly placed a hand over his mouth as if he just had a thought, but in truth it was just a sly way to do a hidden drool check. As Sofia dropped down into a chair, Ram's gaze was forced to take in her small waist, her flat stomach and her in-your-face D-sized breasts that if he didn't know any better would swear were calling his name. Just her being in the room erased his previous annoyance, but it didn't mean that he was just going to let her blatant lie slip past him.

"Somehow I doubt inconveniencing me troubles you in the slightest," he said, returning to his chair.

She smiled as if to validate his assessment. "Let's just get down to business, shall we?" She flipped open a fat folder and started reading the contents as if it was the first time she'd seen the documents. He doubted that, since it was well known that she went over everything with a fine-tooth comb. But while she pretended to be engrossed with what was written on the page, Ram took a brief moment to mentally photograph her flawless face. Her long lashes looked like two perfect black fans and her strong cheekbones and long flowing black hair hinted at the American-Indian heritage that was buried some-where in her family tree. He could sit there for the rest of the day admiring individual parts of her just as he could sit back and appreciate the entire package. Most of the time, he liked to do as much of both as he could.

Sofia drew a deep breath. "I guess the best way to tackle this is to decide who is ultimately in charge of which department in order to avoid overlap in duties."

"Actually, Jacob and I have already discussed that part. I was under the impression that you were bringing me some of your client files to this meeting."

Sofia's head snapped up. "Excuse me?"

Hit with the full force of her beautiful brown eyes,

Ram sucked in a long breath. It was already bad enough that he had to sit there and pretend that her Marc Jacobs perfume wasn't working a number on his senses, but to pretend like those eyes, those cheekbones and that beautiful, full mouth wasn't causing his pants to fit a little tighter in the inseam would require better acting chops than he possessed. He coughed and then pulled his gaze away from her. "I came here to help lighten your load. Jacob said—"

"I'm not about to turn over my clients to you. Are you crazy?"

Ram blinked and stared back at Sofia silently for a moment.

"Do you know how *long* it took me to develop my list? Do you have any idea how much work it involved to develop a rapport with my clients and studio heads?"

"I think I have some idea, yes." Ram shook his head. "You know it's not my first time to the rodeo here," he said with a laugh, trying to lighten the mood. It didn't work.

Sofia leaned back in her chair and calmly folded her arms beneath her very lovely breasts and said simply, "No."

Ram forced his gaze up from her creamy brown cleavage peeking through her white top and met her steady gaze again. "No?"

"Good. We understand each other." She slapped her folder shut and jumped up from her chair. "Now that we got all that settled, I have some work to do." She flashed him a frosty smile and attempted to leave.

"Whoa, whoa, whoa." Ram instantly popped up and snaked a hand out to grab her by her wrist.

Sofa stiffened while her gaze dropped down to his offending hand.

Without her saying a word, he got the picture and released her. "Sorry."

She turned and squared off. "Look. Let's get something straight. I'm against this merger."

"Clearly."

"And I think the way you and Jacob went about this was sneaky and underhanded. And since you and my uncle cooked this whole thing up behind my back, if there's anyone's client list you should steal it should be his."

"Steal?"

"I don't need your help and I didn't ask for it," she continued. "This whole thing was a big mistake and I suspect that it's just a matter of time before my uncle realizes that, too. And until that time, I'd appreciate it if you just stay the hell away from me. Are we clear?"

"Sofia—"

"It's Ms. Wellesley, thank you."

He blinked unbelievingly. "Are you for real?"

She simply lifted one of her perfectly arched and groomed eyebrows to telegraph that she was dead serious.

"All right." He stepped back. "In that case, no. It's not clear," he said in the same dead tone that she used. "As president of A.F.I., this merger makes *me* second in command of our new business together. Jacob being number one, of course."

Her eyes narrowed.

"So just in case you're having a hard time connecting the dots that means that *you* work for *me*. And I'm no longer asking you to produce your client list. I'm telling you.

If I don't have the list in my office before five o'clock today then I'll simply have your assistant compile the list and *I'll* chose which ones you keep and which ones will be divvied up to the other agents."

Sofia's eyes bulged in shock. "You can't do that!"

"Watch me." He turned toward the conference table, snatched up his briefcase and then headed toward the door.

"Five o'clock, Sofia. I wouldn't advise you being one minute late."

He could feel her eyes blazing a hole in the back of his head as he exited the conference room, but at this moment, he really didn't give a damn.

Chapter 3

"Just who in the hell does he think he is?" Sofia fumed as she stormed back down the hallway to her office, feeling as if smoke was coiling out of her ears. Ramell had the nerve to insinuate that *she* worked for *him?* Had the world gone crazy? What was up was now down and vice versa? "Give him my client list? It'll be a cold day in hell!"

An intern looked up and then rushed to move and jerk his mail cart out of Sofia's path before they were both bowled over. The practically comical scene caught everyone's attention, except Sofia's. She was too busy challenging the strength of her Christian Louboutin heels as she continued to pound them against the agency's marbled floor. Never in her professional life had she allowed *anyone* to strong-arm her, and she wasn't about to let Ramell Jordan be the first.

Her boss. Ha! That would be the damn day. The more she thought about his smug attitude back there in the conference room the more she wished that she had said something that would've put him in his place. Anything to wipe that satisfied look off of his face. Sure, he might be decent looking or even handsome by industry standards. Six foot one, close-cropped hair, sexy goatee and fit enough to bounce a quarter off any portion of his body—but none of that meant she was going to allow his well-honed charm to work on her.

No, sir.

So what if most industry insiders liked him and she had a few unsuccessful tries at poaching a few of his clients. It just proved that he was good at fooling people. And she didn't even want to get started in thinking about the harem of women he'd collected over the years, never settling down with one for longer than a few weeks. That's a major red flag.

Never mind that she hadn't been able to maintain any serious relationship herself. Circumstances are different for women. Men usually run off screaming from professional women. It had been her experience in Hollywood that men tended to like their women young and dumb, or at the very least women who put in the effort to pretend to be dumb around them. She didn't play that game.

Sofia reached her uncle's office and breezed inside without saying a word to his assistant, Elisa, who was just a little too slow to stop her.

"Um, Ms. Wellesley," she called out feebly as Sofia marched right past her.

"We need to talk," Sofia declared, interrupting Jacob in the middle of his practice golf swing.

Her uncle let out a long breath. "Meeting over so soon?" Jacob glanced at his watch. "I figured that it would be at least another five minutes before Ramell pissed you off."

"I'm sorry, Mr. Wellesley," Elisa said from the door.

"It's all right." He waved her off. "Just shut the door behind you."

"Yes, sir." Elisa rushed to do just that.

"What? Was she supposed to play goalie and block me from coming in here?"

Jacob set aside his golf club as he admitted, "She was at least supposed to give me a heads-up."

"Very funny." Sofia folded her arms. "Just like I find it *hilarious* that Ramell Jordan seems to be under the illusion that he's my boss."

"Oh, good Lord." Jacob headed over to his desk and removed the bottle of Tums he kept in the bottom drawer.

"Want to tell me what that crap is all about?"

"Well, I guess *technically* he is sort of…kind of, your boss. Technically speaking."

"Come again?" she asked, cupping her ear. Sofia wanted to make sure that she heard her uncle correctly before she snapped, crackled and popped off all up in his office.

"Sofia, just listen. Now, I know that you're upset."

"Try pissed. In fact, I think I've just discovered a whole new level of pissed off. I've been busting my butt for years now trying to make full partner, or even take over the family business, and now you go and throw a monkey wrench like this at me. That man out there now has more pull and say in my own father's company than I do! How could you?" She stomped her foot, feeling a tantrum coming on, which was completely unlike her. Sofia prided herself for always being calm, cool and collected, but today's surprises were making that impossible.

"Calm down, Sofia. When I retire, I fully intend to turn the presidency over to you. Ramell knows that and he knows that he will remain vice president."

"But until then…"

"Until then…well, yeah, I guess *technically*—"

"There you go with that 'technically' stuff again." She tossed up her hands. "This isn't going to work. It's just not going to work," she said as hysteria started creeping into her voice. She had worked too hard to cut Ramell Jordan out of her life only for her uncle to undermine all of her efforts now.

"Sofia, what's the big deal? Ramell is a fine businessman with a lot of good and creative ideas to help take this company to the next level. We've known his family for years. They're good people."

"Ha!" She rolled her eyes.

"What is that supposed to mean?"

"Emmett and Ramell Jordan are not to be trusted. I know that for a fact. They have always had their eye out for this company and now you've just handed it over to them on a silver platter without so much as a fight."

"Yes. Emmett Jordan has always expressed an interest in merging our two companies together. And there has always been an interest on our end to do so."

"Not by my father."

"I think I'm a little more qualified to know what my brother wanted and what he didn't want," Jacob charged back. "I did, after all, start this company with him. I'm also the one who kept the business afloat long before putting you on the payroll."

"Why do I keep getting the distinct impression that you're trying to force me out of the company?"

"Because you're too stressed out and it's making you paranoid." He marched over, turned her around by her shoulders and directed her back toward the door. "This discussion is over. Just trust me on this one. Now get back to work, and try not to stress yourself out too much."

"But—"

"No buts. Just do me a favor and *try* to get along with Ramell."

"I don't know if—"

"That's all. Thanks," he said, pushing her out the door and then closing it behind her.

"How rude." Sofia huffed and stormed off toward her office.

Sarah glanced up from her desk and caught the look on Sofia's face. Instantly she was on her feet, anticipating a list of duties to be rattled off to her.

"In my office," Sofia barked, breezing past her assistant so fast that a small gust of wind ruffled the stacks of papers on Sarah's desk.

"Yes, ma'am. Right away." Sarah grabbed her iPad and rushed in right behind her boss. When they entered the office Sofia seemed content to just pace in a circle. It wasn't just a regular *oh, I'm trying to think* kind of pace. No. Sofia Wellesley looked more like a dangerous wild animal plotting her next attack.

"Is everything all right?" Sarah asked, backing up. If Sofia was going to pounce she didn't want to get too close.

Suddenly, uncharacteristically, Sofia stopped pacing and began to smile. "Sarah!"

"Yes, ma'am?" Sarah asked, taking another cautionary step backward.

With her smile still abnormally wide, Sofia walked over to her assistant and linked her arm through hers. "How do you feel about taking a vacation?"

"Excuse me?"

"You heard me. I want you to leave. Take the rest of the month off."

"A month?" Frowning, her assistant's brows started to stitch together.

"Yes, a month." Sofia insisted as she brightened. "You deserve it. How long have you been working for me?"

Sarah shrugged and stammered, "Um—five years."

"Five years," Sofia repeated. "And you get what—two weeks vacation a year?"

"Well, actually I haven't actually had a vacation in three years."

"Three years?"

"We both haven't," she reminded Sofia.

"Humph." She frowned at that for a moment. "Well there's no time like the present, don't you think?" Sofia started out, directing Sarah back to her desk. "Now you grab your things and I'll just see you next month."

"What? You mean leave right now?" Sarah double-checked.

"Absolutely."

Sarah stopped and dug her heels in. "Okay," she said tentatively. "Am I being fired? Did I do something wrong?"

"No," Sofia reassured her. "It just occurred to me that I've been working you too hard. Your family lives in New York, right?"

"Y-yes. But—"

"Then it's a perfect time for you to go drop in for a visit." Back out at Sarah's desk, Sofia helped the girl by grabbing her purse and leather laptop bags. "Oh, and I need to change your computer pass code." Sofia rushed around to her assistant's computer and started keying in numbers.

Sarah's eyes glossed over. "Are you sure I'm not being fired? Whatever I did wrong, I can fix it."

"You're not being fired. You have my word on that." Sofia popped back up and started escorting her toward the door. "Go. Have a good time. I want you nice and refreshed when you come back."

"Um. Okay," Sarah said. What else could she say? But Sofia didn't just walk her to the door, she walked her all the way to her Honda hybrid and even stood in the parking lot and waved goodbye.

When Sofia returned to her office, she couldn't help but dance around her office like she'd just scored the final touchdown in a Super Bowl game. Hips shaking and arms waving, she couldn't wait to see the look on Ram's face when she told him that Sarah wouldn't be available to compile for him her prized client list and she'd changed the pass code to ensure that no one else could generate the list, either.

"I feel bad that I don't have any cash on me so I can make it rain up in here."

Sofia jumped and spun around to see her new *boss* leaning against her door frame. "What are you doing in here?"

"Well, I was enjoying the show. I think you missed your calling. You should've been a dancer."

"And you should have been a jerk. Oops! I forgot. You are a jerk." She rolled her eyes and marched to her desk. "Now if you're finished annoying me...I'm busy."

"Busy getting that list together, I hope."

Sofia cocked a smile. "Tell you what. Why don't you hold your breath and just wait for it?"

"All right. Five o'clock." He tapped his watch.

"I'm not sure if that time frame is going to work for me," she said, flashing him a smile. "I'm really very busy, so you're going to have to wait for Sarah to prepare it."

He glanced over his shoulder to Sarah's empty desk.

"But don't bother looking for her. She's on vacation… for a while."

"Aww. Well, that was awfully nice of you, seeing how you work her about as hard as you work yourself."

"Thank you, vice president," Sofia said, before adding under her breath, "of the peanut gallery." She motioned for him to leave her office. "Now if you don't mind."

He didn't move. "Well, I hope Sarah has fun wherever she's going. I'm so glad I got her to compile that list before she went."

"What? You did what? When?"

"After our meeting while you were in the office with Jacob."

Sofia's jaw nearly hit her desk.

"You know, I see why she works for you. She's fast and efficient." Ram winked at her. "I'll review it and get back to you." And with that he strolled off, whistling.

Chapter 4

The Latin Grammy Awards were being hosted in Las Vegas. Limelight Entertainment Management represented a number of Afro-Latin musicians that were nominated for everything from Best New Artist to Best Latin Album of the Year. The awards were always held in November—a good six months after the crazy award season in Los Angeles. It doesn't mean that it was any less hectic—and this year it was doubly so for Sofia because she had foolishly sent her assistant on vacation and she was dealing with a temp, Stewart, that seemed permanently hyped-up on caffeine, had dyslexia when it came to writing down numbers, and had a habit of dropping more calls than a crummy cell-phone provider.

If there was one silver lining to this dark cloud, it would have to be that she had managed to avoid Ramell Jordan for the past seven days. How on earth her uncle thought she was going to be able to control her blood pressure with him around, she never knew.

After Stewart screwed up with Armani on which date she needed her awards dress to be delivered and failed to mail out an e-vite to the nominees for Limelight's pre-award private party, Sofia's patience was pretty much ready to snap when the car that was supposed to take her to the airport never showed up.

"What the hell? Did he think I was supposed to hitch a ride?" Sofia yelled, rushing to throw her bags in the back of her sister's car.

"Calm down," Rachel said, laughing. "It's all good. I don't mind dropping you off at the airport."

Ever since her engagement to Ethan Chambers, it seemed like nothing bothered Rachel anymore; not the drama of working on the set of *Paging the Doctor* or the hectic pace of putting a wedding together or even having her love life splattered across the pages of every tabloid across America. Growing up, Rachel wanted nothing to do with the spotlight so of course life dealt her a hand where she'd fallen in love with the hottest star on television. But when push came to shove, love triumphed.

Rachel glowed like a woman in love and Sofia was surprised to feel a prick of envy. That was unlike her, too, since she truly wanted the world for her baby sister. And if there was anyone who could give her the world, it was Ethan. Her future brother-in-law was a rarity in this city: a genuinely good man who valued family.

"I got to get Sarah back here pronto or I'm going to pull out every strand of hair on my head dealing with Stewart."

Rachel laughed and started up the car. "Sounds like you've finally met your match with Ramell Jordan."

Sofia's eyes nearly rolled out the back of her head on that. "Puh-lease. That'll be the day."

Rachel glanced over at the passenger seat while Sofia hooked her Bluetooth on her ear and started powering up her iPad. "What's the deal between you and Ramell, anyway? You act like the man is our sworn enemy or something."

"There's no deal. Trust me. I just have to put up with him until Uncle Jacob comes to his senses. And I hope to hell it's soon because the two of us in one office isn't going to work." She tapped her ear and immediately transitioned into her professional voice. "Hello, Akil. It's Sofia. How's it going? Are you and Charlene going to make it to the award ceremony this weekend?"

"You know it," Akil Hutton boasted. "My first nomination for that joint I produced with Pit Bull. I'm all over it, baby." Akil and his label, Playascape, were the hottest players in the game at the moment and Sofia was thrilled that her newest client, and Rachel's best friend, Charlene Quinn's debut CD was going to drop this spring on the label. Then the surprise of all surprises; while Charlene was down at Akil's Miami home studio she won the megaproducer's heart and landed an engagement ring.

"Good. I trust you're bringing Charlene?"

"Of course. Every man needs someone gorgeous on their arm. In my case it's going to be my beautiful fiancée."

Sofia felt another twinge of jealousy, but she covered it by saying, "That's great. I can't wait to see you both there. Make sure you swing by the pre-award ceremony. Maybe we can set it up for Charlene to do a set. Give the people in Las Vegas a little teaser of what's to come."

"Yeah. Yeah. We can make it do what it do," he laughed.

"Good deal. Catch you later. You can reach me on my cell if you need anything." Sofia tapped her ear and rushed to finish her fourth counteroffer to Larry Franklin for Ethan's next contract.

Rachel shook her head. "Does your brain have an off switch?"

"Not that I'm aware of," she laughed, but then suddenly experienced a wave of vertigo. "Oh, no." She pressed a hand against the side of her head.

"What's the matter?" Rachel asked, glancing back over at her sister.

"Nothing. I'm… I guess I just got a little dizzy there."

"Are you sure you're all right? Do I need to pull over?"

"Don't you dare. I have to make this flight. I'm probably just dizzy because I skipped breakfast. I'll grab something on the plane." Her finger went back to zooming across the tablet on her lap.

Rachel went back to shaking her head. "Did you get your prescription filled?"

Sofia looked over at her.

"Uncle Jacob told me," she said, answering the unspoken question.

"Figures. I love him dearly, but lately I swear the man is trying to run my life."

Rachel shook her head. "He's just concerned about you. We all are. Your workload—"

"Oh, Rachel, not you, too." Sofia pinched the bridge of her nose.

"Yes, me, too. You're the only sister I have and I'd kind of like to keep you around a little longer…or at least until you fulfill your duty as maid of honor at my wedding later this month."

"Figures." The two sisters laughed. After another twenty minutes of navigating through L.A. traffic, Rachel pulled into the private airstrip in Burbank where Limelight usually shared a chartered private jet with a list of other high-profile industry insiders. Given how her day was going so far, she had no idea why she was surprised to find that her wonderful temporary assistant *didn't* book her on a flight to Las Vegas.

"Please say that you're joking," Sofia moaned. She had already had her bags unloaded from her sister's car and Rachel had already taken off.

The pretty, plus-size woman behind the counter fluttered a sympathetic smile at her. "No. I'm sorry. And we're all booked up. Everyone is trying to get to the awards ceremony for the weekend."

"I know. That's where I need to get to." She let out a sigh and then tried to rein in her mounting frustration. If she got her hands on Stewart, he was a dead man. "There has to be something we can do. The chances of me getting out of LAX today will be close to impossible."

"I don't know, ma'am. Like I said, every flight is completely booked."

"Are you sure? There has to be some room. I can sit in the back with the stewardess. Hell, I can be a stewardess. Anyone want some time off? How hard can it be to serve drinks?"

Still shaking her head, the lone booking agent held firm.

"I don't believe this," Sofia said, jerking away from the counter only to come face-to-face with a smiling Ramell, dressed casually in a pair of black jeans and a white short-sleeved top. Instantly, Sofia's gaze zeroed in on his arm's bulging bronze muscles. What Ram looked like in a suit versus what he looked like dressed down were two totally different animals, this one much more dangerous to her peace of mind.

When her eyes shifted across the wide span of his chest, her hand started twitching at her side. She had a sudden curiosity of what it would feel like to run her fingers across it or even lay her head against it.

Ram cleared his throat and Sofia's gaze jumped up to his mirrored aviator sunglasses. "Is there a problem?" he asked.

"No," Sofia lied.

"Yes," the woman behind the counter contradicted. "Ms. Wellesley is looking for a flight to Las Vegas. Unfortunately, we're all booked up."

"Oh, is that right?" Ram's smile stretched wider. "If you're looking to hitch a ride, you're more than welcome to ride shotgun with me."

She hesitated.

"It's not a private jet. It's just my own personal plane."

"What? You're a pilot?"

He chuckled. "I got my pilot license before my driver's license."

"I think I'll pass," she said and then tapped her ear to place a call. "Stewart, I need a car."

Ram shrugged his big shoulders. "All right. Suit yourself." He turned and started for the hangar.

"You know what, Stewart. Just give me the number. I'll call them. You just call the airline and—scratch that—get me the number and I'll call them, too." She asked for a pen from the frowning woman behind the desk and jotted the numbers down. "Thank you." She tapped her ear and pulled out her phone to start dialing.

"Excuse me," the counter girl said, interrupting her.

"Yes."

"Let me get this straight. You'd rather call and wait for a car to come get you so you can fight traffic over to LAX where you'll wait for a flight that may or may not be available to Las Vegas rather than just get on the plane that's *right there* in the hangar and can have you in Las Vegas in less than an hour?"

Sofia opened her mouth to confirm that was exactly what she preferred to do when the ridiculousness of such a response hit her. She was a busy woman with a million things to do before Sunday night's award show and she was about to throw away a whole day just because she didn't want to be on a plane with Ramell.

"I think I see your point," Sofia acquiesced. She handed the woman back her pen and then rushed out of the hub. "Ramell! Ramell!" Sofia raced as fast as she could in heels. "Did anyone see where Ramell Jordan ran off to?"

A few of the guys in the hangar just looked up and smiled as she darted by. When she finally spotted Ram strolling casually toward a white and red single-engine plane, she sped up, screaming his name. "Ramell, wait!"

"Seems like I've been doing that half my damn life," he mumbled under his breath before he forced on a smile and turned around. "Yes? What can I *not* help you with now?"

Sofia pulled up, out of breath, which once again drew Ram's attention to her heaving breasts. Good thing his eyes were hidden behind his shades or he would've really embarrassed himself.

"About that, um, flight…?"

"Yes? What about it?" He was not going to make this easy for her.

"Well, I was thinking…" She smiled. "Since you're here and I'm here…?"

Ram folded his arms. "Yeah?"

"Well…I guess it would be pretty silly of me to try to book a commercial flight and fight traffic and whatnot."

"That sort of crossed my mind, too. Well, I actually thought it was more like ridiculous…childish…juvenile."

"All right, all right. I get the picture." She frowned. "So can I hop a ride or not?"

It was definitely her attitude that rubbed Ramell the wrong way so he said, "No," before he turned away and continued toward the plane.

"No?" she echoed and then had to chase back after him again. "What do you mean 'no'? You just offered me a ride back there in the hub."

"That was then. This is now." He reached the door of his beloved plane and pulled it open.

Sofia huffed out a frustrated breath. "What's the difference between now and then?"

Ram tossed in his lone overnight bag and turned to face her. "Back then I sort of felt sorry for you. Now—not so much."

"Wh-what?" she sputtered.

Taking a deep breath, Ram crossed his arms. "Has anyone ever told you that you really have a nasty attitude?"

She blinked.

"Well, it can't be towards everyone, I suppose. Seems that most people I talk to actually like you. Your clients and studio executives—they all rave about your work and your professionalism. So that must mean this frosty routine is designed just for me. Though I can't imagine why. I've never been anything but nice to you."

Sofia's eyes narrowed. "Is this about to become a sermon?"

Ram pulled in a deep breath, shook his head and turned away from her. "Goodbye, Sofia. Undoubtedly, I'll see you in Vegas." When he started to climb up into the cab of the plane, Sofia panicked and grabbed him by the arm.

"Wait!"

Carefully removing his shades, Ram turned his head and looked down at the slim fingers that were clutching his biceps.

Sofia tried to swallow what felt like a sharp-edged rock in the center of her throat while an intense wattage of electricity singed through her fingertips. She could practically see the fine hairs on her arm stand up.

"Do you mind?" he asked.

His warm baritone managed to break whatever weird trance she'd fallen into, but just barely. "All right." She lowered her hand and forced on a smile, but Ram just frowned and stared at her suspiciously. "You're right. I've been a little…"

"Bitchy," he supplied.

"Short," she corrected. "I was going to say *short* around you."

He rolled his eyes and waited for her to finish.

"It's just that…you know a lot of this…merging stuff… I don't like it."

"Actually yes, you made that pretty clear. But it still doesn't excuse… Let's compromise and call it rude, shall we? It doesn't excuse you for being *rude*." He glanced at his watch. "Now if you'll excuse me. I have a ton of things to do before the pre-award party *our* company is throwing for our nominated clients." He turned to climb back into the cab.

"Wait!" Sofia grabbed his arm again. "Are you really *not* going to give me a lift?"

Ram continued to pretend that he didn't feel the heat

blazing up his arm when he shrugged off her touch. "Are you really *not* going to apologize for your rude behavior?"

She dropped her hand again and pulled up straight, but the one thing she had trouble doing was getting her mouth to work.

"See you later."

"Okay." Her hand flew back to his arm. "I'm…I'm…" She started coughing.

"You have to be kidding me."

"Oh, God, I need some water." She clutched her throat as if it needed massaging to get the words out of it.

"You need to stop wasting my time." Irritation had finally crept into his voice. "I'm not going to stand for you talking and treating me like I'm something stuck on the bottom of your shoe. Whether you want to recognize it or not I'm a man that has worked and earned a certain level of respect. If you can't deal with that then I suggest you march your butt out there on the runway and hitch out your thumb and see if you can catch a ride that way."

She blinked and then finally whispered, "I'm sorry."

Ram cupped a hand around his ear. "Come again?"

Sofia sucked in a deep breath, closed her eyes and spoke louder. "I *said* I'm sorry." After a long pause of silence, she peeled open her eyes. Ram looked as if he was still weighing whether to accept her apology or tell her just where she could stick her apology.

"I mean it. I'm sorry," she added.

Ram nodded. "Fine. I'll give you a lift on one condition."

She should have known. "What is it?"

"That you keep your mouth shut. I don't want you to so much as utter a sound," he said with a narrowed gaze that made it clear that he was being serious. "Think that you can handle that?"

"Ye—"

"Ah. Ah. Ah." He waved a finger in front of her face. "When it comes to you, as far as I'm concerned, silence is golden."

Sofia clamped her mouth shut and then angrily nodded her head.

"Good. Then you got yourself a deal."

Chapter 5

Forty minutes. Sofia just needed to keep her mouth shut for forty minutes. How hard could that be? Turns out, it was pretty hard. Given the fact that she had lost her parents in a plane crash, flying was never her favorite thing. But for the most part, she could deal with it because of all the travel that was needed for her job. But climbing into this plane, much smaller than anything she'd ever flown in, was another thing altogether.

"How long did you say that you've been flying?" she asked, clutching her seatbelt.

Ram cut her a look.

"I mean…" She glanced around as they neared the runway. "You're sure of what you're doing, right?"

"It's not too late for you to get out," he said.

Sofia opened her mouth but Ram signaled for her to zip it. *Now look who is being rude.* She sulked down in her chair. But when the plane raced down the runway, she slammed her eyes closed and prayed. Five minutes later, she finally felt safe enough to pry her eyes open. By then they were coasting smoothly through the clouds. "Well…okay. This isn't so bad." She exhaled and tried to relax. "I can do this."

Ram just sighed.

"What? Are you going to threaten to kick me out now?"

"Don't tempt me."

Sofia pulled in a long breath while she stared at his strong profile. She tried to hold on to the years of anger that she'd felt for the Jordans. In her head, she could still hear her father yelling and accusing Emmett Jordan of being a backstabber. From that day on, she grouped father and son together. But was that really fair?

She jerked at the rogue question and then squirmed in her seat because she didn't really want her subconscious to answer it.

Ram snuck another glance to his right and noticed how stiff Sofia looked in her seat. "Unbelievable," he mumbled under his breath.

"What?"

"Nothing," he lied with a shrug.

"That was not nothing," Sofia challenged. "What is it? Spit it out."

After a couple of more shrugs, he decided to come clean. "I was just noting how…uptight you are." He looked over at her again and shook his head. "You've changed so much."

She raised her chin indignantly. "I have not."

"Puh-lease. I'm willing to bet that this is the longest you've gone without talking on the phone."

"No, it's not."

"I'm not counting when you're asleep, though I'm willing to bet that you don't do that for very long, either."

"That's not true." Even as she challenged his assessment, Sofia reached for her cell phone to check her caller ID.

Ram laughed. "Look at you."

"What?"

"If you don't know then I'm not going to tell you."

Suddenly self-aware, Sofia shoved her phone back into her purse. "Whatever."

"All I know is that the Sofia that I grew up with knew how to have fun," he said with a note of sadness. "She used to let her hair down. Run. Laugh. Play in a field of wild daisies…and even sneak kisses beneath the big oak tree in her backyard."

Sofia's heart skipped a beat. The picture of that long lost girl sprung vividly into her mind and there was a twinge of longing that came swiftly and overwhelmed her. She pulled her face away and stared out at what seemed like an endless sky of white clouds.

"It's like we're floating in a dream," she whispered.

Ram smiled. "That's why I like flying. When you're up here, the world and all its problems just fade away."

Sofia sucked in a deep breath and listened to just the steady hum of the plane's engine and single propeller. It did sort of have a calming effect and there was no denying the beauty surrounding her. "I see what you mean."

He chanced another look at her and was pleased to see the tension in her face had disappeared and her posture had relaxed. Sofia turned her head, met Ram's gaze and fluttered a smile before she remembered that she was supposed to be keeping her distance. Jerking her head away, she then looked at the time.

Twenty minutes.

"I should have known that that wasn't going to last long," Ram commented.

"What?"

"You keeping your guard down." He let a wave of silence drift over them. "Do you really hate me that much?"

Sofia's mouth sprang open, but then her words got caught up in her throat.

"I see." Ram trained his eyes back onto the sky in front of him and pretended that he didn't feel the slight pinch in his throat.

"I don't hate you," Sofia whispered and cleared her throat. "It's just…" She struggled for the right words and then just ended with, "I don't hate you."

"That's good to hear." He shrugged his big shoulders. "Even though I don't quite believe it."

Sofia squirmed in her chair.

"I guess it doesn't matter," he said, but then thought about it. "But it would be nice if we could somehow figure out a way to have some kind of cordial relationship since we are going to be working together."

She sucked in a deep breath.

"And yes, it's still duly noted that you're against the merger. But that's already behind us. Moving forward, I think the best thing we can do for our employees is to show a united front. I know that's what your uncle and I both want."

Silence.

"Or not," he amended, feeling his frustrations returning. "It's up to you. We can pit the Limelight employees against the A.F.I. employees and see how far that gets us. But I'm willing to bet not far."

Sofia took another deep breath and then said, "I'm being stubborn, aren't I?"

"That's…one word I would've used." He smiled. "If I was going to keep it PG."

That won a second smile from her. Still she was conflicted about letting go of a grudge she'd held for so long against the Jordans. "How about we strike a deal?"

Ram laughed. "It's always about the deal with you, isn't it?"

"What can I say? Negotiating is in my blood."

He nodded. "All right. What kind of deal are we talking about?"

"My client list," she said, crossing her arms. "No dividing it up. My people are my people."

Ram threw his head back and laughed. "Now why didn't I see that coming?"

"I don't know. Maybe you had mistaken me for someone who gives up."

"Never that, baby girl. Never that." He shook his head. "Well?"

He tugged in a breath. "The point in me taking the list was to lighten your workload."

"Do you want to end the stalemate or don't you?"

His eyes narrowed. "I do, but—"

"Good. You want something and I want something. Let's negotiate."

Boxed into a corner, Ram considered his options. The fact that this is the longest conversation they'd had without her storming off or tossing in a few choice words his way forced him to recognize the sweet carrot she was offering. "Your list for peace?"

"That's pretty much it in a nutshell."

"But there's still the issue of you working too many long hours," he said, hedging. "I admit that you're one hell of an agent and a great asset to the company, but let's face it. You can't sustain this workload. You need help and you're too stubborn to admit it or acknowledge it."

Sofia's jaw clenched. "Fine. I'll cut back on my hours."

"To forty hours a week."

"What? Don't be ridiculous. I can do…seventy."

"Lower."

"Sixty-five."

"Lower."

"Sixty?"

"Lower."

"Oh. I give up. You're totally being unreasonable." She shifted in her seat in an attempt to give him her back.

Ram was too busy laughing.

"What's so funny now?"

"You are," he said. "I recall us almost having the same exact conversation when you were telling me that you wanted to date a gazillion boys."

"What?" And then the memory hit her. "Oh." Her face warmed as she blushed. "You remember that?"

His smile returned. "Well, I had asked you to marry me for like the millionth time."

"You were persistent. I'll give you that."

"All the good that did me," he mumbled under his breath. "I believe that was the last day we were technically friends." He paused. "In retrospect I think a simple 'no' would've sufficed."

Sofia started squirming again.

Ram felt he was finally getting to her. "What happened?"

The angry voice rising from her father's den played in her head, but she forced it out and lied. "Nothing."

"Yeah. Okay. I believe that." He clicked and rotated a few buttons. "Buckle your seat belt. I'm taking us down for a landing."

Sofia closed her eyes and for the first time felt really ashamed of her behavior. It had to be jarring for a young Ramell to have his best friend suddenly stop talking to him. And the way she'd treated him since. She almost groaned out loud. She had been so wrapped up in her own feelings and angst that she didn't allow herself to see things through his perspective. Stealing another glance in his direction, she made a decision. "All right. Fifty hours," she said. "And that's my final offer."

Ramell cocked a smile. "Sounds like we got ourselves a deal."

When they landed, Ramell offered Sofia a ride to Mandalay Bay, where the 11th Annual Latin Grammy Awards would be held. It was also where Limelight Entertainment would be hosting their pre-award party and where Stewart had booked her room.

And if Stewart was involved in anything that meant that things were screwed up.

"What do you mean we're sharing a room?" Sofia asked the young gentleman with the Justin Bieber haircut behind the counter. "There must be some kind of mistake."

David, according to his name tag, checked his screen again and then shook his head. "You are with Limelight Entertainment, correct?"

"Yes. But—"

"Then, no. There's no mistake. We have you and Mr. Jordan booked for the media suite."

"Sounds great to me," Ramell said, smiling and grabbing the envelope with their plastic keys.

"Whoa. Wait." Sofia grabbed his arm with a troubled frown. "We can't share a room."

He stared at her and shrugged. "Why not?"

"Real funny, Slick. I don't think so." She turned back toward the counter. "I need another room."

David blinked and then started typing in the computer, but even as he did so he was shaking his head. "I'm sorry but due to the Latin Grammys this weekend, we're all booked up."

She huffed. "Then I'll just have to go to another hotel."

He shrugged. "You can try, but I'm pretty sure that they're going to tell you the same thing. With press, artists and industry people in town for the ceremony, they'll all tell you the same thing. You might find something out on the old strip."

"Oh, God," she moaned. Her cell phone started ringing, but she quickly put it on mute.

"Sofia, it's no big deal. The media suite is a huge room. It's at least…what?" Ram asked David.

"Two thousand square feet," David answered. "There are two bedrooms in it."

"See? It's like an apartment. I'll have one bedroom and you'll have another."

He had a way of making it seem reasonable, but alarm bells were ringing so loud inside her head she could hardly think.

"C'mon," Ram said, turning away. "We both have half a million things to do to get ready for the party tomorrow night."

Sofia remained rooted by the counter as she watched him stroll off toward the elevator bay. *This cannot be happening,* she told herself.

Ram stopped, turned and looked at her. "Are you coming?"

Still trying to turn off the bells ringing in her head, Sofia slowly pushed one foot in front of the other while she mumbled under her breath, "I sure hope you know what you're doing."

Chapter 6

It *was* a big suite. Sofia relaxed a little when she walked through the door and saw that the media room was in fact like an apartment. A pretty nice apartment, at that. They walked through a long foyer with eclectic artwork on the walls and minimal furnishing. That led them to a large living room area with floor-to-ceiling windows. There was a full office area, dining room and then it all split off to a media room that was fully enclosed with a state-of-the-art surround-sound theater.

"Feel safe yet?" Ram asked, cocking a smile and shaking his head.

"It wasn't that I didn't feel safe," she defended. "It was just that…"

"You don't trust me," he supplied, still smiling.

She opened her mouth to lie, but her phone started ringing.

"Saved by the bell," Ramell said before grabbing his bags and heading off toward one of the bedrooms on the other side of the apartment.

Sofia watched him go. Her eyes drifted down his broad shoulders, narrow waist and then finally his firm butt that damn near hypnotized her. Geez, did this man live in a gym?

"Aren't you going to answer that?" Ram asked without a backward glance.

"Oh!" She blinked out her trance and answered the phone. "Hello."

"Ah, Ms. Wellesley. Thank goodness. We're having a problem with the caterer for tomorrow's party," Stewart said, sounding like he was on the verge of a heart attack. "Plus the party planner hasn't arrived yet and the hotel is insisting that we can't have fire-eaters in this place."

"What? I never asked for any fire-eaters." She smacked her hand against her head and wondered what the hell she did to get cursed with this assistant. "You know what? Don't touch anything. Don't call anyone. I'll be down in a minute." She hurried off to put her bags in the other bedroom, but when she came back Ram was standing in the media room in just a pair of shorts, socks and sneakers. She nearly tripped out of her designer pumps at the sight of his bare and muscular chest, his chiseled abs and powerful legs.

Ramell Jordan had definitely grown up.

Ram slipped a DVD into the media console and turned to see Sofia rooted behind him. He waved a hand in front of her after a few seconds. "Hello?"

Sofia blinked and then shook her head, but even then she wasn't sure that she had successfully broken her trance because he was still standing there before her half-dressed.

"I was naked."

His eyebrows rose in amusement.

"I mean—" She coughed and cleared her throat. "I was just about to go downstairs. We're having a few issues with the chest." Cough. "I mean party."

He smiled. "You need some help? I was just going to do this workout DVD, but if you need…"

"No. No. Don't worry. I'm on it. I can handle it."

He frowned. "I'll go get dressed."

"No! Really I got it. I'm sure it won't take but a few minutes." He strolled back toward his bedroom with Sofia's gaze following him again. Once he was out of sight, the spell had finally been broken and Sofia could unroot herself from the center of the suite.

"What the hell?" She pressed a hand against her chest only to discover that her heart was beating like a drum. "I have to get out of here."

Not waiting for Ram, she rushed out of the suite and down to one of the conference rooms Limelight Entertainment had rented out for their pre-award show. She ushered her useless assistant aside and delved into fixing all the problems he'd created.

In between talking with the caterer and apologizing to the very lovely fire-eater that her services wouldn't be needed, Sofia took call after call from clients and studio executives. When suddenly the energy in the room shifted and the hairs on the back of her neck stood straight up, Sofia tossed a glance over her shoulder to see that Ramell had entered the room. She felt a twinge of disappointment because he actually had the nerve to put on more clothes. How ridiculous was that?

She continued to watch him while he moved through the room, talked to a few people and even shared a laugh or two. Despite the conversation streaming through her Bluetooth and her nodding to the caterer, Sofia found herself mentally undressing Ram. She remembered vividly what those muscles beneath that T-shirt looked like, just like she was sure that she could probably grate a block of cheese across his abdomen. Suddenly, she was unbearably hot.

"Is the air conditioner working in here?" She fanned herself.

"Excuse me?" her client asked through her Bluetooth.

"Sorry, Larry. I wasn't talking to you." She glanced around and then reluctantly waved Stewart over.

He rushed over like an overeager puppy. With his big, brown, bewildered eyes, he actually sort of looked like a puppy, too. "Yes, ma'am? You need something?"

Sofia hit the mute button on her call. "Check with someone about the air conditioner. It's hot in here."

He frowned. "Really? I was just thinking it's a bit chilly."

She huffed and rolled her eyes. "Will you please just go do what I ask?"

"Yes, ma'am. I'll get right on it." He actually saluted her and ran off.

She turned back toward the caterer only to see that she had moved over to Ramell along with the party planner, seeking to get his final approval on Sofia's changes.

What the hell?

She took her call off mute and said, "Larry, I hate to do this to you again, but I'm going to have to call you back."

"Does that mean we have a deal?"

"I'll call you back," she insisted and then walked over to Ramell. "Did I miss something?" she asked, interrupting Caryn midsentence. Both sets of eyes zoomed over to her. "I put the party together every year."

Ramell smiled. "And I'm sure that you've always done a wonderful job. But this year I'm here to help."

He signed something for Caryn and then asked, "Do you mind giving us a few minutes alone?"

Caryn nodded and then flashed a smile at Sofia before tiptoeing off.

"What gives?" she challenged.

"Nothing." He shrugged. "I'm just giving you a hand since two doesn't seem like it's quite enough."

Sofia's spine stiffened. "What does that mean? Are you saying that I dropped the ball or something?"

Realizing that he'd put his foot into his mouth, Ram tried to backtrack. "No. No. We've already been over this, remember?"

"Yeah." She stretched the tense muscles in her neck. "We've also been over the fact that I didn't ask for your help."

Ram's smile melted off his face. "That's because you're stubborn." When her face darkened he knew that she was just seconds from exploding. "Can't you just relax? Or don't you know how to do that anymore?"

"I—" Her phone rang. She reached for it only for Ram to snatch it out of her hand. "What are you doing?"

"They can leave a message. We're talking. You and me," he informed her.

She blinked and started sputtering.

"I need you to understand something. I gave you back your client list, but my objective is still to lighten your workload. You can go along with it or we can upend that truce we've had for the last—" he glanced at his watch "—two hours and go back to our respective boxing corners."

She sucked in a breath and lifted her chin. "I just don't like being pushed around."

"And I don't like pushing you," he said in a softer

tone. "I really don't, but I feel like you're forcing my hand on this."

She scoffed.

"Unbelievable." He shook his head. "I knew that you were a workaholic but this is ridiculous. What do I need to do? You want me to hog-tie you and stuff you in your room upstairs to make you take a break? Is that it?"

"What?"

"Because I'll do it." He tossed up his hands. "Hell, why not?"

She stepped back from him. "You wouldn't dare!"

He leveled a stern look at her that made it impossible for her to discern whether he was joking or not. Hit with another wave of vertigo, Sofia wobbled around on her heels.

Ram quickly reached out and steadied her. "Are you all right?"

"Yeah," Sofia lied and then tried to push her way out of his arms, but the steel grip he encased her in refused to budge.

"Someone bring us some water," Ram snapped to no one in particular.

Everyone scrambled. The next thing Sofia knew she had her pick of at least fifteen water bottles. "Uh, thanks," she murmured, accepting one.

"Drink," he ordered.

For once, she did what he said. The moment the cold water slid down her throat she sighed out loud, but it was questionable whether it did anything to cool her down or cure her vertigo. In fact, she started to suspect being locked in Ram's arms and feeling the hard ridges of his chest up close and personal were only making things worse.

"How do you feel?"

Ram's intense gaze bored into hers to the point that she was having a difficult time getting her breathing under control. "Fine," she lied again, and attempted to push away again.

Ram loosened his grip, but he didn't let her go. "That settles it. I'll take care of the party. You go upstairs and lie down."

"Ramell—"

"That wasn't a request. I'm telling you." The look he gave her dared her to argue back. "I got this. Get upstairs. Take a nap. I'll be up there in a little while and I'll check on you."

"I'm not a child."

"Then stop behaving like one," he snapped back.

She wanted to argue back, but what was the point? Ramell was proving that he was willing to lock horns and go toe-to-toe with her. But feeling that they were the center of attention, Sofia knew that it was time to back down. "All right. Fine. I'll go take a nap or something."

"No 'or something.' A nap." He finally released her, but she remained pressed against him for a few extra seconds as if her body wasn't really ready to leave.

With a weak smile she stepped back. "I guess I'll just catch up with you later." She reached to retrieve her phone, but Ramell held it back.

"No. I think I'll just hold on to this."

"What?"

"The last time I checked, you don't need a phone in order to take a nap."

She crossed her arms. "It's not like there isn't a phone in the suite."

"Maybe not, but without an address book, I'm thinking that you'll be limited on who you can call."

She opened her mouth to argue again, but stopped when she watched him huff and start to roll his eyes. "Fine."

"Good. I'll check on you later." He tossed her a wink and then strolled off.

Frowning, Sofia watched him go, her mind undressing him once again. "Snap out of it," she hissed, and then rushed out of the conference room. Once she was away from Ramell her head started to clear.

"Ms. Wellesley," Stewart shouted and raced down the hallway toward her. "I talked to the hotel management and they said that they will send someone to check on the air conditioner." A big, eager smile bloomed across his face. "Is there anything else I can do for you?"

"I, um… Actually, just go ahead and take the afternoon off. Mr. Jordan will be taking over the preparations this evening so that actually gives us some time off."

Stewart's bushy eyebrows jumped up. "*You're* going to take some time off?" he asked, practically laughing.

"What?"

"Look. I know I haven't been on the job long, but I was told that you didn't believe in taking time off."

She frowned, feeling insulted. "Who told you that?"

He shrugged as if it was no big deal. "Everyone at Limelight…and everyone at the temp agency…and I think I might have read it in the trade papers, too."

"Come on, I'm not that bad." Sofia laughed, but Stewart just gave her a timid smile. "Am I?"

"I don't think that I've been around long enough to say," Stewart answered tactfully.

"Well played. I get the point." She marched off with

her feelings still bruised. "Everyone acts like I don't know how to relax," she mumbled. "I know how to relax." Her gaze darted around the beautiful hotel. It was filled with people laughing and smiling—just generally having a good time.

"I know how to have a good time." She shimmied her shoulders a bit to try and relax them, but then started to feel silly. At the elevator bay, she hit the up button and waited. A second later, a laughing couple waltzed up next to her to wait, as well. But Sofia started to feel uncomfortable when they started kissing. She turned her back toward them and shook her head. She never really cared for people who got carried away with public displays of affection.

The elevator bell dinged and Sofia hopped into the compartment and pushed the button for the twentieth floor several times. The couple was so into trying to swallow each other's tongues that she breathed a sigh of relief when the doors started to close.

"Wait! Hold the door!" someone shouted.

The couple's lips unsuctioned and the guy jammed a hand between the doors before they could close all the way.

Damn.

"Thanks," Ramell said, appearing out of nowhere and springing into the elevator.

"Not a problem, man." Mr. Don Juan cheesed and then escorted his girl inside the compartment, as well.

Ram's eyes drifted over to Sofia. "Good. You're actually on your way up to the room."

"Why you coming to check on me so soon?" Sofia asked as the elevator doors closed.

"Now why would I do that?" He mustered a faux innocent look and blinked his eyes at her.

Sofia didn't have a chance to answer because Mr. Don Juan suddenly hiked up his lady's leg with one hand and hit the floor panel with his other hand. Eight floors worth of lights lit up. "Oh, my God," she moaned in sync with the woman that was busy getting felt up.

Ram glanced over at the couple and chuckled.

"It's not funny," Sofia hissed, annoyed.

"Oooh." The woman moaned as her lover now concentrated on grabbing her ass and unbuttoning her blouse with his mouth.

"You're right. It's not funny," Ramell whispered.

"Thank you," Sofia said, satisfied.

"It's actually kind of hot," he said.

"What?"

Just then the woman's bra spilled out of her top and the man's mouth lowered so that he could run his tongue along the lacy edges.

Sofia gasped while Ram cocked his head to try and get a better look. "Will you behave?" She shoved him by the shoulder.

"What?" Ram laughed.

The elevator doors opened on the third floor and Sofia ran out like the damn thing was on fire. "I can't believe this!"

Ram followed her. "What's with you?"

"Hey, you two don't want to watch?" Mr. Don Juan asked as the doors started to close again.

Ram looked at Sofia as if the answer depended on her. *"No!"*

"Suit yourself," the man said, and then returned to trying to peel his girl out of her clothes.

After the doors closed, Ram turned and looked at her. "Well, that would have been interesting."

"You're joking. Please say that you're joking." She hit the button for another elevator.

He shrugged his shoulders. "It's Vegas," he said. "People do things that they don't normally do. You know that."

She shook her head. "Men!"

"What? What did I do?" Ram couldn't stop chuckling. "Those two could be married for all we know."

"No rings."

"You did a ring check?"

"That's better than what you were checking out. A couple of more seconds and you would've been nipple bobbing, too."

"Now I'm offended," he said, placing a hand against his chest.

"Sure you are."

"I am. Anyone who knows me knows that I'm more of a leg man." He deliberately let his gaze drop to her long legs. "And if you ask me, you have the best pair I've ever seen."

Sofia blushed, but was spared from having to make a comment when another elevator arrived.

Ram followed her. "So you're really upset about that?"

"It was…inappropriate."

"And I take it that you've never done anything inappropriate?"

"Well…not like that." She frowned, not even able to imagine herself ever losing so much control that she would behave like a twenty-dollar trick. "I have a little more self-respect than that."

"Then like what?" Ram asked.

"What do you mean?"

"Tell me about a time when you've done something inappropriate."

Sofia drew in a deep breath and did a quick search of her memory banks.

"Nothing?"

"Wait a minute. Let me think," she said. They arrived on their floor and she waltzed out the elevator. She was still thinking when she slid her key into the door of their suite and hadn't come up with anything.

"How about something spontaneous?" Ram chuckled. When that only deepened her frown, he decided to let her off the hook. "Never mind. I don't want your brain to start short-circuiting."

"So maybe I haven't done anything that's technically inappropriate or spontaneous. Big deal. It doesn't mean that I'm a prude or anything."

"All right. If you say so."

"It doesn't," she insisted.

He shrugged his shoulders and started to walk off.

Suddenly hit with a burst of inspiration, Sofia grabbed Ram by his hand and pulled him back. When he turned laughing, she cupped both sides of his face and laid a kiss on him that was so powerful he couldn't help but let out a grunt of pleasure. He raked one hand through her thick hair and settled the other against the small of her back. Ram couldn't believe how sweet she tasted or how soft her small curves were. Was this a dream?

Sofia pulled her lips back all too soon but he chased after them for another intoxicating dose. It only lasted for a few extra seconds before she pushed back.

"There," she whispered, while gulping in air. "Is that spontaneous enough for you?"

Before he could answer, she stepped past him on wobbly knees and quickly rushed toward her room before she spontaneously ripped her clothes off.

Behind her, Ram watched her go with a widening smile. Things were finally moving in the right direction.

Chapter 7

Sofia couldn't sleep, not for a nap or even later on that night. All she could think about was that damn kiss. It had to have been some trick of her mind to make her think that the man tasted like chocolate and honey. And even while she lay tossing in her bed, she kept running her tongue across her mouth for any residue he might have left. That kiss disturbed her peace of mind and she wondered if she could ever view him the same way again.

It also seemed like the more she told herself not to think about it, her brain just kept looping the memory of her cupping his face and then moving in on those incredible soft lips. Those few little stolen kisses they used to share under the big oak tree at her parents' old estate was nothing to compare to what Ramell delivered in the living room of that suite. If she kept it up, she was going to drive herself crazy.

She had kissed him to prove that she could be spontaneous and step out of her comfort zone. Now she feared that she'd just opened Pandora's Box. Even knowing that, she wanted to kiss him again. There was a part of her that wanted to prove that what she felt was a fluke—a trick of the mind. Another part of her wanted to kiss him because she hoped like hell it hadn't been a fluke but something greater, something more.

The second the sun rose the next morning, Sofia showered, dressed and zoomed out of the suite so fast it was amazing she hadn't left skid marks. All she knew was that she needed to get as far away from Ramell as she possibly could. Her first pit stop of the morning was to get breakfast inside the hotel's restaurant, Verandah. The minute she entered the Mediterranean-style restaurant and the smiling hostess led her to an available table out on the terrace, her racing heartbeat settled a bit.

"Sofia!"

She glanced around and then spotted Charlene Quinn waving a few tables over. "Hey!" She popped out of her chair and went over to say hi to her newest client. When she reached her, Sofia leaned over and gave the glowing singer a hug. "How are you, sweetheart?"

"Great. How are you? I tried to call you when we arrived but my calls kept going to voicemail."

Sofia lightly tapped her hand against her head. Ramell still had her cell phone. "I'm so sorry about that. Did you need anything?"

"Aww. Look who we have here," Akil Hutton approached the table. "How you doing, baby girl?"

Sofia laughed as she now exchanged hugs with the super producer. "You know me. I'm still out here swimming with the sharks."

"I hear that," he said, taking his seat and then leaning over to plant a kiss on Charlene's glossy lips.

They look good together. "I know I said it before, but I want you two to know that I'm really happy for the both of you."

"Thanks," Charlene cooed, her right hand entwined with Akil's.

They were so adorable together that Sofia couldn't stop smiling at them. "So. Are you all set to perform this afternoon at our pre-awards gala?"

Akil bobbed his head. "Yeah, we set everything up with your man, Ramell."

Sofia laughed, but it sounded a little off-key even to her ears. "Ramell Jordan is *not* my man." She tried laughing again but it was still sounding like a misfired weapon.

Akil frowned. "Nah, I meant it as a figure of speech. He's your business partner, right?"

"Oh, yeah. Right." *Open mouth, insert foot.* "I knew that. My man."

Akil shared a look with Charlene and then smiled back up at Sofia. "Anyway, like I was saying, we set everything up with Ramell. We're going to do a sound check around two and then we'll be ready to go on at five."

"Sounds good." Sofia gave them both a thumbs-up. "I guess I'll just see you at the party."

They said their goodbyes and Sofia rushed back over to her table and ordered herself a stack of buttermilk pancakes. Given the fact that she generally burned the candle at both ends most days, her lifestyle afforded her the luxury of being able to eat whatever she liked. So she ordered a large stack of buttermilk pancakes and link sausages. She was practically salivating when they arrived at her table. After thanking the waitress, she figured she had about fifteen minutes before she needed to meet up with Stewart and get her day going.

When the list of things that she needed to get done before the pre-awards gala started scrolling through her mind, Sofia crammed food into her mouth as fast as she possibly could.

"Mind if I join you?"

Sofia glanced up with a sausage poking out of her mouth.

Ramell smiled. "You know, you could've woken me up. Breakfast is the most important meal of the day."

Cheeks crammed with pancakes, Sofia gave him a half apology but then felt a wave of panic when he took a seat.

"Now that's an interesting look," he chuckled. "The chipmunk cheeks look good on you."

The waitress returned and set his breakfast of French toast and scrambled eggs down in front of him.

"So how did you sleep last night?"

Sofia's eyes narrowed. She had a sneaky suspicion that he knew damn well that she hadn't slept a wink. When he continued to wait for an answer, she lied. "I slept like a log." She smiled animatedly.

His eyes twinkled. "Glad to hear it."

You're playing with fire. Sofia tried to swallow her food but suddenly realized that she needed help.

"Here. Have some of my orange juice." He pushed his glass toward her.

"Thanks," she murmured around the breakfast that was clogging her throat. She quickly gulped down half the glass and then panted when she finally managed to clear her pipes.

"Better?" His neatly groomed brow stretched over his forehead.

She nodded and dabbed the corners of her mouth with her napkin.

"Are you in some kind of hurry or do you usually eat like a starved animal?"

"Ha. Ha. Very funny."

"Well, it was either those two options or…you're try-ing to avoid me so that we don't have to talk about that kiss we shared yesterday."

Sofia shoveled in another hearty helping of pancake into her mouth so that she wouldn't have to respond.

Ram laughed so hard his head nearly rocked off his shoulders. A few curious gazes drifted toward their table and Sofia suddenly wished that she could shrink down to about two inches.

"Do I really make you *that* nervous?"

"Don't be ridiculous," she barked and then started to choke.

Tears practically brimmed his eyes as he watched her weak performance.

"Actually, I don't have much time to eat. There's a lot I have to do before the party and the award show."

He sobered up a bit. "Anything I can help you with?"

"No. I have everything under control. Or maybe I should ask whether you need any help with the party. I know things can—"

"Nope. Everything is fine and going according to schedule."

She frowned. "Nothing ever goes according to sched-ule."

"They do if I'm handling it," he said confidently.

"Right." She tossed down the rest of his juice and then scrambled up from the table. "I'll catch up with you later."

"Looking forward to it."

For the next few hours Sofia remained busy, with Stewart getting some of her clients to press junkets, and answering emails on her iPad. Most of her workload was difficult without her phone, but she lacked the courage to ask Ramell for it back. She didn't have a stack of pancakes on hand to help her through another round of questions about that kiss.

Of course that kiss never stopped looping in her mind, either. It happened so much, in fact, that people were constantly snapping their fingers in front of her face and asking if she was all right. A little after noon, Stewart reminded her that her hair and makeup artist was scheduled to meet with her in the suite so she rushed up to go get ready for the afternoon festivities. Everything was running smooth until the Armani representative, Robyn, showed up.

"That's not the dress I ordered," Sofia said frowning. "I requested the white ball gown with the big butterfly bow in the back."

The petite rep blinked in surprise and then quickly scrambled for her paperwork. "I have here that you asked for the gold drape halter."

Sofia sucked in a breath. She could literally feel her blood pressure rising. "Where are my pills?" She rushed off toward the bathroom and downed one of the much-hated pills.

"Are you all right?" Robyn asked nervously when Sofia returned to the room.

"I will be," she said, pulling in a few measured breaths.

"I'm not sure what to tell you," the rep said. "I spoke to Stewart myself and—"

"Stewart? All he was supposed to do was arrange the delivery date—not select my dress. *I* had selected my dress." *Breathe. Breathe.* "You know what? Never mind. What do we have to do to fix this? How fast can we get the other dress here?"

Robyn blinked and then glanced at her watch. "I'm sorry, but I'm afraid that just can't possibly happen. Your gala is in less than an hour."

Breathe. Breathe. That was hard since at that moment all she wanted to do was find Stewart, wrap her hands around his thick neck and squeeze.

"Don't you want to just try it on?" Robyn asked.

"It doesn't look like I have a choice now." Stripping out of the hotel's robe, she quickly stepped into the gold dress and glanced into the full-length mirror while Robyn zipped her up. Her anger immediately dissipated.

"I think it looks beautiful on you," Robyn complimented.

Sofia turned and assessed herself from different angles. She actually liked it better than the dress that she had picked out originally. "Looks like Stewart actually got one right." She shook her head. "Amazing." The dress was short, hitting her around mid-thigh, and the shimmering gold color reflected beautifully off her mocha skin. And it felt fun and flirty when she did practice turns.

After filling out the paperwork for the dress, Sofia rushed to put on her accessories while the woman took her leave. When Sofia exited from her bedroom, Ramell was in the living room sliding into his tuxedo jacket. They stopped and stared at one another. At that moment, Sofia was convinced that Ramell Jordan looked good in everything.

"Wow. Don't you look amazing," he said.

She blushed—that was something she had been doing a lot of lately. "Thank you. You don't look so bad yourself." Approaching him with slow, measured steps, Sofia noticed that Ram's tie was slightly off-center. "Here. Let me help you with that."

Ram smiled when her slim fingers quickly went to work with his tie. Being this close he was able to get a good whiff of her perfume. On her first go around, she actually made the tie worse off than it was before so she had to try again. While she concentrated on the tie, he kept drinking in her beautiful profile while fighting the urge not to kiss her again. The more he kept trying not to, the more he wanted to do it.

After a minute, he started to give in to gravity and lean forward. She would probably stop him, slap him or give into the kinetic energy he knew that she had to feel flowing between them. When he was within an inch of her lips, her fingers stopped fiddling with his tie.

"What are you doing?" she whispered.

"Something spontaneous." His lips gently landed against hers and stirred up old feelings deep within him. She moaned first and then he pulled her closer. Thrilled and surprised that she was allowing herself to go with the moment, Ram experienced a renewal of hope of what was possible between them.

Their lips only pulled apart because of the necessity for oxygen. And even then he pressed his forehead against hers so that their breaths could commingle.

"What are we doing?" she asked, panting.

"Something that we should've done a long time ago." He reached up and brushed the side of her face.

"But I...I—"

"Shh." He kissed the tip of her nose. "Don't worry. I'm not trying to rush you or anything. Understand?"

She slowly nodded.

"Take your time. I'm not going anywhere." His hand moved subtly from her cheek down to beneath her chin where he tilted her face upward gently. "But know this, I do want you. I always have…and I always will."

He watched her large brown eyes widen and she pulled back just a bit, but didn't run off screeching toward the bedroom. At least that was a good sign. He gave her a wink and then offered her his arm. "Shall we go?"

Sofia hesitated for a second, drew a deep breath and then finally looped her arm through his. "I guess I'm as ready as I'll ever be."

He cocked his head, hoping her answer held a double meaning. When they arrived downstairs for Limelight's Official Pre-Award Gala, they were both thrilled to see that everything had come together perfectly. The event's color scheme was black and gold; it was a nice blend of fun and sophistication. Only after arriving did Sofia realize that they were the same colors that she and Ramell were wearing.

As their guests entered the room, Stewart and a few interns working with the party planner directed people over to the table where hundreds of goodie bags were lined up.

Over the speakers played the music of all the Latin Grammy nominations for the evening. The infectious rhythms instantly had Sofia rocking her hips in time to the beat.

Ram turned toward her and started dancing with her. "Looks like you have some good moves. Should we take this to the dance floor?"

She laughed. "I don't think so. This is as good as these moves get right here. A dancer I am not."

His gaze raked over her. "I beg to differ."

Sofia couldn't quite get used to this constant flirting that they were now engaged in. "Well, maybe I'll just give you a rain check."

"All right. But I will cash that sucker in before the end of the night." He winked. A tray of champagne floated by and Ram quickly chased it down and then offered her a flute. "Let's make a toast."

"That sounds like a good idea." She accepted the glass. "What shall we drink to?"

"To us," he said, simply.

Her brows rose.

"…and our new business merger. May we enjoy years of success together."

She relaxed a bit and then tapped her glass to his. "To us."

Their eyes locked over the rim of their flutes while they each downed a sip of champagne. Just a few short moments later, they separated as they networked through the crowd. At exactly five o'clock, Akil Hutton took to the small stage and introduced his newest artist to the Playascape label.

The guests applauded as Charlene Quinn made her way over to the microphone. Feeling slightly giddy, Sofia couldn't wait until Charlene opened her mouth and shocked everyone with her powerful voice. When she did there was a collective gasp. Charlene wasn't the barely legal teenybopper that could only carry a note with the help of Auto-Tune, which was all the rage in music nowadays. Charlene was a beautiful and welcome throwback artist who could do things with her voice that could only inspire envy. Listening to the emotional song "The Journey," Sofia's gaze drifted across the room and had no problems finding Ram in the crowd.

Luckily there was another tray of champagne drifting by so she quickly snatched up a glass and drank its contents just as Charlene was hitting the song's climactic ending. The room erupted into thunderous applause. Charlene smiled humbly and thanked everyone before stepping off the stage.

The second glass of champagne must have gone straight to Sofia's head because suddenly she was feeling…good. She looked across the room again and locked eyes with Ramell.

Damn good, in fact.

Chapter 8

The Eleventh Annual Latin Grammy Awards was a unanimous hit. The evening was filled with spectacular music and dance. All of the performers were magnificent and the cheers from the crowd just made the evening feel like a four-hour-long concert. Akil Hutton won his first Latin Grammy and gave an emotional shout-out to the new woman in his life, Charlene Quinn, and then of course reminded everyone to look for her debut CD coming out in the spring.

After the show ended, everyone started drifting out of the venue to head for some of the many sponsored after-parties. Sofia and Ramell made their way over to the Eye Candy Sound Lounge. Sofia loved its high-tech touch tables that allowed people to project images over the dance floor. Ram wrapped an arm around her waist and shouted over the music.

"I think I'll take that dance now!"

"You got it." Sofia quickly tossed back her chocolate martini and then slipped her hand into his. With the multicolor-lighted disco floor and the strange electronic images floating overhead, Sofia was experiencing a sensory overload—and she loved it. She threw her hands up in the air and rocked her body to the beat like she didn't have a care in the world.

Never being more than a few inches away, Ram matched each erotic thrust of her hips with one of his own. In no time at all it was just them and the music. Sofia was saying things with her body that she never dared to say aloud. If he touched her hip, she'd touch his. A few times, she'd turned around to roll her butt up the front of his crotch, swivel her hips and then spin away.

Ram was so turned on that he couldn't think straight. He had never seen this side of Sofia before. She was sexy, wild and making him horny as hell. After about an hour on the dance floor, they returned to their table and ordered a few more drinks.

Sofia ordered another chocolate martini and when Santana's "Smooth" blasted through the speakers, she climbed on top of the table along with a few other girls and shook her moneymaker for all it was worth.

Ram bobbed his head along with the music and mouthed the chorus when his eyes met with Sofia's. *Give me your heart, make it real. Or else forget about it.* The seductive smile she shared gave him such a strong hard-on, it was a wonder that he didn't just sweep her off the table, toss her over his shoulder and take her back to their suite. But he made sure that she could read that thought in his mind.

Eventually, she did hop down and Ram was right there to catch and spin her around. There was a skip in his memory because the next thing he knew they were actually at a roulette table, a game Sofia claimed she had never played before, but was suddenly begging to play. Thrilled to see her smiling and having a good time,

Ram removed a few Benjamins from his money clip and handed them over.

The croupier exchanged the money for chips with the pit boss watching and then asked everyone to place their bets. Sofia took all of her chips and placed them on five.

"Are you sure?" Ram asked.

"No. But that's why they call it gambling," she reminded him, and then planted a loud, smacking kiss on his lips.

"Then let's let it ride."

"No more bets," the croupier called and then proceeded to spin the wheel.

Sofia locked her arms around Ram's neck and proceeded to watch intently as the white ball was dropped into the spinning roulette. "Are you having a good time, Mr. Jordan?"

"Actually, I'm having a wonderful time," he answered, sliding his hands up and down her back.

"Five! The lucky number is five!" the croupier called out.

Just as Sofia was about to plant a kiss onto Ram's lips, she realized the number that had just been called.

"Five! That's me! That's me!" She started bouncing up and down. The entire table erupted into cheers while Sofia performed a minidance and then smacked Ram hard on the rear end.

Caught off guard, he jumped and then laughed at her antics. They played for a few more rounds, the crowd cheering as Sofia's chips really started to mount. More drinks flowed and the next thing Ram knew they were at the craps table. Sofia developed her own dance and threw the dice down the stretch. Each time she would draw a seven and their entourage would grow even larger.

"You're hot tonight," Ram commented, shaking his head.

"Yeah? So what are you going to do about that, lover boy?" She playfully pulled on his tie so that she could draw his lips closer. When she laid another kiss on him, the table went wild with hoots and hollers.

"God, I have to bring you to Vegas more often," Ram panted when she finally released him.

Sofia just smiled. "Let's go find another dance floor."

"Your wish is my command." He handed over his V.I.P. card and told the pit boss to cash them out and that they'd pick up their winnings later before leading her and their entourage out of the casino and over to another after-party at Pure nightclub.

As the hour ticked later and later, both Ram and Sofia's dancing grew hotter and hotter. They drew many eyes and much finger pointing, but neither paid any attention to it. They were both yin and yang, grinding on the dance floor and just enjoying the night. Sofia couldn't remember the last time she had ever felt so free, so alive. Every time Ram's gaze roamed over her body she felt beautiful and sexy. If she had her wish, this night would never end.

Somewhere along the line, someone in their newfound entourage suggested going to a club called Jump! So they all piled into a stranger's limousine and ended up at another high-tech club. The surprise was that it was a strip club, but not just any strip club.

"Oh, hell, no," Ramell said and turned right back around toward the door.

"Wait. Wait." Sofia grabbed him by the arm and dragged him back. "C'mon. This could be fun."

Ramell groaned as he allowed her to turn him back around. His frown deepened at the sight of the muscled and oiled men all pumped up and gyrating on the stage. "I don't want to watch this."

Sofia ignored his complaints and pulled him along. He wasn't the only one. A lot of the guys that had played tagalong were also trying to make their way back toward the door. However, the women were going buck wild, including Sofia, who continued to drag Ramell closer toward the stage.

He hung his head and hoped that this was just going to be a pit stop. When the dancer finally left the stage with his teeny-weeny briefs filled with dollar bills, he expelled a sigh of relief.

"You should go up there," Sofia yelled above the crowd.

"Say what?" He tried to pull back.

"C'mon." She smiled. "You can do it." She kept pulling him toward the stage despite his horror.

When the women saw what she was doing they all started cheering.

"What's this now?" the DJ blasted over the club. "Is it amateur night on the stage?"

The women screamed louder while Sofia shoved Ramell harder.

"C'mon. You know you got the body," she teased.

"I'm not getting up on that stage."

The DJ spoke out again over the loudspeaker. "Let me give you a little something to dance to, my man." He began to spin a popular new song and the women in the club damn near went into hysteria.

"Fine. If I have to get up here then so do you," Ramell said as he grabbed Sofia by the wrist and pulled her onto the stage alongside him.

Suddenly, the lights dimmed and a spotlight was directly aimed at the couple. Sofia stood in the center of the stage, giggling until she felt a feathery touch drifting down her arm. She shivered but then she was quickly spun around to see Ram rip the buttons off his shirt with one-hard jerk and then do a sexy body wave that had the women screaming so loud it made her eardrums ring.

Ram sent his shirt sailing into the air and rocked his hips as he pulled up his white T-shirt to reveal his perfectly bronze chest with his tight, mountainous muscles.

Without thinking, Sofia reached out and smiled at his dewy texture. Smiling, Ram spun her around and pressed her back against his chest while his large hands dropped to her thighs and then slowly inched their way upward. The heat that blazed up Sofia's body was so intense that beads of sweat dotted her hairline and rolled down the side of her face.

The women that were screaming around the stage no longer mattered. Sofia was losing her mind because she alone could feel Ram's hard-on grinding against her round bottom. It was suddenly hard for her to breathe. His hands inched higher and when he was just a flick away from exposing her Victoria's Secrets, he whipped away from her again to perform a few more body waves and hip rotations.

Money rained down onto the stage despite the fact that Ram never took his eyes off of Sofia. He crooked his finger and beckoned her toward him. When she stood inches from him, he unsnapped the top button of his slacks and offered her, and her alone, a peek inside. Curiosity may have killed the cat, but Sofia wasn't about to pass up a golden opportunity. So she peeked and her jaw nearly hit the floor at his impressive size.

The women went wild. They all wanted to see what she saw. But with her face heating up, she finally slapped a hand in front of his pants and prevented him from peeling those bad boys off. Suddenly, she wasn't in the mood for sharing. "Don't you dare."

"Problem?" he asked, wickedly.

She grabbed hold of his wrist and tugged him off the stage.

"Boo!" The jilted women shouted, but a giggling Sofia and Ram paid them no mind as they tried to make their way to the door. They were still laughing when they piled into a cab and headed back to Mandalay Bay.

"You know I look ridiculous, right?"

She glanced at him without his shirt and T-shirt and decided, "Actually, I think I prefer you like this."

"Really?" He dragged her over to his side of the cab and pressed her against his chest.

"We can always arrange it so that I could see you like this more often," she said, walking her fingers up his chest.

Ram's brows jumped. "I'm listening."

Smiling up at him with her hand pressed over his heart she asked, "Ramell Jordan, will you marry me?"

Chapter 9

At three-thirty in the morning, Sofia and Ramell stumbled into the Viva Las Vegas Wedding Chapel, giggling and clinging on to one another. Behind them, Akil and Charlene entered, shaking their heads. They were still dressed in their gown and tuxedo, only Akil had draped his jacket around Charlene's exposed shoulders as they came in from the night. It was clear that they didn't know what to make of this latest development. They were surprised when Ram called them as they were leaving yet another after-party. Both of them looked exhausted and might've been headed for bed had Ram not called and asked if they wanted to serve as witnesses to his wedding.

"Are you two sure that you want to do this?" Akil asked.

Charlene nodded. "Yeah. This seems kind of sudden. Maybe you guys should just…sleep on this?"

Sofia laughed and wrapped her arms around Ram's waist. "Don't be silly. Ram and I have been planning to get married for…" She looked up at him. "How long?"

He smiled. "A gazillion years."

They erupted into giggles while Charlene and Akil just looked at each other and shrugged.

A black Elvis Presley impersonator emerged from a curtain of multi-colored beads with a grin as wide as Texas. "Evening, folks. What can I do for you on this early morning?"

Sofia and Ramell took one look at the man in his be-dazzled jumpsuit and had another fit of giggles. This time, even Akil and Charlene joined in.

"Are we looking to have a double wedding this morning?" he asked eagerly.

"No. It's just us," Sofia answered excitedly.

"First, do you happen to have a shirt I can buy or rent?" Ram asked.

"Sure. We can hook you right up," Elvis bragged and then disappeared into the back.

While he was gone, Sofia and Ramell peppered each other's faces with kisses. To casual observers they looked like young lovers who couldn't keep their hands off of each other. When Elvis returned he held up two suits. One was a pale blue suit complete with bell bottoms and satin lapels. To add insult to injury, the accompanying white shirt had enough ruffles to do Liberace proud. The other suit was a black and silver sequin number that was equally hard on the eyes.

"Just a basic white shirt will do," Ram said, snickering. "I may be drunk but I'm not *that* drunk."

Elvis shrugged his shoulders. "As you wish." He disappeared and returned with a brand new white dress shirt still in its package.

"Perfect."

"Great." Elvis clapped his hands together. "Now let's see about getting you two married."

For the next ten minutes Elvis showed the couples rings and different wedding packages. They settled on the Elvis Blue Hawaii Special, mainly because it came complete with two traditionally garbed hula dancers. Sofia and Ram giggled their way through the entire ceremony. Still they managed to get their I Do's out and were immediately showered with rice while Elvis busted out with his microphone and launched into a jacked-up rendition of Blue Hawaii. He didn't really bother trying to sound like the King of Rock 'n' Roll. If anything he sounded more like Isaac Hayes. But it didn't matter. Nothing really mattered at that moment.

They were married.

Amazingly, after they left the chapel they all stopped at another club so they could share a celebratory drink. There was more dancing involved and Sofia stopped nearly everyone she saw to show off the simple silver band and declare that she was indeed a married woman now.

Cheers went up and cameras came out. Sofia and Ram made several silly poses. At long last when the hour ticked closer to five o'clock, Sofia struggled to keep her eyes open.

Ram stretched up a brow. "I don't believe it. My little Energizer Bunny is actually wearing down?"

"Mmm-hmm." Sofia looped her arms around Ram's neck and nibbled on his lips. "I think it's time we get back to our honeymoon suite."

"Aww. Honeymoon suite, eh? I kind of like the sound of that." He kissed her and explored her mouth like it was the eighth wonder of the world. She moaned and melted against his body.

"Get a room," a member of their second entourage shouted, causing everyone to laugh around them. In dramatic form, Ramell swept Sofia up into his arms and received a round of applause.

Sofia smiled against his lips. "I'm so happy right now."

He met her gaze. "That's all I ever wanted you to be."

"Good to know." She snuggled closer. "But if you want to see me ecstatic then I suggest you get me to our room, lover boy."

"I'm on it." He turned toward the group. "Good night, everyone. Me and the missus have plans."

"Woo-hoo!" they all cheered.

"Say good-night, Sofia."

"Good night, Sofia," she chimed, giggling.

With that, Ram swooped out of the club and carried her all the way over to the hotel portion of the luxurious casino. In the elevator, Sofia insisted that she wanted to be the one to punch the number for their floor, only for her to do it with her left big toe. "Hey! What happened to my shoe?" Not until that moment did she even realize that she was just wearing one.

Ram frowned. "I have no idea."

"Oooh," she pouted. "But I loved that shoe."

"Don't worry," he said, nibbling on her lower earlobe. "I'll find it for you."

"You promise?"

"Yeah. I promise. Now kiss me."

"Gladly." She turned her head and captured his addictive lips in another soul-stirring kiss. Sofia loved kissing this man. She loved how her thoughts would get all woozy and how her body would heat up and tingle from the tips of her toes all the way to the ends of her hair.

Neither one of them heard the elevator again or even saw another couple step into the small compartment along with them. They were in their own world where only they existed. Ram lowered her legs, but kept her body pressed up against him and one wall of the elevator.

Sofia couldn't stop moaning as she felt her husband's hands roaming up her long legs and traveling up her inner thigh. When his seeking fingers skimmed along the edges of her lacy panties, she quivered. But when he shifted them over to the corner of her thigh and then dipped his fingers into the dewy lips to tease the tip of her sex, she nearly came unglued.

"You like that, baby?" he asked, abandoning her kiss-swollen lips in order to concentrate on her sexy scented neck.

"Uhm, hmm." Sofia's eyes fluttered open and she was finally able to see that the same couple they had shared an elevator ride with yesterday was now gawking at them. In normal circumstances she would have been embarrassed, but right now all she could do was giggle.

Ram lifted his head. "Oh. So this is funny to you now?"

She shook her head and then pointed over her shoulder.

He turned and then offered the couple a smile and a wink. "Morning," he said, lowering his hand from beneath Sofia's dress. A bell dinged and the door slid open to offer their escape route. "Have a good day." He took Sofia's hand and together they raced out of the elevator.

Sofia clamped her other hand over her mouth and started laughing so hard her sides hurt. It didn't help that she was hobbling with one shoe on and one shoe off. "Did you see their faces?"

"Forget about them." He waved it off and slid his key card into the lock and then surprised her by sweeping her back into his arms.

"I believe that this is tradition," he said, and then picked her up to carry her over the threshold.

"Weeee!" She waved her hands high over her head as Ram then proceeded to spin her around. Suddenly everything was funny so they just looked at each other and cracked up. Soon enough their laughter faded and their smiling eyes shifted into desire.

"Well, Mrs. Jordan, what would you like to do now?"

Those wonderful tingles returned. "I don't know. I was sort of hoping that we can do what most newlyweds do on their wedding nights."

He stretched one eyebrow high up on his face. "See. That's the reason we're so perfect for each other. We think alike." He kissed her again. "My bedroom or yours?"

"You choose." She started pulling on his shirt, popping off one button at a time.

"Let's start off in your bedroom. Maybe we'll go to mine on round two."

"And for round three?"

"Damn. We might have to stop for a bowl of Wheaties and a vitamin B shot."

"You do what you have to do, baby." She drew his lips in for another kiss while he walked her toward her bedroom. Unfortunately, since he was distracted by her hungry kisses, he whacked her head against the wall as he moved down the hallway.

"Oww."

"Oh. I'm so sorry." He chuckled. "Are you okay?"

Laughing herself, she rubbed the top of her head only to have him do it again when he made a turn into her bedroom and she hit the door frame.

Thump!

"Ouch. Are you trying to kill me?" she laughed.

"When you're with me, I want you to see stars, baby," he joked, and then finally set her down.

"One way or another." She laughed. Like before, their laughter slowly faded and the chemistry that had always existed between them started to crackle. Suddenly she felt small standing in front of him. But not vulnerable. The idea of being devoured by a man of his size and strength actually triggered an anxiousness that had her entire body vibrating. One part of her wanted to say *don't hurt me,* while the other wanted to shout *take me however you want me.*

"Turn around," he ordered.

With a smile, Sofia did.

Gently, he swept her long hair over her left shoulder in order to expose the back of her neck. Lightly, he planted small kisses along her shoulders while he slowly unzipped her dress. When he peeled the thin straps from her shoulders, her breathing thinned and she became lightheaded once again.

"Do you know how long I've waited for this night?" He moved toward her collarbone. "How long I've dreamed about making love to you?"

She shook her head though the question intrigued her.

"A gazillion years," he said, spinning her around as her dress fell to the floor. Before she could respond, he crushed their lips together. In his head it was as if the heavens had opened their golden gates. He made quick work of unhooking her strapless bra. When it fell to the floor and her full breasts stood at attention before his greedy eyes, he knew without a doubt that he could die a happy man tonight.

"You're so beautiful." He cupped her breasts with his

large hands and then smiled when he felt her tremble. "So beautiful," he repeated, rubbing the pads of his fingers against her nipples. In no time at all they were as hard as marbles and she was panting like she was in the middle of a marathon.

"Do you mind if I taste you?"

"Please," she begged.

Ram's head dipped low and then he sucked one hard nipple into his mouth, lightly scraping the sensitive flesh against his teeth. She hissed and then quivered, letting him know that he had set off a mini-orgasm. He did it again and received the same results. Her trembling hands cupped his head, her fingers raked through his close-cropped hair. He eased her down onto the bed, their hands and mouths exploring one another.

Sofia no longer cared that she could hardly breathe. She just knew that she needed Ram inside her as fast as possible. However, he wasn't on that same game plan. His slow and deliberate moves made it clear that he was in no hurry. He wanted to taste and savor her for as long as possible. Her heart raced like a thoroughbred in the Kentucky Derby. It all seemed like so much but not enough at the same time.

While Ram feasted on her breasts, she lowered her hands from his head and glided them down his neck and then across the wide span of his back. But that was as far as she could go since he started to inch down her body, his mouth planting wet kisses directly down her center. The pleasure was so intense that tears started to leak from the corners of her eyes.

Ram discovered her sensitive spots were her right nipple, her belly button and the tiny area on the back of her left knee. To him she looked like a lost angel, quivering and thrashing among the bed's pillows. He took one leg and slipped off her lone metallic shoe before peppering kisses around her ankle and then working his way upward. Her moans grew louder when he reached her thighs. By the time his lips brushed against the crotch of her panties, she was calling on God. But what he longed to hear was his name falling from her lips.

His hand roamed to her slender hips and then peeled her delicate panties off. With the morning sun now peeking through the windows, he liked the way the golden rays highlighted the V of brown curls between her legs. It was like her own private halo.

"So beautiful," he whispered again while parting her legs. Her glistening pink bud peeked through her brown lips. Ram sucked in a breath as he reached down and spread her open for a better look.

With a groan, he dropped his head and lapped his tongue gently against her feminine pearl. Instantly her knees rose up while she sank deeper into the bed.

"Oh, Ram," she sighed.

His heart took flight at the sound of his name falling from her lips. Ram's light laps became a quick and steady drumming. The sweetest honey he'd ever tasted dripped and then poured out of her body until it completely coated his tongue. And still it was not enough.

He settled further down the bed until his abs lay flat against the mattress and her legs were hooked over his shoulders. He looked like he was just settling in for a good meal.

However, Sofia's long legs wouldn't stay still. They kept fluttering on the side of his head like a big butterfly. Then an unmistakable pressure started to build in her lower belly and her manicured toes started to curl. Her eyes sprang wide open as if suddenly realizing that it was all too much. No way could she handle what was coming.

"Ram. Ram, baby." She started inching up the bed.

He knew what was happening, but he showed no remorse. Grabbing hold of her hips, he locked her in place and then transformed his drumming tongue into a whirling tornado.

"Ohh, ohh, yes." Sofia reached out and grabbed hold of the sheets as if somehow they would anchor her down.

"Oh, yes! Oh, yes!"

It went from a tornado to a hurricane in two seconds. The cry that ripped from her throat was undoubtedly heard in the suites surrounding them, but neither one of them cared. After the explosion, Sofia's body continued to tremble with aftershocks.

Ram sapped up the rest of her honey and unlocked her legs that had clamped around his head and then climbed his way back up her body.

"Oh, God. I've never felt anything like that before," she panted.

The compliment inflated his ego. "I've just gotten started," he promised.

"No," she said, shaking her head. When he frowned, she added, "I want to do something for you first." She shoved at his shoulder and rolled him over onto his back. Smiling and giggling, she took the top position.

Ram stared up into her beautiful face and still had a hard time believing that any of this was real. Twenty-fours hours ago, he'd just barely gotten her to agree to a truce and now she was his wife and in a few minutes she would completely belong to him.

"You're not the only one who knows a few tricks," she told him.

"Is that right?" He couldn't help but grin.

"Uh-huh." She leaned down and started raining small kisses across his chest. "Oh, God. You smell incredible," she moaned.

"I'm glad that you approve." He chuckled.

Sofia's mouth roamed lower. "Mmm-hmm. You taste good, too."

Slowly, she sank lower.

Ram started evening out his breathing in anticipation of his new wife's next move. But then the kisses grew lighter and softer and then he couldn't feel them at all. He waited a moment and then opened his eyes. "Sofia?"

Silence.

He pushed himself up onto his elbows and looked down. Sofia's head lay across his stomach, her arms relaxed against his side and her breathing slow and steady. *Is she asleep?*

"Sofia?" He reached down and shook her.

"Mmm," Sofia moaned and poked her lips like she was giving him an air kiss. In the next second, she snored. Loudly.

Ram dropped his head back down against the pillows and started laughing. "I guess my little Energizer Bunny has finally conked out."

Covering his face with his hands, Ramell went ahead and had a good laugh. When that was over, he carefully sat back up and awkwardly maneuvered himself up from under his wife. After that, he climbed out of bed and picked her up so he could tuck her in. But before he could join her, he took a very cold shower in her bathroom. It was a sad substitute. When he got out and wrapped a towel around his body, he could already tell that he was cruising toward one hell of a hangover. But damn, he had fun.

Just as he was about to exit the bathroom, his gaze drifted over to a medicine bottle. He picked it up and recognized the name of the blood-pressure medicine because his father used the same brand name. *Did Sofia take this before drinking last night?* He glanced back out into the bedroom, wondering.

Chapter 10

Riiiinnng! Riiinnng!

Sofia groaned and tried to bury her head deep beneath the pillows. Somehow that only caused the ringing to grow louder. It didn't help that her head felt like it had been crushed beneath an avalanche of rocks. She groaned louder and shot her hand out to the nightstand and consequently knocked a whole lot of things onto the floor. A cacophony of noise caused her to flinch and smack her hands onto the pillows in another lame attempt to drown out all sound. But that didn't stop the ringing.

Riiiinnng! Riiinnng!

This was it. She was going to die. That had to be what was happening to her. Something shifted next to her. She didn't even care what it was as long as it could stop that damn ringing before her ears started to bleed. Something started to climb over her. It was large and heavy and managed to press her deeper into the bed. Great. Now she had the choice of either the noise killing her or being crushed to death. Whichever it was she prayed that it would be quick.

"Hello?"

Sofia frowned at the growling baritone. It was foreign

and familiar at the same time. But it didn't concern her enough to try and lift her head from beneath the pillow.

"What do you mean who is this?" the baritone asked. "Who are you?"

Couldn't this floating voice keep it down? Couldn't he see that she was too busy trying to die peacefully over here?

"Oh, hey, Rachel."

Rachel? Didn't she know a Rachel?

"You must be looking for your sister," he groaned. "Hold on."

The weight was lifted off of Sofia and she pulled a little more oxygen into her lungs. Before she could seize the opportunity to drift back off to sleep, something started shaking her. Were they in the middle of an earthquake?

"Telephone," the baritone said.

Sofia groaned, wanting to tell the floating voice to keep quiet. Surely any minute the ceiling was about to cave in on them. That would be an interesting way to go. Finally the shaking stopped.

"Sofia, it's your sister," the voice persisted.

Sister? She tried to think for a second and then slowly she was able to recall something about her having a sister.

"Sofia." The bed started shaking again.

She was seconds away from just starting to cry. "Will you please stop yelling?"

There was a rumbling chuckle. "I'm sorry, baby. But your sister is on the phone."

Baby? Sofia attempted to lift her head, but it plopped back down when it felt as if it weighed a ton. Suddenly, the pillows were magically lifted and the cold phone was pressed to her ear.

"Talk," the voice instructed.

"Hello," she croaked and then cringed at the sound of her own voice. Was she speaking through a megaphone?

"Sofia! What's this about you getting married?" Rachel shouted. "It's all over the trade papers here. Everyone has been calling me all day. Charlene called and told me that she and Akil attended the wedding. What happened? What's going on?"

Rachel hurled questions at her so fast that Sofia questioned whether or not her sister was even speaking English. "I don't...I don't know what you're talking about."

"I'm talking about you getting married! I can't believe it. You beat me and Ethan down the aisle."

Did she just say that Ethan was beating her? Sofia attempted to sit up again. This time succeeding in that she was able to prop her back against the bed's paneled headboard, but there was still no way for her to pry her eyes open. "I'm sorry. Now what did you say Ethan did?"

"What? Ethan didn't do anything. I said that you and Ramell beat me and Ethan down the aisle. I can't believe it! I always suspected that he had a thing for you, but I never dreamed that you two would elope in Vegas."

Sofia's head was pounding so hard that her little sister's sentences weren't making any sense. But her heart quickened at the thought of Ramell eloping. *Her* Ramell? Well, he wasn't technically hers but... "Slow down, Rachel. You're not making any sense. Who did Ram marry?"

Silence.

"Rachel?"

"Are you joking?" her sister asked.

"Joking? You're the one that called me. I'm trying to understand what the hell you're talking about. Oh, God. Someone shoot me. My head is about to split open."

There was another beat of silence before Rachel tried again. "Sofia, are you all right?"

Silence.

"Sofia?"

"Um." Sofia rubbed her head and tried to recall the previous night, but instead she started drifting back off to sleep.

"Sofia!"

"Aah!" She jerked the phone away from her ear and dropped it. "Stop all that yelling," she groaned and then tried to rub the pain away. Next, she grabbed the comforter and slid back down into the bed. When she tried to pull the bedding over her head, she got hit in the face with the phone. "Oww." She placed the phone up to her ear. "Hello?"

"Sofia, what the heck is going on?"

"What do you mean what is going on? What are you doing calling this early in the morning, anyway?"

"Early? What are you talking about? It's five in the afternoon. I've been calling you all day."

"Five? It can't be that late. I have to be back in L.A. at—" she yawned "—some time."

"Sofia, focus!" Rachel snapped. "We are talking about you and Ramell getting married."

"Ramell is getting married?" Her heart quickened. "Whoa."

"What?"

"I think I just experienced déjà vu. It seems like we just had this conversation."

"We did just have this conversation," Rachel said. "Ramell *did* get married."

"To who?"

"To you!"

"Me!" Sofia laughed, slapping a hand over her forehead. "Don't be silly! Where would you get that ridiculous idea?"

"But…wasn't that him who just answered the phone?" Rachel asked.

"No…that was…" Sofia drew a blank. "That was…" The floating baritone resurfaced in her mind. *Who was that?* Her head swiveled to the left, over to the huge lump that was buried beneath the covers.

"Sofia?" Rachel inquired.

Sofia didn't answer, mainly because her heart had now found a new home in the center of her throat. With her head still pounding and her hand sweating, she reached out and grabbed the top of the comforter and slowly started to pull it off from whatever or whoever was lying beside her. When the bedding inched away and revealed Ram's peaceful sleeping face, she screamed, dropped the phone and scooted sideways so fast that she toppled out of bed and hit the floor with a thud.

Ram jumped up like a toasted Pop-Tart. "What? What's going on? What's happening?" His head swiveled around while his hands went into instant defense mode like he was about to karate chop the first thing he saw.

"What are you doing in my bed?" Sofia barked.

Ram's head jerked to his right, but when he saw the bed empty, he had to lean all the way over to the heap piled on the floor. "What are you doing down there?"

"I asked you first." Not until his gaze began to roam over her did he realize that she was naked. "Close your eyes!"

"What?"

"You heard me. I said close your eyes!" He started laughing at her. *"Now!"*

He tossed up his hand and closed his eyes. "All right. All right. They're closed. Are you happy?"

Sofia reached up and snatched the comforter from off the bed and covered herself. "I'm still waiting for an answer," she snapped. "What the hell are you doing in my bed?" It no longer mattered that her head felt like it had its own personal jackhammer drilling away or that in her fall she jerked the telephone cord out of the wall socket. She needed answers and she needed them now.

"Well?"

"I don't think that I understand the question," he said, leisurely lying down on his side. "I know that I'm a little hungover right now, but I definitely remember you inviting me into this bed."

"I most certainly did not!"

"You most certainly did. When I carried you into the suite, I asked you 'My bedroom or yours?' and you said, 'You choose.' Then I said, 'Let's start off in your bedroom. Maybe we'll go to mine on round two.'"

Sofia gasped. "Liar!"

"What?" He laughed, not taking her charge seriously. "You even suggested that there might be a round three. Which there wasn't, by the way."

Her eyes grew larger with each word he said. "Are you saying that we…me and you…*had sex?*"

Ram's frown deepened as if he didn't know how to take this strange interrogation. "Well, I guess that would depend on your definition of sex."

"What do you mean?"

"Well, we definitely flew past first, second and maybe even third base. It was sliding into home where we sort of fell apart."

Sofia grabbed her head. She was still having a hard

time trying to process any of this. "But why…? I don't understand. Why would I…? Why would we…?"

"Well, it is what most people do after they get married."

"Get married?" She jumped up onto her feet but forgot the comforter.

Ramell's smile returned when his gaze caressed her small curves. "No worries. We can easily just pick up where we left off," he said, peeling back the sheets so that she could see that he was hard and ready.

Sofia gasped, but her eyes zoomed in on Ram's thick and sizable member. For a moment she experienced a surge of recognition.

He started patting the bed. "Don't worry. I won't bite…unless you want me to."

His body was like a huge magnet and Sofia felt herself pulling toward him. But she quickly slammed her eyes closed and tried to shake off whatever spell or voodoo had come over her. "This is not happening," she recited to herself. "This has to be a dream…or a nightmare… or something."

"Careful," he warned. "I think you're on the verge of hurting my feelings."

Sofia's eyes flew back open and, sure enough, Ram was still lying on the bed in his beautiful birthday suit. "Oh, my God." She dropped down and snatched up the comforter again. But it was one sudden move too many. Her stomach rolled while her gag reflexes were activated. She dragged the comforter up with one hand and then slapped the other hand across her mouth to buy a little more time while she raced toward the bathroom.

"Are you all right?" he asked.

She didn't get far before tripping over the long comforter so she dropped it and continued her race toward the toilet. Once there, she dropped to her knees and proceeded to expel the many drinks she consumed the previous evening. "Oh, God," she moaned when she managed a half of a second to breathe. A moment later, she was hit with another wave of soured alcohol.

"Poor baby." Ram retrieved a face towel from one of the racks and quickly wet it with cool water. Once he had wrung it out, he made it over to the toilet and started pressing it against Sofia's hot face and neck.

Sofia glanced over at him and was relieved and a little disappointed that he'd put on a pair of boxer shorts before coming in to help her.

"Shh. It's going to be all right," he assured her while he pulled her long hair out of the way. "Just try to take deep breaths."

She closed her eyes and tried to follow his instructions. When the towel started to warm, he rushed back over to the sink and ran cold water over it again. It took a while before everything started to settle down and she was able to look up at him. "Are we really married?"

He nodded. "If memory serves me correct."

She didn't know whether to throw up again or start crying. How could something like this happen? Why couldn't she remember… "Wait. Was it by a black Elvis impersonator?"

A smile lit Ram's face. "Aww. You do remember."

Sofia turned back toward the toilet and threw up.

An hour later, Ramell helped bring his hungover wife back from the brink of sickness. He pumped her full of fruit juice and crackers to get her amino acids up. After that he gave her some Excedrin for her headache and then helped her to the shower. Through it all, he had to admit that he liked taking care of her. While she was in the shower, he ordered himself a minibuffet since they had missed both breakfast and lunch.

He started cleaning up the bedroom while he waited. It was busy work so that he didn't have to think about what Sofia would say once she came out of the shower. Judging by her reaction to the news of their marriage, he had very little hope that they would reach their two-day anniversary.

He plugged the phone back into the wall just as the bathroom door swung open. Ram looked up to see Sofia draped beneath a white hotel robe that was at least two sizes too big. Even with her hair wet and no makeup, she was still the most beautiful woman he'd ever known.

"We need to talk," she said.

"I had a feeling you were going to say that."

The phone rang. He picked it up because it was already in his hands. "Hello."

"Ramell," Jacob Wellesley roared. "What's this I hear about you marrying my niece?"

"Uh, Jacob! Hello!" He glanced over at Sofia.

Her eyes bugged out as she started shaking her head.

"Well?" Jacob demanded.

Ram couldn't tell whether his new business partner was mad or just sincerely wanted an explanation. "Yes, sir. About that, I'm sure it has come as a bit of a shock but—"

"Shock? Hell, I'm wondering what on earth took you so long!"

"Yes, I, um… What did you just say?"

"I said that it took you too damn long." Jacob laughed.

"I can't tell you enough how thrilled Lily and I are about this latest development."

"Oh, really?" He looked back over at Sofia who was now mouthing questions to Ramell, trying to figure out what her uncle was saying.

"This just means that I made the right decision in merging our companies together. Plus, it means that our business is still technically family-owned. I have to be frank with you, I've been up nights worried about all of this. Now I feel as if a giant load has been taken off my shoulders."

"It does?" he asked.

"What?" Sofia whispered, creeping over to him.

Jacob continued. "I was up every night. Doing this deal made me feel like I was somehow stabbing Sofia in the back. She has worked very hard in the company and in a lot of ways I should have made her full partner years ago. At the same time, all those hours she puts in had us all worried. Now that you two are going to officially be a team, well…I know that you're going to look after her best interest and not let her take on too much. Frankly, I think you are a godsend."

Ram smiled. "I can't tell you how much it means to me to hear you say that, Jacob."

"You love her, don't you?" Jacob asked.

Ram's gaze caressed Sofia's face while he spoke from the bottom of his heart. "For as long as I can remember."

"I knew it!" Jacob's laughter thundered through the phone so loud that Ram had to pull it away from his ear for a second. "Is she there right now? Her aunt and I would love to talk to her."

"Yes. She's right here."

Sofia shook her head and backed up.

"He wants to talk to you," Ram insisted.

"No. No." Ram thrust the phone under her ear. "Noooo— Hi, Uncle Jacob." She forced a smile into her voice, but gave Ram an evil look.

"Congratulations, Sofia," Uncle Jacob boasted. "I was just telling your husband how thrilled your aunt and I are about this wonderful news! Even though I question the venue you and Ramell selected. A black Elvis impersonator?"

"What? How did you—"

"It's all over the news. The media followed Akil Hutton and his new girlfriend there thinking that they were about to get hitched and instead got tons of footage of you and Ramell getting married. It's a little unconventional, I admit, but it looks like it was a lot of fun."

"We were on the news?" Her gaze shot back over to Ram.

"Don't look at me," he hissed. "You're the one that proposed to me."

Sofia covered her hand over the phone. *"What?"*

He shrugged. "I take it you don't remember that part, either."

"Clearly. I was drunk out of my mind," she hissed. "Why didn't you stop me?"

"You seemed fine to me. Besides, I was drinking, too," he reminded her.

"Hold on, Sofia," Uncle Jacob interrupted her next retort. "Your Aunt Lily wants to talk to you."

"Wait, Uncle Jacob."

"Sofia?" Her aunt's soft voice drifted over the line. "Baby, is that you?"

Sighing, Sofia dropped down onto the bed. "Yes, Aunt Lily. It's me."

"Baby, I'm so happy for you," she sniffed. "I've always suspected that you two had strong feelings for each other. And I prayed for so long that someday you both would get together."

Sofia frowned. "You did?"

Her aunt laughed. "Please. I think we all did. I remember back in the day that boy must've proposed to you every day of the week. Your mother and I used to find it adorable."

The mention of her mother instantly brought up many conflicting emotions that glossed her eyes with tears.

"Aww. You used to tease that boy mercilessly," Lily said. "Personally, I'm thrilled that he hung in there. You two are perfect for each other—but for a while it seemed like you were determined not to realize it."

Sofia didn't understand where all this was coming from. People thought that she and Ramell were perfect for each other? Sure, once upon a time she used to fantasize that one day they would get married, but that was a long time ago. She was only a child.

"Aunt Lily, I think that there's something I should tell—"

"The only thing I hate is that we all couldn't be there—Elvis impersonator and all."

"Yeah. About that—"

"So you have to let me throw you two a big reception. It'll be tight since we're still planning Rachel's wedding and all, but you *have* to let me do this. I've been looking forward to this day for so long."

A long pause hung over the phone while Sofia tried to come up with the right words. Instead of admitting that she was just seconds from telling Ram that she wanted an annulment, she said, "We would love for you to throw us a reception, Aunt Lily." Her gaze jumped back up, this time to see Ram's startled face. "Nothing would make us happier."

Chapter 11

While Ramell and Sofia headed to Los Angeles, they were still dancing around just how they were going to handle this whole marriage thing. Their cell phones and emails were overflowing with congratulatory messages from friends, colleagues, studio executives and even tabloid magazines and bloggers. For a moment, they were being treated as if they were celebrities themselves. The embarrassing part was just how much of their wild night was documented.

In a world of camera phones, it seemed that everywhere and everything they did that night ended up somewhere on the web. Ramell made it clear that he liked the ones with her dancing on club tables. For Sofia, it was the video of Ramell's debut strip performance.

"I would've gone Full Monty if you would've let me," Ram said while he flew them into the private airport.

"That would have played well on *Entertainment Tonight*," she chuckled.

"I want to know why you stopped me," he said, glancing over at her.

"Maybe because even in my drunken state I realized that we needed to hold on to *some* dignity."

"Or maybe you didn't want to share me with all those

other women," Ram suggested. "I kind of like the idea of you being possessive."

"Oh, please." She straightened herself in her seat while her fingers flew across her iPad. She was rapidly transforming back into her old self, with her ever-present Bluetooth hooked onto her ear and her ability to type ninety words while still holding a separate conversation.

Ram shook his head. "Do you have to do that now?"

"Do what?"

"Work. We have a lot of stuff to figure out, Mrs. Jordan."

Her fingers tripped over themselves at the sound of her new title. She wanted to be irritated, but the truth of the matter was that her heart quickened a little bit whenever he called her Mrs. Jordan and parts of her even tingled a little. *What the hell is going on?* She glanced over at him and met his smiling eyes. One thing was for sure, Ram certainly didn't seem bothered by landing himself a new wife at all.

She forced her gaze away and coughed. "What sort of stuff do we need to figure out?"

"Oh, I don't know. Things like…where are we going to live?"

"What?"

"You don't think that it might be a little strange if we return home and go back to living in separate houses?"

"I guess that's a good point," she conceded, and then thought about it for a moment. "How about my place?"

"You live in a high-rise."

"Yeah, so?"

"So. Now that we're a married couple maybe a house is more appropriate?"

"Meaning your house," she said, crossing her arms.

"I do happen to have one available," he reasoned. "And you don't have to worry, I have excellent taste. It's not your run-of-the-mill bachelor pad."

"Says you."

"Says everyone. It was actually featured in *Architectural Digest* last summer. Of course, I had to take down the sex swing, but if you want we can get it out of the attic."

Her head whipped back over to him.

"It was a joke. Ha. Ha. We're supposed to laugh at jokes, remember?" Ram reached over and elbowed her playfully. "You really need to learn how to lighten up."

"Have you ever thought that maybe you play too much?" she challenged. Now she had to try to get the image of her riding on his swing out of her mind, even though she was partly intrigued.

"One can never play too much, sweetheart."

It was the endearments that were doing her in. *Baby, sweetheart, honey, Mrs. Jordan.* Each one sounded and felt like a lover's caress and was undoing the foundation of everything she thought she knew about herself.

"So would you like to go out with me when we get back home?" Ram asked.

"Excuse me?"

"Well, it sort of just occurred to me that despite our knowing each other for all our lives, we haven't officially gone out on a date."

"We don't have to date." Sofia shook her head. "We're married now."

He laughed. "Yeah. I guess we sort of put the cart before the horse here. But I'd like to take you out. Plus, I hear that married couples are bringing dating back with a vengeance."

She shook her head but a smile curved across her lips.

"Does that mean we have a date?"

Sofia tried to stifle the small flurry of excitement fluttering in the pit of her stomach. Why was she feeling like this and why couldn't she stop it? Self-discipline was something she prided herself on, but since Ram charged back into her life it'd been more or less thrown out of the window entirely.

"Yes? No? Maybe so?" he asked.

"Well where do you plan on taking me?"

"Ah. Ah. Ah." He took his hand off the controls to wave a finger in front of her. "I want it to be a surprise."

She lifted her eyebrows but still couldn't wipe the smile off her face. "All right. Fine. May I at least know when this postmarriage date is going to take place?"

"Sure. How about tomorrow night?"

"Oh. I don't know if I can do tomorrow night." She pulled up her calendar on her iPad. "I think—"

"Whatever it is, cancel it," he said.

"What?"

"You heard me. Cancel it." He gave her a look that made it clear that he was being serious. "I think that with everyone knowing that you're a newlywed they will be more than forgiving of you canceling whatever it is you seem to think is so important."

"My business *is* important."

"You mean *our* business, right?"

She opened her mouth to continue arguing, but once again realized that there would be no point. Ramell had a cool, logical answer for everything. "Fine. I'll cancel."

"Great! See, now that wasn't so hard, was it?"

She folded her arms with a huff and pretended to be annoyed. At least that would have been true a few days ago. Lately, she was finding his take-charge attitude to be a real turn-on. Maybe there was something else in her blood pressure medication because ever since she started taking those things, she hadn't been acting like herself at all.

With just a few minutes left in their flight, Sofia leaned her head back and closed her eyes. But she was totally unprepared for the images that splashed in her mind. Images of Ram sliding off her shoes and of him kissing her on her ankle and then working his way up her inner thigh. Her body started tingling like crazy. She drew in a soft breath, sure her body temperature was rising.

The pictures inside her head were so vivid she swore that she could feel his fingers peeling her panties from her hips. She squirmed in her chair.

"So beautiful," his voice echoed inside her head as he parted her legs. When his head dropped in between them, Sofia's eyes sprang open.

Ram looked over at her, concern written on his face. "Are you all right?"

Panting, Sofia placed a hand over her heart and stared at him.

That only made his frown deepen. "Sofia?"

"Y-yes. Yes. I'm fine," she lied. *Was that a dream or a memory?*

He gave her a look that said he didn't believe her, but he let it go.

They touched down at the airport and they were both surprised to see a few photographers waiting there, snapping away.

Sofia was thrown off guard. While her agency may represent some of the most talented people in Los Angeles, the spotlight rarely hit her personally nowadays. It was a little reminiscent of the days after her parents' death. She couldn't imagine why anyone would be interested in the life and times of a Hollywood agent in the tabloids, but there they were.

Ram quickly escorted her to his white Porsche and peeled out of there as if he was trying to qualify for a drag race. While he played speed racer, Sofia glanced around the spotless, leather interior.

"What?"

She shrugged. "Nothing. I was just thinking that this is the sort of car a confirmed bachelor would drive."

"Well, just say the word and I'll trade this puppy in for a minivan in a heartbeat."

He grinned devilishly at her and she had the sneaky suspicion that he meant it. *Kids?* Things were definitely moving too fast for her to wrap her brain around. They were going to start dating after getting married and now they were going to discuss kids before they had sex? Or did they have sex already?

Another image of Ram's head dipping low to suck one of her nipples into his mouth filled her head along with him running his teeth lightly against the sensitive tip. She twitched and her panties grew moist. She covered a hand over her mouth when she could hear her own sighs echoed in her ears.

"Are you sure you're okay?" Ram asked.

"Yes," she said as she started fanning herself. "Don't you have an air conditioner in this thing?"

"It's cool and the windows are down," he said.

"Well…I'm hot." She reached over to the console herself and put the air on full blast.

Ram just gave her a stern look and then shook his

head. What man really understood women, anyway? He was trying to wing this whole marriage thing himself. So far, Sofia hadn't said anything about getting an annulment, but she wasn't exactly acting like a gushing newlywed, either. Hopefully on their first official date tomorrow, he could put all his cards on the table and convince her to really give this marriage a try. He knew in his heart that he could make her happy. He had known it for years. But if she still needed time, he was more than willing to give her as much of it as she needed.

He arrived at her penthouse at the Beverly Hilton. She tried to just hop out of the car and grab her own bags, but Ram wasn't having any of that. He parked and insisted on bringing his wife's luggage up to her penthouse.

"That's not necessary," she insisted.

"Oh, it is necessary. And besides, I *want* to do it." When she folded her arms, he added, "You need to get used to letting a man take care of you."

He placed a finger against her mouth before she could say anything to argue with him. "I'm not talking about financially. I'm talking about emotionally." Their eyes locked. "Everyone needs someone to love and to hold. Someone to share their darkest secrets with. To laugh and play with." He reached up and cupped the side of her face. "You know—how we used to do."

Sofia stared into Ramell's eyes and was instantly transported back to a time when she trusted him with all her secrets, a time when she knew without a doubt that one day they would be together forever. That moment in time now felt like it was yesterday. And in many ways, he was the same Ram, waiting on her to hand him her heart.

"You love me," she said. It wasn't a question.

He smiled. "I have *always* loved you." He leaned down

and slowly drew her lips into a kiss. It started off soft and slow but it quickly heated up to the point that their mouths delved into each other like they were completely ravenous for one another.

The next thing Sofia knew she was sliding her arms up around his neck so that she could pull him closer. Yes, he tasted like chocolate, and yes, he was the most addictive thing she'd ever known, but most importantly, he tasted like love. Sweet, heady and completely intoxicating. Now that she recognized the taste it consumed her and knocked down walls that she never even knew she had erected. When she managed to pull their lips apart, her chest heaved like she had just traveled the entire world in less than sixty seconds.

Ram's devilish smile slid into place. "Now may I help take your bags up to your penthouse, Mrs. Jordan?"

Hell. She forgot that they were still standing in the parking deck. What happened to her hatred of public displays of affection? "Yeah. That would be nice."

"Good." He kissed the tip of her nose. "I kind of like convincing you to see things my way." Ram grabbed her bags from the trunk and when they turned to head toward the building, Sofia's sister stood there smiling.

"Rachel." Sofia blinked. "What are you doing here?"

"What else? I came to see you." Rachel walked over to her older sister and drew her into a hug. "The last time we talked I think it's safe to say that you were a little…out of it."

Sofia laughed. "That's putting it nicely." She kissed her sister's cheek before she pulled out of her arms.

"But after seeing that kiss, I know now that there's absolutely nothing to worry about." Rachel turned toward Ramell. "And I guess that makes you my new brother-in-law," Rachel said, sweeping her arms open wide.

Ram lowered Sofia's luggage and quickly embraced Rachel in a hug. "Hey, I always wanted a little sister." And just like that the two clicked. They had always known each other, but the recent marriage made them instant best friends. Ramell retrieved the bags and together all three of them walked up to Sofia's penthouse.

When they entered the luxurious apartment, Ram asked where the bedroom was and Sofia hesitated. She had another jolt of everything moving so fast, but then shook it off to show him the way. Rachel stayed in the living room to give them a few minutes of privacy.

In the bedroom, Ram set her bags on the bed and took a look around her peach-and-gold bedroom. "Nice."

"Thank you."

"It's not as nice as mine, of course, but it's nice."

"We're having a contest now?"

"I'm just saying." He shrugged his shoulders. He walked over to her and swung his arms around her waist. "Make sure when I come and pick you up tomorrow that you pack enough clothes to stay at my house for a while."

She drew in a deep breath.

"I have more than one bedroom, you know. There's no pressure."

Sofia flashed the simple band around her finger. "No. There's just a wedding band."

"Hey," he said with a sudden note of seriousness. "You know me. I'll wait as long as you need me to."

She did know that, had known it for a long time. "Thank you," she whispered.

"No. Thank you."

"For what?"

"For finally asking *me* to marry *you*."

Chapter 12

The next morning, Sofia strolled through the office doors of Limelight Entertainment Management wearing a big smile. Almost everyone she passed in the building seemed to go out of their way to stop and offer their congratulations and well wishes. Sure, there was one or two of them that pointed or snickered about the Elvis impersonator or the small clip of Ramell giving her a strip dance—which, had, incidentally, generated hundreds of thousands of views online.

But none of that bothered her. She was too excited about her date tonight. Not even Stewart, who had screwed up her coffee order and dropped a very important director's call four times in a row, could upset her. It turned out she wasn't on her A-game, either. While Larry Franklin was still trying to lowball her on Ethan's next contract, her mind was still trying to figure out what she was going to wear that evening. When she left for work that morning, she had narrowed her selection down to seven dresses.

"Sofia, are you still there?"

"Huh, what?" She blinked out of her stupor.

Larry cleared his throat. "I'm sorry. Was I boring you?"

"No." She started to apologize but stopped. "But I'm

still disappointed in the offer." Sofia had no idea what he'd offered, but it was her job to press for more, anyway, so her answer couldn't have been wrong.

"All right, all right. I give. We'll accept your last counteroffer. Does that make you happy?"

She perked up. "Extremely."

"I'll have legal draw up the contracts," Larry huffed, and she could tell that he was lighting one of his favorite illegal Cuban cigars. "I have to tell you, Sofia, I had hoped that marriage would have softened you a little."

"There you go thinking again, Larry. I told you that was a dangerous proposition." They shared a brief laugh and then ended their call. A second later, Uncle Jacob knocked on Sofia's glass door. She glanced up and smiled. "It's about time you rolled in," she said, glancing at her watch.

"Actually, it's my day off. I only came in to see you," he said, strolling over to her desk. "Two days after your nuptials and you're already back to work? I was hoping that marriage would've curbed some of your workaholic ways."

"Seems everyone has been hoping that marriage would change me," she said, a little irritated at that discovery.

Uncle Jacob's kind face crinkled at the corners. "Not change you. I just want you to slow down and smell the roses." He moved around her desk and opened his arms. "In my eyes, you and your sister are perfect."

Sofia stood and embraced her uncle. Because he was her father's twin, it had always been easy to view him as both her uncle and her father. With him around, she could never forget her father's face. And when she wanted to see her mother all she had to do was look in the mirror.

"I come bearing news of your wedding reception," he said after they had exchanged a long hug.

"The wedding reception." Sofia sank back into her chair. "You know Aunt Lily really doesn't have to go to any trouble. In fact, I'm sure that she has to be up to her eyeballs helping Rachel plan her wedding."

"Nonsense. We want to celebrate both of your unions." His smile doubled in size as his gaze started to shimmer with tears. "I know that your parents have to be smiling down on you two right now. I've only met Ethan a couple of times but I know that he and your sister are going to be happy for a long, long time. And as for you…" He reached down and tweaked her nose. "I've known for a very long time how Ramell has felt about you. I don't think anyone who has ever been in the same room with you two didn't know that one day…" He waved his finger and then winked.

Sofia smiled but dropped her gaze.

"But how do you feel about him?" Jacob asked. "Do you love him?"

She took her time thinking the question over. She thought about the years that she had foolishly blamed Ram for the things his father did. It had been unfair, but at the time it was the only way she knew how to cope.

"Sofia?" Jacob pressed, concern starting to seep into his voice.

"I think I've always loved him…in some way," she finally said. "Given how I've treated him, I'm not sure that I deserve him."

Jacob chuckled. "We all deserve love, Sofia. Don't you ever forget that."

She nodded and let his words wash over her.

"As for your reception, it's next Friday and then

the week after that we all head out to Napa Valley for Rachel's wedding and for Thanksgiving."

"Next Friday?"

"It was going to be sooner than that but Emmett is out in New York and won't be back until that Wednesday so we settled on Friday."

Sofia's hands tightened on the pen in her hand. "She's inviting Emmett?"

Jacob paused and then said softly, "Well, he is Ramell's father. It only seems right to invite him to the wedding reception."

Sofia clenched her teeth together in order to prevent herself from saying something nasty. But the effort was hard and it instantly brought on a headache.

Jacob watched her reaction and then seemed to struggle with something. "Sofia, maybe it's time we had a little talk about Emmett Jordan," he started, propping a hip up on her desk.

"No," she said sternly. "The last thing I want to do is talk about that man."

"But—"

"I mean it," she snapped, feeling her face heat up. In the brief three days she had to think about this marriage, she hadn't given much thought on how she was going to have to handle *him* being her new father-in-law. The only solution that popped in her head right now was to keep the same game plan that she'd always had: stay the hell away from him.

"Well, thank you, Uncle Jacob. I'll definitely tell Ramell our schedule."

Uncle Jacob's brows hiked up. "He's not here? You left him home alone?"

"Actually, he mentioned something about needing the day off to plan for our first date."

Jacob laughed. "Well, in that case I guess it's all right. You have any idea what he has in mind?"

"None." She thought about it. "Maybe I should be worried?"

"Or," Jacob said, standing again, "maybe you should be excited."

Sofia didn't work a full day, something that should have been marked in the history books. Instead, she begged for her favorite hairdresser to fit her in. After that it was a rushed manicure and pedicure and then an eyebrow threading before racing back to her penthouse to decide on what to wear.

"What happened to my other Prada shoe?" she wondered aloud while she searched her bags. After another twenty-minute search, she gave up and went for her black Jimmy Choos and a black Chanel dress.

Their date was for eight o'clock and that was exactly when her doorbell rang. She gave herself a last casual glance in the mirror and went to answer the door. She started off with a casual stroll, but when the bell rang a second time, she ended up doing a light jog to the front door.

When she opened it, Ram stood on the other side in a black suit with one hand in his pocket and the other one mysteriously behind his back. "Good evening, Mrs. Jordan."

That wonderful feeling of warmth rushed through her body again. Once again, Ram looked good from head to toe and she had to force herself to stop staring. "Evening."

"Mind if I come in?"

She stepped back with a smile. "Absolutely. Come in."

When he strolled through the door, his signature cologne filled her senses and weakened her knees. His white smile and kissable lips had her heart tripping in her chest. When on earth had he learned to turn her on so quickly? "I brought something for you," he said.

"Oh?" She closed the door behind him.

Ramell gently pulled out a bundle of daisies. "I didn't think I'd be able to find them in November," he admitted.

Tears stung the back of her eyes while her smile tripled in size. "My favorite."

"I know." He stepped closer and tipped her chin. "I remember." His head slowly descended until their lips locked together. His broad chest felt wonderful pressed against her. Her heartbeat became erratic. If this was all that he had planned, then he wouldn't get any complaints from her.

This is crazy. But despite that, she was willing to see where this wild and unexpected ride was going to lead her. *Everyone deserves love.*

Ram pulled back and then kissed the tip of her nose. "Are you ready to go?"

Not sure that she could speak, she nodded. But when she tried to walk, she still wobbled a bit. *What on earth is this man doing to me?*

"Where are your bags?"

"Uh. I haven't actually had a chance to pack yet," she informed him, looking for a vase that would fit her short stemmed bouquet. "It took all of my free time just to get ready."

His gaze roamed over her again. "Don't worry about it. It was worth every second." He offered her his arm and then escorted her out of the penthouse.

"Am I allowed to know where we're going now?" she asked when he opened the passenger-side door of his car for her.

"No." He tossed her a wink and then shut the door. A few minutes later they were on the road and cruising down the highway.

When it became clear where Ram was taking her, a fresh wave of tears filled her eyes. "I don't believe it."

Ram reached over, took her hand and kissed it. "Are you upset?"

Sofia shook her head as she stared at her old childhood home. The white three-story mansion nestled on a grassy knoll looked exactly as she had remembered. In a lot of ways it was as if time had just stood still. For years she kept promising herself to come by the old estate, but always allowed herself to get caught up with work or some other social function. A part of her also believed that the memories would be too painful, but now that she was standing there she couldn't stop smiling. Only belatedly did she realize that the lights were still on.

"Does someone live here?"

"Not exactly." Ram climbed out of the car and rushed to the other side to help her out.

Taking his hand, Sofia looked up into Ram's soulful eyes and felt like she was stepping out of his car and into a dream. Again, she wondered at the magic he seemed to be able to cast over her at will. How she had been able to fight it as long as she had would probably be a mystery to her for the rest of her life. But right now, at this moment, she just allowed it to consume her.

"Our table awaits," he said.

Sofia cocked a curious smile, but floated along beside him as he escorted her around the house. Once they made it to the backyard her gaze immediately zoomed to the large oak tree where she and Ramell used to steal childhood kisses. Tonight, a round linen-covered table with two flickering candles sat beneath it. Next to it a single waiter and a violinist awaited them.

"Oh, my God." Sofia clutched a hand over her heart and a fresh wave of tears threatened to ruin her makeup. She glanced to her left and met Ram's gaze again. "It's beautiful."

"Believe me, it pales next to you." He leaned over for another kiss. Each time he did it was as if heaven had momentarily touched down on earth. When their lips pulled apart, he escorted her the rest of the way to their waiting table. He'd pulled a few strings to get Patina to cater this evening. It was Sofia's favorite restaurant according to her sister. And he made sure to have her favorite meal prepared. "I can't believe that you went to all this trouble," she said as he pulled out her chair.

"It was no trouble at all. I wanted to do this." When she sat, he brushed his lips lightly against her shoulders. When her soft skin trembled beneath his touch, his chest swelled with love and his confidence soared. He took his seat and allowed the stirring music from the violin and the evening's cool breeze to wrap around them while their waiter busied himself removing their silver trays.

"You're quite the romantic," Sofia said, blushing.

"I hope you don't mind."

She shrugged shyly. "I guess there are worse things in the world."

Ram couldn't stop looking at her. He could sit there all night watching the evening's gentle breeze play with her hair. Between the candlelight and the moonlight, she looked like she'd just descended from heaven.

"Stop." She shook her head, looking uncharacteristically shy.

"Stop what?"

"Stop looking at me like that."

He laughed. "And just how am I looking at you?"

Her cheeks stained red as she shook her head. "You're making me self-conscious."

"I'm sorry, but I can't help it. I've never had a wife before."

Her eyes met his again, but something flickered in them that scared him for a moment. "What is it?" he asked, wanting to tackle any problem head-on.

"Well, I guess…I'm wondering, what are we doing? It's not like we really meant to get married, right?"

The question shaved a few inches off of his smile.

"I mean when I started receiving all those calls and Uncle Jacob seemed so happy…I couldn't bring myself to tell them…"

"Tell them what?" His voice dropped as he prepared for her to say something that was going to tear him apart.

"I couldn't tell them the truth."

He sat silently during a few bars from the violin before he could bring himself to ask. "And what is the truth, Sofia?"

Her eyes started shimmering with tears while she tried to find the right words. "That's just it. Our truth is complicated."

He breathed a sigh of relief. "Not on my end." Ram reached across the table and took her hand. "My truth is that I'm thrilled that we're married. I love that you have my last name because I have loved you my whole life. And I have a sneaking suspicion that you feel the same way about me. I just never understood why you insisted on fighting it."

In a flash, Sofia remembered poking her head into her father's study and seeing him enraged and yelling and hurling accusations at Ram's father. A lump swelled in the center of her throat while her gaze lowered to where his hand held hers. Their fingers looked so perfect entwined together. "It's so complicated."

"So complicated that you can't even tell me?"

The only other person Sofia had ever shared what she'd seen and heard that night with was her sister, Rachel. And now her new husband was asking and she didn't know how to go about repeating those words to him. It was his father, after all, and as far as she knew they were very close.

"You know…maybe it's just best to kind of leave it in the past," she decided. "Tonight…we should be celebrating our first date." She chuckled, hoping to lighten the mood.

He smiled. "Moving forward, I guess what I need to know is whether we're seriously going to give this marriage a try—or is this some kind of charade we're just putting on for family and friends because…what? Because we don't know how to tell them that we got drunk and did something wild and spontaneous?"

She blinked.

"Do you want an annulment?" he asked. "Tell me now because I don't do charades." And there it was. His cards laid out on the table.

Sofia drew a deep breath while her head started to spin.

"It simple," he said. "Do you want to stay married to me?"

Chapter 13

In an instant Sofia was transported back to that last time they were in this backyard, Ramell standing in front of her with a bundle of wild daisies and asking her if she would marry him. And just like then, her stomach filled with butterflies while her heart skipped around in her chest. He stared at her with the same intensity, the same confidence and the same amount of love.

"I honestly don't know," she whispered and then slowly bobbed her head. "I guess we could give it a try—for the time being."

Ram tossed down his linen napkin and jumped up from the table. He walked over to Sofia's seat, pulled her up and crushed his mouth against hers. Holding any stream of conscious thought was impossible so she didn't even bother to try. She just floated around in an endless abyss of desire.

"You don't know how happy you just made me," he whispered, coming up for air. "I've waited my whole life to hear you say those words…soberly." They laughed while he continued to cup her face. "I promise you that you won't regret this." He kissed her again and swirled her in time to the music.

"I have another surprise for you," Ram said softly.

Sofia pulled back. "Really? I don't know if my heart can take any more surprises."

"Just one more." He gently turned her around so that she faced the back of her old home. "I was thinking about that conversation we had about whether we should live at your place or mine."

"I thought you said—"

"I bought this house," he announced.

Sofia's mouth opened and remained like that for a long moment before she finally asked, "What?"

"I bought this house today." He lowered his arms to her waist while he waited for her response. At the sound of a soft sniffle, he jerked toward her. "I'm sorry. I didn't mean to upset you."

Shaking her head, Sofia placed a hand over her mouth while silent tears rolled down her face.

"We don't have to move here," Ram said, desperate to fix the situation. "My place is fine. Or we can live at your place. I don't care. I'll live wherever you want to live."

Sofia spun toward him and wrapped her arms around his neck. "No. It's okay. I love it. It's just so overwhelming. Thank you." She sobbed gently against his chest before lifting her head up and receiving the kiss she sought. This time her lips were salted with tears.

"Would you like to go inside?" he asked.

She quickly nodded and then grasped his hand before they took off in the direction of the back doors. Of course none of the old furniture was there, but the house still felt like home with the rented modern furniture. "It's so…perfect."

They strolled through the house while recalling different childhood stories. Like when they used to make chocolate chip cookies or colored Easter eggs with Sofia's mother. Upstairs, she stopped at what used to be Rachel's baby room and then her room. She touched the walls where her mother used to mark how tall she was growing.

"I don't know why I haven't visited this house more often," she whispered, shaking her head. "I kept telling myself I would but…"

"Too busy?"

She glanced over at him. "No lectures this evening."

He surrendered by tossing up his hands. "Agreed."

They continued their stroll until they reached the master bedroom. Sofia's heart contracted because she remembered so many nights that she had run to this room for the comfort of her father's arms to protect her from bad storms or nightmares. But like the rest of the house, her parents' old furniture was gone and in its place a California King four-poster bed with royal blue silk sheets sat like a regal throne toward the back of the room. She stepped farther into the room while Ramell hung back.

Sofia glanced at the walls, the windows, the crown molding—but her gaze kept creeping toward the bed. "Can I ask you a question?"

Ramell cleared his throat. "Of course you can."

"It's about our, um, wedding night."

"All right." He leaned against the door frame. "I hope I can help."

"Do you know whether we…you know?"

His brows hiked while a different kind of smile inched across his lips. "Did we make love?"

"Well…I know that you said something about first and second base."

"Don't forget about third," he said.

Sofia swallowed. "Remind me what third base is again."

Within the blink of an eye, the flirtation in his gaze

transformed into something primal—hungry. "Third base is when I lay you down and start kissing you from the heel of your foot, up to the back of your calf—where you're ticklish by the way—then up the inside of your thighs. I watch you quiver for a while and then I travel further up while I peel your panties from your hips and then spread you legs open so I can...enjoy the taste of your inner beauty."

Hit with a sudden heat wave, Sofia's knees started to wobble. Her mind had replayed the images in her head while he talked. "So it wasn't a dream," she whispered.

Ram locked gazes as he shook his head. "No. It was paradise."

She licked her lips. "Can you take me there again?"

With a moan, he strolled across the room. When their bodies connected, he was fire to her dynamite. Sofia felt as if she was being devoured. Ram's hot mouth latched on to her pearled nipples while his large hands spread her silken legs open. She tilted her head back as far she could against the pillows in hopes of tugging in a few streams of oxygen. It worked for a few seconds but then she decided to take her chances with the fire by leaning forward so she could rain kisses against the top of Ram's head.

He continued to nibble and suck while slowly working a finger through the soft, wet V between her legs.

"Oooooh," Sofia sighed and lifted her hips to allow Ram to slide a second finger into her smooth flesh. Her world spun as he rotated his fingers until he could hear her body's juices start to make smacking noises. By then his head was directly over her soft, springy curls and he wasted no time unrolling his long tongue to taste the honey within.

Melodic moans rolled off of Sofia's lips and seemed to blend effortlessly with the violin that still played outside their window. She closed her eyes, surprised by just how much her body was trembling. It was like an earthquake that didn't have an end in sight. She gave up her quest for oxygen and welcomed the idea of death by pleasure as her first orgasm started to churn at the base of her body.

Unbelievably, Ramell's tongue sank deeper, hitting the G-spot that supplied all her body's honey. His tongue flicked, rotated and flicked again, causing Sofia to clamp her hands around Ram's head. She was both pushing him away and locking him in place at the same time.

Then, an explosion. She tried to scream out but her voice failed. Her toes balled like fists and her knees squeezed Ram's head like a nutcracker. While waves of euphoria washed over her, Ram struggled to pry her legs back open. When he finally succeeded, he climbed back up her body and chuckled against her neck. "Remind me to strap you down next time."

Before her aftershocks had fully subsided, Ram brought her back to the brink again by working in one, two and then three fingers into her slick honey pot.

When she started to thrash again, Ram's mouth made its way back to her breasts. "Oooh, Ram," she recited. Each time she said his name, he picked up the pace until his entire hand was as wet as she was.

The pleasure was too much, too intense. Just when her second orgasm was about to slam into her, she lifted her hips high to give Ram better access. Next thing she knew she was hitting her head hard against the headboard and trying to escape Ram's wicked fingers. "Wait. Please," she begged. "I need to catch my breath."

"Is that right?"

Panting, Sofia could tell that his ego was swelling out of control. She put on her best sexy smile and then brushed his hands from between her legs. "All right, Mr. Jordan. Your head game is on point." She rolled him onto his back. "But you're not the only one with skills, you know."

Ramell laughed. "Careful now. The last time you started bragging, you left a brother hanging."

Sofia frowned. "What?"

"You fell asleep kissing my stomach."

Embarrassment heated her face. "No. I didn't."

"I'm afraid so." He laughed and drew her in for a kiss. "It's okay, baby. The kissing was nice. The cold shower was another story."

She pushed him back down onto the bed. "Well, there won't be any cold showers tonight." Sofia climbed on top and straddled Ram's trim hips. Gazing down at him, he looked like a chocolate deity and she definitely had a sweet tooth. Lowering her head, Sofia slowly and deliberately ran her tongue over his chest.

"Ooh. Now that's nice," he said, folding his hands behind his head so he could watch her work her magic. And it was a sort of magic, that the way his body tingled wherever her tongue roamed. When she glazed over one of his hard nipples, a thin sigh seeped out of his chest and he grew even harder.

Sofia floated down his body like a feather. For a brief moment her open legs and pink pearl brushed against his iron-hard erection, and despite the momentary pleasure, she kept moving down until his thick and mountainous length stood tall before her face.

"Oh, my goodness," she moaned, staring in awe. Curious, she wrapped one hand around him and smiled when she saw that her fingers just barely made it around the base.

"You sure you know what you're doing down there, sweetheart?"

Sofia's brows jumped at the challenge. She immediately rolled out her tongue and then slowly dragged it up and then down his straining flesh. The muscle quivered and jumped. When it did, it bounced against Sofia's lips. Laughing, she tried again. Her tongue went up and down, soliciting a moan and then a hiss from Ramell. To push him over the edge, she opened and relaxed her jaw so she could sink her mouth over the fat, mushroom-shaped head. She sank down as far as she could, held him and then squeezed the muscles in the back of her throat.

Ram called out to the Almighty and then raked his fingers through her long hair.

She released him, bobbed her head up and then sank back down before he had a chance to catch his breath. He hissed, groaned and then latched his hand on the back of her head as she now set a steady but maddening pace. Periodically she would stop, squeeze and then bob again.

Words of love, lust and a few things in between tumbled out of his mouth. Chances were he didn't know what he was saying. And now that the shoe was on the other foot, he was having a hard time trying to lie still. He was going to come and he didn't want that.

"Okay, baby. You can stop," he half begged while he attempted to pull her up.

She warded off his hands for as long as she could,

but when it was clear that he was seconds from exploding, Ram reached down and pried her off of him. Sofia came away laughing.

"Ah. So you think that's funny?" He pinned her beneath him and then smothered kisses against the crook of her neck while his wet erection slapped against her core. "I know how to make you serious," he said.

"Do you now?" She giggled and squirmed.

"Uh-huh," he said seductively, his hardness rubbing against her spot without his help. "Now that I have educated you about reaching third base, what do you say we take this on home?"

Instead of answering, Sofia reached down in between their bodies and grabbed hold of him and guided him directly into her silky walls. It was a bold maneuver, but the minute Ram started to sink into her body, her eyes widened and her body started to tense at his length and width. The combination of pain and pleasure caused pearl-size tears to form and roll from the corners of her eyes.

Ram stopped. "Are you okay, baby? You need me to stop?"

"No. Please. Don't stop," she panted, rolling her hands around his waist and urging his hips to sink lower.

He curled his body so that he could kiss the tracks of her tears while still submerging deeper. The pleasure of feeling her vaginal muscles pulse in time with her heartbeat had Ram's mind spinning like a pinwheel. Breathing became a chore while he fought for control. If he started moving too soon, he risked becoming a two-minute brother and that would be one hell of a way to start off his marriage.

Luckily, Sofia was still trying to adjust to his size, so

together they had an undeclared time-out. Soon enough the kissing returned and Ram started to rock her slow and deep. Sighing, she thrust her head back and then lifted her legs to wrap them around his trim waist. Together they found a rhythm and lost themselves in the splendor of each other.

Euphoric, Sofia alternated between calling out for God and Ramell. Tears of joy continued to roll down her face.

"Do you love me, Sofia?" Ram asked, his hips now a human drill.

"Y-yes," she cried. "Oh, yes."

"Then I want to hear you say it, baby."

"I—I love you, Ram, baby."

"I love you, too." He dropped his head lower, sucked in a nipple and hammered and licked until his ears rang with her screaming his name. He hiked her legs higher and enjoyed the sound of their bodies slapping together. At long last an orgasmic cry seemed to tear from her very soul while her mind spun into sweet oblivion. Two deep strokes later, Ram growled and clenched a large fistful of the bedding while he exploded inside of her.

For long minutes afterward, neither one of them could speak. They just lay there, hot and sweaty, clinging to each other. The sound of the violin was still playing somewhere off in the distance. They both seemed to realize that at the same time.

"That dude is working for his money," Ram laughed, climbing out of the large bed.

When he rushed over to the window, Sofia rolled onto her side and ogled his perfect behind and low-swinging manhood. She smiled at the knowledge that he now belonged to her. She belonged to him. They belonged together.

Ram opened the window and let out a loud whistle. "Yo, man. You can head out."

The music finally stopped and Sofia snickered and shook her head. "How long has he been out there?"

"I don't know." Ram glanced at his watch. "Wow. It's one in the morning."

"No!"

He bobbed his head as he headed back over to the bed. Once there, he grabbed her and pulled her close. Their bodies snapped together like two missing pieces of a puzzle. However, before he could get round two started, Sofia's stomach growled like a starved lion.

She gasped and then covered her face in embarrassment.

"I take it that means you're hungry," Ram laughed.

"Well, we never did have dinner and we did burn up quite a lot of calories," she reminded him.

"Then let's see what we can do about that." He kissed her on her collarbone and then climbed back out of bed. After a quick shower together where they played just a little more than they concentrated on getting clean, they were left having to wrap their wet bodies in clean sheets instead of drying off with towels because they couldn't find any. When they descended the large staircase, they looked like a college couple about to attend a toga party.

The surprise was seeing that their waiter had moved their outdoor dinner party back into the house. Sure they had to remove it from the refrigerator and heat everything up in the microwave, but it was still food for the starving husband and wife. For the next hour they laughed and reminisced about a time long gone. It felt good opening up to one another. To Sofia, it even felt like she had her best friend back.

It was perfect.
Almost too perfect.
Surely, the other shoe had to drop.

Chapter 14

Sofia woke with the sound of birds chirping outside of her window. She sighed, smiled and tried to snuggle closer to the muscled body lying next to her. If she could carry a tune she might've just busted out singing "I'm Every Woman."

"So how long are you going to lie there and pretend that you're asleep?" Ramell asked.

Sofia's smile stretched wider as she fluttered her eyes open. "I thought that *you* were asleep."

"Are you kidding me? We've been waiting a couple of hours for you to wake up."

"We?"

Ram nodded downward and Sofia's gaze followed its direction to see her husband's early-morning erection. "Oh, my." She arched a brow and reflexively licked her lips. "Is this something I can look forward to every morning?" She reached down and slowly pulled the top sheet until it slid off of Ram's impeccably chiseled body. His length stood straight up like a black obelisk.

"I hope that's not a problem," Ramell said, cupping her chin with his fingers and then tilting it upward so he could have his first kiss of the day. The first brush of his lips was sweet but then when his tongue swept inside her mouth a familiar heat rushed up her body and pure passion took over.

Before she knew it, she was swinging her leg across his waist while he sat up in bed so he could stretch his hot mouth over her full breasts. Sofia was as wet as he was hard and it made it easy for him to enter her quickly and thoroughly. Sofia smiled and rolled her hips in a figure eight so that Ram's steel rod could hit her four walls perfectly and caused a few sighs to blend with her moans. They were going at it like they had been lovers all of their lives. She arched her back further until she could grab hold of his ankles. Honey gushed between her legs with each grind and thrust, causing their bodies to make loud, exotic popping and squishing noises.

"That's it, baby. That's it." Ram skimmed his fingers down the front of her body and then dipped them in between the wet folds of her lips and she thumped back against the pads of his fingertips.

"Oh. You feel good, baby," he praised. "So damn good."

"Yeah? You like that?" she asked.

"You know that I do," he panted.

"Well, I have something else for you," she said. Sofia maneuvered and turned around with their bodies still connected. Her knees remained on both sides of his hips, her legs curled behind his back while she lay down in between the V of his legs. Then she started to grind.

And Ram lost his mind.

He watched the incredible sight of her perfect round ass while it bounced, flexed and rotated until his toes started to tingle. "Oh, damn." Ram parted her cheeks so he could watch as he flowed in and out of her to the precise rhythm that was playing inside his head.

Sofia panted, thrashing her head from side to side, but still working her hips, pelvis and vaginal muscles so that there was no mistake as to who was in control. "You feel so good."

Not as good as you feel. He closed his eyes for a second and bit his lower lip when the pleasure intensified. *It should be a crime for anything to feel this good.* Then again, if it was a crime then he would just have to get locked up. Ram would risk anything and everything for mornings like this.

Sofia practically hissed as her vaginal muscles tightened. The next thing she knew, her moans skipped up the musical scale until she hit a high C. When the beginnings of her first morning orgasm stirred in her belly, everything started to tremble like she was a human earthquake.

"Are you about to come?" Ram asked, locking his hands down on her hips.

Sofia tried to answer, but all she could manage was a few more moans.

Ram was glad to hear it. He was close, too, and he didn't want to blast off before she did. A few more rolls of her hips and Sofia cried in ecstasy. Ram followed shortly after, growling with pleasure upon the intensity of his release.

Spent, Ram fell back onto the bed's pillows like a chopped tree. Sofia chuckled and struggled to get her feet from beneath him. He didn't help because he couldn't. She had sapped every drop of energy out of him, but he was happy and satisfied. "I could die a happy man right now."

Sofia chuckled while she still lazily rolled her hips. "What are you doing to me?"

Ram hitched up one side of his face while he slid his hands all around her beautiful brown behind. "If you're trying to get a brother to fall in love with you then you can quit. That happened a long time ago."

Sofia pushed herself up and spread her legs out until she had the perfect cheerleader split over his still hard erection. "Then maybe I just want to make sure that you stay that way."

"You weren't playing when you said that you had tricks." He sat back up and wrapped an arm around her waist while he scooted over to the edge of the bed and then stood up with their bodies still joined.

"What are you about to do?" Sofia asked, laughing.

"You'll see," he chuckled. "Plant your feet on the floor."

She did as she was told while he turned so that she leaned over the bed. From there he took hold of her arms held them up from behind her like they were a pair of reins and then started thrusting his hips. Each time he would slap against her lovely bottom, she would bounce forward but his tight hold on her arms prevented her from falling onto the bed and ensured her springing back for another hard thrust.

"Ohh." Sofia's mouth sagged open while a new wave of ecstasy washed over her. She dropped her head and then watched as her full breasts bounced and jiggled while the friction from their bodies soon had her weak in the knees. More importantly, her muscles started to tighten, and caused Ramell to moan her name.

"Kiss me," he said, holding still long enough to release her hands so she could erect her top half and turn her face over her left shoulder to receive his hungry kiss. While their mouths caressed and their tongues dueled,

Ram eased a hand down the front of her body where his fingers slithered through her dewy curls. Feeling her quiver and swallowing her moans, Ram rotated his hips and gently massaged her core.

In need of oxygen, Sofia broke their kiss to suck in deep gulps of air. Ram's lips found a new home against the curve of her neck. Before she knew it, she was popping off orgasms back-to-back, followed again by Ram's release. When they finally fell onto the bed, they were laughing and gasping for air. Neither of them were sure who went to sleep first, but when they woke again, Ram joked, "We're really late for work."

"Work?" Sofia sprung up. "Oh, my God, what time is it?"

"Huh, what?" Before he could process what was happening, Sofia had bolted out of bed and slammed the door to the bathroom and he could hear her turning on the shower. "Wait. Come back." He rolled out of bed, peeked at his watch and went after her.

In the bathroom, he opened the glass stall and walked inside. "Here, let me help you," he offered, reaching for the soap.

"Only if you're really going to help and not try to distract me. I need to get to the office."

"Why?" he laughed. "It's already past noon. We might as well go ahead and take the day off."

Sofia stopped scrubbing beneath her breasts to stare at him as if he'd lost all his marbles. "Take the day off?"

Ramell hiked up a brow. "What? You have taken a day off before, haven't you?"

"I've taken vacation before, yes, but it's been a while."

Now it was his turn to lower the soap and stare at her

as if she'd just sprouted a second head. "You've never played hooky from work before?"

"And why would I want to do that?"

"Because it's fun?" He shrugged his mountainous shoulders.

She shook her head and rolled her eyes. "No. I actually take my work seriously."

"Well, not today," he said, turning her around and soaping down her back. "Today you and me are going to play hooky."

"What? Are you kidding me? I probably have like…a million emails and phone messages by now."

"They can wait until tomorrow," Ram said. "And don't bother to argue with me. I'm not going to take no for an answer."

She did argue, but in the end he won.

After their shower, they returned to Sofia's penthouse so she could change clothes. "How casual are we talking about?" Sofia asked.

Ramell followed her into her bedroom. Upon seeing the queen-size bed, he instantly dove on top of it. "You know before you move out we're going to have to test the springs on this one."

She turned and settled her hands on her hips. "And why is that?"

"Because it's a bed. Do we really need another reason?"

"You're insatiable."

"And that's a bad thing?"

Sofia held her hand up and gave him the brick wall. "I'm ignoring you."

Ramell laughed. "Whatever. Just grab some jeans and a shirt. Nothing fancy."

"Uh-huh. You still haven't told me where we're going," Sofia said, pulling out a pair of Chip and Pepper jeans. "I think I have the right to know where you're dragging me off to."

"Dragging? I offer you a day of fun and leisure and you call that dragging you?"

"Tell me where we're going and let me be the judge of whether it's going to be fun and leisure."

"No." He climbed off of the bed. "You'll say no so you can run back to your precious little office where you can listen to actors and directors whine, or so that you can fleece more money out of studio executives."

"What can I say? Work is my spice of life."

Ramell shook his head as he moved over to his wife and pulled her into his arms. "Not anymore. Now I'm the *new* spice in your life." He leaned forward and nibbled on her ear. "Just like you're the new spice in mine."

Sofia wanted to pretend that his warm breath against her skin wasn't affecting her, but her moans slipped out before she had the chance to stop it.

"You know we can try that bed out now instead of later."

"I knew it. You don't really have anything planned for today."

"We just decided to play hooky an hour ago—and yes, I know where I'm taking you."

"Then tell me."

Ramell shook his head and then smacked her on the behind. "Change your clothes. I'll wait for you in the living room. If I see naked skin then we'll never get out of here."

"Oh, really?" Sofia slid the straps of her dress off of her shoulders.

Ramell quickly slammed his eyes shut and then turned away to feel his way out of the room. "I will not be tempted," he said as he made his way out. "Just hurry up so we can go."

Sofia laughed as she watched him being silly. Again, it felt good to just be able to laugh and play the way they used to do. All those wasted years of holding that damn grudge while she and Ramell could've… She stopped. Could've what?

Her gaze fell to the small wedding band on her left hand and she knew the answer to that. How many times had Ramell proposed when they were children? How many times had she wanted to say yes, but played hard to get because that was what her mother had coached her to do?

Then, just as quickly as it came, Sofia dismissed the thought. They were just children. There was no way of knowing whether their puppy love would have survived elementary school, let alone junior high and high school. The odds of that happening had to be something like a million to one. Or a gazillion to one, she corrected herself. She laughed softly and then went back into her closet for a pair of Nikes.

When she emerged from her bedroom, she found Ramell in the kitchen rinsing off some strawberries. "Hmm. You know a man in the kitchen is like an aphrodisiac to a woman."

"What the hell do you think I'm in here for?" He held up a strawberry and then watched her hungrily as she took her sweet time opening her mouth and sliding it in tip first.

"You're a damn tease is what you are," Ram said, plopping the red fruit into her mouth and stepping back. "But I'm onto you. Are you ready to go?"

Sofia reached over to the fruit bowl and picked up a banana. "I'm dressed, if that's what you mean." She took her time peeling the fruit.

Ram watched, completely fascinated, as she then tilted the banana toward her mouth. This time her tongue performed a little dance that involved licking and swirling her tongue around the tip. By the time she took a healthy bite, he was rock hard and was seconds away from grabbing her and spreading her out on the counter for a different kind of meal.

Instead, he pushed the fruit aside, took her by the hand and led her toward the front door.

Sofia laughed. "Is there a problem?"

"Yeah. You play too much."

"I thought there was no such thing as playing too much?" Sofia said with a wink, tossing his words back at him.

"Oh, wait, wait." She stopped and started back toward the bedroom.

Ramell tossed up his hands. "What is it now?"

"My cell phone. I need to grab my cell phone off the charger."

"Oh, no." He rushed after her and grabbed her hand again. "No cell phones. No computers. No gadgets of any kind."

"But—"

"And no buts. We're playing hooky, remember?" He started dragging her toward the door. "Hooky means no work."

"I don't know if I like hooky," she said, poking out her bottom lip.

Ramell opened the front door and smiled. "You say that now, but trust me, you're going to forget all about that phone soon enough."

Chapter 15

They played hooky at Venice Beach. Blue ocean and an azure sky, it was like most of California—beautiful year-round and always crowded. There were a ton of things to do. There were several vendors selling crafts, drawings and every type of junk food one could imagine. But it was the street performers that really caught their attention and entertained them.

At the Sidewalk Café, Ram and Sofia grabbed a light lunch and had fun checking out the eclectic crowd. Clearly mohawks were making a comeback. As well as spandex.

"Now you know I want to get you on some skates," Ram said, munching on some hot wings.

"Oh, no," Sofia started shaking her head. "That's not going to happen."

"Oh, *yes,*" he contradicted. "You owe me."

"Come again?"

"Yeah. Just when we got old enough to go hang at the skating rink without chaperones, you dumped me. Remember that?"

"This wouldn't happen to be the same skating rink you took Connie Woods to, would it?"

Ramell's eyebrows raised in surprise. "Oh, so you knew about that, did you?"

"Of course I knew about it." She stiffened and straightened her shoulders. "I also heard that you and Connie were caught necking in the back of the rink next to the boy's bathroom."

He choked.

"Uh-huh. You didn't think I knew about that, too, did you?"

"More like I didn't think you cared," he challenged, leaning back in his chair and smiling at her. "Now I just need to figure out if you're just giving me grief or if you're actually jealous."

"Now why would I be jealous of that ten-year-old tramp? For all I know she's probably pulling tricks down on Hollywood Boulevard nowadays."

"She's not pulling tricks. She's a Broadway actress."

Her head jerked toward him. "And how do you know that?"

"She's an A.F.I. client…which I guess now makes her a Limelight client."

Sofia worked her jaw while she reached for her lemonade. "I never knew that. Does she work under her real name?"

Ram laughed. "What? You think I'd tell you now? Look at you."

"What?"

"My lips are zipped. You're not going to go back into the office and drop her from the company." He laughed.

She shrugged. "I don't know what you're talking about. I was just going to check and see how she was doing…see if she's a good fit for the company."

"Chill out, Sofia. It was just a kiss—a peck, really."

"Uh-huh."

"Actually," he said leaning forward. "I kissed her hoping that the news would get back to you." He reached across the table and picked up her hand.

"Yeah. Likely story," she said, pulling away playfully, but he held firm.

"I have no reason to lie," Ram said. "I had to do something. You refused to talk to me—even at your parents' funeral."

Sofia dropped her gaze and just stared at their connected hands.

"I'm sorry about that," Ram said, quickly wishing he hadn't brought up Sofia's parents.

A silence drifted between them and Sofia could tell that he wanted to pursue his line of questioning and for a few seconds her stomach looped into knots. The last thing that she wanted to do was to ruin their playful mood to start talking about what happened back then. Plus, she still felt uncomfortable at the possibility of having to tell Ramell about his father and her mother—especially since his parents were still married.

"Anyway…Connie and I are just good friends," Ramell said, returning to the subject at hand.

She sensed that he changed the subject for her. Sofia glanced up and met his intense gaze. He was clearly trying to read her like a book. "Don't."

"Don't what?"

"Don't stare. It makes me uncomfortable."

"Then what do you propose I do when I want to let you know that I'm sitting here remembering some of those tricks you showed me this morning?" Ram said, attempting to steer the conversation in yet another direction.

She blushed.

"Do you have any more?" he asked.

It was her turn to lean back and level him with a sultry look. "Maybe."

"Well, then, before we get to that, first I think we need to fill in a few blanks."

So much for thinking that she had dodged a bullet. "What sort of blanks?"

"Well, I know a lot about the ten-year-old you, and I definitely know a lot about the—"

"Watch it."

"The *mature businesswoman* side of you, but there a few questions I should know…seeing that we're now man and wife."

"All right. Shoot."

"Okay." He set his beer back down. "Is yellow still your favorite color?"

"It's one of my favorites. I tend to like coral or peach a little bit more nowadays. How about you? Is blue still your favorite color?"

"Guilty. Favorite song?"

"'Purple Rain.' You?"

"I'm all over the map on that. But if pressed I'm really feeling that joint Charlene and Akil performed at our Pre-Award party."

"'The Journey,'" Sofia said, nodding. "Yeah. I have a feeling that's going to be a big hit for them."

They continued through the standard line of questioning until they eventually reached some stickier topics.

"What was the longest relationship you've ever been in?" Ramell asked.

Sofia shrugged.

"C'mon. You can tell me," he pressed.

"John Davis. We dated when I went to Cambridge.

When we were together, I was too busy to notice that he was a complete jerk. Once I graduated and we spent, like, a whole week together, I noticed."

Ram chuckled.

"What about you?" she asked.

"That's easy. I've been in love with one woman my entire life."

Sofia blushed again. "I'm flattered. But we haven't been in a relationship that entire time so come out with it. Who was it and how long?"

He rolled his eyes back and thought about it for a second. "I guess that brings me back to Connie."

"You dated Connie?" she asked incredibly. "I thought you said that it was just a kiss."

"It was just a kiss that night," Ram clarified. "We dated in college for about three months."

"Three months is your longest relationship?"

"Like I said, I've been in love with one woman my entire life. No one else has ever come close, so…"

"So you've had a lifetime of booty calls and one-night stands?"

"Something like that." He started shifting in his chair. "Hey. Don't hate on me because you didn't come around soon enough."

"Look. You're the one that chose this line of questioning."

"Good point. So let's get off this subject before I have to look this John Davis dude up and put him out of his misery."

"Right. And you know Ms. Connie is going to be looking for another agency to represent her when I get back to the office, right?"

Ramell threw back his head and laughed. "Whatever. Come on. We're going skating."

"Uh, wait. I don't know about this," Sofia protested, but Ramell tossed money down on the table and then grabbed her by the hand. Next thing Sofia knew they were renting skates, helmets, knee and elbow pads.

"I'm going to look ridiculous in all of this."

"You're going to look safe," Ram said.

"Then how come you're not wearing all this stuff. I look like a tall three-year-old."

"Because I know what I'm doing. You haven't been on skates in years."

"More like decades," Sofia clarified.

"Then there you go." He stood up and turned to help her.

Sofia was up for a full minute and then her long legs tried to roll in two different directions. She screamed and then made a desperate lunge for Ramell. He grabbed her and tried to hold her up, but then he toppled over along with her. When they hit the concrete they immediately burst into laughter like pain was funny.

"Well, at least you got busting your butt out of the way pretty quickly." Ram laughed and then helped her back up. "Are you all right?"

Sofia was still laughing so hard that she was crying. "Yeah, I'm fine. I can do this," she affirmed, and then took a deep breath.

"Are you sure?" he asked, helping to wipe away a few tears.

She shook her head no, but said, "Yes."

Thirty minutes later, while she was still a trembling mess on wheels, Ram tried to convince her that she was ready for him to remove his hands.

"No. Don't let go," she begged.

"You're doing fine," he said.

"Wait! Don't!" She started to tremble harder. "Don't do it, Ram," she begged. "I swear I'll never forgive you."

"Is that a fact?" he asked.

"Yes! I'm not trying to break my neck out here."

"You're not going to break your neck."

"How do you know?"

"Because you're already skating by yourself," he informed her, rolling out to her side so that she could see that she was now skating on her own.

Sofia's eyes nearly bugged out as she glanced down. "I'm skating!"

"I know! Look at you."

Her head jerked toward him as she proclaimed again, "I'm skating by myself!"

"I know!"

"I'm skating by myself," she announced to everyone on the boardwalk.

A few people stared at her but some of them clapped. A big smile exploded across Ram's face at seeing her so happy. Soon they were skating and eating candied apples like a couple of kids. The day breezed by to the point that Sofia was sad to see the sun set. But with Ramell standing next to her and staring at her that sadness was replaced by desire.

"You ready to go home?" he asked.

Home. They had a home together. The whole thing was just so strange to her. It was blowing her mind and stealing her heart at the same time.

"Yeah. Let's go."

Sade's "Soldier of Love" played softly from the speakers that Ramell had set up next to their new bed. After taking a long shower together to wash the day's dirt and grime away, the newlyweds stood in the center of the room, lips locked and smelling like Ivory soap and baby oil. The more their tongues tasted the hungrier they became.

Ramell moaned while his hands made light circles along Sofia's lower back. His touch was so feathery soft that it caused goosebumps to rise across her body. Her nipples hardened and ached, but they were nothing compared to the iron pipe that was pressing against her brown, wet lips.

Unable to resist, Sofia's slender fingers drifted down between their bodies. She took hold of his oiled rod and started stroking him. Though their mouths were still connected, she felt him gasp. She smiled against his lips. She might not be able to win an argument with him, but she sure as hell held power over him when their clothes came off.

Wielding some of that power, Sofia pulled their lips apart and nibbled her way across his strong jawline until she reached his right ear to whisper, "I want to taste you." She blew a cool stream of air against his lower earlobe. He shivered and then stretched a couple of more inches in her hand. "Oooh. That's a good boy." Slowly her knees dipped until they kissed the floor.

With her head at waist level, Sofia continued to rotate and stroke Ram's thick erection. Just gazing at its smooth length and fat mushroom head made her mouth water. Putting on a timid act, she leaned forward and just swirled her tongue around the tip like it was a piece of candy.

Ramell hissed and stepped forward, hoping that she would open her mouth wide. She didn't accommodate him. Instead, she ran her tongue along the side and then rolled under and slid back up toward the tip. "You're trying to kill me," he panted.

"Now why would I want to do that?"

"I don't know. You must hate me or you wouldn't torture me like this."

"Torture?" Her wonderful tongue moved to the other side. This time inching along at a snail's pace. "I don't know what you're talking about." She glided over a small vein near the top and felt Ram jump reflexively. Sofia smiled and then did it again. Same reaction.

Convinced that she'd found a small sensitive spot, she concentrated on that area, licking and sucking until Ramell's large hands gently grabbed fistfuls of her hair. Showing no remorse, Sofia stretched her mouth over the head, but made sure her tongue massaged the hell out of that vein.

Ram rolled up onto his toes. Not wanting to come yet, he summoned superhuman strength to jump back and spring himself free from her divine mouth. "You know I'm going to pay you back for that, don't you?"

Sofia put her innocent face on as she blinked up at him. "What did I do?"

"That's not going to work." He took her by her elbows and pulled her up from the floor and before she could process what he was about to do, he lifted one of her legs and pressed it high against his chest so that she had to balance her weight on one leg and lean against him. Ram reached down and squeezed his fat head in between her melting brown sugar and hissed slowly.

Like before, Sofia's mouth sagged open at his initial entry. He was thick, heavy and felt so damn good that a few tears streaked down the corners of her eyes.

With one hand on her stretched leg and the other

one on her hip, Ramell started moving. "How does that feel, baby?"

Sofia couldn't speak and didn't bother to try. She was too busy enjoying all the feelings that he was working out of her body. She was on a fast train to ecstasy and he was definitely driving.

"Uh-huh. I have you now, don't I, baby?" His hips stopped stroking and started pounding. "You're not the only one with power in this bedroom, sweetheart." To prove his point, Ram stopped long enough to get a good hold so he could go ahead and lift her completely off the floor and then just bounce her body on top of his length.

It was too much. Sofia could feel her orgasm brewing. When it finally exploded, she threw back her head and released a strangled cry. Ram was right behind her, but with everything rushing to one area, his knees weakened. Finally, his orgasm hit him like a truck and his legs went out from underneath him.

They tumbled to the floor with his body absorbing most of the impact. After the initial shock wore off, they laughed. Like when they fell during skating earlier, once they got started, it was hard to stop.

"I love you so much," Ram said, pulling her close and planting a kiss against the top of her head.

Sofia smiled in the dark, but she was still waiting for that other shoe to drop.

Chapter 16

The next week floated by like a dream. When Sofia and Ram weren't making love, they were trying to patch together plans for their future. When Sofia informed her family about Ramell buying her parents' old home, everyone expressed their joy and excitement for having the house back in the family, especially Rachel. Sofia became obsessed about redecorating and Ram kept dropping hints about them having a real honeymoon.

So caught up with creating their new life together, Sofia started spending less and less time in the office. It didn't mean that she was off her game; she still made and closed some great deals for her clients, but she started spending less time on her BlackBerry and Ram declared their bedroom a no-electronics zone, so the iPad and the laptops had to stay in her new home office.

If there was one thing that was starting to cause Sofia some anxiety it was the wedding reception her aunt Lily was planning. It wasn't the list of friends and colleagues that her family invited—it was the fact that Emmett Jordan was going to be there.

Ramell picked up on her apprehension but Sofia struggled with confessing about its source. After all, Emmett was Ram's father and it was clear that the two of them were close. Sofia told herself that she just needed to suck it up. It was just going to be one evening. Surely, she could handle that. If she could glue on fake smiles for Hollywood pow-wow meetings and parties, she could grin and bear being around that lying, backstabbing jerk.

Sofia didn't know how her aunt pulled it off on such short notice, but their wedding reception was booked at the Beverly Wilshire in the heart of Beverly Hills. Both Ramell and Sofia hoped for just a small event with their closest friends and family. Somehow that equaled over a hundred people in her aunt's mind.

Sofia selected a lavender Stella McCartney gown that was all classic chic and timeless on her willowy frame. Her long hair hung in soft, structured waves over her bronze shoulders. When her small team of stylists finished getting her ready and she descended the staircase, Ramell literally stood at the bottom with his mouth hanging open. Everyone chuckled at his reaction while Sofia simply blushed.

An hour later when they strolled arm and arm into the Beverly Wilshire, the beautiful couple was greeted with an enthusiastic round of applause before being surrounded and congratulated on their marriage. It was at that moment that it truly sunk in for Sofia that she was indeed a married woman. The idea was both scary and thrilling at the same time.

Uncle Jacob and Aunt Lily swept their way over and showered Ram and Sofia with hugs and kisses.

"I'm just so happy for the two of you," Lily said, blotting away her tears before they had a chance to ruin her makeup. "You're both just so beautiful together. I know in my heart of hearts that you two were destined to be together."

Ramell's arm draped around Sofia's slim waist and then pulled her closer. "That's what I keep telling her." He smiled at her and couldn't resist leaning in for a quick kiss.

A few minutes later, Rachel and her fiancé, Ethan Chambers, approached. With their own wedding a week away, the happy couple glowed with love.

"It looks like we're going to be brothers soon," Ethan said to Ramell, thrusting out his hand.

"I'm looking forward to it," Ramell said, pumping his hand. "But I'm also expecting you to take good care of Rachel here. If not, I would hate to have to hunt you down."

"That would make two of us," Uncle Jacob cut in.

Ethan pulled at his collar to let them know that he could feel the invisible noose they were threatening him with. "I don't think that you guys have anything to worry about." He pulled Rachel close and captured her with a kiss.

Ramell frowned and then glanced over at Sofia. "I think we can do better than that, don't you?"

Sofia smiled. "I don't know. Do you think?"

Ramell straightened his arm and then in dramatic form grabbed Sofia, dipped her back so that she kicked one foot up and then laid a kiss on her that was reminiscent of the old black-and-white classic movies. When he finally lifted her back up, the entire room erupted into applause.

Ethan and Rachel laughed at their antics.

"Since this is your reception, I'm going to let you win this round," Ethan joked.

Ramell winked. "Smart man."

Emmett Jordan's voice boomed as he approached. "Hello, son!"

Instantly, Sofia stiffened. Her gaze shifted to Rachel who, with one glance, telepathed silent support.

"So you finally did it!" he laughed, whacking his son on the back. "You finally married her. I have to admit I was beginning to have my doubts. Then again, women can't resist the Jordan charm."

Ramell laughed as he returned his father's hug. "I'm glad you could make it, Pop."

"I wouldn't have missed it for the world. Well, I did miss the wedding," he reminded him.

"Sorry about that, Pop." Ram tightened his hold around Sofia's waist. "It was sort of a spontaneous thing."

"Is that right?" Emmett's gaze finally drifted over to his new daughter-in-law. "My God. You look so much like your mother," he said, shaking his head.

Sofia was already on a low simmer and her smile was starting to wilt.

"How about a hug?" he asked, stretching his arm wide.

She'd rather gouge her own eyes out with a pitchfork, but it was time for the big Hollywood agent to put the acting chops she'd learned to work. After making Emmett wait for a couple of awkward seconds, she finally stepped into his embrace. However, she didn't allow for his arms to stay around her for long as she quickly removed herself from his embrace. She caught Ramell's frown from the corner of her eyes, but she refused to look at him. Instead, she forced her lips to curl back up so that she could ask to be excused.

"I just need to dip into the ladies' room for a second," Sofia said, stepping away from Ramell's side.

"I'll come with you," Rachel offered. She gave her fiancé a brief kiss and then peeled herself out of his arms.

The two sisters rushed from the small circle just shy of leaving skid marks. Seeing their speed most of their guests started parting like the Red Sea to avoid being run over. Sofia couldn't get away fast enough and could barely manage to fill her collapsing lungs with much needed oxygen as she reached the ladies' room.

"Are you all right?" Rachel asked.

"I will be," Sofia said, pulling in several more deep breaths. "I swear I can't stand that man!"

"I know," Rachel said, rubbing her back in hopes of calming her down. "It's just for one evening. You can do this."

"And after tonight?" Sofia challenged. "What if he's around all the time? What if Ram invites him over to dinner once or twice a week? What if they get together and hang out in the media room for football and basketball games?" Heat rushed up her chest and neck as she worked herself up into a frenzy. When she started feeling lightheaded and woozy, she grabbed a hold of the vanity to support herself.

"Calm down, Sofia. Calm down," Rachel urged. "Deep breaths. Take deep breaths."

After feeling the tips of her ears burning, Sofia took her sister's suggestion and started taking in deep breaths and expelling them slowly.

"That's it. Calm down," Rachel coached. "You can do it."

Bit by bit, Sofia's face cooled as she calmed down.

Rachel smiled. "There you go. Do you feel better?"

Sofia nodded and then hugged her sister. "Yes. Thank you. I really appreciate it."

"You know I'm always here for you." Her sister smiled. "But as far as dealing with your new father-in-law, I think you're just going to have to talk to Ramell and tell him how you feel about Emmett."

"Yeah. I should really tell my new husband that I can't stand his father. That should go over well."

"There's something to be said for honesty. You can't go the rest of your lives together trying to avoid the man. Ram is going to understand—he might even be able to help you two work this thing out."

Sofia stiffened. "I do not want to work anything out with that man."

Rachel tossed her hands up. "I understand. But you're going to have to talk to Ramell about the situation regardless. There's no getting around that."

She hesitated, but after her sister cocked her head and stretched her eyebrows up at her, Sofia had to admit that she was right. "I'll do it tonight."

"Good," Rachel said, giving her another hug. "Now are you ready to go back out there?"

She sucked in one more deep breath and then nodded.

"All right. Let's go get them, tiger." Rachel draped her arm around her older sister's shoulders and then led her out of the ladies' room.

They hadn't taken more than a couple of steps outside the door before Emmett Jordan cornered them.

"Sofia, do you think that I can talk to you for a few minutes?"

Sofia dropped all pretense of a smile. "I don't think that now is a good time," she said coldly. But when she attempted to step around him, he blocked her and Rachel's path.

"It will only take a minute."

"Then call my office and make an appointment."

Emmett shook his head. "My God. You really do hate me," he said, frowning and shaking his head. "I think I've always suspected it since you had walked in on—"

"I don't want to talk about this right now!" Sofia yelled as she tried to move around him again, only for Emmett to pull the same stunt and block off her exit.

"Wait!"

"Will you stop doing that?" Sofia snapped and stomped her foot.

When a few heads swiveled in their direction, Rachel leaned over and whispered, "Take a deep breath. It's going to be all right."

Sofia followed her sister's instructions. "Look, Emmett. This isn't the time or the place for this."

"I just want to clear the air. I think that there's a huge misunderstanding that's gone on for far too long. And now that…well, we're family…"

Sofia stiffened again. Why couldn't this man get it through his head that she didn't want to talk to him?

"…and family is important to me…" he continued as he stepped into her personal space.

Alarm bells rang in her head as she quickly jumped back and held up her hands like stop signs. "Emmett, we're not about to have this conversation."

Rachel stepped forward. "Mr. Jordan, maybe this isn't such a good time."

"Is there a problem over here?" Ramell asked, threading his way into the circle.

"There's no problem," Sofia lied.

"I think there's a big problem," Emmett contradicted. Ram frowned.

"What's going on?" Uncle Jacob and Aunt Lily now joined the loop.

Sofia's blood pressure shot up as she placed her slim fingers against her temples.

"I was just trying to talk to Sofia about a few things," Emmett pressed.

"And I said that I didn't want to talk right now," Sofia hissed. "I don't want to talk to you *ever.* Period. End of story."

"Sofia," Ram said, stunned. "What's gotten into you, sweetheart?" He moved closer to her and wrapped his arm back around her for support.

"Nothing has gotten into me. Will you just drop it?" She tried to pull away, but he wouldn't have it. "Will you let me go? Stop trying to control me!"

"What?" Ramell's arm fell away from her waist.

"Maybe we just need to go into another room real quick so that we can talk," Uncle Jacob suggested. "Clearly, we do need to clear the air about a few things."

What had gotten into everyone? Didn't they just hear her say that she didn't want to talk to this man?

"I don't know," Rachel hedged. "Sofia is getting pretty upset. Maybe we should do this another time."

"Well, I, for one, want to know what the hell is going on," Ram said, his gaze still searching his wife's face for the harsh rebuke that she'd just lashed out on him.

Sofia wanted to apologize, but at the same time she felt as if she was being cornered. And now that her family was all looking like she was the freak in a freak show, she relented so that she could just get this whole thing over with. "Fine." She tossed up her hands. "Five minutes."

Emmett had the audacity to smile now that he'd gotten his way.

"Let's just go into this room over here," Uncle Jacob said, pointing off to the side.

Unbelievably, in the middle of their own wedding reception, the family smiled and excused themselves to their few friends and family so that they could dip into a room off from the grand room.

Ram took a chance and swung his arm back around her waist. She allowed it, but she was still irritated. This was the very thing that she had hoped to avoid for years, now it was worse than she had ever imagined it. Instead of privately telling Ram her issues about his father, she now how to air her grievances in front of her whole family. Once they were all piled into the other room, Uncle Jacob closed the door.

"First of all," Jacob began, turning toward Sofia, "I'm sorry that we have to do this this evening, but clearly it's time that we deal with a few things, a few things that… your aunt and I had hoped to avoid." He reached over for his wife's hand.

Sofia folded her arms. "My problem isn't with you or Aunt Lily. This is about Emmett and him alone," she stressed. "It's about how *he* stabbed my father in the back. It's about *him* sneaking around with my mother!"

"What?" Ram thundered, turning toward his father.

Emmett's hands came up as he stepped back. "That is not true!"

"Yes, it is," Sofia contradicted him. "I was there, remember?"

"What? You saw them together or something?" Ram asked.

"No." Sofia shook her head. "I was there that day my father called him out on it." Her gaze swung back to Emmett. "You remember that?"

Emmett lowered his hands as sadness crept over his face. "Of course I remember that day. But you got it wrong, Sofia. Just like your father got it wrong. And in the end he didn't believe any of that nonsense. He was just lashing out."

"No." Sofia shook her head. "He called you out for the lying backstabber that you are!"

"Sofia," Aunt Lily gasped.

"It's true, Aunt Lily. Come on. You were there, too."

Ram's head swiveled to his father. "Dad, is it true?"

"No," Emmett said simply.

Uncle Jacob stepped forward. "He's telling the truth, Sofia. You were too young at the time to understand what was going on. For a long time I thought that you'd forgotten about that day. Heck, I have sometimes forgotten that you had walked in there that day. Given that the accident was just a couple of days later, we—your aunt and I—just concentrated on being there for you and your sister. And part of being there for you was also trying to shield something from both of you and the crazy media attention we generated at the time. I knew that you were angry, but I didn't understand the depth of this until the A.F.I. merger."

Sofia tried to keep up with the conversation, but none of it was making any sense yet.

Jacob drew a deep breath. "What you walked in on that day…was an intervention."

"A what?" Sofia frowned.

"An intervention for your father," he said, moving closer. "There's no easy way to say this, girls, but your father had a drinking problem."

Sofia started shaking her head. This was all a big lie.

"We had all gathered there that day to confront him.

At first I didn't think anything of it. And I was his twin. I always thought that I knew everything about him. We've always had such a strong connection. You know that. We were best friends our entire lives. People used to label him the fun one and I was the serious one of the two. Then one day the cracks started to show and then there started to be too many to hide. He started losing money and the business we had poured all our blood, sweat and tears into was threatened. He was gambling, taking out loans I didn't know about. The next thing I knew we were surrounded by creditors.

"Your mother, Lily, tried several times to convince him to go to AA, but your father wouldn't hear of it. He didn't think that he had a problem. When it was clear to all of us, except to John, that Limelight was teetering on the edge of bankruptcy, *I* approached Emmett about a possible merger. When John found out he became convinced that Emmett was trying to steal the company from him. Unfortunately, he found out the same evening that we had staged the intervention. And he came in drunk and belligerent. He said a whole lot of stuff that he didn't mean."

Sofia kept shaking her head. "My father wasn't a drunk. How can you say that?"

Aunt Lily stepped forward. "Sofia, I know all of this is a big shock, but what you heard—"

"What I heard was not the truth!" She pushed back out of Ram's arms. "I remember my father and he was not a drunk. He was loving and caring—"

"Yes," Uncle Jacob said. "He was all those things— but he had a problem." He drew a deep breath. "Which is why he finally agreed to go to rehab…in Colorado."

Both Sofia and Rachel gasped.

Jacob nodded. "*That* was where he and your mother were going when their plane crashed. He was going to get help."

Aunt Lily wiped tears from her eyes. "There hasn't been a day that any of us hasn't wrestled with the cruel irony that the only reason that they were even on that plane was to try to save his life. I know how much you love and cherish the memory of your father, Sofia. That had a lot to do with our decision to not tell you about his problem. And it isn't fair to Emmett for you to believe those wild accusations your father tossed at him. They weren't true and he doesn't deserve it."

"No." Sofia continued shaking her head. "It's not true. It's not. My father was a good man. He was a hard worker and…"

"Yes, yes and yes," Lily said. "But he was still just a man. A man that needed help."

Tears started pouring down Sofia's face and she couldn't stop shaking her head. "Why would you? How could you?" She placed a hand over her mouth.

"Baby." Ram reached for her but she jumped out of his grasp.

"Don't touch me," she snapped and then tried to suck in a deep breath. Instead she started hyperventilating. "Don't ever touch me." Her gaze zoomed back to her aunt and uncle and she wanted to lash out at them, too, but couldn't get the mean words off her tongue.

Rachel rushed to her side. "Sofia, honey. You're turning red. Try to calm down."

"How can I calm down when they're saying…" She shook her head. "I don't believe it. I refuse to believe it. My father was not a drunk. He was a good man and I'm not about to just stand here while you all drag his name and his memory through the mud! I won't! I—" Just then the room started spinning and there didn't seem to be enough oxygen for Sofia to breathe.

Ram rushed forward to his wife just as she started to sink toward the floor. "Sofia!"

Chapter 17

Ramell didn't wait for the paramedics to be called. Once Sofia collapsed, he spent a full minute trying to wake her up. When she wouldn't wake he swept her into his arms and raced out of the room. *"Please get out of the way."*

A collective gasp rose above the glittering Hollywood elite while they quickly jumped out of the way. The Wellesleys and Ethan Chambers all raced right behind him as Ram jetted out of the Wilshire. Less than twenty minutes later, they all piled into Cedars-Sinai Hospital Emergency Room. Upon seeing an unconscious woman draped in his arms, doctors and nurses rushed toward him and then pried her out of his arms.

"What happened?" A young man, dressed in a pair of blue scrubs, who looked like he was barely old enough to have a driver's license, started checking Sofia over.

"I'm not quite sure. She just fainted," Ram said and then a memory flashed. "It might have something to do with her blood pressure. I know that she's taking something for it."

The young man nodded, placed her on a rolling gurney and then pushed Sofia's eyelids open.

"Is she going to be all right?" Ram asked, hovering over the doctor's shoulders.

"She's going to be fine, sir," the man said, plugging his ears with his stethoscope and then checking Sofia's heartbeat.

Everyone was rushing around at warp speed, but Ram made sure that he stayed on top of everything that was going on. It was difficult because every time he looked down at Sofia lying on the gurney, she looked so small and vulnerable that it was causing a tight constriction in his chest and his eyes to feel as if someone had poured battery acid in them. He didn't like seeing his wife like this and he was angry about his part in getting her so upset. She had made it very clear that she didn't want to talk to his father and they had all insisted that they try to clear the air about her father's past.

It was a lot of startling information about a man she had spent her entire life idolizing. Ramell had known about Limelight's near bankruptcy once upon a time, but his father certainly never told him that it was because John Wellesley had a gambling and alcohol problem. Maybe because his father always knew about his feelings toward Sofia and possibly feared he would tell her about it. Apparently they had all agreed to bury John's demons in order to protect his children.

The media coverage was intense when John and Vivian passed, but the paparazzi back then was a different animal and not every rock was overturned on their personal life. If it had been, surely John's problems would have been splashed everywhere. Instead the coverage just focused on the tragedy and the fate of the children. Now he wished he would've known. Knowing now that she had walked into that intense intervention and misunderstood all that she heard, it made sense why she fought their companies' merger as hard as she did.

Now he finally understood why she had ended their friendship. All those years he thought it was because of something he had done.

Twenty minutes later, Sofia was wheeled into a private room and their entire clan followed closed behind. Not long after that, Sofia moaned and her eyelashes started fluttering.

"She's waking up," Lily said, clutching her left hand.

Ram held her right one. When Sofia opened her beautiful brown eyes he was finally able to pull in his first full breath and offer up a prayer of gratitude. He lifted her hand and brushed a kiss against the back of it before smiling and speaking softly, "Hey, baby. You gave us quite a scare. How are you feeling?"

Their eyes locked and a string of pear-shaped tears slid down the side of her face. But instead of answering, she pulled her hand free from his and then turned away from him.

His smile melted as confusion and disbelief crashed in on his hopeful expression.

Lily swept Sofia's hair from her face while Rachel and Jacob crowded around the bed. "The doctor says that you're going to be all right," Lily informed her. "Your blood pressure was elevated pretty high and…well, baby. We're so sorry. We didn't mean to upset you so badly. We just—"

"I don't want to talk about it," Sofia croaked, but then started coughing.

Ram turned toward the small table next to the bed and quickly poured her a small plastic cup of water and then offered it to her.

Still coughing, she hesitated for a moment, but then gave in and accepted it, along with his help, when he pressed it up against her lips. She started off with small sips, but then ended up gulping it down. He poured her another cup, but she waved it away.

"Feeling any better?" Rachel asked.

Sofia nodded, but there were still tears rolling down her face. After a minute, she spoke. "I appreciate you all being here, but I need some time alone."

Everyone opened their mouths to say something, but she cut them off cold. "Please."

Their gazes shifted among themselves, but this time they were determined to respect her wishes. "All right," Ram said. "We can all just step outside, if you like."

She shook her head. "No. You don't understand. I don't want you all to wait outside. I need time…without any hovering."

Her words were like steel bullets through his heart. "Sofia, I think we need to talk."

She swallowed, but still refused to look at him. "And we will. Just not right now."

No one moved.

"Please," she begged again. She closed her eyes but her tears soaked through her long lashes.

Struggling to understand, Ramell lowered his head and brushed a kiss against her turned cheek. In that moment, he knew that his marriage was in trouble. He pulled away from her while the pain in his heart nearly became unbearable, but he released her hand and backed away.

Jacob, Lily, Rachel and Ethan also started drifting away from the bed and then they all marched toward the door with their heads hung low. But before they all ushered out, Sofia spoke, "Rachel…you can stay."

Rachel gave them a sympathetic look but turned back

and rushed to her sister's side. The rest of them were clearly dismissed. Heart broken, pride shattered, Ram left the hospital with his own tears streaming down his face.

Chapter 18

Sofia left the hospital with a new prescription and a doctor's warning for her to manage her stress better—which she answered by throwing herself headlong back into work. However, this time she refused to step one foot into Limelight Entertainment. She returned to her penthouse and worked out of her home office. She didn't want to see her aunt and uncle or even Ramell and Emmett. She couldn't. Just like she couldn't wrap her brain around the man they portrayed her father to be.

Every time she closed her eyes, all she could remember was the father that would take time to play tea or dress up with her—even when he was tired. She would remember the times he would read her bedtime stories and fill her head with fantasies about princes and princesses. Her father was everything to her. Everything.

He was kind, handsome and strong. Even now she remembered how she used to feel like she was on top of the world whenever she would ride on his shoulders. And so many people loved him. They used to have parties at their house all the time. She remembered sneaking down to see all the Hollywood stars of the time in their beautiful clothes—laughing, smiling…and drinking.

Sofia snapped out of her reverie in time to hear an

offer from a studio executive buzzing in her ear. "What kind of deal are we talking about?" she asked, standing up from her office chair and waltzing over to the window to stare out at the cityscape. "I don't know. That sounds awfully low," she said, even though she wasn't listening to what Frasier was offering. It didn't matter. Her job was to play hardball.

That was pretty much her routine for the next few days—that and screening her calls.

What Sofia was going through wasn't Ramell's fault. It wasn't even her aunt and uncle's fault. It was the foundation of who she was and what she believed crumbling beneath her that made her question everything—especially everything that had happened in the past month. Work didn't comfort her, but it kept her busy. And being busy kept her from breaking down.

But just barely.

However, the more she linked back into her own routine, the more she started distancing herself from the decisions she'd made in the past month. Getting married in Las Vegas the way she did. How cliché could they get? Hardly anything she'd done since Ramell merged his way into her life was like her. Making out in public places, dancing on tables and drinking and blacking out—who was that girl?

Much later that night, Sofia attended a small viewing party for a new movie from a popular director. She smiled. She laughed. She went through the motions. But her heart just wasn't into her performance.

She just wanted to make an appearance and then head back to her place, but as luck would have it, her uncle was also attending the party.

"You've been avoiding me," Jacob said.

Sofia sucked in a deep breath. She wasn't ready for this. "I know. I'm sorry."

"I know this isn't the place, but I really wish that we could sit down and talk. Maybe after your sister's wedding tomorrow. Your aunt and I would *really* like to talk to you about why we kept certain things from you."

"I know why. I just…can't get myself to believe it. And I can't believe I had everything so wrong for so long. I'm just trying to adjust." Sofia shrugged. "It's going to take some time."

He nodded as if he understood. "Still. Your aunt would like to hear from you. She's blaming herself for a lot of stuff right now and I don't think that's fair. Everything we did we did out of love. We may not have always gotten it right, but no one is perfect."

"I know that."

"Do you?"

Sofia frowned and then finally recognized the look on her uncle's face as disappointment. That wasn't something that she was used to seeing from him.

"I'm just going to say this and then I'm going to let it go. I loved my brother. Being twins, we shared a strong bond. There was nothing I wouldn't do for him and I know that he felt the same way about me. He was a good man. And just because he struggled with an illness didn't make him any less of a man. In the end he recognized that and he was going to get help. He did it for me, for your mother, and most of all he did it for you and your sister. John loved both of you so much that he wanted to be the best father he could be. And nothing we told you the other day should change how you feel about him, how you've always felt about him."

Jacob's words of wisdom caused a tear to skip down

her face. She quickly brushed a finger beneath her eyes and sniffed. "You're right," she admitted. It all suddenly became crystal clear to her. There was no point in trying to fit a square block into a round hole. People were complicated and they had many different sides to them.

"We'll talk after the wedding tomorrow," her uncle said, even though it sounded like a question.

"I'd like that." She leaned forward and brushed a kiss against his cheek. "And I'll call Aunt Lily tonight."

"Thanks. She'd love that."

"I was hoping I would run into you here."

Sofia stiffened with her drink pressed against her lips when she recognized the voice behind her. Her heart hammering, she slowly turned around and met her husband's tense and probing stare.

Uncle Jacob cut in, "I'll just leave you two alone." He stepped back then turned and drifted into the crowd.

"You look good." Ram's gaze roamed over her simple blue dress. "I hope that's not alcohol. It doesn't mix well with your medication, you know. And I don't want you running off and marrying someone else."

"Ramell," she whispered.

"Ah. So you do remember me. I was worried there for a moment since you haven't returned any of my calls." He smiled but it didn't reach his eyes.

"I was going to call."

"Good to know."

"I just needed some time." She glanced around to make sure that they weren't drawing too much attention.

"Time for what?" he challenged, sliding a hand into his pocket. Somehow he managed to look aloof and pissed off at the same time.

"To think," she answered, lowering her voice further. "I just got hit with a lot, you know, all at once."

He bobbed his head. "Yeah. I believe I was there. You know this is generally the time when a couple tries to come together. If you're hurting then I hurt." Slowly his smile melted. "But what *kills* me is that after all these years you still don't come to me. Not when we were best friends and not when we're man and wife."

"Ram—"

"No. Let me finish." He cleared his throat and lifted his chin. "You have a habit of just putting me on a shelf and then going on about your life. And like a fool I just let you do it."

Sofia frowned as cracks in Ramell's controlled expression started to show. "That's not...that's not what I'm doing."

"Don't insult me, Sofia. Every night I go to *our* house, hoping that you'll be there. And you're not. You've gone back to your penthouse, back to your beloved job, and back to ignoring me and my calls."

Fear clutched Sofia's heart. Seeing the sincerity in Ram's eyes forced her to let her guard down and she could finally see herself through his eyes and she could feel what he was feeling right now. She stepped forward and reached for his hand, but he stepped back.

"You don't have to say anything. I'm going to make this easy for you, Sofia. I'll file for an annulment. Clearly this whole marriage thing was a mistake."

"No, Ram. That's not it at all."

He shook his head. "That is it. Look. I'm going to be honest with you, Sofia. I love you. I always have and I always will. But I can't continue to do this with you. I can't keep waiting for you to love me as much as I love you. I just can't. I'll talk to Jacob. I can transfer to work out of our New York office. That should make things easier and we won't have to worry about running into each other at the office."

"Ramell, that's not necessary."

"For me it is. It will just make all of this a lot easier, for the both of us."

He stepped forward and then planted a kiss on her forehead.

"Goodbye, Sofia."

Chapter 19

The next morning, Sofia woke with red, swollen eyes. She had spent the whole night staring at the phone and drenching her pillow with tears. The few times that she managed to drift off to sleep her mind would replay the scene of Ramell telling her that he was going to file for an annulment. Each time it repeated she would experience the same stabbing pain in her heart. But what had she expected? She was guilty of everything that he'd accused her of. She cut him off when they were children over some stupid misunderstanding and then she did the same thing again these past few days. And because of what? Because she couldn't handle hearing that her father wasn't perfect?

Ramell was right. Why didn't she turn to him in her time of trouble and not away from him? It wasn't like she didn't trust him. She did. She trusted him with her life. Climbing out of bed, Sofia shuffled to the bathroom to see how bad the damage was. It was worse than she thought. Bed head, red eyes, puffy nose—she looked like a train wreck and she had to be on a plane to Napa Valley in a couple of hours.

She headed for the shower even though all she really wanted to do was go back and climb into bed. But there was no peace there, either. Her thoughts tortured her as she scrubbed and rinsed. *I can't keep waiting for you to love me as much as I love you.* Sofia's tears blended with the hot water spraying down from the showerhead. By the time she turned off the water she was rubbed raw and her fingertips looked pickled.

Realizing that she needed to hurry, Sofia attempted to pick up the pace, but she was sluggish at best. When she got into her car, she had every intention of going straight to the airport but the minute she hit the highway she drove to her old house instead. "Please be here. Please be here," she prayed feverishly. In the driveway, she'd barely put the car in Park before hopping out and running into the house.

"Ramell," Sofia shouted as she jetted through the house. She kept calling out for him as she ran from room to room. He wasn't there. When she reached their bedroom, she was shocked to discover that his clothes weren't there. Not in the walk-in closets, not in the drawers—not anywhere.

"Oh, my God. What have I done?" Sofia slapped a hand against her mouth while a fresh wave of acid tears started to burn the back of her eyes. She needed to fix this. But how?

Think. Think. She fixed problems all the time. Being a good agent meant being a problem solver. *I don't think I can solve this one.* Sofia walked over to the bed and sat down for a few minutes. In the back of her mind, she knew that she needed to get over to the airport. Her sister was getting married that afternoon, but the other part of her wanted—no—needed, to find her own husband. She needed to stop him from filing an annulment.

Torn, she hopped up from the bed and returned to her

car. While she drove out to the highway, she picked up her cell phone, took a deep breath and called Ramell. Hopefully, he wasn't so mad at her that he wouldn't answer his phone. At least that was her prayer...until her call went to voicemail. She was about to hang up but then waited too long and heard the beep. "Uh, hello, Ram. It's me. Sofia." She cleared her throat. "Look, I've been thinking a lot about what you said last night. You know the whole thing about you thinking our getting married being a mistake and you, well, you know—"

Beep!

"Damn it." Sofia tossed her phone over to the passenger seat and then slapped a hand against the steering wheel in frustration. Heartbroken, she made it over to the private airport. She was twenty minutes late, but her uncle held the private jet until she got there. She quickly apologized for her tardiness and climbed aboard.

Actually, she had a lot of apologies to make, she realized upon boarding the plane, the first one being with her aunt Lily.

"Don't worry about it, baby," her aunt said, cupping her face. "All that matters is that you're all right."

Sofia wasn't all right, but she had worried them enough. Plus, it was supposed to be a happy day. Rachel's day. She was going to put a smile on her face and be there for her little sister. When the plane took off, Sofia glanced out the window and stared out at the white fluffy clouds. Ram said that all his troubles faded when he was in the sky. She waited for that feeling to come over her now. But there was nothing on earth that was going to make her feel better about losing the best thing that had ever happened to her.

Nothing.

* * *

The beauty of Napa Valley rolled past Sofia without her noticing. She sat in the car next to her aunt with her thoughts tumbling over the mess that she made with Ramell. Beside her, Aunt Lily exclaimed at the vineyards they passed while riding up to the Chambers Winery.

"This is such a wonderful place for a wedding." Lily clasped her hands together. "I know I'm going to cry."

Jacob chuckled. "You always cry at weddings."

"True. But today there's going to be some real waterworks."

"Don't worry about it. I come bearing handkerchiefs." He wrapped his arm around his wife and delivered a quick kiss against her temple. He noticed his other niece brooding on the other side of the car, but held his tongue. When they arrived at the Chambers' breathtaking château, he helped his wife out of the car and then lingered to offer a hand to Sofia. He already suspected what was going on but he asked, anyway. "Everything all right, Sofia?"

She instantly plastered on a fake smile. "Fine. I'm doing just…" She met his knowing eyes and came clean. "I messed up," she admitted. "I messed up badly."

Jacob pulled in a deep breath and slid an arm around her waist. "Is there anything I can help you with?"

"I wish that you could, but…I don't think anything can fix this."

He cocked his head. "It's not like you to just give up."

"I know, but—"

"Then don't start making it a habit now." He squeezed her waist as they headed toward the front door.

Sofia let her uncle's words hang in her head. The more she thought about it, the more she drew strength from them. They were quickly introduced to Ethan's parents as well as his older brother, Hunter, and his six-year-old niece, Kendra. They were a beautiful family that was clearly a close-knit unit. And when Livia Blake entered the room and slid an arm around Hunter, Sofia felt a kick. It wasn't jealousy this time, but longing.

Excited, Lily clasped her hands together. "Well, I hope everyone is ready for a fantastic wedding,"

The women said their goodbyes to the men and headed off to a separate wing of the house that was temporarily dubbed the bridal suite. Rachel, who was sitting in a chair with a hairstylist, jumped from her chair, screaming, *"Guess who's getting married today!"*

"You are," the women screamed back and then rushed forward for a group hug. Music, champagne, hors d'oeuvres, before long there was a full party in swing. Sofia's mood lightened. She loved seeing her baby sister so happy. Rachel positively glowed while she recounted the story of how she and Ethan met and fell in love on the set of *Paging the Doctor*.

"Well, it's not like I'm the only one getting married." Rachel turned toward Charlene and then all the ladies in the room followed suit.

Charlene cradled her hands on her thick waist. "I wasn't going to say anything. It's your day."

Rachel waved that comment off and reached for her girl's hand and thrust it toward the other women. "Bam! Look at that sucker."

All the women blinked at the mammoth rock that Akil had put on her finger.

Sofia's mouth hung open just like the rest of them and she wondered how she hadn't noticed the ring when she first saw her. It was just that big. "That *definitely* says that you're off the market," Sofia said and all the women laughed.

"And what about you, Livia?" Charlene asked. "Have any news that you'd like to share with us ladies?"

You've got to be kidding me. Sofia turned her head toward Livia, who was now blushing as hard as Charlene.

"What? You want me to talk about this? *Bam!*" She thrust out her hand, also adorned with a beautiful, equally sizable diamond.

"And?" Rachel prodded.

"And…Hunter and I should be hearing the pitter-patter of little crawling feet by summer."

There was a collective "Oh, my God" before everyone rushed to hug and congratulate Livia. At least now Sofia knew the real reason why Livia had recently quit the business.

"And let's not forget my big sister, Sofia," Rachel chimed.

Sofia shook her head. She definitely didn't want the attention on her.

"She recently got married, too," Rachel continued.

Sofia hadn't gotten around to telling Rachel that Ram was filing for an annulment. And she certainly wasn't about to tell her right now, either.

"Let's see the ring," one of her sister's friends said.

Sofia glanced down at the simple band that she and Ram picked out during their quickie marriage and couldn't help but smile when she thrust it forward. "I believe that it was the best one Elvis had in his display counter," she chuckled.

"Well I can testify that it was certainly an interesting ceremony," Charlene said. "And after taking a peek at that video clip floating around, at least Akil and I now know why Ramell wasn't wearing a shirt when we showed up."

Sofia slapped a hand across her face while the women laughed. "So much for what happens in Vegas stays in Vegas."

Luckily Sofia was soon spared any further inquiry about her marriage and she went back to just celebrating Rachel's day.

"Oh, I wonder if Uncle Jacob remembered to write his toast," Rachel said. "The last time I talked to him he said that he hadn't gotten around to it."

"I'm sure he has," Sofia reassured her.

"I don't know. Uncle Jacob likes to ad-lib a lot, and he's not as good at it as he thinks he is."

The girls laughed. "Sofia, can you call him and check?"

Sofia grabbed her purse, but then remembered that she had left her cell phone in the passenger seat of her car. "I'm sorry but I don't have my cell phone with me."

Instantly, everyone stopped what they were doing and gawked at Sofia.

"What?"

"All right. Hold up. Who are you and what have you done with my sister?" Rachel asked with her hands on her hips.

Sofia frowned at all their stunned expressions. "What do you mean?"

"You never forget your phone," Rachel told her. "Never."

Sofia thought about it. Lately she hadn't been as much of a slave to her gadgets as she used to be and…it felt good. "Hollywood can wait…every once in a while," she said with a wink.

Everyone applauded.

After makeup, manicures and intricate hairstyles, the women all shimmied into their dresses in time for the wedding photographer to usher them to a designated area and take the first round of pictures. Rachel looked like an angel floating around in her white dress and striking poses.

When the women finished taking their pictures, they headed back toward the bridal suite. Bringing up the rear, Sofia and Charlene were laughing as Livia told them adorable stories of her soon-to-be stepdaughter. It was clear to everyone that she was going to make a wonderful mother. They turned down the wrong corner and ran directly into the groom and the groomsmen.

"Afternoon, ladies," Ethan greeted.

Sofia sucked in a startled breath when her eyes zeroed in on Ramell.

"Ooops. I guess we should have taken that left turn at Albuquerque," Livia laughed. "But first—" she rushed over to Hunter "—let me just steal a quick kiss."

The small group laughed…all except for Sofia and Ramell, who were both left standing off to the side. "What are you doing here?" she finally asked.

Ram cleared his throat and forced on a smile. "I, uh—"

"I invited him," Ethan said. "After all, in about an hour he's going to be my new brother-in-law." He gave Ramell a good, hearty whack on the back. "Besides, I had a cousin that had to back out at the last minute and it just all worked out."

Sofia swallowed. There were a million things going through her mind at the moment and she couldn't settle on a single one to say. Their laughter died down and an uncomfortable silence started to hug the group.

"Well, we're just going to head on back to the blushing bride," Charlene said, tugging on Livia's arm.

"Yeah. We don't want them to think something happened to us."

"Can I come with?" Ethan joked.

"No." Charlene waved a finger at him. "It's bad luck to see the bride before the wedding."

Ethan tossed up his hands. "Fine. I guess we'll just go get our pictures taken."

The bridesmaids and the groomsmen started to part ways. Sofia's moment was about to pass her by. *Stop him! Stop him!*

"Ramell, can I talk to you for a moment?" she said so quickly that it sounded like one long word.

Ram stopped in his tracks and turned back to face her.

"Please?" She glanced at the others and then tried to swallow the large lump in the center of her throat. "It'll just take a moment."

No one waited for a brick to fall onto their head. They quickly scrambled out of the hallway. Sofia hesitated because she had the distinct impression that Ram wanted to leave, as well. Was it too late?

"I…" She stopped, feeling her throat closing up on her. She closed her eyes at the threat of tears. "I've never been at a loss for words," she said and tried to laugh at herself, but even that fell flat.

"Maybe that's a sign, too," Ram said.

Eyes shimmering, she looked up to see tears shining in his eyes.

"Love isn't supposed to be this hard," he said.

Sofia shook her head. "I think you're wrong about

that. If it wasn't hard then everyone would have it. Love is hard to find. Love is hard to wait for. And in my case it was hard to recognize. And even harder to appreciate." She sniffed and then backhanded a few tears. "I'm…I'm sorry. I'm just so damn sorry about how I've treated you. You were right about everything you said last night. You've always been there for me, even when I convinced myself that I didn't want you to be. I took you for granted and there's nothing…nothing I can say can ever excuse that."

Ramell nodded and lowered his gaze.

"But you never had to wait for me to love you. I've always loved you. And if you give me another chance, I promise to prove it to you every day for the rest of our lives. I don't want you to move to New York and I don't want an annulment."

"Sofia—"

"No. Please let me finish." She reached for his hand and then took comfort from the fact that he didn't snatch it back from her. "You mean more to me than even I knew at first. It wasn't until I was faced with the possibility of really losing you that I realized just how much you're a part of me. I love kissing you, making love to you. Hell, I even love fighting with you. But I can't… I absolutely can't imagine myself going back to living without you. Not this time." She took a timid step forward and slid her hands flat against his chest. "Please. Give me a chance to love you the way that you deserve to be loved. I'll work less hours. I promise that I'll never put you on a shelf again. I'll—"

"Sofia—"

"Don't say it's too late." Tears streamed down her face. "I don't know what I'll do if you say that it's too late."

She searched his eyes for any sign that he still loved her, that he still wanted her.

Ramell lifted her hands from his chest and brought them up to his lips. In that moment she feared that this was it. Her second rejection in two days.

"Do you know how long I've waited to hear you say that?" He leaned forward and pressed their foreheads together. His hands trembled as he cupped her face and then kissed her with all the love he felt in his heart. "Are we really going to do this? For real this time?"

Sofia pulled her hands from his grip and then threw her arms around his neck. "Yes! I love you so much." She leaned up on her toes and kissed him with every ounce of love and passion that was in her body. She gave and received so much that her whole body trembled like the last autumn leaf blowing in the wind.

When they both had to come up for air, Sofia held him tight while Ramell whispered against her hair. "I love you so much."

"I love you, too." Relief rushed through her like a tidal wave.

"I want to marry you," he said. "The right way. With family and friends around us to celebrate and witness our love."

Sofia laughed and cried at the same time. "I'll marry you anywhere, anytime."

"Harrumph."

Sofia and Ramell pulled apart to see Jacob standing nearby, smiling.

"I hate to interrupt but the photographer is waiting." He winked and then walked off.

Sofia and Ramell stole another kiss before they reluctantly pulled apart. "I guess we better get back to the wedding," she said.

"Save a dance for me?" he asked.

"I'll save all of them for you."

Thirty minutes later, everyone was in their places and watching Rachel float down the aisle. Sofia had never seen her sister look more beautiful. When she met Ethan in front of the minister and linked their hands, everyone sighed at just how beautiful the couple was together. When it came time to recite their vows, Ethan choked up a bit and every woman's heart swooned.

"I now pronounce you man and wife. You may now kiss the bride."

Ethan stepped forward and drew his wife into his arms, made a dramatic dip and then kissed Rachel passionately. While the wedding party cheered, Sofia and Ramell's gazes found one another. There was so much love in his eyes, Sofia could drown in it.

At the wedding reception, Ramell swept her into his arms and pressed their cheeks together. Sofia still struggled to keep her tears at bay when she reflected on just how close she came to losing the best thing that had ever happened to her.

"No tears," Ramell said, kissing their salty tracks.

Sofia smiled. "Don't worry. They're happy tears."

"Yeah?" He smiled. "Then those might be all right."

They floated around the dance floor, sharing Rachel and Ethan's special day and feeling like it was truly the beginning for them, as well. In a lot of ways, that was exactly what it was.

The beginning of happily ever after.

Epilogue

A year later...

Sofia sat on the edge of the doctor's table with her cell phone tucked under her ear while her fingers raced across her new iPad as she fired off one contract counteroffer after another. "Sorry, Larry, but that's not going to happen. You've only locked down Mary Bell for one season of *Paging the Doctor*. She's a big hit. The fans love her. If you want to lock her down for another four years then you're going to have come up with a figure that doesn't insult my intelligence." She only half listened to Larry Franklin's response because she knew that this was the part when studios started crying broke.

"Larry, if you feel that way then we can just let the contract run out and I can dedicate more attention to the numerous *movie* offers that have been flooding my in-box."

"Damn, Sofia. There you go beating me up again. I hoped that you becoming a mother was going to soften you up a bit."

"Are you kidding? Not with these hormones."

Larry laughed. "All right. All right. I can go up another ten percent. But that's it."

That managed to put a smile on her face. "I'll confer with my client and get back to you," she said noncommittally and then disconnected the call. But then her phone started ringing again. She was about to answer when Dr. Perry's voice startled her.

"You think you can fit in time in for your check-up?"

Sofia jumped and then flashed him an apologetic smile. "Sorry about that." She quickly put her phone on vibrate and set it and her iPad down.

Ramell unfolded his arms and grabbed his wife's electronic gadgets. "Yes, please forgive my wife. She gets a little carried away sometimes."

Sofia glanced over at him. "Hey, I'm doing better. I've cut my work hours in half and only work three days a week."

"And I appreciate that, baby." He leaned over and kissed her before returning his attention to their doctor. "So what's the news, Doctor?"

Dr. Perry smiled at the loving couple. "I'm going to ask once again. Are you two sure that you want to know the sex of the baby?"

Sofia and Ramell smiled as their arms drifted around each other's waists.

"We're sure," Sofia said, giddy.

"All right. Then just lie back and let's get you hooked up."

Minutes later with her belly jelled down, Sofia and Ramell stared at the sonogram monitor in awe. When Dr. Perry pointed out the tiny little head and feet of their child, tears rushed their eyes as more love filled their hearts.

"Oh, my God, baby. Look." Sofia reached for Ram's hand. "That's our baby."

"It sure is." Ram nodded and then planted a kiss against her forehead.

Dr. Perry pointed at the screen. "And this here tells me that you two are about to have…a boy."

Ramell dropped his wife's hand and pumped his fist high into the air. "Yeah! Yeah, baby!"

With tears streaming down her face, Sofia laughed at her husband's antics and then beamed when he then wrapped his arms around her and smothered her with kisses. "I take it that you're happy?"

"Are you kidding me? You've made me the happiest man in the world."

She smiled as she cupped his handsome face in her hands. "And you've made me the happiest woman. I love you."

"I've loved you for a gazillion years," he said tenderly.

"And I'll love you for a gazillion more," Sofia whispered, and sealed that promise with a kiss.

* * * * *

The first two stories in the *Love in the Limelight* series, where four unstoppable women find fame, fortune and ultimately… true love.

LOVE IN THE LIMELIGHT

New York Times bestselling author

BRENDA JACKSON

&

A.C. ARTHUR

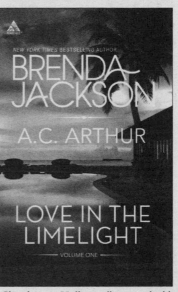

In *Star of His Heart*, Ethan Chambers is Hollywood's most eligible bachelor. But when he meets his costar Rachel Wellesley, he suddenly finds himself thinking twice about staying single.

In *Sing Your Pleasure*, Charlene Quinn has just landed a major contract with L.A.'s hottest record label, working with none other than Akil Hutton. Despite his gruff attitude, she finds herself powerfully attracted to the driven music producer.

Available now wherever books are sold!

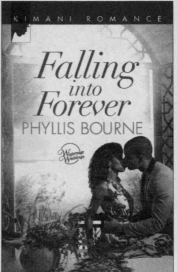

His kisses unlocked
her inner passion…

Red
Velvet
kisses

Sherelle
Green

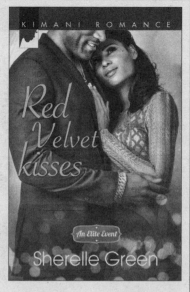

Meeting gorgeous Micah Madden while lingerie shopping leaves
event planner Lexus Turner embarrassed yet intrigued. Only a
man like Micah could make her feel this good, which is why she is
determined to keep her distance…but he's determined to uncover
the woman behind her buttoned-up facade. And with Lex's ex swiftly
moving in for a second chance, Micah will have to open up in ways
he never dared before….

An Elite Event

"The love scenes are steamy and passionate,
and the storyline is fast-paced and well-rounded."
—*RT Book Reviews* on *IF ONLY FOR TONIGHT*

HARLEQUIN®
™ www.Harlequin.com

*Available November 2014
wherever books are sold!*

KPSG3791114